Indefatigable, Linyi [...] approach to Nikko, [...] seconds, when the alarms sounded.

"Nelson, what have we got?" asked Price.

"Eight fusion-drive signatures, likely missiles, originating approximately zero point zero two light-seconds out. Accelerating rapidly. Three are targeting *Indefatigable*, three on *Linyi*, and two on *South Dakota*. Radar emissions detected, likely for targeting. Estimated time to impact is two minutes. Initiating evasive maneuvers, activating radar jammers, and deploying chaff."

Price knew the drill. The AI Nelson could respond much faster than a human in a defensive situation, so it was given near-complete flexibility for defending the ship. Price could override, of course, but in most cases that would be the complete wrong thing to do. Humans were still rather good at strategy and offensive tactics, but defense required too much to happen too quickly for their limited response time.

"Were they launched by ships? What's their origin?" asked Price.

"Unknown. There are no signs of any ships near where the missiles originated, so they could be sleepers activated by our approach," replied Nelson.

Drones, Price thought. *Set to take out whoever came to help the colonists on the world they attacked. Great.*

THE
SPACETIME
WAR

✦

LES JOHNSON

THE SPACETIME WAR

Copyright © 2021 by Les Johnson

A Baen Books Original

Baen Publishing Enterprises
P.O. Box 1403
Riverdale, NY 10471
www.baen.com

ISBN: 978-1-9821-9220-4

Cover art by Don Maitz

First printing, August 2021
First mass market printing, December 2022

Distributed by Simon & Schuster
1230 Avenue of the Americas
New York, NY 10020

Library of Congress Control Number: 2021036507

Printed in the United States of America

10 9 8 7 6 5 4 3 2 1

To those who believe
that tomorrow can be better than today
and are willing to work to make it happen.

THE
SPACETIME
WAR

PROLOGUE

Price had technically been all over the solar system, from near Mercury to Venus and Mars, through the asteroid belt (where there really wasn't much to see unless you looked really hard) to Jupiter, Saturn, Uranus, and Neptune. He'd never been to the dwarf planet Pluto or its distant cousin, Eris, but he suspected his job might take him near them someday. That's why his colleagues found it odd that on his one-month leave from the Commonwealth Space Navy he would choose to take a pleasure cruise on the *Grandiosa* through the Saturnian system. What they didn't realize was that flying by a planet the size of seven hundred Earths was not the same thing as visiting it and its moons up close and personal, and he had never had the chance to disembark to walk anywhere but the Moon, Mars, Phobos, and the asteroid Vesta—all locations where the Commonwealth Space Navy had bases. Now he would. He and about fifty other passengers were just beginning their second week of their month-long tour of the Saturnian system, and they would soon have their first shore leave on Titan. Granted, they would only be going to the research outpost and tiny visitor's center that the cruise ship company had built there, but they would nonetheless be walking on its surface and hopefully see one of the moon's famous methane lakes up close and personal. Price's excitement grew at the thought, but that visit was not for another few days.

Tonight was the weekly captain's dinner, and for the last hour beforehand, Price worked out in the *Grandiosa*'s variable-gravity exercise facility. There were people on board who lived on or in places other than Earth and were therefore accustomed to something less than the standard one Earth gravity. For this reason, most cruise ships, including the *Grandiosa*, tuned their artificial gravity systems to roughly fifty percent of Earth normal, a fairly reasonable compromise. Forcing those from Mars, whose bodies were accustomed to one-third gee, to live under a full Earth gravity would almost be cruel. As it was, the Martians onboard were suffering even under the compromise. But for people who had to return to a one-gee environment after a month aboard ship, that meant incorporating at least an hour each day of rigorous exercise under one or more Earth gravities to maintain muscle tone and bone strength. True, there were those who would probably spend the month at half the pull of gravity to which there were accustomed to feeling like superheroes, leaping high and relishing in sensing body strength reminiscent of their younger years, but they would pay the price when they returned home until they reacclimated. Price would have to return to his ship, where one Earth gravity was standard, and he could afford no such downtime. His workout was focused and intense; not something he enjoyed, but something he knew he had to do. It also made him hungry for whatever food would be served at the captain's dinner.

Being military, Price felt odd calling the casually dressed man with a flippant attitude "Captain," but that was the protocol and Price knew all about following protocol even if it seemed stupid or nonsensical. Captain Lomax claimed to have been in the US Space Navy, but Price doubted it. He had been around other civilians with similar backgrounds as himself, and none were as nonchalant and complacent about their job responsibilities, no matter what they were, as this man. If the ship did not have an AI to keep the systems running, Price doubted the man had the competence to do anything aboard ship, let alone be its skipper. But, of course, he kept those thoughts to himself.

The captain's dinner was being held in the dining hall, as was every meal, but for this occasion, the alcohol was a cut above the usual, meaning it was actually pretty good and not just acceptable, and the food was excellent. The one thing Price could not say anything negative about was the food. Being used to navy fare, the excesses of a cruise ship's buffet were almost obscene—and he loved every minute and every bite of it. Tonight was no exception.

Overhead, visible through the fully retracted shutters, was Saturn. *Oh. My. God. It's beautiful,* thought Price for the umpteenth time as he stood on the deck, wine in hand, mouth slightly agape, as he beheld the giant planet with its majestic rings. It wasn't the first time he'd seen it, but it was the first time he had seen it this close. And tomorrow they would pass through the Cassini division, a nearly three-thousand-mile-wide gap in the rings, allowing them to see the rings from below and above before they boosted for Titan.

"It never gets old, does it?" asked his dinner companion, who had arrived unnoticed, by Price anyway, about which he felt somewhat embarrassed. She had asked him to join her for dinner, and he did not want to be rude. Her name was Miranda Runyon, and Price knew that just about every other unattached man on the ship had noticed her, and probably some of the attached men as well. She was stunning, and they'd developed the beginnings of what might be a budding relationship since they met over lunch three days before. He had, of course, noticed her before, but it was she who had approached him—he was flattered.

"No, it doesn't. I don't believe I would ever get inured to it," replied Price, taking his gaze from the majestic rings of the planet to the spectacular figure that was his date. She was wearing a black dress that was quite modest in what it concealed, revealing more about her personality in the process. He motioned for her to take a seat, which she did, and he followed suit. There were four other people at their table, already engaged in chatting with ever increasing volume as more people crowded into the room.

They exchanged some casual banter—catching up on the events of the day, introducing themselves to the others at the table, some of whom they had already met but whose names were long forgotten—and ate their way through the first few courses of what was promising to be a very satisfying evening meal. As with previous conversations, Miranda gently probed about Price's job, and in response he gently deflected. He did not want to talk about his military service, because he found that people's attitudes toward him changed when they found out he was the captain of a warship. The men inevitably wanted to know more about his ship's speed and weapons, and the women started treating him less as "Winslow Price" and more as the desirable "Captain Price." Granted, there was a time that Price had wanted to attract the immediate affection of the fairer sex, regardless of why, but that time was in the past. What he wanted now was for more meaningful relationships based on who he was, not what job he happened to have. He knew Miranda was independently wealthy and part of a small group of investors who were taking the cruise to celebrate some big deal they had recently closed that had something to do with diamond mining on an undisclosed asteroid somewhere in the main belt.

The dessert, coffee crème brûlée, was being delivered by the attendants when Captain Lomax, in his ridiculous looking dress "uniform" got up to speak. He began with his usual attempt at humor, to which some in the room politely guffawed, and then began speaking about the upcoming visit to Titan. He was not saying much of anything new, and Price had already tuned him out. Unfortunately, his date was listening in rapt attention. When Price simply could not bear it any longer, he leaned toward Miranda and whispered into her ear, "I need to use the loo." It was all he could do to not call it *the head*, but for some reason, civilian women did not seem to like the term. "If you don't mind, please request a refill on the tea. I'll be right back."

"Sure thing. Don't be long," she replied, smiling, as she turned her head back toward the captain, waiting expectantly for him to say something interesting. He knew she might have a long wait and hoped that by the time he returned, they would be back to having their dinner conversation. He quite enjoyed her company.

As he departed, he noted that none of the other guests gave him a second glance. They, too, were listening to Lomax and his showman-like self-aggrandizing.

The head was not far from the banquet hall and was thankfully deserted.

After completing his business, he began the short walk back to the banquet hall and stopped about ten feet outside. Just inside the door, one of the stewards, who had just been bringing tea and dessert to his table, was pulling a Mark IV laser pistol from under the serving table and using his other hand to pull the door closed behind him. Price knew he had only seconds before the steward glanced over his shoulder and saw him. Not seeing many options and knowing that people are capable of discerning motion in their peripheral vision, Price opted to instead just stand still next to the hallway wall and hope that the steward wouldn't see him. Plan B was to make a dash for the hallway to the right, which he might be able to do if he were noticed. He figured the odds were about fifty-fifty for him making it to the hallway without getting lasered.

Thankfully, the steward only gave a cursory glance down the hallway before closing the door, not noticing that Price was there. Only after he heard the *thunk* of the door closing and being sealed did Price dare to move. He doubted his movements could be heard through the wall and door that separated the hallway from the banquet room since it, and all doors and walls onboard the ship, were rated against vacuum and extremely substantial.

As he moved down the corridor and toward his stateroom, Price began going through the various plausible reasons that a steward would be armed with a military-grade laser pistol and sealing off the banquet room and found none that made any sense whatsoever except for the obvious. This was either a robbery, blatant piracy, or terrorism. And since he had heard no commotion, no alarms or people fleeing the banquet room, Price had to assume that the steward was not acting alone. Not good.

The hallways had been eerily empty, which was not unexpected since just about everyone went to the nightly gala dinners. But somehow the stillness now seemed ominous. He entered his room without being seen, or so he surmised, since no one had come for him yet. But he might not have much time. There were cameras everywhere on the ship, and if anyone were looking, he could not be missed. The first thing he would need to do after calling for help would be to do something about the cameras. He would not be able to do anything if he were tracked and caught.

In his stateroom, Price had no weapons or much of anything else that would help him do anything about whatever was happening, but he did have his emergency transceiver. Vacation or not, he was an active-duty officer in the Commonwealth Space Navy and that meant he could be recalled at a moment's notice and had to be reachable anywhere in the solar system. He had granted himself some discretionary time without the bulky interplanetary transceiver, which, though it fit in the palm of his hand, was too cumbersome to carry around all the time. He was looking forward to the day when there were enough relay stations in the solar system to allow his ear implant to assume this function as well. As was his routine, he had planned to return to his room after dinner, alone or not, to check for messages. Whatever was happening, he had to get word to the navy or civil authorities.

He activated the transceiver in military-only SOS mode, which would send whatever message he recorded to the existing network of relay spacecraft which would, in turn, identify the active Commonwealth and allied military ships nearest to his location for receipt of the message. Given that he was at Saturn, he knew that there was a relay station on Titan that would get the signal boosted and on the network. After he sent his message, telling them all he knew at the moment, which was not much, he pocketed the device and quickly grabbed a few items that might come in handy. He found himself wishing for his sidearm, but of course, he had not brought it with him. He was on vacation. Military or not, law-abiding citizens were not allowed to bring lethal weapons on cruise ships. That, of course, did not stop the pirates. Fortunately, he did bring his old-fashioned utility knife, which now provided a comforting bulge in his right pocket. As weapons went, a utility knife would be no match for a laser. But that was all he had, and he would have to make the most of it.

The problem with the message he sent, and the anticipated reply, was time. Given the speed-of-light delay, unless there was a navy ship serendipitously in the neighborhood, it would take minutes to tens of minutes for his message to go out and to receive a reply from whatever ship responded. He simply could not risk that he had not been seen coming to his stateroom to wait for their answer. He had to move. Now.

His next stop would be propulsion engineering. If this was even a halfway organized takeover, then the bridge would be compromised for sure. The pirates might not have enough people to also control the propulsion and engineering section. Price also knew that cruise ships like this one were not designed with the functional redundancy of a navy vessel that had to have an auxiliary control room ready to run the ship in the event the bridge were destroyed. No, the best he could do from propulsion engineering was get the team there to shut down the fusion power system, effectively stranding the ship on whatever course it was currently taking. Since he had not felt any of the telltale vibrations of the fusion drive kicking in, he had to assume they were still in Saturnian orbit. Orbital mechanics would allow them to remain there for months to years without any additional boosting. Disabling the drive should be a safe thing to do.

He quickly moved away from his stateroom and toward his target, taking as much of a circuitous route as he could manage to get there in case he was being tracked. He did not want to give away his target destination too easily.

Clank! Thud.

The sound of a hatch opening just ahead of him was

unmistakable. Price looked quickly at his options and retreated a few steps to the corridor intersection through which he had just passed. He pulled out his utility knife and made himself as inconspicuous as possible against the wall in the adjacent corridor.

He heard the clank of the hatch being closed and the footfalls of a single person coming down the corridor he had just vacated. Knife at the ready, he waited.

As the approaching man walked past, Price saw that he was armed with a laser sidearm, fortunately still in its holster. Not wanting to kill him without being able to interrogate him about whatever was going on, Price opted against using his knife. He instead threw himself forward and tackled the man. Having the benefit of surprise, Price quickly pinned the interloper on the ground, prone, and kept him there using his body weight. Price had one arm around the man's neck with his hands clasped together in an oxygen-depriving choke hold. His captive began to struggle, but Price held firm and not-so-gently increased the pressure on his neck, momentarily restricting his airflow. The pirate gasped and quickly stopped struggling. Price relaxed his grip, but only slightly.

"Do exactly as I say, and you might live to see tomorrow," Price said, increasing slightly the pressure on the man's neck, allowing him to again experience a lack of air. He grunted in what Price took to be acquiescence.

"Good man," said Price as he relaxed his choke hold only enough to allow the pirate to get enough air to talk.

"How many of you are there?" Price asked.

"Enough," he said.

Price again increased the pressure on the man's neck.

"Now, now. There may be enough of you to do whatever it is you have planned, but there aren't enough of you here right now, are there?"

"Go to hell."

Price increased the pressure on the man's neck to the point where his reflexes took over and he again began to struggle. Price did not relent until he felt his body go completely limp. He did not want to kill the man, but he did need him out of action. Price knew from his training that he hadn't killed his captive, just momentarily incapacitated him. He let the man's body slump to the ground and quickly removed the sidearm from his limp form.

What do I do with you? Price thought as he looked around the corridor for an answer, finding it only a few steps away at the door to another passenger's stateroom. Grasping the man under his arms, Price dragged him into the stateroom and quickly cut the room's bed sheets into thin strips, tying his captive where his legs, arms (which were behind his back), and neck were all connected in what Price knew from personal experience (but that was another story) was an extremely uncomfortable and completely incapacitating position. If he tried to loosen his arms, the strips of sheet would increase the pressure on his neck, reducing his air supply—something the man would probably be loath to do after nearly being strangled moments before. Price also gagged him, for obvious reasons.

"Thanks for the sidearm," Price said as he opened the stateroom door and exited, continuing his journey to the propulsion section. The ship was fairly large, as private ships go, and followed a fairly standard layout common to just about every ship flown to date. Finding the propulsion section aft was fairly straightforward. As Price made his way there, he received a reply message to his SOS:

"Message received. The HMSS *Belfast* and the CSN *Jinggang Shan* are en route to Saturn and should be there by twelve hundred hours. There has been no contact from the *Grandiosa*. We've asked the staff at the Titan visitor's center to send a routine query to the ship and will let you know what they hear back. You are advised to use caution and not intervene unless ordered to do so by the captain of the *Belfast* upon its arrival."

Not intervene? Price thought as he noted that the message said he was "advised to use caution and not intervene," not *ordered* to not intervene—a huge difference that gave him a great deal of leeway and gave his superiors a convenient "out" should he do something that ended poorly. Price's concern was that whoever had taken over the ship would decide to leave orbit for someplace else before help arrived. Once they did that, the ship would be extremely difficult to track, placing everyone's lives in even more jeopardy. No, he needed to disable the ship's propulsion system as soon as possible.

Being a clean, well-kept, and state-of-the-art ship, everything was labeled, and there were direction markers everywhere showing what was where with convenient "You Are Here" displays. Following these helpful guides, Price arrived at the sealed door to "Main Propulsion." It was closed and had the appropriate markings, warding off lost tourists from all the potential dangers that lay within, including "fusion by-products, gamma rays, and high-strength magnetic fields." He knew that if the fusion reactor was functioning according to spec, none of these were a real danger.

Not seeing any alternatives, Price drew his newly acquired laser sidearm, made sure his utility knife was readily accessible from his belt, and opened the hatch.

He was immediately greeted with the familiar loud hum of high-power electronics and high-strength magnetic fields with a hint of ozone in the air. Where there should have been two crewmen tending the local workstations, there was instead one immobile man lying on the floor, face down, his head cocked at an unnatural angle. He was not dressed like a member of the crew. Price looked quickly around the room, trying to figure out what was going on, when he noticed a familiar red dot centered on his chest.

"Put down your weapon, raise your hands, and step forward two feet," said a woman's voice from somewhere nearby—*above*? Knowing that whoever had placed the laser sight on his chest could probably pull the trigger faster than he could react and find her, he complied. His captured laser pistol clanked on the floor, its sound muted by the humming and the acoustics of the room. As he raised his hands, Price glanced upward and saw the source of the command, standing on the catwalk one level up. She held a laser pistol similar to the one he had just dropped, still pointed directly at the center of his chest, and was flanked by what looked like ship's engineers slightly behind her, one on each side. She was clearly protecting them.

Price looked at the body in front of him and then back toward the woman with the pistol. He decided to take a chance. "I'm on your side. My name is Winslow Price, Commonwealth Space Navy, here on leave. I took this gun from one of the pirates and came here to disable the propulsion system."

"Would that be Captain Winslow Price of the HMSS *Indefatigable*?" she said, not wavering in her aim. She spoke the King's English with an Indian accent, which her dark complexion and coal-black hair complemented.

"Yes. And you have me at a disadvantage," said Price, looking down at the target spot on his chest and then back toward her. "Actually, two," he added.

She lowered the pistol, the red target disappearing as she engaged the weapon's safety. "Anika Ahuja, first officer of the INS *Mumbai*," she said. As she did so, she asked the two engineers, one man and one woman, to get back to their posts.

"Captain Price, it would seem that we think alike," Ahuja said as she followed the two engineers down the ladder from the catwalk to the ground floor.

Now that he could see her in the light and not be too distracted by the laser she had previously held pointed at his chest, he was struck by how beautiful she was, and he did recall seeing her at some events earlier in the cruise, but none lately.

"Right, you can tell me how you know who I am later, but I am curious how you pulled this off," Price asked, looking at the pirate's body sprawled on the floor.

"I suspect my plan was similar to yours. Get here to disable the ship before they can take us somewhere difficult to find, but I beat you to it. I didn't feel like going to dinner tonight; I've been sick these last few days and hardly away from the facilities in my stateroom, if you know what I mean. Today was the first day I actually felt better and probably could have come to dinner. I was dozing when my comm sounded. It was my roommate, who had switched on her transmitter from the banquet hall just after the pirates made their move. At first, I didn't know what was going on, but it became clear after a while that the background noise I was hearing was the whole point. She was letting me know what was happening without saying anything. Once I heard them threaten to kill the captain, I knew I had to do something. That's when I decided to come here," she said.

"And him? How did you manage that?" asked Price, pointing to the man on the floor who Price now assumed was dead.

"Despite centuries of progress, men are still distracted by their hormones. I came through the hatch acting lost, making sure that my shirt had one too many buttons undone, which distracted Mr. Pirate over there into thinking I was both hapless and harmless. From there it was easy. He allowed me to get too close. Bang, boom. Too bad for him," she said.

"Remind me to not let you get too close," said Price.

She smiled. "You won't. Not unless I want you to. Now, while they are shutting down the propulsion system, do you have any ideas of what we might do next?"

"I think one of us, maybe both, should make sure they finish the job and then get our engineer friends hidden away somewhere so the pirates can't find them. Once they realize they are stranded, they may not be too happy. From there, I don't know. I contacted the fleet and two ships are on the way. They should be here in about nine hours," Price said.

"Nine hours can be a long time if some pissed-off pirates are running around loose. From listening to Kathryn's audio feed, they seem to be after a digital file carried by some group of business people who are onboard. Something about an asteroid and diamond mining," she said.

"Miranda," said Price.

"Miranda? Who is that?"

"My dinner date. She and her colleagues are on this cruise to celebrate some sort of big diamond-mining deal they just closed," Price replied.

A flicker of—regret?—Price was not sure . . . crossed Ahuja's face, quickly replaced by one of determination.

"How did you get out of the dining room? It sounded like they had it locked down pretty tight," she said.

"I had to go to the head—but for very different reasons than yours. I was on my way back into the room when I saw one of the stewards pull a weapon out and close the door. Five seconds sooner, he would have nailed me. I was completely unarmed and unprepared. But that's history. The cavalry is on the way, and we need to do something to make sure no one gets hurt."

"What about the gun?" she asked.

"One of the pirates gave it to me. He can tell you the whole story later," replied Price.

Looking toward the engineers, Ahuja asked, "How much longer? We need to get you two out of here and to a safe place."

"Ten minutes, twelve tops," said the woman as she rapidly manipulated the touchscreen interface in front of her. As she spoke, the pitch of the electronic whine filling the room began to shift from high to low, indicating that the power in the system was dropping.

"Wait a minute, stop. Keep the power up. We don't want the pirates to know we're here yet, and I have an idea," said Price.

"They are going to find out when he doesn't check in," said Ahuja, pointing to the dead man lying on the floor.

"Him and the goon I left tied up in one of the staterooms," said Price as he turned to face one of the engineers. "You can control the life-support systems from here, correct?"

"Yeah, sure. You want me to shut it down?" asked the other engineer, turning to face Price and Ahuja.

"No. But I do want you to reduce the oxygen levels in the air enough to cause everyone to pass out."

"Uh, yeah, we can do that. But it will affect us here too," said the woman.

"You have emergency space suits here, right? Put them on," said Price.

"There are suits on all levels of the ship," said Ahuja. "Once the pirates figure out what's going on, putting them on will be the first thing they do."

"But it won't do them any good," said Price.

"Why not?" Ahuja asked.

Price raised his laser pistol and looked at it. "Because you and I are going to all the suit lockers and lasing each and every one of them while we seal our new friends up nice and safe in here," he said, again nodding toward his pistol.

She smiled. It was a wicked smile.

"I'll take that as an affirmative," Price said to Ahuja before turning his gaze back to the engineers. "Once they figure out what is happening, the pirates may try to contact you to make a deal, threaten to kill hostages or something. Don't answer. If you don't answer, they won't know if you heard them or not. It would be best if you didn't hear them."

"Ah, okay," said the woman, looking at her colleague who nodded in affirmation.

"Can you lock down the escape pods?" asked Ahuja.

"Uh, yes. We are not supposed to. It's illegal to lock them down while we are out of space dock," the male engineer replied.

Ahuja's look of incredulity would have made the most dissident of teenagers proud.

"Ah, yes. I guess they won't cite us under these circumstances, eh?" he said.

"If they do, then tell them that we ordered you to do it," said Ahuja.

"Yes, ma'am," the engineer said as he turned away, presumably to initiate the lockdown procedure.

"Once you change the oxygen levels, go ahead and power down the reactor to below the minimum needed to drive the engine. No matter what happens, they cannot be allowed to navigate away from here," said Price.

"We understand," the female engineer said.

"First Officer Ahuja, are you ready?" asked Price.

She again gave him the most-wicked smile and said, "I'm ready. Let's go."

Three hours later, everyone on the ship except for Price, Ahuja, and the two engineers were sound asleep. Six hours after that, the *Belfast* arrived, followed thirty minutes later by the *Jinggang Shan*. There were no additional injuries or deaths by the time the seven pirates were taken into military custody and removed from the ship. Captain Lomax, still full of himself, said that if the passengers were willing, the cruise would go on, citing an immediate return to Mars as the only alternative—which, itself, would take five days. The passengers decided to continue, with many offering to fill in for the now missing "stewards" who had been taken into custody. The owner of the cruise line sent a message promising to refund everyone's money, improving spirits. The only thing Price didn't like was how the stories of what happened during the whole ordeal were now subtly shifting, giving an ever-more prominent role in the events that unfolded to Captain Lomax. Price was not necessarily looking for glory, nor was Anika, but their self-deprecation left the door open for Lomax to take the spotlight.

Price cordially parted ways with Miranda—not feeling at all guilty since there were many other suitable, and quite eager, companions she might have the company of for the rest of the trip—and instead he began spending as much time as possible with Anika. They got to know each other quite well. Quite well indeed.

CHAPTER 1

Fourteen months later

Pirates.

He hated them. Captain Winslow Price, captain of Her Majesty's Spaceship *Indefatigable*, was assigned to this quadrant of the solar system for the very purpose of deterring piracy, which had been a growing problem for the burgeoning space economy since, well, nearly since its beginning. Whenever people engaged in commerce, it seemed there were people engaged in schemes to steal what was not theirs. On Earth, most thought that piracy was something from ancient history and imagined it in almost a reverential, idealized sort of way. Captain Hook, Blackbeard, pirates in fiction and fictionalized reality, were almost larger-than-life characters. Of course, the real pirates of old Earth were nothing but scum, and the space pirates were no different. He knew this intellectually, and the events fourteen months previously had given him personal experience. The events on the *Grandiosa* had been a turning point, of sorts, with pirates getting more daring and brazen.

The spacefaring countries of Earth built and maintained space navies for waging war. Thankfully, in the years Price had been in the navy, there had never been a war. But there had been sporadic engagements with pirates, and they were getting more deadly. The pirate ships that raided interplanetary shipping and the growing number of incoming and outgoing interstellar cargo ships were getting bolder and more aggressive thanks to however they were gaining access to the latest weaponry. A few years ago, pirates could, at best, have a few missiles to either disable or threaten their ponderously slow targets—or board, and try to take them over, as they did on the *Grandiosa*. Today, or more accurately, two months ago, pirates based God-only-knows-where raided an outgoing freighter and when they apparently didn't find on board what they were looking for, they killed every member of the crew. After that, it was decided that the warships would now become more of a coast guard, assuring safe passage through the shipping lanes of space—all gazillion square miles of it.

That was the mission upon which Price and the *Indefatigable* were now engaged. They were escorting the outbound freighter, *Hudson Cavalier*, on its way from Mars to Nikko, one of the settlement worlds, where it would unload whatever cargo it was carrying and then make the return trip home, or to another colony, filled with goods from its current destination. Unfortunately, there were not enough warships to escort every ship in the solar system and there were certainly few, if any, at the settlement worlds to escort the ships once they arrived there. But it was a start.

Price was into the second month of his current

deployment and was very much looking forward to its end. He loved the navy and being in space, but he also loved Anika. The events of fourteen months ago changed his life—for the better. In an ideal world, they would be here together, but life was far from ideal and it certainly was not fair. His relationship with Anika had moved very quickly, and they never seemed to have enough time together. Her deployments were as long as his and their time together was limited to when those deployments did not overlap. The result was a series of brief, passionate, and intense interludes that left them both longing for more. *Someday* . . .

Hudson Cavalier was about two thousand miles from the *Indefatigable* and had been for most of the last two days. The ships traveled together as they made their way outbound to the orbital radius of Jupiter where in two hours the freighter and the *Indefatigable* would activate their Hawking Drives and make the jump to the Nikko settlement. Jupiter's orbital radius of five astronomical units was the closest to the sun that one could safely use the Hawking Drive. As a stardrive that relied upon warping spacetime to allow nearly instantaneous travel across light-years, the massive gravity wells of stars proved to be a noise and disturbance source from which one had to be a safe distance. Stars significantly warp spacetime and the designers of the Hawking Drive said that "bad things would happen" if you activated the drive too deep into a gravity well. There was some margin in the required Jovian distance requirement, but not much. The minimum safe distance was known as the Oppenheimer Limit. So far, the trip had been quiet and uneventful.

"Nelson, is there any nearby traffic?" He was speaking to the ship's AI, Lord Nelson. For simplicity, Price left off the "Lord" part. To him, it was a bad name for an AI. The last thing people want to feel is subservient to a machine intelligence and calling it "Lord," even if it was only an honorific bestowed upon the AI's namesake, just felt wrong.

"Nothing of note," said Nelson.

Price noted that and breathed a bit of a sigh of relief. Maybe their increased show of force was having the desired effect and the pirates were standing down. Maybe. Maybe not. But it looked like this assignment would be a quiet one—at least for this leg of the journey. He once again reviewed information about their destination, confirming that they would arrive within a few light-seconds of Nikko's shipping station, the *Hakudo Maru*, located near that system's Oppenheimer Limit.

What kind of day will I have today? Governor Saito asked himself as he emerged from his aircar that had just autonomously parked itself atop the landing pad reserved for himself and his lieutenant governor, Riku Ito. The pad was on the roof of the newly completed capitol building that had finally replaced the one first erected after the founding of the Nikko settlement nearly one hundred years before. He and his staff had just moved in a little over four months ago, and he wasn't yet tired of its newness and all the amenities lacking in their previous office. Saito wondered how he had ever been able to survive without the sauna that adjoined his office and the onsen in the courtyard. The architects had selected the location of the new capitol building so it could take advantage of the area's natural hot spring to fill the onsen. *Civilization finally arrives to Nikko!*

The day was glorious, with bright orange starshine and little humidity, and he could see things with clarity not possible on a normal day. From the snow-covered peaks of the New Suzuka mountains to the east and the coastal basin to the west, he again realized what a blessing it was to be on a new world that would never be despoiled like Earth was before the development of cheap, abundant energy and nearly one hundred percent recycling of, well, nearly everything. He stopped briefly to scan the mountains for signs of hikers, but then decided that no matter how clear the air might be, his vision would never be able to distinguish individuals from the trees and rocks at this distance.

Nikko was one of the first extrasolar settlements established and, as such, it now had one of the largest populations other than Earth. With nearly half a million residents, about five percent of which were on farms scattered throughout the countryside near the capital, Nikko in no way felt crowded like Tokyo and Kyoto, which Saito had been able to visit once, just before his selection as governor. In old Japan, there were still too many people crammed into too little space for his liking. During that trip, he had put the uncomfortable claustrophobia that he felt at being among so many people aside so that he could attend to the matter for which the Nikko Corporation had summoned him. He had known he was a candidate for the job of planetary governor, but he didn't expect being named to the position while he was there. When the announcement was made, Saito actually had second thoughts about accepting it, doubting his ability to effectively run a planetwide government that was really part of the Nikko conglomerate. His talent was in being a CEO and making money. Assuming the responsibility for the trash being sorted into the correct categories and picked up on time was not on his resumé at the time. Now it was. That was what made his days most interesting. He never knew if the day's most pressing issue would be civil or corporate. On Nikko, these were intertwined since its inception.

Nikko, the planet, was settled by multiple ships sent from Japan over a nearly seventy-five-year time span. Named for both the corporation and the city from which its founding family originated, Nikko was a rich and prosperous world, made so by manufacturing many of the goods needed by the smaller and more recent settlements being established through the growing sphere of human expansion into the galaxy, and by its innovation. The integration of government and corporation—with the traditional Japanese commitment of workers to the company and vice versa—resulted in new technologies and consumer product ideas being developed here and sold, with quite handsome profits, back on Earth. Earthers seemed ever eager to buy and use the new neuro-sim implants that were designed and developed just a few kilometers away from the capitol building. These, and the injectable nanobots that had single-handedly increased the human life span by more than a quarter of a century due to their ability to repair cellular telomeres and stave off senescence, had made the company and the settlement quite wealthy. Saito had, of course, shared in the profits.

He made his way to his office, passing a few other people and the ubiquitous cleaner bots winding up their overnight tasks making sure the office space was clean, neat, and fresh each morning for the hundreds of employees that would eventually arrive and begin their workday. As was his custom, he was at work at least an hour before most of his colleagues and staff.

He entered the office and immediately got to work by reading the various flash reports provided at the end of yesterday's workday, summarizing the issues that would need his attention or involvement, or at least awareness, as the week continued. One in particular caught his eye.

Five large ships had emerged in the outer solar system late yesterday afternoon without any advance warning and without any of the standard beacons that usually included the ship's registry and cargo manifest. Since they had emerged not far from the *Hakudo Maru*, Nikko's shipping station in the system's asteroid belt, their arrival seemed ordinary enough. That was the first stop of just about every ship bound in system. It was highly unusual to have more than one ship arrive at a time, let alone five, and none identified themselves. *Probably some sort of communications glitch,* he thought. *Perhaps on our side. We'd better do a system check.* Saito assumed it was unlikely that all five ships had their beacons fail or turned off, so where other than in their ground systems could the problem be?

Saito made a mental note to ask space traffic control at the *Hakudo Maru* if they had been able to make contact.

He would bring that up at the staff meeting. He moved on to the next flash report about, of course, the drainage problem on the eastern side of the city. The recent heavy rains had flooded a few residential blocks and they were clamoring for a fix to the problem. *My work never ends,* he thought as he immersed himself in sorting through the electronic to-do list that was his morning pre-staff meeting routine.

The *Indefatigable* and *Hudson Cavalier* made their jump to Nikko without incident, with both ships arriving less than five thousand miles from the *Hakudo Maru*. Price was looking forward to visiting Nikko, even if he would only see it from high orbit. Earthlike worlds were few and far between and he relished seeing as many as he could.

Lieutenant Carlin Stuart, his XO, was on his last deployment before taking his new assignment as an instructor at the Commonwealth Space Naval Academy back on Earth. Price couldn't figure out why someone as accomplished as Stuart would remove himself from the line where he stood a good chance of promotion to captain his own ship. That is, he couldn't understand it until he met Stuart's wife. They were a perfect match and wanted to start a family. So when the job opportunity groundside came open, he applied for it and was selected. Price was happy for them, though Stuart would be sorely missed.

"Lieutenant Stuart, send our entry report to the *Hakudo Maru* and give them our regards," said Price.

"Yes, sir. Message away."

"Captain! There are five unknown ships within ten

thousand miles of our position, and they appear to be attacking the *Hakudo Maru*," said Stuart abruptly.

"Go to General Quarters and bring up the tactical display," said Price, his training kicking in without even having to think.

The image on the screen did not paint a pretty picture. Nikko's shipping station was shown in the center, with five red bogies rapidly converging on it from roughly twelve o'clock. The *Indefatigable* and *Hudson Cavalier* were moving slowly toward the station from eight o'clock. All of the ships were well within missile range, making the current situation immediately perilous. On the top right corner of the screen was a telescopic view of the *Hakudo Maru*. The station was obviously seriously damaged, with a gaping hole on the side facing them—the torn structure ragged and blackened. As Price was watching, the telltale flash of a nuclear detonation consumed more than half of the remaining structure. It was highly unlikely that anyone could still be alive there. *They are almost right on top of us*, Price thought.

"Order the *Hudson Cavalier* out of here," said Price. "Get her the hell away from here."

"Nelson, do we have a firing solution on any of the attacking ships?"

"Yes. But the launch window closes in less than thirty seconds. Based on the current velocities of the attacking ships relative to ours, they will be well past the *Hakudo Maru* and out of missile range after that."

"Launch two anti-ship missiles at whichever ship we have the best chance of hitting; nuclear weapons are authorized," said Price. Nelson nearly instantaneously verified Price's voiceprint, as was required to authorize the use of nuclear-enabled missiles. Moments later, the two missiles were in space and accelerating toward their target.

"Captain, bogey three just launched two missiles toward the *Hudson Cavalier*," Nelson said.

Price could now see the flowing yellow dots on the tactical display showing the gently curved path the enemy missiles were flying toward the unarmed cargo ship the *Indefatigable* was there to protect. "Nelson, put us between those missiles and the *Hudson Cavalier*, flank speed. Launch decoys and bring the Gatling guns to bear." Electromagnetically actuated, the Gatling guns could spew a relatively thick wall of depleted uranium pellets in the path of the missiles as they neared the ship, with a high likelihood that any missile getting that far would impact one of the pellets and be damaged or destroyed by the kinetic energy released during the impact.

The timing would be tight. Price could see the location and trajectory of the slowly accelerating *Hudson Cavalier*, the missiles, and the more rapidly accelerating *Indefatigable* on the screen. Ahead of each was an estimated trajectory, showing that the *Indefatigable* would meet the incoming missiles just seconds before they would otherwise impact the *Hudson Cavalier*. The seconds ticked by, simultaneously seeming to move at a glacial pace and at breakneck speed. Finally, Price heard the thrumming of the Gatling guns being activated. He knew that next thing he and his ship might feel would be either nothing, which would mean they successfully intercepted and destroyed the incoming missiles, or a likely lethal explosion ripping the ship to pieces. *Tick. Tick. Ti—*

"Missiles destroyed," said Nelson, as the yellow blinking lights on the tactical display winked out and Price exhaled, not realizing until then that he had been holding his breath.

"Is the *Hudson Cavalier* clear?" asked Price.

"If the enemy vessels don't have more capable systems than ours, then yes. However, based on the brief engagement, it is impossible to say with any certainty what their capabilities might be."

"Lieutenant Stuart, order the *Hudson Cavalier* to immediately reverse course and return to Sol. Tell the captain that he is to contact the Commonwealth Space Navy via the SOS network and fill them in as soon as he returns. We are going to remain here to see what we can do, if anything," Price said.

The display showed the five rapidly departing bogies, the slowly accelerating *Hudson Cavalier*, and one very damaged *Hakudo Maru*.

"Bring up the radar at full power. Let's see what we can learn about these ships using the best sensor systems the Commonwealth can muster. It will also let them know that a warship is in system. Maybe that will give them second thoughts," said Price. He knew he was likely engaging in willful self-delusion, but when there was little hope, long shots were worth trying. "Take us over to what's left of the *Hakudo Maru*. Maybe by some miracle there will be survivors."

Today was not a day for miracles.

✦ ✦ ✦

Governor Saito was on his second cup of coffee when the door to his office opened and his minister of defense, Eichi Hayashi, entered hurriedly, bowing as soon he crossed the threshold.

"Saito-chizi, we received an urgent message from the *Hakudo Maru* and then abruptly lost contact with the station. They reported being under attack," said Hayashi.

"Under attack? Are you sure?" asked Saito as he rose from his chair.

"Yes. Before we lost contact, the *Senchō* reported that several missiles were launched from the ships that arrived late yesterday and that two had already hit vital areas of the station," said Hayashi, again bowing as he delivered the bad news. "Routine telemetry from the station ceased at the same moment. I fear they are destroyed."

"Fifty crew. Were there any survivors? Do we know anything more about the ships? Did they make contact and issue demands?" asked Saito.

"Unfortunately not, Saito-chizi. However, our radar confirms they remain inbound for Nikko," said Hayashi. "We also have confirmation that the Commonwealth warship *Indefatigable* arrived at about the time of the attack escorting an inbound cargo ship. Her captain is looking for survivors at the wreckage of the *Hakudo Maru*."

Saito looked at the clock and saw the Council of Ministers meeting was to convene in about an hour.

"Inform the ministers. I want to know everything we can about the incoming ships, what happened to the *Hakudo Maru*, and our options," said Saito.

"Yes, immediately," said Hayashi as he again bowed and backed out of the room.

Saito knew that his options were few. There hadn't been a major war on Earth for nearly 150 years, and he knew of no escalation in tensions between Japan and the other major power blocks. If war had broken out, then they would surely have received word via some sort of drone message or a fleeing ship. Furthermore, he knew that none of the other settlements had the resources to build five ships, let alone warships. *So, who were these attackers and what did they want?*

Saito's hour passed quickly as he, in a whirl of activity, cleared his calendar, personally contacted several of his key advisors beyond those who would be in the meeting of the Council of Ministers, and began forming the basics of a plan.

When he entered the council chamber, the various members rose, bowed, and then returned to their seats. Saito took his customary seat at the head of the table and wasted no time in starting the discussion. The ministers had already been briefed by Hayashi.

"Hayashi, when will the five ships arrive? More precisely, based on what we know of their attack on the *Hakudo Maru*, when will we be in range of their weapons?" asked Saito.

"Five days and twelve hours," replied Hayashi, his tone simple and matter-of-fact.

"And they still do not respond to our radio and laser comm messages?" asked Saito.

"No response. We are broadcasting in every major Earth language, trying all known frequencies, using digital and analog signals, as well as Earth-standard laser wavelengths," replied Hinata Maeda, Minister of Internal

Affairs and Communications. She was the newest member of the council and one of the most energetic. It was the twenty-second century and still Japanese women had to struggle to gain acceptance at the highest level of industry and government. Maeda never let it deter her ambitions and never raised sexism as an issue. Saito liked and respected her.

"What about commercial shipping? Are there any interstellar-capable carriers in the system that can get here before the Kurofune arrive?" Saito asked, giving the interlopers a name for the first time. It was a name that would resonate with the council and the general populace. Saito was shrewd and always chose his words carefully and with forethought. Kurofune were what his Earthborn ancestors and countrymen called the ships belonging to European vessels arriving in Japan in the sixteenth and nineteenth centuries. The Kurofune, or "black ships," forever altered—Saito would say destroyed—the Japanese way of life.

"Yes, Saito-chizi. There is one cargo ship in the system, the *Asama Maru*, it departed yesterday bound for Earth," said Ryusei Aoki, the Minister of Interstellar Trade and Industry. Aoki had served on the council for many years and was one of Saito's most trusted confidants. "And then there is the Commonwealth warship, the *Indefatigable*. It arrived during the attack on the *Hakudo Maru*."

The ministers all looked up expectantly with the hope of salvation stemming from the arrival of the *Indefatigable* showing on their faces.

"It would be best to not place too much hope in what the Commonwealth ship can do. I spoke briefly with her captain and he informed me that that even if he were to boost at maximum acceleration, the soonest his ship could arrive at Nikko would be at least a half day behind the Kurofune. And he was reluctant to commit even to that. One ship against five are not good odds," said Hayashi.

"He cannot simply do nothing!" blurted one of the ministers.

"He also cannot risk his life in a futile gesture that would likely end in failure and the loss of his ship," said Hayashi.

"And what of the *Katori*?" Saito asked.

"The *Katori* is in orbit and ready to go," replied Hayashi. "But it is a rescue ship, not a warship. Though the crew are technically soldiers, the ship has only a point-defense laser system and in their annual training exercise, they use it on derelict ships, not to . . . to . . . well, shoot at someone."

Saito remained silent and, out of respect, the rest of the council sat patiently awaiting his response. The world had changed since he arrived at work this beautiful morning and he knew that the most difficult decisions of his life would be made in the next five days. Perhaps the most important, those affecting the lives of the people on Nikko, might be decided in the next few hours.

"We will immediately begin transmitting on all available communications channels the unconditional surrender of Nikko. The *gaijin* showed no mercy to the crew of the *Hakudo Maru*, and we can expect them to act similarly when they arrive here. We don't know what they want, but we do know they kill without provocation and with impudence," said Saito. "Maeda, see that the message begins transmission as soon as this council is adjourned."

"Yes, Saito-chizi," she said.

"See to it that the outbound cargo ship is immediately ordered to return to Nikko. The ship's cargo holds are to be emptied and filled with as many evacuees as possible. Priority is to be given to children and a few caregivers. I want them outbound to the Oppenheimer Limit opposite the arrival trajectory of the Kurofune ships. They are to proceed to Earth with haste. And coordinate everything with the captain of the Commonwealth ship," said Saito.

"Saito-chizi, a cargo ship can carry a few hundred people, at most. There are more children than that in this prefecture alone," said Maeda.

"We must save who we can. The Ministry of Home Affairs should come up with a plan to select the children and caregivers who will evacuate on the cargo ship. The next step is the orderly evacuation of the cities. Please provide a plan by the end of the day. I will address the people tonight. Please alert the 'net providers that I will be preempting all of their programming for an important announcement."

"And the *Katori*?" asked Hayashi.

"I will let you tell me how to best deploy the *Katori*," said Saito. Like the captain of the Commonwealth ship, he did not want to send the crew of the *Katori* to their deaths, but if they could find a way to use the cruiser to slow down or weaken the Kurofune, then he would do as he must. At this time, he had no idea how to use the small ship. He would leave that to his experts, Hayashi specifically, to provide a recommendation.

Four hours later, after recovering no survivors from the wreckage, Price was in the CIC with Lieutenant Stuart and his tactical officer, Lieutenant Ashley Gold, to review what they had learned so far and to discuss options. Nelson, as usual, was also in attendance.

"I need options," said Price. "My gut tells me we should boost for Nikko at maximum thrust to do as much damage as we can. My head tells me that would be a suicide run and that the strategic move would be to remain here, observe what happens, and then return to Sol with as much intel as we can gather. What am I missing?"

"Sir, based on the damage to the *Hakudo Maru* and what we learned in their missile attack on the *Hudson Cavalier*, it appears that their missile tech is at least comparable to ours. From their drive signatures and trajectory, I would say the same for their propulsion system. Combine this with their tonnage and the fact that there are five of them, I would say your head is giving you the best course of action. To follow and engage them would be a suicide run and likely not alter whatever intentions they might have," said Gold. She was not one to mince words.

"I agree," said Stuart. "We need to gather as much intel as we can and then return to the solar system as quickly as possible. We don't know if this incursion is part of a larger attack or an isolated event. As we speak there could be dozens of these ships inbound toward Earth or attacking other settlements."

"If this is part of a larger, more coordinated attack, then we should consider departing now in case we are needed elsewhere—with better odds," added Gold.

A surprise attack on an unsuspecting Earth was a terrifying thought and a risk Price was not prepared to take.

"Very well. I will inform the governor that we are departing for Earth and assure him that we will be back as soon as we can—in force," said Price. He knew that the promise was hollow and would be perceived as such by Governor Saito. Nikko would be on its own.

Six hours later, the *Indefatigable* was at the Oppenheimer Limit and jumped for home.

Five days passed quickly. Too quickly.

The Kurofune were only minutes away from what Hayashi and his experts had calculated would be the outermost reach of their missiles—if they were to attack and used the same weapons that destroyed the *Hakudo Maru*. The people of Nikko had no idea of the hostiles' real capabilities or intentions. Saito was in the council chamber, which had been converted to a war room from which he and his ministers had spent the last several days planning their response to the incoming ships. There was not much they could do in terms of defense. Their strategy was more disaster preparedness and response planning.

The population of Nikko City had taken the news with surprising collective calm. Some people and families evacuated to the countryside, but most decided to remain in the city. The Ministry of Home Affairs used a lottery system to determine which families, mainly their children, would be evacuated. The ship carrying them was now underway on its voyage out of the star system and toward Earth. Hopefully, he would soon be able to give the recall order and reunite these children with their parents. The ministry also established a plan similar to what the British did in London during Earth's World War II and evacuated several thousand children from the city to willing families living on the many farms away from town where they would be presumably safer than in the city itself.

In the event the Kurofune, whoever or *whatever* they were, decided to occupy the planet, the Ministry of Defense organized each prefecture in Nikko City around appointed civil defense chiefs who were responsible for assuring that their regional populations remained stable and responsive to any directives issued by the civil authorities, while simultaneously organizing resistance wherever and whenever possible, should the need arise. Armed resistance would be exceedingly difficult since there were virtually no personal weapons to be found on the planet outside of the police. With no predators on the planet that had ever posed a threat to the colonizing humans, there had been no need for self protection in the populace.

Hayashi's plans for the *Katori* were similarly weak, though it was not for lack of trying. Saito knew there wasn't much the cruiser could do to stop the Kurofune, but he had held out hope that the Ministry of Defense would come up with something useful. They did not. Rather than commit the crew's lives to any sort of useless defensive maneuver, he ordered it to proceed to the

Oppenheimer Limit but in a direction opposite to that from which the invaders were arriving. It was to remain there until called home or it became apparent that it should make its jump to Earth. The Kurofune were not displaying any performance, speed, or maneuverability beyond what human ships could achieve, so Saito felt reasonably confident that the *Katori* and the cargo ships were safely out of harm's way.

Saito was extremely concerned about the lack of a response from the hostile ships. Every possible means of communication with them had been tried, continuously, for the past several days. Their response: *silence*.

Saito sat with his ministers as they watched the projection of the Kurofune ships' trajectories cross the line they thought to be the outer range of their weapons. Saito realized he had been holding his breath and then released it after the ships were noticeably across the line. Maybe . . .

His hopes were soon dashed by Hayashi.

"Missile launches detected," he said, his voice deadpan.

Saito cringed and asked, "How many?" He knew the number of missiles launched was likely immaterial. From what they could tell, the *Hakudo Maru* had been destroyed by nuclear weapons, not kinetic projectiles. Whoever the interlopers were, they had used nuclear bombs without hesitation.

"Five. The computer projects they are bound for Nikko City and the surrounding region," said Hayashi.

Saito wondered how many of the people in the city were able to find shelter that would protect them from a nuclear explosion. He also wondered if they should even try.

The radiation and devastation that would accompany such an attack would be horrific, especially since there were precious few areas on the planet where any form of civilization existed that could provide post-attack relief. He knew that there were scattered settlements around the planet that were not technically under the government's control, but they were sparsely populated and mostly organized around subsistence farmers—without any sort of infrastructure. Perhaps it would be better to die in the initial attack than during its aftermath.

"How long do we have until the missiles arrive?" asked Saito, again just going through the motions. Everything seemed to be moving in slow motion.

"One hour, Saito-chizi," Hayashi replied.

Fifty-nine and a half minutes later, five twenty-megaton fusion bombs exploded in the air over Nikko City, one after the other, instantly killing Saito and nearly everyone in a twenty-five-mile radius and millions more within hours.

After detecting the explosion, the *Katori* activated its Hawking Drive and jumped to the Earth's solar system.

CHAPTER 2

Price was running through the possibilities that awaited him and the other ships in the fleet as they entered the star system and made way for the Nikko settlement. For him it was a bittersweet return, having had to depart without being able to do a damn thing to help them just over a week ago. He and the seven accompanying ships were a significant fraction of Earth's space-worthy defense fleet that hitherto was fighting only bureaucrats for its continued existence.

The fleet, a conglomeration of ships from multiple countries, had been hastily assembled after the ships arrived from Nikko telling of the attack upon it. No one knew who the attackers were, their motivations, or their capabilities other than that they had entered the Nikko system and destroyed both the system's cargo hub and, from what they could tell from the long-range imagery provided by one of the ships that escaped, the settlement on the planet. Fortunately, when Price had returned to Earth, it was at peace and there were no signs of invasion.

News of the attack on Nikko had spread rapidly, in governments and among the general population on Earth, and across the many habitats and mining ventures scattered throughout the solar system.

Though there had been no signs of the attackers in the solar system, the situation could have quite easily become dire if the interlopers at Nikko were to suddenly appear there. The *Indefatigable* and every other warship in the system had been on high alert. Price joined two of the other Commonwealth ships and took up station near Vesta in the asteroid belt. Fortunately, the nations of Earth, after quickly determining that the attackers were not some sort of sneak attack by a terrestrial country, had agreed to coordinate the defense of Earth with each sending their warships to different regions of the solar system, in and out of the ecliptic, so that they could respond quickly should the attackers materialize anywhere within five to fifteen astronomical units of Earth. The United States' vessels were split between Mars and the Moon; China took its ships and split them evenly at roughly two AU distance from Earth above and below the ecliptic plane. The remaining countries had divided ships among various positions on the other side of the solar system from Earth to allow nearly 360-degree spherical protection. Operating on so little information, no one had known if this would be enough.

Finally, Price received new orders. A task force consisting of ships from each major space power on Earth would assemble near the orbit of Jupiter, but on the other side of the sun from the gas giant, for a jump to the Nikko system.

Of course, the Americans were in charge, as they seemed to always think they should be. Some traditions were just expected, and this was one. The flagship, the USSS *South Dakota*, was commanded by Admiral Li Wei. Price knew Wei and found him to be smart, capable, and typically American—Wei was a first-generation American, born of Chinese-immigrant parents. With Americans, you never knew what ethnicity you would be encountering. There were two American ships in the hastily assembled fleet, the *South Dakota* and the *Maryland*. The Commonwealth provided the *Indefatigable*. China sent two ships, the *Benghu* and the *Linyi*. The remaining ships, one each, were sent by Japan and the United Arab Emirates, the *Fuji* and the *Mubarraz*. The remaining ships were held in reserve to protect Earth.

All the warships were built and fielded to protect each nation's space assets from other Earth nations. Though some thought encountering extraterrestrial civilizations was a possibility and reason enough to build a defensive fleet, most did not. The failure of anyone to detect any signs of intelligent life beyond Earth, after over 250 years of looking, made policy makers, and those that controlled the purse strings, believe that the risk of hostile aliens was so small as to be infinitesimal. Lately, most nations were questioning the expense of maintaining even the few warships in their respective fleets. There had not been anything close to a global war on Earth since World War II—two and half centuries in the past. If humanity had outgrown war, why continue to build tools of war? Thankfully, the zeal for realizing a peace dividend had not quite taken hold. Every ship was now needed.

It took some time for the participating countries to agree how the fleet would coordinate command, control, and communications, or C3. In space naval operations, like any coordinated military operation, good C3 was essential. Without it, each ship would be operating independently, perhaps unknowingly firing upon a friendly ship, and mostly in the blind. Operating together, any fleet of ships had an effectiveness much greater than the sum of the capabilities of each individual ship. Price suspected that the technical problems, the control and communications part of C3, were overcome quickly. Engineers, when given a task, were good at working things out. It was the command part that probably took the most time to negotiate, with America and China wrangling over who would be in charge. The good news was that the C3 problems had been resolved and they were now underway.

Price, a student of military history, could not help but muse about how difficult such a multinational coordination would have been if carried out in an earlier era before real-time language-translation software became universal. It was still true that most people at least spoke English as a second language, a fact that remained a sore spot for the French and an annoyance to the Chinese.

The fleet jumped together to the Nikko system and took up station about 1.4 light-hours from the central star—at about Saturn's distance from Sol. Far enough to not violate the Oppenheimer Limit and to give them a good chance of arriving undetected. From here, they would assess what was going on in the system and determine their next moves. They desperately needed to know what they were headed into.

Each ship checked in via secure optical laser comm which could only be intercepted if you were in a direct line of sight and had your optical detectors set to look for a laser signal at the correct wavelength. There was not a more secure communication system available. The fleet was intact, in communication, and sharing data from their radar and optical sensors. Despite the differences in technologies and resulting capabilities, Price and the other captains in the fleet were getting a good sense of the tactical situation in and around Nikko.

There was no sign of ongoing conflict. Since they arrived, there had been no detection of the X-ray, neutron, or gamma-ray emissions characteristic of a nuclear explosion. They knew that several such explosions happened when Nikko was attacked, but the attack had apparently long-ago ceased.

Furthermore, there was no indication that the hostiles were nearby. Nikko's only quasi-warship, the *Katori*, had recorded the drive signatures of the incoming ships and found them to be surprisingly similar to their own fusion drives. None of the Earth ships currently detected operating fusion drives anywhere within their lines of sight. Of course, they were almost one and a half light-hours from Nikko's star and that meant they were seeing events that happened within the last one and a half hours as they looked inward. Looking outward, to avoid being surprised by anything or anyone waiting further out system, they were seeing what happened in the last several minutes, hours, and days—depending upon how far out they were able to gaze. There was no such thing as "real time" data when operating across such large distances and that made military planning even more complicated.

Price and his crew were at General Quarters and had been since entering the system. Based on the tactical situation, Price could now relax—a little.

"Secure from General Quarters," Price announced as he unbuckled from his chair. The ship's artificial gravity did a good job approximating one Earth gravity when the ship was stationary or under thrust to about three gees, but at higher thrust levels, the crew would notice inertia's inevitable effects. The artificial gravity also did not work during a Hawking Drive jump, causing momentary weightlessness every time the drive was used. For these reasons, it was standard practice for crew to be strapped in whenever possible.

"Sir, we have a message from the *South Dakota* and Admiral Wei," said Price's XO, Lieutenant Oliver Green. Green and Price had never served together before this deployment, but from what Price could tell, Green was professional, proficient, and not terribly social. When they had conversed over dinner in the wardroom, Green never allowed himself to be at ease. Price gave him the benefit of the doubt, this being their first time to serve together, but he was also concerned. Officers that were strung that tight often snapped.

"Let's hear it," said Price.

"Yes, sir," replied Green, keying the video to the main bridge screen, temporarily turning off the tactical display. Wei's image appeared, the 3-D visualizer making it appear that he was on the bridge speaking to Price directly.

"Captain Price, the *Indefatigable* and the *Linyi* will accompany the *South Dakota* inward to survey Nikko and search for survivors. I want the fleet to remain on high alert, but I see no need to maintain General Quarters. There do not appear to be any imminent threats, but we cannot take for granted that the hostiles have gone. They might just be sitting out there somewhere watching, like we are now. Once we light up our fusion drives, we will be announcing our arrival to anyone in the system. I am ordering all remaining ships to maintain their position with drives powered down, and they are to use only passive sensors. The only ships that will go active will be those of us inbound. I see no need to give away the actual size of our deployment. Trajectory information is being sent to your AI. Let me know if you have any questions," said Wei as his image winked out and was replaced by the tactical map of the system. The three ships that were to go inbound were now highlighted in yellow on the display.

"Nelson, I assume you have what you need to take us in?" asked Price.

"Yes, Captain. The formation and trajectory data are uploaded and plotted, awaiting the command to execute from Admiral Wei," replied Nelson. Nelson, unlike most AIs that Price had worked with, was often reticent to speak unless asked. Price was not yet sure if that was a good thing or a bad thing. Time would tell. Each AI had its own limited, preprogrammed personality and each took some time to get used to. Calling Nelson an AI was really a misnomer. So far as Price knew, no one had succeeded in creating a truly self-aware artificial intelligence. Nelson, and other AIs like him, came close but they were still nothing more than complex computer algorithms with a preprogrammed personality matrix overlaid to make them easier for humans to interact with. Of course, if one did become truly self-aware, how would anyone know?

Like three dancers converging on the stage, the *Indefatigable*, *South Dakota*, and *Linyi* fired their fusion thrusters and began their looping, minimum-energy trajectory toward Nikko and whatever awaited them there. Admiral Wei was apparently not in a huge hurry; the ships were limiting their acceleration to fifty percent of maximum, about two Earth gravities. Fast enough to get to Nikko within a few days, but not so fast as to be reckless. *If only we could use the Hawking Drive within a gravity well,* thought Price, not for the first time. The remaining ships held their relative position, minimizing emissions to reduce their likelihood of being detected.

Price used the time they spent traveling into the system to run combat simulations, pitting his tactical officers against various adversaries created by Nelson. With nearly instant access to the ship's enormous digital library of military history, Nelson was able to come up with many modernized variations of historical battles to throw at Price's crew. In some, it was *Indefatigable* fighting alone; in others, as part of a larger fleet with Nelson playing both the adversary and simulating the movements of the other human ships as they took commands from Price. In one that Price recognized afterward as a recreation of the Battle of Gaugamela, with the fleet defending Earth substituting for the Persians and the alien ships assuming the role and tactics of Alexander the Great, the Earth fleet lost rather spectacularly—just like the Persians. Price and his crew were able to win about half the simulated battles, and he suspected that Nelson might have allowed them to win some of those to not totally demoralize him and his crew. The experience was humbling and incredibly useful. In the age of space travel, mankind had never fought a war in space.

In the early days of interstellar travel, after the discovery of the Hawking Drive, there had been a few skirmishes over mining rights to some particularly attractive asteroids that were providing supplies to the burgeoning industries springing up in near-Earth space. It was impractical to bring all of the raw materials needed at the lunar and Mars shipyards out of the planetary gravity wells, so entrepreneurs did what entrepreneurs do—they innovated new business models and found that mining asteroids for the same raw materials was less expensive and could form the backbone of an entirely new supply chain. Along the way, there were disputes as to who "owned" what and in a few cases that led to the dispute being resolved the old-fashioned way—by force.

The dispute that almost triggered a real shooting war was over Oliver's Asteroid, a near Earth asteroid rich in platinum, tantalum, vanadium, and other elements that were commanding a high price at the shipyards. Price did not remember the names of the companies involved, only that one was registered in the United States and the other in Brazil. Both filed claims to the asteroid within hours of each other, not an easy thing to do considering the paperwork and processes involved, and both rushed to emplace their mining equipment on the asteroid accompanied by "protection" provided by ships from their respective countries. Tensions rose as the claimants' voices grew louder and more belligerent and eventually someone on the US ship fired on the Brazilian ship, putting a railgun-launched depleted-uranium spike through their hull which then, unfortunately, caused a containment failure of their fusion power plant. There was not much left of the Brazilian ship. Failure to contain a sustained fusion reaction makes for a bad day on a ship.

Back on Earth, Brazil put its planes in the air flying toward the southern US border. Fortunately, the US president at the time got on the hotline to his Brazilian counterpart and they agreed to cease hostilities and allow an international court to settle the dispute. The US ended up paying reparations to the families of the dead Brazilians and forced its mining company to share mineral rights at the asteroid with the other claimant. Though it successfully averted a war, Price seemed to remember that this particular president lost his reelection bid largely based on his handling of the conflict.

The bottom line was that that no one from Earth had experience fighting a real shooting war in space. The closest they had come was when the *Indefatigable* intercepted the missiles meant for the *Hudson Cavalier*; fortunately, the weapons systems and the people performed as they were supposed to. They had the ships, but their crews were completely green. And they were soon to be going against someone, or something, that might have a lot more experience at such things than they did. Price found the thought unsettling, and he was sure his concerns were shared by Admiral Wei.

Price was all too aware that his crew knew the same history and they were all too aware of their inexperience. Running the simulations kept them on their toes and hopefully helped prepare them for what would undoubtedly be unpredictable tactics by their unknown adversaries.

Indefatigable, *Linyi*, and *South Dakota* were on final approach to Nikko, at a distance of about two light-seconds, when the alarms sounded.

"Nelson, what have we got?" asked Price.

"Eight fusion-drive signatures, likely missiles, originating approximately 0.02 light-seconds out. Accelerating rapidly. Three are targeting *Indefatigable*, three on *Linyi*, and two on *South Dakota*. Radar emissions detected, likely for targeting. Estimated time to impact is two minutes. Initiating evasive maneuvers, activating radar jammers, and deploying chaff."

Price knew the drill. Nelson could respond much faster than a human in a defensive situation, so the AI was given near-complete flexibility for defending the ship. Price could override, of course, but in most cases that would be the complete wrong thing to do. Humans were still rather good at strategy and offensive tactics, but defense required too much to happen too quickly for their limited response time. If jammers, maneuvers, and chaff did not stop the missiles, then the only thing left was the point-defense Gatling guns. Of course, no one wanted a missile carrying a nuclear warhead to get that close . . .

"Were they launched by ships? What's their origin?" asked Price.

"Unknown. There are no signs of any ships near where

the missiles originated, so they could be sleepers activated by our approach," replied Nelson.

Drones, Price thought. *Set to take out whoever came to help the colonists on the world they attacked.* He shifted in his chair as the time seemed to pass in slow motion.

"Estimated time to first impact, one minute. Activating Gatling guns," said Nelson.

Price could feel the ship thrum as the fifteen Gatling guns on the starboard side of the ship began throwing hundreds of thousands of tiny pellets toward the incoming missiles at eight kilometers per second, roughly the orbital velocity of a spacecraft circling the Earth. At that speed, any missiles not fooled by the chaff would impact the wall of uranium in a few seconds and uncomfortably close to the ship. Close, but far enough away to mitigate the worst of a nuclear explosion.

Price was still in his chair, but he could feel the beads of perspiration growing on his brow and on his back. He felt helpless in the face of an impending storm.

"One missile has locked onto chaff and is now veering away. Make that two," said Nelson.

"Two down, one to go," said Price as he looked at the tactical display. He could see the tiny red missiles converging on his ship and the others on the 3-D display. The ships were close enough together that the speed-of-light delay would be small, and he could be sure he was seeing everything in almost real time.

"Thirty seconds," said Nelson just as the tactical display showed the remaining missile converging on *Indefatigable* wink out. He continued, "The final missile targeting us was destroyed without detonation. The *Linyi* successfully spoofed all the missiles that targeted her. She is also undamaged."

Price looked at the tactical display and saw that one of the missiles previously converging on the *South Dakota* was now moving away, likely following some piece of chaff or decoy. The other was getting closer and closer to the flagship when it, too, winked out. However, the display showed that it, unlike the missile that got near *Indefatigable*, detonated in what the sensor indicated was a nuclear explosion.

"Did she suffer any damage?" asked Price, wiping his brow.

"The *South Dakota*'s AI indicates that the ship suffered no damage," replied Nelson.

"Do we have any updates from the admiral?" asked Price.

"None. We are still on course to Nikko and decelerating. We should enter orbit in roughly 1.5 hours," replied Nelson.

"Take us to GQ2 until we're safely in orbit and know the composition of every rock, pebble, and piece of debris within two light-seconds of our position," said Price as he unbuckled from his chair and rose to his feet. It was time to pace. He did his best thinking when he was on his feet moving and not tethered to a chair—sometimes rank hath its privileges.

After a few moments, Price turned to Lieutenant Gold and stared thoughtfully at her before he began to speak.

"Lieutenant Gold, I want you to work with Nelson and see what else you can figure out about the attackers. We learned a lot from our first engagement, and this is an opportunity to learn more.

"Look at the spectral analysis of the drive signatures. I want to know how they were propelled, how they were targeted, and since one of them detonated close to the *South Dakota* we should be able to get a yield curve. It would also be good to know how the data we collect compares with the data collected by the ships that escaped from Nikko. They were further away, but we should be able to use their observations to help fill in the gaps from our sensors. Based on what we have seen, our attackers appear to be at about the same technological capability as us. But I need that confirmed."

"Yes, sir. I'm on it," replied Gold as she turned toward the console in front of her.

"After we achieve orbit, I want to know everything you can tell me that you've learned about the attackers and the status on Nikko," said Price as he resumed his pacing.

CHAPTER 3

From space, Nikko looked like a peaceful, beautiful Earth that never was. Sprawling deep-blue oceans surrounded unfamiliar continents. Wispy white clouds streaked across the planet's disk, and the ever-so-thin haze of the planetary atmosphere could be seen on the limb, especially visible as the *Indefatigable* orbited and moved from eclipse into daylight. When flying over the shadowed nightside of the planet, there was no sign of civilization. No artificial lights betrayed the location of cities as one would readily see on Earth and many of the settlement worlds. Nikko looked pristine. A world waiting for intelligent life to move in and make its own.

Only it was not supposed to be this way. Nearly a century ago, intelligent life had moved in and settled the world. Humans, mostly from Japan, had come to Nikko and established a small, but thriving settlement, and there should have been evidence of its existence for the three Earth ships to see from a mere five hundred kilometers above. Instead of settlement, they observed its remains.

Shortly after entering orbit, *Indefatigable* uncovered the aperture of its five-meter telescope and began taking pictures of the area where Nikko City should have been. Instead of buildings and busy thoroughfares, the pictures showed ugly, blackened ruins still smoldering from the nuclear fire that had enveloped them. Instead of the orderly green patterns of agriculture that should have been all-too evident all around the city, there were instead huge brown streaks that looked like someone had taken a dirty finger and smudged the image. From above, they saw nothing but death with no signs of intelligent life. Beyond where the attack had occurred, the world was largely untouched. The native flora looked like the humans had never arrived.

Price knew that some people might have escaped the conflagration by fleeing to the wilderness, but he had no idea of how to find them and doubted that a ground search and rescue was in Admiral Wei's immediate plans. They needed to assess the damage, render assistance if there was anyone in evidence of needing it—which there was not—and then return to Earth with as much information as possible to help the brass figure out what to do next. Price felt like he had been kicked in the gut.

They had completed three orbits, taking almost five hours to gather data, when it was time for the ships' captains to meet with Admiral Wei. Price took the meeting in the CIC with his XO and tactical officer.

On the screen, Wei's holoimage, and that of Captain Meng from the *Linyi*, were to Price's left and right, respectively. Price was projecting only his image, but like he chose to have his senior officers at his side, he knew that on each ship there were others present as well. This was not unusual since the meeting was not "eyes only." The meeting was being sent by laser comm to the remainder of the fleet, still waiting in passive mode in the outer solar system. The time delay alone would prevent their direct participation even if they were not under orders to remain quiet and passive.

The meeting began with a quick assessment of the damage to the settlement, largely reinforcing what Price had already determined and affirming his conjecture that there would be no attempt made to scour the surface for small groups of survivors. That would come later, should a rescue ship be sent for that specific purpose. The orbiting ships had broadcast radio messages, hoping for a response from someone on the surface, but there was none. Either there were no survivors, or they had no ready access to radio.

"Based on the evidence, it appears that the attackers have a level of technology surprisingly similar to our own. The nuclear explosions that destroyed Nikko City and the one that detonated near the *South Dakota* have yields comparable to what we deploy on our ships. Spectral analysis of the exhaust plumes from the missiles that were launched against us again match fairly closely with what our ship-to-ship missiles employ. Their acceleration and overall flight performance do not appear to be that much different either. All in all, if we hadn't been able to account for all of the Earth's warships, I would say that Nikko was attacked by another terrestrial power," said Admiral Wei.

This caused the three captains to eye each other warily,

not with suspicion, but certainly with anticipation of perhaps seeing an unexpected reaction. Price immediately felt bad about his own reaction and the paranoid thoughts that Wei's comment evoked.

"Admiral, that just doesn't make sense," said Price, voicing a thought he had been harboring since the failed missile attack. "We know these ships aren't from Earth. We would know if any terrestrial power had launched them and none of the settlement worlds have the infrastructure to build them—yet. In a few years, maybe. And of all the ones that might have been able to do so, Nikko would have been at the top of the list."

"Go on," said Wei.

"What are the odds of humanity encountering aliens that presumably evolved into an intelligent, tool-using species and developed space travel and war-making capabilities at the same level as ours and at the same time that we did? We have always thought we might encounter other life in the universe, but it would make sense for that life to be at a completely different level of development than us. They should either be ahead of us in their science and technology or behind us. The odds of us encountering aliens with roughly the same capabilities as we are probably about zero, or so close to zero that it doesn't matter," said Price.

"But aren't the laws of physics the same everywhere? Doesn't it make sense that any tool-using species might come to the same understanding of the universe and develop comparable tools using those laws? Why should we assume they would arrive at something completely different?" asked Captain Meng.

"Oh, I agree. The laws of physics are the same. And I would not be at all surprised to see an alien species develop similar technologies to ours. But I would expect that to have happened thousands or millions of years ago or thousands or millions of years in the future. Hell, I wouldn't have this reaction if in two hundred years we were to encounter them and say, 'How quaint! They are using the same drives we first used two hundred years ago.' But that is not the case here. We are encountering them *now*; at the *same time*, we are using the *same* technology. That is just . . . improbable," said Price.

"Improbable or not, it's real," said Wei, regaining control of the meeting. "We need to return to Earth as soon as possible with the data we've gathered and hope that someone in military intelligence can make sense of it all. We depart in two hours to rejoin the rest of the fleet and return home. The trajectory information will be relayed to your AI. Any questions?" asked Wei.

There were none.

Two hours later, the fusion drives of the *South Dakota*, the *Linyi*, and *Indefatigable* lit to propel them for their outer solar system rendezvous and trip home.

Hidden by the glare of the Earth ships' fusion drives, twenty-five additional missiles ignited their own propulsion systems and began following. While the Earth ships had been assessing the capabilities of their enemies, so had the computers of the powered-down missile swarm that had been planted near Nikko for this very purpose. They, too, had cataloged the capabilities of *their* adversary's shipboard defenses and had developed tactics to exploit the weaknesses they found. As they departed, being careful to avoid detection by moving too far from the Earth ships' fusion exhaust plumes, the robotic missiles and their limited AIs, like true predators, had a plan.

"Incoming missiles!" exclaimed Lieutenant Gold at the same moment that Nelson sounded the call to General Quarters.

Price was in his chair reviewing the technical details they had been able to glean about the attackers and quickly switched gears to respond. He pulled up the tactical screen and immediately did not like what he saw: at least fifteen missiles were rapidly converging on the *South Dakota* and five each on the *Linyi* and *Indefatigable*—all from aft. The one direction where their ability to detect the fusion plumes of enemy ships or missiles was more difficult when they were under thrust, their own plumes potentially masking those of any attacker.

Nelson was already reacting, taking evasive action with the ship and deploying chaff. Unfortunately, these missiles had been able to get a lot closer than the previous batch and that left precious little time for the ship to take evasive action, forcing it to instead rely on spoofing and point defense.

"Forty-five seconds to impact. All five missiles are still converging on us," said Lieutenant Gold.

Price could see that the chaff was having no effect and at the same moment again felt the vibration of the Gatling guns attempting to detonate the hostiles by throwing up a wall of kinetic energy projectiles between *Indefatigable* and what was coming at her.

Price saw one of the hostiles wink out from the tactical array, then another. Three left.

"Thirty seconds."

Price felt the artificial gravity strain as Nelson increased the ship's acceleration to four gees. With a compensation limit of just over three Earth gravities, Price felt the pressure of the extra gees not being nulled pushing him into his chair. The crew knew their jobs and had trained for this. If they were all at their stations, then they would be buckled in and spared the gyrations the ship was now attempting to evade the missiles.

The vibrations grew as Nelson increased the rate of fire, making the pellets yet more dense and reducing the likelihood of a breakthrough. Another hostile winked out on the tactical screen. Two remained.

"Ten seconds," said Gold.

The ship shifted like it had been bumped and the aft sensor array went offline. Price knew this was probably due to a premature detonation of a nuclear weapon. Close enough to unleash hellish radiation, but not necessarily close enough to cause physical damage to the ship. Any crew members on that side of the ship probably just received a sizable and dangerous dose of radiation.

The next bump took the primary power systems offline, plunged the bridge into darkness, and turned off the artificial gravity generators. He heard the sound of someone on the bridge puking. Annoying, yes, but not one of his major concerns. As the emergency power kicked in and artificial gravity resumed, down became down again and the depressurization alarm sounded. *If that was not a direct hit, then it was damn close,* thought Price as he recovered from the thrashing.

"Nelson, damage report," said Price.

There was no response.

"Lieutenant Gold, by my count that was the last missile. Please tell me there are no more," said Price.

"Unknown, sir. Aft and port sensors are rebooting. The first nuke took both sensor arrays down. I'm getting no data from the starboard sensors at all," said Gold, who was working so rapidly on her console that Price didn't think he could keep up even if he tried. He did not try. He had other, more pressing matters on his mind.

"Lieutenant Green, I need a damage report and I need it fast. Are we losing atmosphere on the bridge?" asked Price.

"No, sir. The depressurization is localized starboard where it looks like we took an almost direct hit. The missile must have detonated next to our outer hull. From what I can tell, the starboard Gatling guns, the mess, medical bay, and most of our non-ammunition stores are . . . gone. The explosion tore a hole in the hull and severed some of the power lines from the reactor room. The reactor and propulsion system are undamaged. It is too early to estimate casualties," said Green.

"So, we are wounded and temporarily blind. Any news from *Linyi* or *South Dakota*?"

"No, sir. Laser comm is also down, both broadcast and receive. And there have been no radio transmissions since just before the attack," replied Ensign Murphy. Murphy was on duty at the signals station.

"Murphy, find out why Nelson isn't responding and fix him if you can," directed Price.

"Yes, sir. I have already started a diagnostic and the

preliminary results show that the first nuke overloaded some of his circuits and the second took him down entirely. His core processors are completely powered down."

"Can you reboot him?" asked Price.

"I can try, but the manual says he might come up fine or, well, not at all. There's a chance the blast wiped his experiential memory and he'll be completely reset," responded Murphy.

"Give it your best shot," said Price, wondering what a freshly activated AI would require in terms of situational awareness to be of any help at all and not wanting to think about the potential loss of the AI's Nelson personality. Price had grown to be comfortable with it. *Him,* he corrected himself.

The next seven minutes seemed like hours. *Indefatigable* was literally flying blind, damaged, and almost helpless.

"Captain, the aft and port sensors are back online," reported Lieutenant Gold.

"The comm system just came back online as well," said Murphy.

As they spoke, the tactical display partially reappeared. Partially, because the starboard side was just showing as empty and black with no data. Price was momentarily relieved that no fusion signatures were visible anywhere close by. The relief was replaced by dread as he realized that the signatures of *South Dakota* and *Linyi* should have been readily visible. They were not.

The *Linyi* was still on the main screen, inactive and unmoving, but physically there. The *South Dakota* was nowhere to be seen, on screen or tactical. That could only mean one thing.

"Murphy, raise the *Linyi* however you can and send a sitrep by laser comm to the rest of the fleet immediately. Also inform them that they are not to attempt a rescue. I don't want them firing up their fusion drives until we are sure there aren't any more of these damned missiles out here waiting for new targets," said Price.

Admiral Wei and the *South Dakota* were dead; there was no other explanation for them not showing up on the tactical display. *Indefatigable* and *Linyi* had each barely survived five missiles, let alone the fifteen that Wei faced. They had arrived wanting to better understand their enemy's capabilities and now they knew. While the Earth and her adversary were technologically comparable, the attackers were much farther ahead tactically. The Earth fleet's inexperience in fighting a space war was made clear today, and they had better learn from it pretty damn quick or they would be in trouble. Deep trouble.

"XO, I want this ship moving again as quickly as possible. We might be too late to help the *South Dakota* but maybe not the *Linyi*," Price said.

"Murphy, let me know when you raise the *Linyi*. Find out if they need help and make sure they can still receive our IFF code. I don't want their defense systems to see us and think we're the enemy," he continued.

Both acknowledged their orders and focused their attention back on their work. Price activated his monitor and began annotating the ship's status reports with his personal observations, He wanted to get this info to every ship in the fleet in case there were more surprises awaiting them before they got home. That way, at least one of the ships might return to Earth with all the valuable intel they had gathered so far. They had paid dearly for it.

"Sir, I have comm with the *Linyi*. Their primary communication array is damaged, so they are patching through one of their low-gain antennas. The signal is weak, but the link closes. Their damage is much worse than ours. Their AI is down, as is the fusion reactor. They are on auxiliary power and have no maneuvering capability," reported Ensign Murphy.

"Can you connect with Captain Meng?" asked Price.

"Sir, Captain Meng is dead. Captain Cai is in charge," replied Murphy.

"Captain Cai?" asked Price, not familiar with the name. He had learned the names of the bridge officers on the *Linyi* and Cai was not one of them.

"She's the *Linyi*'s medical officer," said Murphy.

Price winced. If the ship's doctor was in command, then the *Linyi* must have lost a lot of her crew.

"Let me speak with her," said Price. It took only a moment for the connection to be made. It was audio only, no video.

"Captain Cai, how may we render assistance?" asked Price.

"Captain Price, I'm glad we were able to reach you. It is an awful mess over here. I have assumed command. Captain Meng and the bridge officers are dead. We need to evacuate the ship, and we have a lot of crew either too injured to move themselves or who are trapped aft that we need to free. The fusion-reactor containment failed, and the radiation levels are going up back there pretty fast," she replied. Price was impressed by her coolness despite being thrust many levels up the command chain to be the highest-ranking officer on the entire ship. He was also impressed by her English. She had obviously spent some time in America or studied there due to her American accent. If the *Linyi* were not a Chinese ship, he would have thought the person with whom he was speaking was from the USA.

"Is the ship in immediate danger of any sort of explosion? Would I be risking my ship if I were to come alongside to get your wounded?" asked Price.

"One of my engineering techs says he doesn't think there is an immediate danger. The reactor cannot explode and any gas buildup that might cause one is venting to vacuum. That whole area is open to space through a gash torn in the side of the ship by one of the explosions," she replied.

Great, her engineering tech says it is safe. That means her engineers are either dead or severely wounded. Price knew that the navy's techs were well trained and that he could *probably* trust his assessment, but he would rather have heard it from someone higher up the technical chain of expertise than "tech." But if the tech was all they had, then that was good enough.

"Very good. We will be there within the hour. How many of your crew transfer shuttles are operational?" Price asked.

"Three. The others were destroyed," she replied. Price could hear her telling someone trying to get her attention to wait. He needed to let her go—she had more pressing matters to attend to until his ship arrived.

"Have them prepped and ready to start sending over

your wounded as soon as we arrive. We will send over some of ours to help with the transfer. And Captain, prep the rest of your crew to abandon ship. We need to get everyone off the *Linyi* and onto the *Indefatigable* for the trip home. And we have to do it quickly."

"Yes, sir. We will be ready," she said.

Price cut the connection and turned to Lieutenant Gold.

"Lieutenant. I do not want any more surprises. They know we are here, and they hurt us. If there are any more of them or their damnable drones still around, then I want to know about it. Turn the radar to full power and light up everything nearby. I want a full IR scan to see if anything out there is emitting heat and, if so, then I want to know how much and whether it might be a risk. When we are boosting to rest of the fleet, I do not want the remaining ships to be caught by surprise like we were. Everything within a few light-minutes of this ship and every Earth ship in this system needs to be found, identified, cataloged, and deemed a threat or not as soon as possible," said Price.

The rescue and transfer of the wounded from the *Linyi* took nearly a day. A day well spent, considering they saved over one hundred lives. The *Linyi* left Earth with a complement of 253. They removed as many bodies as they could, but nearly one hundred had been lost to the vacuum of space and were unrecoverable. There were no survivors from *South Dakota*.

Indefatigable's radar, infrared, and optical survey of nearby space revealed no additional alien ships or missiles present. The rest of the fleet loudly announced their presence by illuminating everything within forty light-minutes of their location with their network of high-power radar. From what they could tell, there were no more hostiles.

Despite Murphy's best efforts, Nelson never came back online. The AI did, but not Nelson. Most of his subsystems and subroutines rebooted without incident, but the core processor, that which housed the highest functioning portions of what created the being they knew as Nelson, never fully returned. Price hoped that the engineers at the lunar shipyard would be able to restore his personality and recent memory.

Indefatigable lost seven crew members in the battle and its aftermath, six immediately and the seventh just after the survivors of the *Linyi* finished coming aboard. Seven letters to seven grieving families that Price would have write on the return trip.

It took another seven days to rendezvous with the fleet, covering a distance of just over seventy light-minutes, or 1.3 billion kilometers. It then took all of one microsecond for the Hawking Drive to get them back to the Sol system.

Every night during the relatively slow crawl to the Oppenheimer Limit before jumping home, Price laid awake thinking of what he could have done differently—and of Anika, the love of his life who was waiting on him back at the lunar base. He would be returning safely to her, but what of the hundreds of men and women who died from this surprise attack? How many husbands, wives, lovers, brothers, and sisters would not be coming home this time? What about them?

Round one went to the enemy, whomever or whatever they were.

CHAPTER 4

Once they were back at the Sol system, it took four long days for the fleet to reach the orbit of Mars where some ships broke formation for their respective shipyards there. *Indefatigable* was able to keep up with the undamaged ships despite the pounding she had taken and continued to Luna for repairs. From the outside, she looked far worse than she performed. Price was exceptionally proud of his crew and how they supported those that had joined them from the *Linyi*.

On their way in system, they held multiple secure VR conferences with the members of the combined Earth Defense Force leadership. The EDF was hastily assembled to coordinate the multinational defense of Earth from the still-unknown threat they faced. The first VR sessions were painful. The light-speed delay in this discussion made what might have otherwise been a very intense one-hour debrief stretch out to a torture session that lasted most of the day. Since they arrived in system at approximately five AU, fortunately on the same side of the Sun as Earth, the signal transit time was just over thirty minutes—each way.

Each day the transit times decreased as the fleet's physical distance to Earth shrank. And each day the questions from the EDF grew more repetitive until Price found himself missing the respite provided by the longer light-speed delays.

Indefatigable docked at the lunar orbiting shipyard without incident and was immediately swarmed by the repair crews that awaited her. The ubiquitous self-propelled hard suits began photographing, measuring, and assessing the exterior damage from the outside while a veritable army of engineers and technicians gathered at the embarkation lounge to await their time to board the wounded ship.

The *Linyi* refugees were offloaded and the *Indefatigable*'s crew sent to the Commonwealth's Marius Hills base and dormitories on the lunar surface by shuttle. Located deep within a long-dormant lava tube, a veritable city had sprouted around the military bases there. The Commonwealth, USA, and India all chose the safety of being buried underground here for the nonweaponized parts of their respective bases. Though technically a member of the Commonwealth, India chose to establish a separate base, continuing the tradition of independence begun in the mid-twentieth century. Beside, over, and under the bases in the Marius Hills, the entrepreneurially spirited from Earth had built a sprawling city of nearly fifty thousand civilians. Anything a soldier wanted was available there, priced according to the demand and the degree of illegality. China, asserting its sovereignty and

independence, chose to have its lunar military base at the
Shackleton crater near the south lunar pole. Ferrying the
crew from the *Linyi* to there would take some time.

Price and his senior officers had quarters both on the
surface and at the orbiting shipyard. Price, eager to see
Anika as soon as possible, hastily made arrangements to
travel to the surface where he knew she would be waiting
on him. Her leave was nearly over, and they would have,
at most, two days before she had to ship out and they
would again be apart.

For Price, seeing the Earth from lunar orbit was the
second-best sight in the universe. The first was seeing
Anika's face resting asleep in the bed beside him. *The
forbidden relationship.* That is what his closest friends
and some fellow officers had called it. *You cannot have
a relationship with an officer of a foreign-flagged navy
ship and retain your commission,* they had said. Price
smiled. Forbidden relationship? *That is not what I
would call it . . .*

He and Anika had been together for more than a year
and were, for all practical purposes, married, except, of
course, for the fact that they were not. Nor would they be
able to get married until one or both resigned from
military service. Neither had had to lie to their clearance
officers about their relationship since, in what was
peacetime, the rules about interservice relationships had
been *somewhat* relaxed and their respective militaries
might have been overlooking theirs after the events on the
Grandiosa. Both services had benefitted from good press
when their off-duty officers made headlines for foiling a

robbery/hijacking and saving the cruise ship and her crew. Now that they were at war, that might change.

Price had already given her a ring, which she accepted, but they agreed she could not wear it until they were able to make their relationship public and get married. She often wore it when they were in private, like she was now. Her rhythmic deep breathing, some might say her snore, briefly paused as she shifted her body, and then resumed. Price never tired of seeing her look this relaxed. Thinking of her light brown skin, black hair with just a few wisps of gray, and ever so perfect chin with the little dimple in it were what helped carry him through the recent mission to Nikko and the catastrophe that it was. He was thankful she and her ship, the *Mumbai*, upon which she served as XO, had not been on the same deployment. He knew he, *they*, could handle themselves professionally on a joint deployment and not allow their personal lives to interfere with their professional duties as soldiers in different, but allied, space navies. As he lay next to her, Price was glad that he didn't have to do that just yet.

Her eyes popped open and she smiled. She knew of his sometimes habit of watching her sleep and had come to be okay with it. At first, she said it was unnerving. Then she acquiesced. Now she seemed to actually draw comfort from his gaze. Truth be told, he just could not believe she was with him. The only area of his life in which he currently felt like an imposter was in the role of Anika's partner. Fortunately, she was gracious enough to help him get over his imposter syndrome.

"Still thinking of the mission to Nikko?" she asked.

"No, just thinking of you and how lucky I am."

"Hmm. Well, my leave is almost over, and I'll soon have to get back to the business of my ship. I have a long list of 'to do's the captain asked me to accomplish today before I get back to *Mumbai*," Anika said, sitting up in bed.

"Tonight will be our last night together. A lot has happened since we left Nikko. Everything has changed. From the beating we took there, I'm more than a little surprised the aliens haven't already dropped into the solar system and attacked us here," said Price.

"We're ready. Well, as ready as we can be," she said.

"Anika, you know that's not true for the same reason we took such a beating at Nikko. Why didn't we think there could be mines or drones waiting to attack us? How could we allow our ships to have sensor blind spots aft? The whole situation would have turned out very differently had we taken the right precautions," Price said.

"Look at me," she said. "It wasn't your fault. It wasn't Admiral Wei's fault. Unmanned armed drones are mines and are banned under UN protocols just like land mines are banned back on Earth and have been since the twenty-first century. You didn't think of it because you were trained to fight another human enemy. You and I are trained to fight an enemy that has the same constraints and thought patterns as we. This enemy is unconstrained. They used nuclear weapons on Nikko's helpless civilians, for heaven's sake."

Price knew she was correct, but she was not *right*. He was in command of his ship and responsible for his crew. He should have thought through all these contingencies and realized that they were dealing with someone or something not constrained by the same thought patterns and moralistic concepts. *That would not happen again.*

"Do you know anything about your new orders? Are you staying in system?" asked Price.

"I do. They came last night. The EDF wants to send recon missions to some of the settlements we haven't heard from lately to check on them. There are three that have strong ties to India, and I suspect *Mumbai* will be sent to look in on them, one at a time," Anika said.

"Can we spare the ships?"

"I don't believe they are planning to send more than one ship at a time to any particular settlement unless there is reason to believe the aliens will be there. The general plan is to transit into the outer part of the star system, well outside the Oppenheimer Limit to avoid detection, look around, and then make way for the settlement. Once there, we will have to warn them about the war, if they don't know already, which they probably won't or why else would they be sending us to make contact?" Anika replied.

"And if the aliens are there?"

"We don't engage. Under that situation, the orders say we are to transit back to Earth and report. Just like you had to do."

"Anika, I know you. If you see helpless civilians being nuked from orbit, I just cannot imagine you ignoring the situation, dispassionately turning around, and leaving. Hell, I can't believe I did that."

"You had no choice. If you had, you and your crew would most likely be dead. I will do whatever Captain Padmanabhan decides—just like you."

Price knew that Anika was as committed to her chain

of command as he was to his. Only now, with the creation of the EDF, hers was now his and vice versa. He also knew that under those circumstances, she would look for any possible wiggle room in her orders that might allow her a chance to save lives. She was one of the most clever people he had ever met, and if she had been the one at Nikko, then she might have found a way stop the slaughter. It still pained him to have left Nikko defenseless against the marauders.

"Shall we plan dinner at Mario's?" asked Price, changing the subject. Mario's was the restaurant in the commercial side of the shipyards in which they had enjoyed many a romantic dinner. It was there that Price had proposed and given her the ring. Though only a year ago, it seemed like another age. Another life. Before the war.

"Sounds great. I'll get my shower and catch breakfast at the corner snack bar as I head out," she said as she got out of bed and moved toward the small apartment's shower.

"Mind if I join you?"

"For breakfast or in the shower?" she asked, tilting her head just slightly in the way that Price had come to recognize meant she was being flirtatious.

"Both," he said.

It turned out to be a long and satisfying shower.

Anika's first stop wasn't for work. She took a tram to the shopping district where she had arranged to buy a gift for Winslow. He loved to read books. Not the standard eBooks that ninety percent of the population found to be just fine for reading, but rather an old-fashioned hardcover book printed on paper, for heaven's sake. For not an insignificant price, she had arranged to have sent from Earth a signed copy of Marcus Greer's last book, published nearly seventy-five years before. The best she could find and afford was a third printing of the classic. She had located a few signed first editions, but they blew through her budget by a wide margin. Greer was a military historian turned space buff and his book, *Strategy and Tactics of War in Space*, had inspired the strategy and tactics for space war before space war had even really become possible. The book was required reading at all the space military academies, and she'd heard Winslow mention more than once how much he would enjoy reading a paper version of the book, even though he had already read the eBook at least a dozen times. Well, now he would get the opportunity to do just that. She was still looking for a paper copy of Forester's *The Happy Return* but had found none she could afford.

The Marius Hills shopping district could have been mistaken for a twentieth-century shopping mall if it weren't for the comparatively low gravity and the ever-present lunar dust. Since the Apollo days, the dust had been a problem. It clung to everything despite the best cleaning and filtering systems. From the grit on the floor to the long-ago-stained walls and ceiling, the dull gray dust was commonplace. It was also a health risk. In addition to getting on and in just about everything, it was impossible to not breathe it. Like "black lung disease" used to be common in coal miners back on Earth, Lunar Dust Disease was a growing health issue on Luna. Anika knew that to mitigate the problem, the Indian military had a three-year lifetime limit for those living or visiting the Moon. Once your time on the surface totaled three years, anywhere on the surface and anytime in your life, you had to return to Earth and would never be approved to go to the Moon ever again. Not all countries had such strict limits and the increasing demand upon the lunar medical facilities dealing with the complications of Lunar Dust Disease was a growing problem.

The importer who arranged delivery of the book was at first very professional and aboveboard. Since he required half of the book's cost up front, she had researched him fairly well to not lose her money with a fly-by-night merchant that could easily vanish off-world at any given time. After the transaction was complete, he not-so-subtly suggested that he could arrange for other, not-so-legal, items if she desired and, of course, if she had the money. All that dropped when she let it be known that she was the second-in-command of a warship and not interested. She was not too surprised by the offer. The black market was alive and well all over the Moon.

As she departed, clutching the carefully wrapped hardcover book in her left arm, her comm pin sounded.

"This is Ahuja," she announced as she answered the call.

"Ma'am, this is Swati Prasad in Colonel Lal's office. The colonel wants to see you as soon as possible. How soon can you get to his office?"

Anika looked at her datapad, quickly found the closest train access tunnel, and calculated how long it would take to get back to the base before she replied. "I can be there in thirty-five minutes."

"See you then," Prasad said, ending the connection.

Anika did not waste any time pondering why the colonel wanted to see her. He just did and, being a good soldier, she dropped all her other afternoon plans and set out at a fast pace to get to Colonel Lal's office sooner than she had announced. Anika liked margins, even in travel time.

She made the journey in just under thirty minutes, straightening her civilian clothes as she walked through the opening into the colonel's outer office. She hoped the colonel didn't mind. She was still, technically, on leave. She had been in Colonel Lal's office before, frequently, for staff meetings, planning sessions, and the occasional one-on-one with Lal. He was a good man and a capable manager who seemed to make the lunar base run smoothly and efficiently. She liked him personally but did not really know much about his military expertise. Like just about everyone else in the Indian Space Navy, Colonel Lal had risen through the ranks in a time of peace. He was a good manager and bureaucrat...

Despite the best efforts of office workers everywhere on Luna, military or civilian, it was impossible to give a pressurized office on the outer periphery of the base the look and feel of an office on Earth. The base filled an ancient lunar lava tube, which meant the outer edge contours were all natural. The outer mold lines of the pressurized wall melded with the contours because they were made from a flexible graphene nanofiber that conformed to the wall shape as it was pressurized. The colonel's office made the contours of the lava tube immediately obvious and, in its own way, visually interesting and appealing. As she entered the room, to the left were two distinct rock bulges that the colonel had used as shelving, placing various mementos and photos at odd angles to conform with the contour of the bulge. Immediately behind his desk was a two-foot-deep indentation in which he had placed the office safe. The ceiling was remarkably high, well over the standard eight feet because of a bulge in the ceiling. Up there, facing down, were two flatscreens that showed the view of the Earth as it would be seen, she supposed, if one were standing directly above on the surface.

The colonel looked up from his computer screen, acknowledged her presence and motioned for her to take a seat where she sat quietly and patiently, waiting on him to begin the conversation. He looked back at the screen, read intently for another few seconds and then looked back at her.

"I apologize for summoning you on the last day of your leave, but it is important," said Lal. To Anika, Lal looked like a commanding officer. He had the requisite square jaw, was the right indeterminate age of fortyish to fiftyish, had black hair cropped short with streaks of gray, and a deep, booming voice. He was also strikingly handsome, an observation not lost on Anika or most of the female officer corps.

"It is perfectly all right, sir. I am just wrapping up some last-minute errands before I have to depart," she replied. What was she supposed to say? *How dare you bother me on my last day of leave?*

"I'm placing you in command of the *Mumbai*, effective

immediately," Lal said, his gaze squarely on Anika's eyes, making her instantly aware that he was going to make a decision about her based on how she reacted to the astonishing news of her assignment. "You need to get on board her today and prepare to depart tomorrow as planned."

She did not blink.

"Yes, sir," she replied, wondering what happened to Captain Padmanabhan, with whom she had been serving for the better part of a year. He was a capable captain and one for whom she had respect. True, his temper sometimes got the better of him, but he always managed to tamp it down and not allow it to overtly influence his decisions.

"I suppose you are wondering what happened to Captain Padmanabhan?" asked Lal.

"Yes, sir. The question did cross my mind," she replied honestly.

"Conduct unbecoming an officer. He was relieved of command this morning. Please don't ask for any more details. There will be an official inquiry," said Lal.

"Yes, sir. Thank you for the information," she replied, without breaking Lal's gaze. Though some would have been troubled by the prolonged eye contact, Anika took it for what it probably was—a measure of how she reacted to the news combined with a little bit of alpha-male assertion of dominance.

"There is another matter," said Lal, finally backing off from the staring contest to momentarily consult his datapad. "And that matter is named Winslow Price."

Anika had been expecting one of her superiors to bring up her relationship with Winslow long before now.

"Sir?" she replied.

"Having the captain of an Indian warship sleeping with the captain of another major power's ship is highly unusual and improper. We have overlooked it long enough, and if word spreads too far, some might even call it treasonous," said Lal.

"Sir, are you asking that I break off my relationship with Captain Price as a condition of my being appointed captain of the *Mumbai*?" she asked, this time initiating the eye contact to assess *his* reaction.

Lal leaned back in this chair and sighed before speaking. "Yes. Otherwise, you will likely be reassigned to Earthside by someone higher in the chain of command and I won't have a say in the matter. You are one of my best officers and the one I believe best suited to command the *Mumbai*. We need you. India needs you. Hell, Earth needs you."

"And if I refuse?" she asked, with a dew of perspiration forming on her brow and back.

"*Captain* Ahuja, do we really have to go there?" asked Lal, heavily emphasizing her title.

Her mind raced. She had known this day would come and had rehearsed so many times the lines she would say, *Thank you sir, but I must resign. I love Captain Price and we intend to be married.* Or a variation, *I respectfully decline and will request reassignment to a position where I can fulfill my oath and be with my future husband.*

The words that came out of her mouth were quite different.

"Yes, sir. I will inform Captain Price and report for duty on the *Mumbai*."

"Very good, Captain. Dismissed."

Anika gave the requisite salute and departed from Lal's office. As she left, a flood of emotions and thoughts began to pour over her. She was thrilled at the fulfillment of her lifelong dream—being named captain of a ship in the Indian Space Navy. She, the daughter of an herbalist in Munsiyari, was soon going to have a ship to call her own. The dream she nurtured for years as she stared at the stars from atop the snow-capped peaks that surrounded her home in rural India was becoming real. The thrill barely had time to register before the remorse overcame her. Winslow. She loved him. How would he ever understand? Was this the right choice? Why did she have to choose between her career and the man she loves? And how could she decide so quickly?

Suddenly, the book she was carrying seemed to weigh far more than it had when she arrived at Colonel Lal's office. How would she break the news to Winslow? Hand him the book, wish him well and say, "See you later?" She had to report to the ship today, which meant there would be no time for a protracted dialog. They had dinner plans that would have to be canceled. Her mind raced with all that she now needed to accomplish before reporting for duty on the *Mumbai* and she was overwhelmed. Would he ever understand that her accepting the captaincy of the *Mumbai* was not a rejection of him? They could cool off their relationship and begin again after this crisis was over and one or both left their respective posts. How would he react?

Before she knew it, Anika was standing outside the door to their shared apartment. She took a deep breath, placed her palm on the pad to unlock the door and entered. The lights were out, which meant Winslow was out and about. *Thank God,* she thought. It was then that she realized what she was going to do.

They both knew that her leave was ending and that she would be departing tomorrow. Chances were that by the next time she arrived at Luna, he would be on the *Indefatigable* and deployed somewhere or another. That meant there was plenty of time for her to figure out how to break the news to Winslow. And a lot could happen in that time. They were in the middle of a war, after all. She looked around the room, found a pen, and began to inscribe the book she had just purchased. She then called up her apartment avatar and began recording a message.

"Dearest Winslow. A lot happened this morning and I don't really know where to begin. The biggest news is that I have been named captain of the *Mumbai* and asked to report to the ship today. I am so excited. Unfortunately, that leaves us no more time together as we had planned. By the time you see this, I will be on board buried in the details of preparing for tomorrow's departure. It will be difficult not being the XO and instead being the one in the chair. On the nightstand is a gift that I know you will enjoy. I wish I could be here to give it to you in person, but that is not to be." She paused and then concluded with, "I love you."

Coward, she thought.

CHAPTER 5

"Captain Price, the engineers have been working around the clock to get *Indefatigable* spaceworthy and in better shape than ever before. Your sensor data from the mine attack was extremely valuable, for both future defensive and offensive capabilities and tactics." Speaking was Julian Stephens, the engineering director of the Commonwealth's lunar shipyards. Stephens was an engineer's engineer with his thin frame, hawkish nose, and flat-topped, closely cropped hair. His appearance was what could only be described as "standard engineer— timeless." He could have been picked up and dropped back in time in virtually any era post-1900. He was also one of the smartest people Price had ever met.

Stephens was at the front of the briefing room eagerly pointing to various features on a virtual 3-D rendering of the *Indefatigable* that hovered next to him, responding to his every command of movement left, right, up, or down, with so many zooms in or out, that Price was almost dizzy. It was profoundly good news that the ship was not only repairable, but easily so. The damage that appeared extensive was mostly in areas of the ship made from modular components that were easily replaceable. Price was eager to get back aboard and see the repairs himself, but that would have to wait at least another week.

"Your inability to see the drones coming aft was particularly disturbing. We knew that the radiation from the fusion torch would make it difficult, but not impossible, to detect lower-emission vehicles within an approximate three-degree cone from the plume's centroid, but how did the enemy know this? True, this wavelength-specific blind spot is basically the same on all the Commonwealth and many of the other Earth ships for the same reasons, primary of which is that we all use a variation of the same fusion propulsion system design. You were not, however, totally blind in this region. Your aft sensors were blinded, overloaded, at only a few specific wavelengths—those at which Commonwealth-designed fusion torch emissions are brightest. Other Earth ships have slightly different emission characteristics, but not radically so. Emissions peaks at those wavelengths is partly driven by the fundamental physics of the fusion reaction and partly driven by history and the evolution of a specific system design," Stephens said.

"Excuse me, Dr. Stephens, I have a question," said one of the other briefing attendees to Price's right. Price did not know the questioner's name, but he knew that the speaker served aboard *Indefatigable*'s sister ship, the *Australia*. He might not have made the connection as quickly had the man not spoken with such a thick Aussie accent.

"Yes?"

"Please expand on what you mean by 'history and evolution of the design.'"

"There are myriad decisions made by the physicists and engineers who first designed the basic torch we use and the many iterations of improvement and refinement that have been occurring since we began using them several decades ago. For example, the primary direct byproduct of the hydrogen/hydrogen fusion reaction is helium. The reaction is not one hundred percent efficient so there will also always be leakage of unfused hydrogen isotopes into the plume as well as trace amounts of the materials used to construct the fusion drive itself. These elements are superheated and emit light at specific wavelengths. The ratio of hydrogen to helium and between the various hydrogen isotopes emitted is specific to the design, as are the other trace elements emitted. A separate group of equally talented engineers started with the same basic reaction, but using slightly different materials in the reaction chamber or the exhaust channel would almost certainly result in a noticeable variation in the ratios of expelled hydrogen and helium and the leaked trace elements. This would result in the plume having a hugely different spectrum and intensity. The *Indefatigable* should have only been blind in that very narrow viewing region to the exhaust plumes of other Commonwealth ships. Your sensors would have been able to detect plumes from Chinese-designed fusion propulsion systems because their specific design evolved away from ours and we know what their emissions look like." Stephens paused and reoriented the projected ship so that the audience was looking straight up the business end of its fusion torch.

He continued, "The enemy missiles were either extremely lucky, exceptionally good guessers, or had inside knowledge of our capabilities. From what we can tell, the missiles maneuvered into your blind spot over a period of time using nonfusion propulsion, which your sensors didn't detect, and then adjusted their emission plume to exactly match that of *Indefatigable*'s, making them invisible to your sensors. According to their sensor data, the same thing happened to the *Linyi* and, most likely, to the *South Dakota*. It is my opinion that of the three options I offered, the only one that makes sense is that they have been watching us for a very long time. Long enough to know the limitations of each country's shipboard sensors and to have a design such that they could adapt to whichever ship they happened to be targeting."

"You are saying that the missiles were designed to target specific ships with specific known emissions characteristics? You are sure that this isn't just some generic capability they have that just happens to make us vulnerable?" interjected someone from the back of the room whose voice Price didn't recognize.

"If I were to hazard a guess, and that is exactly what I was asked to do by Commonwealth intelligence, then I would say yes. Each ship was independently targeted by a missile that knew the weaknesses of that particular ship, or at least its design heritage or country of origin," Stephens replied.

"Can you fix the problem?" asked Price.

Stephens turned to Price and for the first time today, smiled and nodded.

"Yes, Captain Price, we can. We are adding three sensor pods to your ship that will be mounted on the outside circumference about midway between fore and aft. The pods will have cameras pointing aft to look for other ships' fusion plumes. They will be 120 degrees apart and when their images are combined, they will have the ability to see anything within the region of the former blind spot. No one sensor will be able to view the complete three-degree cone, but taken together, you will no longer be blind there."

"Dr. Stephens, I'm also concerned about the ability of our point defenses to take out the missiles. The system seemed to be quickly overwhelmed," Price said as he kept Stephens' attention.

"Unfortunately, that isn't a problem with a quick fix. To replace or redesign the weapons systems on a ship like *Indefatigable* would take months, more likely years. I'm sure the weapons group is busily coming up with devious new systems for future ships, but there simply won't be anything new to help you or any other Commonwealth ship anytime soon," Stephens replied, walking to the other side of the visualization.

"On a rather troubling note, it appears that they had at least some form of artificial intelligence onboard, coordinating their attacks. The way they split into three groups, slowly regrouped into your torch blind spots, and concentrated their attack on the *South Dakota*, which they correctly identified as the flagship, implies that the missiles had much more than the standard autonomous-operations capabilities in our munitions."

This was a troubling development. With the

emergence of AIs in the latter part of the twenty-first century, there was a movement to restrict their access to weapons and they were globally banned from having access to weapons of mass destruction. The countries of the world (or most of them) signed on to the United Nations Treaty on Potentially Sentient Artificial Life which limited the development of self-aware AIs. The treaty also allowed countries to forbid the creation of AIs altogether, which many did for various religious, cultural, or sociological reasons. The USA-, Commonwealth-, and Chinese-aligned countries embraced artificial intelligence to a point. The complex systems that many believed could become self-aware were expensive to create and maintain, leaving the societal niche for their use available mostly to government, the military, big corporations, and the very wealthy. In the military and banking were where most AIs resided.

The most sophisticated AI constructs, like Lord Nelson, were created for the Commonwealth's military. Under the UN treaty, placing AIs on missiles or space mines armed with nuclear weapons was strictly prohibited. Giving even limited-capability AIs complete control of such destructive systems was outlawed from the start and no country on Earth was known to have violated the prohibition. The same farsighted people who drafted the UN treaty before AIs had even been created foresaw the dangers of giving such power to nonhuman potential sentients and acted on it.

They were dealing with a foe who had no such prohibitions.

"Our shipboard AIs can take autonomous tactical

command during combat. How is that different?" asked the Australian officer.

"The AIs on Commonwealth ships, and others like them, often take tactical control during combat operations because of their faster reaction times and the fact that the ships are essentially their bodies. Humans react quickly in fast-moving situations like hand-to-hand combat without consciously thinking about how to move their hands, arms, or feet. Training and human reflexes are the keys to such encounters. Ships and their systems are analogous. It only makes sense to give the AIs *temporary* command and control. The difference is that we have to authorize them to do so and the safety protocols only allow for this tactical control to be temporary, revocable anytime by the ship's human captain," said Stephens.

"Is it possible we are not dealing with biological aliens who happen to have killer AIs but are instead up against just killer AIs? Do we know?" asked another officer from somewhere in the back of the room.

"I'd better let Major Castillo answer that one. She's here from navy intelligence," said Stephens.

Major Castillo certainly did not look like anything like an engineer. She was all military. From her uniform to her very demeanor, she exuded professionalism. Some might call it professional stiffness. She looked like either an intelligence officer or a lawyer.

"It is certainly possible we are dealing with AIs, and if the only data we had was from the encounter Captain Price had with them, then that might be a perfectly reasonable theory. But we do not believe that to be the case. The data from the ships that escaped the Nikko system as it was being attacked showed ships of similar size to our own, maneuvering in such a manner that they would not turn any organic passengers into butter. If there were no biological life-forms on those ships, then there would have been no need to constrain their accelerations and maneuvers as they did. No, we believe the attackers are biological, just like us," said Castillo. She spoke with a French accent, one that was slightly nasal, making Price think she was likely Belgian by birth.

"That really finishes my briefing, so I will now turn over the floor to Major Castillo," Stephens said as he stepped aside and began to make his way from the front of the room to the back.

"Dr. Stephens, before you go, may I ask about my ship's AI? Were you able to restore Lord Nelson?" asked Price.

"Absolutely. I should have told you before the meeting began. We were able to repair the damage to his systems, which were mostly in the data pipes allowing him to communicate. As soon as he was cut off from you and the rest of the crew, he placed himself into hibernation," replied Stephens.

Major Castillo walked to the front of the room and turned to face the rest of the attendees. Price wondered if she had to consciously avoid clicking her boots as she turned.

"Thank you, Dr. Stephens. Please remember that the content of this briefing is top secret and compartmentalized. I am here to give you our assessment of the situation, again in large part due to the data provided by Captain Price and his recent journey to and from the Nikko system," she said, pausing for effect at just the right moment. Price wondered why military intelligence people always seemed to have a flair for the dramatic.

"Ladies and gentlemen, the enemy we face is remarkably like us. It appears that their ships are of comparable tonnage, have comparable propulsive capabilities both in system with fusion torches and between systems with a version of the Hawking Drive. Their missiles and mines appear to contain nuclear weapons of comparable yield to ours, suspiciously so. If we were not sharing data so readily and completely among all the Earth's spacefaring countries, one could reasonably conclude that these attacks were carried out by another terrestrial power and not some alien species. In short, a conspiracy," she said, again pausing.

No one used the pause to ask any questions. Most, like Price, just sat there, listening to learn more. Price assumed she had more to say and he was correct.

"You have all read the reports from the Nikko survivors. To honor them, we have decided to call our adversaries the Kurofune. We assembled the world's leading astrobiologists, xenoanthropologists, sociologists, and other experts to examine the intelligence we have gathered so far and there is only one thing they all agreed upon: that the data we brought them must be flawed in some way. It seems that the probability of us encountering an alien species *now* that just happens to have capabilities similar to our own, very similar to our own, *now*, in all the possible times in history that two galactic civilizations might encounter each other, is, for all practical purposes, zero." She paused again to take a breath and a sip of water.

Price had made the same argument before, just a few weeks ago at Nikko.

"Modern humans have been around for about three hundred thousand years, give or take. In all that time, we have had space travel for only about two hundred years. Out of three hundred thousand years. We live on a planet that is about four and half billion years old. Could evolution have driven two separate species toward intelligence, tool using, and space-travel capabilities that are essentially the same, including in general design, at the same moment in galactic history in a time space of billions of years? The experts we assembled say 'impossible.' And that leaves only one viable alternative explanation. The data provided by the *Indefatigable* is flawed or faked," she said, now looking directly at Price.

The room was so quiet that Price could hear the beat of his heart as his blood pressure rose. He was stunned by the comment, the implied accusation, and was at a momentary loss for words. Realizing that everyone was looking at him to respond, he rose to his feet, composing his thoughts as he did so.

"Major, please elaborate on what you mean by flawed or faked data. Was there some other set of measurements I should have taken as the nuclear missiles were targeting my ship? Or perhaps my crew should have just not bothered with that whole 'defend the ship' thing and instead started taking pictures of the *South Dakota* being ripped to shreds without survivors? Maybe we should not have rushed to rescue the crew of the *Linyi* before their reactor leak poisoned them all? Or are you saying that none of these events actually happened and that we made it all up? I am not really clear on what it is you are saying," said Price, his anger almost getting the better of him. He was every bit as incensed as his tone conveyed.

"Captain, with all due respect, I am merely pointing out the only possible alternative to an impossible scenario. The experts say that the data you provided cannot possibly match reality. Therefore, the data must be in error from either ineptitude or malfeasance."

This time the room was not quiet, several murmurs were evident and more than a few mutterings of "impossible" or something similar.

Before Price could form a reply to what was now a challenge to his integrity and loyalty, the base commander, Colonel Williamson, rose to his feet.

Price had known and worked for Colonel Williamson since he was assigned to the Moon. Williamson was tough, but fair. He was from a military family that traced their service back to the middle of the nineteenth century and was proud of it. He was also known to be loyal to those under his command.

"That is enough, Major Castillo. I will not have the integrity or capabilities of one of my officers questioned in a public forum. If you have issues or concerns about Captain Price, or any of my officers, you need to raise them to me, with ironclad justification, in private," said Williamson, leaning forward as he made his point.

"Yes, sir," Castillo replied, still looking mostly at Price.

"This meeting is adjourned. Dismissed," said Williamson as he moved forward to where Castillo was standing.

"Major Castillo and Captain Price, please remain

here," added Williamson as the other officers filed out of the room. It took only a few minutes for the room to empty. In that time, Price calmed down—a bit.

Colonel Williamson, not wasting a moment once the room was empty, turned his glare toward Castillo as he spoke.

"Major Castillo, I would like to know right now if you believe that Captain Price has done anything improper in the conduct of his duties as an officer of the Commonwealth. But before you answer, if the answer is yes, then be Goddamned sure you have proof."

"Colonel, I am not making a preferral of charges at this time," she replied.

"'At this time.' But you plan to do so in the future?" Williamson asked.

"With the backing of my commanding officer, I intend to review all the records from the *Indefatigable*, interview some of the key witnesses, and then decide what the appropriate next step or steps might be," she said defiantly.

"Is there anything else you would like to tell me or Captain Price?" asked Williamson, who anyone could tell was definitely not pleased.

"Only that Captain Price should tell Ms. Ahuja that I said hello," she replied, staring at Price . . .

CHAPTER 6

Oh, God. Are all captains this nervous? Captain Anika
Ahuja, having assumed command of the *Mumbai* less than
twenty-four hours previously, was taking her ship from
lunar orbit toward the outer solar system where she could
safely engage the Hawking Drive and begin her
reconnaissance mission to New Hyderabad. This was the
exact same bridge upon which she had been serving but
from where she now sat, it looked different. The
difference in appearance, in feel, was not due to where
she sat—she had assumed temporary command many
times for Captain Padmanabhan during the last year and
sat there before. But now was different. She would not be
relinquishing the chair when the captain returned to the
bridge. She was the captain, and the weight of that
responsibility was bearing solidly down upon her. *Maybe
the nervousness will pass with time,* she thought—she
hoped. It would take them five days to reach their
departure point, more than enough time to get used to
her new job. At least, she fervently hoped it would be
enough time.

Her XO, Lieutenant Jenya Chatterjee, was at her new station and did not look the least bit nervous. *There is no reason she should look nervous,* thought Anika. *She has been XO before and knows what she is doing. I hope she doesn't figure out that she, instead of me, is more qualified be the captain of the Mumbai.*

"Mitra, what do we know about the settlement at New Hyderabad?" Anika asked. Mitra was the ship's AI. When Anika first came aboard the *Mumbai* and met Mitra, she did *not* like him. He was too quiet. She generally did not like to be around people who were overly quiet and introspective and found no reason to change her preferences to accommodate a machine intelligence. Over time, she came to appreciate Mitra's quiet competence and to understand that his quietness was simply a personality trait and not a reluctance to get to know her personally. Mitra was just programmed to be an introvert.

"New Hyderabad was settled by a group from India. Funded by the donations of the wealthiest families in the city of Hyderabad, the New Hyderabad settlement ship was the second from India to participate in the diaspora, departing only two months after the Jaipur settlement was established. When the ship departed the Earth system, it was the largest settlement ship at the time, accommodating just over ten thousand colonists. The planet they settled was typical for the time, not too far from Sol and just barely habitable for Earth life. The colonists were eager to leave and, according to sources at the time, they did not want to wait for the survey ships to find that 'just right' Earthlike planet to call home. What they found was a terrestrial planet circling a G2-type star approximately 350 light-years from Earth. The planet is forty percent larger and more massive than Earth, making the increased gravity likely uncomfortable to the colonists and visitors, but not debilitating. All other aspects of New Hyderabad are Earthlike, including the atmospheric constituents, a vigorous magnetosphere, and a tidally locked large moon," Mitra replied, displaying an image of New Hyderabad that Anika presumed had been sent back to Earth in the earliest days of the settlement.

"The records of the settlement for the first ten years are fairly complete. The settlement's leadership during that time sent robotic drones back to Earth with detailed records of the events occurring there: social, economic, political, and environmental. They sent an update drone back each year for the first ten years. In the eighty years since, there has been little contact. They have continually rebuffed efforts to initiate trade and requested that they be left alone," Mitra continued.

"Do the records indicate any sort of disease, disaster, or unrest that might explain why?" Anika asked.

"No," Mitra replied.

Anika was not very troubled that the colonists had not attempted to recently contact the home world. Many early colonists left Earth because they wanted to have nothing to do with from where they had fled. What was troubling about the whole settlement effort was the lack of follow-through from Earth. One would think families, governments, and most of all, commercial entities would want to remain in contact with those that left in case there were new opportunities discovered or new wealth to be made. After all, with a whole galaxy of resources available, the possibilities were endless. But that logic had not prevailed in the real universe. In the practical reality of life and business, there were simply too many settlements, and too many worlds open and available for settlement, for anyone on Earth to go out of their way to force themselves on those already launched.

"Thank you, Mitra. Is there anything else we should know?" Anika asked.

"No, Captain, there is not. I will inform you if anything pertinent comes to my attention," said Mitra.

"Very well. We have some time until we can engage the Hawking Drive, so let's make the best of it with a few drills. XO, I read in your file that you excel at combat simulations. You and Mitra need to create a few for us to simulate these next few days. Plan the first one to occur just after tomorrow's first shift goes off duty," Anika said.

"Yes, ma'am," said Chatterjee, a devious smile forming on her face.

We are going to get along fine, thought Anika as she settled back in her chair to begin the disposition of a mountain of messages. *Being in charge looks like it just means more paperwork. Maybe being captain won't be as glamorous as it looks*, she thought.

Five days and seven simulated battles later, two of which had resulted in the loss of the *Mumbai* with all its crew, the ship activated its Hawking Drive and jumped to the New Hyderabad system.

From forty light-minutes out, space looked basically the same in the New Hyderabad system as it did back in the solar system—black with uncountable pinpoints of starlight in all directions except toward the system's center where its Earthlike star lay. The familiar constellations with which she grew up were absent, of course, but that did not stop Anika from trying to find them. Human brains liked patterns and familiar patterns most of all. She did not allow herself to become distracted by her amateur-astronomer predilections. She had a job to do.

"Mitra, I need a threat assessment," said Anika as she manipulated the virtual viewscreen projected in front of her and the bridge crew, zooming in on the region of space New Hyderabad occupied, or more accurately, the space the planet occupied forty minutes ago. Any glimpse of the planet that they might see would be as it appeared in the past, given the time it took the light to travel from there to the ship's telescopes.

From this distance, they could see the planetary disk, but not much else. She knew that while she was straining to see the light from New Hyderabad and make sense of it, Mitra would have performed a full sky survey, looking for emissions across the electromagnetic spectrum from radio, microwaves, and infrared to ultraviolet, X-rays, and gamma rays. If there were other active spacecraft or nonnatural objects in the system anywhere close to the *Mumbai* or the central star, Mitra would find it. Inactive craft, like mines or remote missiles, were another story.

"Other than the robust radio traffic I am detecting from New Hyderabad, the system is clear of artificial emissions. I must caution, however, that from this distance it is impossible to detect the low-power emissions of drones or missiles like those that attacked the fleet at Nikko," Mitra calmly announced.

Anika was immediately relieved for two reasons. First, New Hyderabad was still there, as evidenced by all the radio noise coming from the planet. Second, there were no other ships in the system, or at least nearby. For the moment, she could relax. She had not taken the ship to General Quarters for the jump because there was simply no need. Space is big. Really big. At forty light-minutes from the star, the chance of another ship being within missile range when they arrived was so low as to be essentially zero. There was no need to go there now because there was no obvious threat. That might change as the ship neared the inner solar system, and Anika had no intention of allowing her ship to be surprised as the *Indefatigable* had been.

Winslow. As her thoughts raced from one threat scenario to the next, the mere thought of the *Indefatigable* made her think of Winslow, changing her mood from pensive to melancholy. She so loved that British man who was so British that he did not even realize he was a living, breathing, walking stereotype. From his penchant for tea and love of naval history to his irrational attachment to the anachronistic royal family and stiff upper lip, he was the epitome of Britishness. Even if she could not understand all his predilections, she loved him from the top of his head to the tip of his toes. And she was going to hurt him. Worse, she had run away to avoid the inevitable hurt that would come when she told him that she had to choose between career and him—and that he lost. No, they both lost. *Winslow. Dear Winslow. How can I do this to you?*

"Mitra, what have you gleaned from eavesdropping on the natives?" Anika asked.

"The settlement world appears to be doing well. Most of the broadcasts are commercial data transfer, some are obviously entertainment, others personal and government communication. There is minimal encrypted traffic and no sign of any sort of heightened alert status," replied Mitra.

"We've only been here ten minutes so they would have no idea they are about to get company," said Lieutenant Charun Patel, the ship's tactical officer. Mitra was good at gathering and synthesizing data, but command and control of the ship's most vital systems remained in the hands of flesh-and-blood people. Lieutenant Patel had served on the *Mumbai* almost as long as Anika and had proven himself to be quite capable. As XO, she had tried to get to know him better, but he always kept his personal life at arm's length. She sensed there was some sort of pain in his background that he tried to avoid by not engaging in any sort of personal exchange beyond the perfunctory. Now that she was captain, she would like to fix that. She wanted to really know her officers and what made them tick. It was that kind of soft knowledge that might make a life-and-death difference in a crisis.

"Lieutenant Patel, do they have any sort of space-based radar array?" asked Anika.

"There are no radar emissions powerful enough to resolve our presence until we are well within the orbit of the planet's moon. We are still too far away for me to assess their space capabilities," Patel said.

"When will they know we are here?" asked Anika, already suspecting the answer.

"From what I can tell, they may remain unaware of our presence unless or until we announce ourselves. There is always a chance that a ground- or space-based telescope might inadvertently spot our thrust plume, but without an active radar system more powerful than anything I have found so far, there is little chance of us being detected," Patel replied.

"Let's keep it that way. I don't want to announce ourselves until we are fairly sure there are not any mines waiting on us and that the locals are friendly. Lieutenant Utreja, plot on a course in system that will put us in orbit around New Hyderabad's moon, but don't execute. I want to first get a better understanding of the locals before I decide if we are going to get close enough for them to do anything that might surprise us," said Anika.

"Yes, ma'am," said Utreja. Utreja was the *Mumbai*'s pilot. And, unlike with Lieutenant Patel, Anika had been able to get to know the affable and deeply philosophical Lieutenant Laj Utreja. He was an astrodynamicist to the core and was perfectly happy talking about the nuances of planetary orbits, Oberth maneuvers, and Hohmann transfers ad nauseum. But when personal matters were brought up, he did not shy away from them. Anika knew so much about Utreja's parents and siblings that she felt like she knew them personally, even though they have never met. And may the gods show mercy if you ever got him talking about Nyaya-Sastra and other Indian philosophies. The man was a walking, talking encyclopedia of esoteric knowledge. Anika thought that a mind that could grasp the nuances of interplanetary trajectories might also be wired to appreciate the more abstract side of living embodied in traditional Indian philosophy, so it sort of made sense. Sort of.

As Anika absorbed the tactical situation near New Hyderabad, or, rather, the lack of a tactical situation, she had a decision to make. If the settlement had truly not been attacked, and if they had no capability to defend themselves, should she announce her presence and warn them of the danger? If no attack came, then the panic that might arise from the warning could do more harm than good. If it did come, and if the populace were warned, what good would it do if they have no way to defend themselves? They had learned from Nikko that surrender did not help. The enemy paid no heed and nuked the planet from space with the obvious intent of killing as many people as possible. Her orders left the matter of making contact and providing a warning to her discretion based on "the circumstances." In other words, it was up to her to screw up when some future politician looked back and assessed her actions in the context of what was yet to come.

Complicating the matter was her order to visit two settlements—New Hyderabad and Jaipur. Given that the Hawking Drive would not allow arriving or departing any system closer than forty to forty-five light-minutes from the local star, and that most habitable planets were within ten light-minutes of the star, actually visiting the settlement in each system would require a minimum of eight to twelve days, give or take. Even if she provided warning, there was not much else she could do to help other than say "good luck" as she left on her way to the next system or back home.

If she were a settlement administrator, governor, or president—she had no idea what form of government or governments were currently in place on New Hyderabad—would she want to know?

Yes. Yes, I would, she thought. That moment of insight then raised the next logical question. Should she take the time to go to the planet for a dialog with the settlement's government or just do it from where they were to save time? From here, the communication would be frustrating due to the speed-of-light time delay, but still advantageous from an overall time-spent perspective. If they did not need to spend days traveling inward to the planet and then back out again to activate the Hawking Drive, precious time would be saved. They needed to minimize the time in the New Hyderabad system and move on to Jaipur. The enemy had not pressed their attack after Nikko, but that could change. The *Mumbai* needed to complete its mission and get back to Earth where another warship might be needed the most.

"Mitra, what language are the colonists primarily using?" Anika asked.

"A bastardized version of Telugu and English, not terribly different from the dialect spoken when they left Earth, though I have intercepted communications completely in Hindi and English, the latter being not so common," replied Mitra.

"You and I need to figure out who is in charge, how we get in contact with them, and what to say so that we aren't misunderstood and nothing gets lost in translation. And we need to do it so that the inevitable back and forth is minimized. We're going to initiate contact from here and then move on Jaipur as quickly as possible," Anika said.

"Certainly, Captain. I can be ready when you are," replied Mitra.

"Let's get started," said Anika as she began dictating her first thoughts of what an introductory message might say.

CHAPTER 7

It took just over two days to conclude the time-delayed meetings with the government of New Hyderabad. Finding out who was in charge was easy, taking Mitra less than a few minutes of parsing the thousands of messages, news broadcasts, and data transfers happening across one of the planet's continents. There were radio sources in other parts of the planet, but very few. New Hyderabad had a prime minister, a parliament, and various semiautonomous regions they called "administrative areas." Overall, the message traffic portrayed a relatively stable, self-sustaining settlement still coming into its own economically. Their standard of living had not regressed much, as had been the fear of many when the colonization efforts began. Establishing an industrial infrastructure sufficient to sustain a twenty-second-century standard of living had been thought to require at least a million inhabitants. So far, here, on Nikko, as other settlement worlds, that had not been the case. On just about all the settlements they had contacted or studied thus far, none had seriously regressed. This was good news for those wishing to continue the effort.

What had not progressed, however, was New Hyderabad's military. They had none. Violence was one of the many reasons colonists had fled Earth in droves. Many were sick of war and conflict; others were idealists who wanted to create a society free of the violent disagreements that had plagued humans since the dawn of history. New Hyderabad was a textbook example. Their constitution forbade them from establishing anything more than a national police force. War they had so far avoided; crime they had not. People were still people. But a police force equipped with stun guns would be no match for a starship dropping nuclear weapons from orbit.

Because Earth's own combined military was relatively small, Anika was unable to offer any concrete promises of military help. She did, however, agree to provide the New Hyderabad government with three drones that could be quickly activated at the Oppenheimer Limit for transit to Earth in the event of an attack. With luck and enough warning time, Earth might be able to send ships to help defend the settlement. If she could spare the ships and were not under attack herself. That was a lot of "ifs."

As Anika prepared the ships for departure from the system and transit to Jaipur, she did ask the prime minister why the settlement stopped communicating with Earth those many decades ago. The answer surprised her.

"We simply didn't care about what was happening on Earth anymore. New Hyderabad was established, our food supplies were more than sufficient to meet the needs of our population, and our industrial base was growing rapidly. Since no one from Earth bothered to reply to our updates or provide an update to us, the government at the time assumed that either the Earth had destroyed itself or nobody cared. So, they voted to stop communicating."

It was a neat and concise answer to the question that had been bothering Anika since before they left Earth. With her mind nearly always racing to the negative side of the possible answer set, she was a bit surprised. When they arrived, Anika's preconceived answer had been that either the settlement had been destroyed or regressed to the point where sending future updates would have been impossible. That they might stop because they simply did not care had not occurred to her. In hindsight, it was perfectly reasonable.

Six hours after the last data dump from New Hyderabad, they made the jump to Jaipur.

Jaipur was the third settlement established by any group from Earth and the first by India. Named after a bustling Indian city back on Earth, the planet was barely in the habitable zone. Jaipur's star was a bit smaller and cooler than Earth's, which meant that the planet the settlers selected was much closer to its parent star than the Earth was to Sol. The conditions on the surface were suitable for humans and biological life, but few would call it generally hospitable. From the data provided to Anika by Mitra, it appeared that those early settlers might have been better off waiting on more Earthlike planets being found before they selected one to call their home. Jaipur was cold, with a daily average temperature at the equator being barely above freezing and little seasonal variation.

The planet had no axial tilt, which might have been a good thing since such a tilt might have led to seasonal low temperatures extreme enough to make the planet unhabitable. The planet also had no moon to stabilize the normal wobbling of the planet's rotation over long timescales, making the long-term climate extremely variable. Jaipur was not very livable.

Nonetheless, Jaipur was not only settled, but it actively traded some of the native biologicals with Earth and other settlements. It seemed that whatever drove evolution on Jaipur tended to infuse the local flora with a compound that produced hallucinogenic euphoria in humans. So far, there had been no serious side effects from the compound, driving up demand in some circles. Despite the best efforts of scientists on Earth and elsewhere, synthetic versions of the compound were inferior in inducing the euphoric effect. This, of course, drove up the demand, and the price, for the real thing. Like the poppy farmers in Pakistan, the farmers on Jaipur were never lacking for a cash crop.

The last shipment of anything to or from Jaipur occurred a little over a month ago, which was on the long side between contacts, but not unheard-of. The frequent contact also meant that the locals would know about the war, making Anika's job just a little bit easier. She was just there to check in and fly the flag, as it were.

Unfortunately, Jaipur ships loaded with the hallucinogenic compound had proven to be a tempting target to pirates. Unfortunate only because of the incidents; fortunate because it meant that Jaipur had a few space-based ships that were armed with which they could defend the planet. They were not warships, so Anika doubted they could stop a determined and well-armed enemy, but they could at least put up a fight.

Upon arrival in the Jaipur system's Oppenheimer Limit, Anika was again momentarily distracted by the beauty of the starscape on the bridge display. She was jolted from her reverie by Mitra's abrupt interjection.

"Captain, there is a problem," said Mitra.

"Explain," she said, now giving the AI her full attention.

"I am receiving no radio traffic whatsoever. Jaipur control should be broadcasting a navigation beacon and protocol for visiting ships, but the frequency band they normally use is silent. From what I can tell, there are no RF emissions from Jaipur," Mitra replied.

"Show me the inner system in optical," Anika ordered. The virtual screen appeared with its usual clarity and three-dimensional projection of the planet and nearby space—as seen forty light-minutes away and as things were on Jaipur forty minutes ago. She did not like what she was seeing. The entire planet was encased in a cloudlike haze.

"Mitra, show me the view from a previous ship that visited here," Anika asked.

Mitra responded by showing the view of Jaipur taken by a merchant ship as it had recently departed the system for destinations unknown with its cargo. The view contrasted with what she saw now in that Jaipur used to have significant and noticeable water and ice cover, plus a few distinctive land masses. By contrast, the new view of Jaipur looked like there was either a planetary dust storm, one hell of a large weather event, or atmospheric dust and debris resulting from a devastating bombardment of the planet. As much as Anika hoped it was one of the former, she feared it was the latter.

"Lieutenant Patel, are there any obvious threats here?" Anika asked.

"I'm still waiting on Mitra's system scan to be complete, but as of now, it looks like we are the only active ship here," replied Patel.

"Lieutenant Patel is correct. I do not detect the drive plumes of any ships and no thermal emissions beyond what appear to be naturally occurring. Like New Hyderabad, if there are any hostile ships here, then they are either quite far away or powered down. However, I urge caution. There is a high probability that the planet was attacked, and we are seeing the aftermath of what has been some sort of planetary bombardment."

That was it then. Another settlement had apparently been attacked and destroyed with hundreds of thousands dead. They could not discern any more details from this distance and there was little point in going sunward to find out more. That might come later when they had the luxury of time and resources. This was not that time. She needed to get back to Earth and report as soon as possible.

"Lieutenant Utreja, spool up the Hawking Drive and calculate a jump that will take us back home," she said.

"Yes, ma'am," replied Utreja as he began the prejump routine.

"Captain, I have detected a distress beacon emanating from the minor asteroid belt approximately eighteen light-minutes from our current location. The signal is weak and highly irregular. It was not there when we arrived, so it is either on a timer, turned on after the light from our arrival reached the source of the signal, or a timing coincidence," Mitra said in his usual matter-of-fact manner.

"Lieutenant Utreja, stand down the Hawking Drive. Lieutenant Patel, what do you think? I don't like coincidences," said Anika as she rose from her chair to approach the projected image of Jaipur with its cloud-shrouded surface. She stretched out her hand, seemingly to stroke and comfort the planet.

"The signal is from one of the Jaipur defense ships. The ship is severely damaged and reports having many casualties. They are requesting rescue," said Patel.

"Mitra? What do you think? Is this for real or some sort of trap?" asked Anika as she continued to stare at the wounded world so many millions of miles away. As she did so, she could not help but think of Winslow's words to her when they were last together: "I can't see you turning around and leaving" when there were wounded to be rescued. *Could she?*

"Eighteen light-minutes is too far for our telescopes or sensors to discern space mines or a powered-down ship, so I have no way of knowing," Mitra replied.

"Mitra, use the optical comm to let them know we are coming to render assistance. There is no need to broadcast our intentions to the entire solar system," said Anika.

At full burn with the fusion drive, it would take the *Mumbai* about two days to reach the damaged ship from their current location. Two days of a very bright fusion plume allowing anyone within two light-days to know where they were and deduce where they were going.

Anika's orders were specific. If the aliens were there, do not engage. If there were people in need of rescue and the aliens were there, do not engage. But in cases where there was no obvious threat and people needed rescue, the decision to render aid was at her sole discretion. Winslow was right; she could not ignore a plea for help. Remote mines or not, she was going to render aid.

"Lieutenant Utreja, take us in. Tell Dr. Pillai to prepare for casualties."

They were three hours out from the damaged ship, which they now knew was one of three antipirate "Space Guard" ships from Jaipur that had engaged the invaders in a valiant, but doomed effort to stop the attack. Anika was in communication with the wounded captain of the Jaipurian ship, *Sachet*. According to the captain, the government of Jaipur knew that they were at risk of attack and came up with a plan to use their limited space self-defense forces to at least make the attackers feel some pain in their attack. From what Anika learned, they were successful.

Since the planetary government did not know when and from where the attack might occur, they kept two of the three ships hidden in the glare of the system's sun at the L1 Lagrange region, one and a half light-seconds from Jaipur. L1 was where the gravitational pull of the star and the planet came together to create a region of space sunward from the planet where a spacecraft could remain without using much propellant. The ships were not powered down since they would need to potentially activate their fusion drives at any time to engage the enemy. They gambled that to any ship coming into the system toward the star, the thermal emissions of a fusion reactor on standby would be difficult to differentiate from the star's emissions. They were correct.

The third Space Guard ship went about its normal duties, acting as a deterrent to pirates and performing space search and rescue, as needed.

Three weeks ago, five of the now all-too-familiar alien ships appeared in the system. The citizenry had already been dispersing around Jaipur as best they could, but the tempo of departures from the cities and towns increased once news of the ships' arrival began to spread.

The alien ships thrusted toward Jaipur while the lone Space Guard ship not hiding at L1 boosted outward to engage them, only to reverse course back to the planet at the last possible moment before any sort of engagement could begin. To anyone observing, it would have looked like the Jaipurian ship decided to not sacrifice itself in what would have otherwise been a suicide attack with little tactical or strategic gain.

Once the alien ships entered high orbit around Jaipur, the lone Space Guard ship placed itself in a highly elliptical orbit that would maximize its time away from the attackers but would set it up for a high-speed pass at the lowest part of its orbit that just happened to occur when the enemy ships would be on the sunward side of Jaipur. Meanwhile, the two Jaipurian vessels hiding at L1 began low-thrust boosts that would have them reach the same region of space as the attacking ships at the same time as the ship in the elliptical orbit. They were counting on the star's infrared glare to hide the thrust plumes of the two

Space Guard ships until it was too late, and they could launch an attack from an unexpected direction, essentially attacking from behind.

It was while this sole military engagement was being implemented that the alien ships began their devastating attack on Jaipur. As on Nikko, the major and minor cities were hit by nuclear weapons, vaporizing them and their remaining inhabitants. Then, the attackers launched a swarm of nuclear missiles at the planet's northern icecap. Huge swaths of ice were vaporized, sending plumes of radioactive steam and debris into the planet's atmosphere, and causing what would undoubtedly be a prolonged nuclear winter, perhaps a century or more in duration.

When the engagement finally occurred, the object of the war was over. Jaipur lay in ruins with whomever survived doomed to freeze or starve during the nuclear winter. As expected, and easily determined by the laws of orbital mechanics, the Jaipurian Space Guard ship's speed increased from its modest one and a half kilometers per second speed at apogee to nearly ten kilometers per second at perigee. The engagement would last only a few seconds, during which both sides would launch missiles and use their point defenses to stop any missiles launched by the other side. As the ships converged on the area where their orbits would coincide and the battle would occur, the two "hidden" Jaipurian ships arrived and completely surprised the attackers from the rear while they were distracted with obliterating a seemingly hopelessly outnumbered defending ship. Each Jaipurian ship launched two missiles, their entire complement, neither of which carried a nuclear weapon. Space Guard ships were designed to deal with pirates and police actions, not fight wars.

As the orbiting Space Guard ship was destroyed, all four of the missiles converged on a single Kurofune ship, with two breaching the target's late-to-activate point defenses. Moments later, after the sneak attack was recognized, one of the two remaining Space Guard ships was destroyed. The third, which the *Mumbai* was now approaching, took a direct hit after it had reached sufficient speed to escape orbit from around Jaipur and place it on an outbound trajectory away from Jaipur and the attacking fleet.

Taken by surprise, the damaged alien ship was apparently beyond repair. As best as the *Sachet*'s captain could discern, the attacking fleet did not pursue him because they were busy offloading the injured from their own damaged ship. Several hours after the brief engagement, the *Sachet* detected the telltale signature of a ship's fusion drive having a containment breach and exploding. He could only surmise that their attack had either directly caused enough damage for the reactor containment to fail or that the ship had been damaged enough to be unusable and was self-destructed. From this distance and without looking more closely at the remaining debris, there was simply no way to tell.

The audacity, cunning, and bravery of the Jaipurian ships reinforced Anika's decision to effect a rescue. These were brave men and women who did not deserve to be left here alone to die in the cold. Not on her watch.

"Lieutenant Patel, Mitra, in less than three hours we will be close enough to the *Sachet* to offload the remaining crew and wounded. This is also the most dangerous part of our mission. Are there any signs of mines or anything else that might threaten us?" Anika asked.

Mitra was the first to speak. "No. I have been reviewing the optical, thermal, and RF data taken by the *Sachet* on its outbound trajectory, and it appears the attackers made no effort to follow them—they or their remote weapons."

Patel simply nodded.

"Very well, I want these brave people offloaded on board as quickly as possible so we can make our next move. Lieutenant Utreja, lay in a course for Jaipur orbit. A low one, less than three hundred kilometers, circular."

"Yes, ma'am," said Utreja, hands flying across the control.

Anika turned to toward to door to leave when Lieutenant Chatterjee approached her and began to speak in a hushed tone, joining the conversation for the first time.

"Captain, I realize you have great discretion in your orders if there are no active enemy forces in the system, but I must remind you that we are to minimize our time here and return to Earth as soon as possible. May I ask what you are thinking with your plan to proceed to Jaipur? Any planetary survivors are likely to be few and exceedingly difficult to find, perhaps impossible to find," said Lieutenant Chatterjee.

"Jenya, I appreciate your advice, as always, and reminding me of my orders. As XO, that is your job. But we have an opportunity here to find out more about whoever it is that is so eager to wipe us out and I intend to take it," Anika said. She then turned to the rest of the crew and spoke.

"Captain Anand said that the one of the enemy ships exploded in orbit around Jaipur. That means there will be debris, perhaps bodies, that could provide valuable intel about the nature of who we are fighting. We have to go in to see what we can recover and return it to the Earth for analysis. We don't currently know anything about the enemy, and this might just be our chance to change that," said Anika.

Lieutenant Chatterjee grinned in response. Anika looked at the rest of the bridge crew and saw similar reactions. They were all eager to get into the fight, and right now, getting intel on an enigmatic and unknown enemy might be more important than any direct military engagement they might get themselves into. Her crew was with her and it felt good.

Now I know why I wanted to be a captain of a warship. To lead a crew like this doing something that really matters.

CHAPTER 8

As a Space Guard ship, the *Sachet* had a crew of eight. When the *Mumbai* arrived, three were dead and two critically wounded. Both would have died soon had it not been for the advanced medical facilities run by Dr. Pillai. It was not that Earth's medical capabilities were better than those available on Jaipur; they were just there and available. Jaipur no longer existed, and the *Sachet* was too small for more than an infirmary. The remaining crew were uninjured, including Captain Anand. The transfer of the crew went quickly, and within two hours, the *Mumbai* departed and set a course for Jaipur. The trip would take just over three days.

Anand and Anika were sharing dinner in her cabin the day after the crew was rescued from the damaged *Sachet*. They spoke as they shared a traditional Indian meal that included lapsi halwa, a sweet dish made from large-grain cracked wheat, cooked with ghee, and sweetened with sugar and cardamom powder. Anand ate like he had not eaten in weeks—which was not far from the truth. The

Sachet crew had stretched their rations to last as long as possible as they drifted, hoping against hope for a rescue.

"Don't get me wrong, any human from Earth would have been a welcome sight, but seeing a ship flying the flag of the home country boosted our morale beyond what you can know. India has grown to mythic status on Jaipur, in fact on Settlement Day we have a traditional..." Anand's pause turned into a painful silence.

"I'm sorry," he said. "For a moment there I was thinking that Jaipur, my family and friends there still existed. But they don't."

"That's all right, Captain. I cannot imagine what you must be going through. Feel free to talk about it or not. Just know that I am here and will listen. Captain to captain," said Anika.

"I will accept your offer on one condition," said Anand.

"What's that?"

"When we aren't on duty, please call me Bhargav," he replied.

"Anika," she said in reply.

"Very good, Anika. Thank you. In my time aboard ship, I tried to learn as much as I could about the attacks but there isn't much. The war, I guess it is now safe to say, seems to be very one sided. They attack and we lose. I hope I am wrong. Am I?" Anand asked.

"You are not wrong, and I believe the public back home is becoming more and more aware of how precarious this whole situation is. We have lost at least two settlement worlds, with many dead, and had several of our ships severely damaged in a trap. Your engagement with them was the first to produce a kill. The tactics were a beautiful thing to see. I would love to speak with the person who came up with it," said Anika as she took another bite of food.

"Lieutenant Laghari, my second-in-command. He was one of those killed during the attack. He had a wife and three children and was a brilliant orbital dynamicist and tactician. In the time we served together, he came up with novel maneuvers that allowed us to stop two pirate attacks on ships outbound from Jaipur. Both times, the pirates didn't know we were on them until it was too late. I will miss him."

"I'm sorry. He sounds like someone I would have been proud to have served with," Anika said.

"When we reach Jaipur, I know your priority will be to learn as much as you can from the remains of the enemy ship, but will you also be able to rescue any survivors on Jaipur?"

Anika paused, carefully considering her next words. "Bhargav, you yourself just noted that we don't know much about who is attacking us or why. And we are losing. What you and your ships did may help us change that and save billions of lives. We are hoping that we find something in the remains of the exploded ship that will be useful to the experts back home. Something we can use against the aliens and turn this war around so no other settlement, or Earth, has to go through what you, your crew, and the people of Jaipur went through," said Anika.

Anand leaned forward, then back, then forward again as he looked like he was searching for the right words to say. Anika sat patiently, not wanting to interrupt his thinking.

"Anika, may I ask you a personal question?"

"Of course," Anika replied.

"Are you married? Do you have a family back on Earth?"

"No, I am not married, but I was planning to be," she said. Thinking of Winslow made her sad, and it must have showed.

"I didn't mean to pry. It sounds like you, too, have suffered a loss. But I must ask you a question. If your loved ones were on Jaipur, would you be able to walk away without trying to rescue them? Someone on the planet is bound to have survived the attacks but from what I can see about the hellish conditions on the surface right now, they probably will not last long."

Anika's thought went immediately to Winslow and the similar dilemma he faced at Nikko. He chose to return to Earth with vital intelligence data that could make a difference in the outcome of the war. Now it was her time to make a life-or-death decision. And she realized that decision had already been made when she accepted command of the *Mumbai* and received her orders.

"Bhargav, I have my orders and I intend to carry them out. Earth needs the data we are about to collect, and they need it as soon as possible. If, by chance, we encounter any survivors in space near the wreckage, we will, of course, do everything in our power to save them. But we cannot take the time to do a limited search and rescue across an entire planet. Even if we found survivors, we could not bring many of them with us on the *Mumbai*. There simply is not enough room. I am sure you understand," she said.

"I do. And I would undoubtedly say the same thing if the situation was reversed," he said.

Mumbai's approach was not unnoticed. Among the debris orbiting Jaipur were five autonomous drones identical to those that damaged the Earth ships at Nikko. Those who placed them were not as confident that ships from Earth would venture close to another destroyed settlement after the surprise attack that had been left for them at Nikko, so they left fewer drones in the trap. They thought it enough to make the Earth ships pay for potentially finding something useful among the debris— should any come along to look. The drones were mostly powered down to render them indistinguishable from the many thousands of pieces of debris that the damaged ship had cast into orbit around Jaipur when its fusion core was detonated. Using their passive sensors to see the characteristic heat signature of a fusion drive, they now knew their time of waiting was nearing an end. Silently, they watched and waited.

"Mitra, we are getting close to entering orbit and I do not want to be surprised like the *Indefatigable*. What do you see? Are there any drones or missiles?" asked Anika, sitting in the captain's chair staring at the three-dimensional trajectory plot projected in the viewing area of the bridge. In the center of the plot was the now-dust-covered Jaipur, being orbited by a cloud of red and blue dots, some with circles around them. The blue and red dots were pieces of orbital debris, presumably from the destruction of the ships that fought there. Those with circles were likely interesting pieces of debris from the destroyed alien ship. It was those pieces of debris that Mitra identified as the most likely to contain information about the enemy and its technological capabilities. Anika planned to use the ship's robotic arms to grapple them into the cargo bay.

"As expected, there are several thermally active objects in the debris field. Most are likely to be pieces of the fusion drive, the reactor core, or the liquid-metal coolant. All would be still radioactive enough to generate a detectable heat signature. If there are any drones, then I cannot discriminate them from among the other debris signatures," Mitra replied.

"Keep me informed. If there is anything that looks out of the ordinary, take immediate defensive action. We will not risk this ship and in no case will we remain for more than twenty-four hours. Let's make good use of the time to collect as much as possible."

"Captain, there is something you should see," said Mitra.

The 3-D image of Jaipur vanished to be replaced by an image from another of the *Mumbai*'s telescopes, this time showing a large piece of metal that was presumably a piece of debris that Mitra was studying. Still attached to the inner walls were what looked like beds, protruding out and into empty space. From this distance, it looked like a toy. A toy that was part of a large, three-dimensional jigsaw puzzle waiting to be assembled. In a way it was, just assembled in reverse.

As the camera zoomed in, the picture became clearer and clearer as the image-processing software made sense of the scattered light it was receiving, Anika saw what Mitra was calling to her attention. Strapped to one of the beds was what looked like a body. The resolution was still rather poor from this distance, but it was clearly a biped with a torso and arms remarkably similar to humans. Anything more than that was lost in the digital noise.

"Lieutenant Utreja, we have our first priority salvage. Take us over there. I want that section of hull brought into the cargo bay as soon as possible," Anika said.

"Captain, the hull fragment is too large to bring aboard in one piece. I recommend we pull alongside and use the cutting torch to sever it into two pieces for salvage. We can get it through the cargo bay door if we cut it in the correct places," offered Mitra.

"Just don't damage the body if that is what it is. I want it intact. Tell Dr. Pillai that he needs to be ready to collect a potential biohazard for return to Earth. I want it in BSL-4 containment from the moment we bring it into the ship," Anika ordered. Biosafety Level Four was the highest level of containment for a likely biohazard.

"The rest of the debris is to remain sealed in the cargo hold at BSL-3 until we return to Earth. Who knows what pathogens might be circulating on that ship that could be normal and healthy for its occupants and lethal to us?" said Anika, eager to see what the adversaries looked like. In humanity's expansion into the galaxy, they had found many planets teeming with life and many planets having biospheres similar to Earth's. But they had never encountered an alien, intelligent, or tool-using species until now. If they were bringing a dead alien into the ship, then she had an obligation to complete the rest of the mission and get home with it as soon as possible.

Three hours later, the hull section was split into two and safely in the ship. Anika invited Captain Anand to join her in the corridor outside the cargo bay for their first look at the alien body through the eyes of the camera mounted atop Dr. Pillai's spacesuit helmet. Once Pillai and his team retrieved the body, they would place it in a graphene-impregnated biohazard containment box that was designed to remain intact even if the entire ship were to crash at high speed into a mountain after reentering Earth's atmosphere from space. Each deep-space Earth ship carried one for just such an event as this. To the best of Anika's knowledge, this might the second time such precautions were ever taken by any of the ships so equipped.

Pillai took his job and safety quite seriously, which meant Anika and Anand had to wait what seemed like an eternity for Pillai and his team to get their suits checked out and the containment box ready. She and Anand passed the time by mostly remaining silent. She suspected Anand was still reliving, or at least pondering, the moments that had brought him to this point. Knowing what she did about post-traumatic stress, she suspected he was beginning to have survivor's guilt. He and his crew would need extensive counseling when they reached Earth—for integrating into a whole new culture and society and for processing the unimaginable losses they had endured.

"Oh my God," said Pillai as he neared the frozen and desiccated body that lay strapped to the bunk. Anika's camera was displaying essentially the same thing Pillai was seeing, and she was without words.

"It's human," said Anand.

Pillai, who could hear them, replied, "I would say a human male, midthirties, with a muscular build who looks to be of central Asian descent."

"Human?" Anika's mind raced for an explanation. "Could this have been a prisoner? Is this a fragment of their ship's security area? Could this be someone taken from a merchant ship or from Jaipur?" asked Anika in rapid-fire succession.

"Captain, I can't know without doing a full autopsy," replied Pillai. "I would also like to determine the cause of death. We don't know if he was dead when the ship decompressed or before."

"Doctor, I don't want to break BSL-4. Your autopsy will have to wait until we get Earthside and have the appropriate facilities. Doing that on the *Mumbai* would place us all at risk," Anika replied.

"Yes, Captain, I agree with you. Chances are they won't let me near the body once we get back, though," said Pillai, not doing a good job at hiding his disappointment.

"You are probably right, Doctor, and I'm sorry."

"No, Captain, you are right. We need to do what's best for the war and that isn't some ship's surgeon cutting up what might be our first alien in a half-assed autopsy. We will get him stowed and sealed," said Pillai.

"Mitra, I'm returning to the bridge. Please get the last of the high-priority salvage onboard as soon as possible so we can get underway for home," said Anika.

"There are only three more that I believe might

provide useful information. One of them has a weak electromagnetic signature that could be a still functioning data pad or some other small electronic device within it. So far, not much in the way of functional electronics has been recovered, making this one important to retrieve. We can have them all safely on board and stowed within no more than two hours," said Mitra.

"Very good, please keep me posted," she said. Anika's mind raced in a thousand directions at once, with thoughts of the captured alien body, the salvage and its secrets to be discovered, the frustratingly long journey back to forty light-minutes from the central star so they could go home, and Winslow, poor Winslow, among them. It was then that she remembered that Captain Anand was next to her. He stood silently and patiently while she, too, was momentarily lost in her thoughts. Anand needed a morale boost.

"Captain Anand, would you like to join me on the bridge? I haven't shown you that courtesy yet, and I'm curious as to your reaction to the differences you might notice between our ships and yours," Anika said as she and the *Sachet*'s captain began walking toward the elevator that would take them to the bridge.

"Thank you," said Anand, coming out of his funk. "I would like that very much."

Using its own low-power laser point-to-point comms system, the drone known as Zeta informed its brethren that it was almost time. It knew this because the enemy ship was approaching with its grappling arm extended, reaching toward the debris that it had attached itself to.

Any minute now, they would fulfill their designed purpose . . .

"Your bridge is far more advanced than ours," said Anand as he looked at the three-dimensional situational-assessment view projected in the forward section. "We've tried to keep up with the developments on Earth, but ours was still a relatively young and cash-poor settlement. When it came to licensing technology, the government tended to put more into bio and biomedical tech than anything else. We needed to stay ahead of famine which always seemed to be nipping at our heels on Jaipur. Military tech for fighting pirates was not high on the list."

"Nor on ours. These attacks caught us completely by surprise," she said.

On the 3-D display, Anika watched the ship's robotic arm grapple one of the last pieces of debris to secure it in the cargo bay. Mitra was able to manipulate the arm much faster than a human, but it was still a painfully slow process given the fragile nature of the debris being captured.

"Captain, the forward IR camera just picked up a glint reflecting from a piece of debris that appears to be coherent," said Patel, tension clear in her voice.

Coherent meant artificial and likely part of a short-range optical communication of some sort. Not good. Anika did not hesitate.

"General Quarters!" she said as she lunged for her seat and grappled with the safety belt. The ship-wide alarm began to sound.

"Mitra, abort the retrieval and find out where that

signal is coming from," she said. She turned to direct Anand toward one of the available emergency seats and saw that he was already in one and fastening his safety belt.

On the screen, the robotic arm released the debris it had been holding and began to retract. In what seemed like slow motion, but happening all too quickly, there was a blinding flash from the debris just released, followed by what felt like an earthquake rumbling through the ship. The decompression and radiation alarms began to sound, raising the cacophony to a new level. The ship shuddered again.

"Four fusion signatures!" shouted Patel, his hands moving rapidly across the controls at his station.

She then heard the short-range Gatling gun point-defense weapons activate, making a sound that was both reassuring and disconcerting. Reassuring in that they were actively defending themselves from attack; disconcerting because she knew what would happen if they failed to do their job successfully.

The view on the situational assessment changed from a real-time view of space surrounding the ship to a tactical map showing themselves at the center and the location of the detected threats. As she looked at the display, three of the fusion signatures winked out and were replaced with the skull-and-crossbones symbol for a kill. Moments later the ship shuddered again, not as violently as was caused by the first explosion, but close enough to likely cause more damage to an already injured ship.

"The immediate threat is behind us," said Mitra.

"Mitra, what is our status?"

There was a few second pause before Mitra responded, a noticeable difference from his normal way of communicating. "The ship is functional with no primary systems offline. Most of the damage from the first explosion was confined to the cargo bay and the area immediately around it. There are three crew missing, presumed lost to space, and no additional casualties. My aft cameras, those you were viewing when the explosion occurred, were momentarily overloaded but have now recovered. The point defenses took care of the remaining missiles with only the last one detonating near the ship, causing minimal additional damage, mostly on the outer hull. The ablatives absorbed most of the energy and will need to be replaced when we are next in space dock."

"Did we lose the body?" asked Anika.

"No. The body is safely in storage, undamaged," he replied. "But we did lose much of the debris we collected, and the cargo doors will not be able to close during the trip home," he said.

"Is that a problem?" asked Anika.

"Having the cargo bay exposed to vacuum will not impede our ability to maneuver in system or with the Hawking Drive. However, we cannot safely land anywhere with a significant atmosphere. The ship could become uncontrollable in atmospheric flight."

Anika was relieved. For the moment they were safe and had avoided another of the alien traps. She was troubled that the shipboard sensors had not detected the bomb, or whatever it was, earlier. She suspected that the EMF they had detected, and thought was functional debris, was what exploded. She knew that Mitra would sort through all the available data and provide her a complete assessment of the likely causes, and she did not want to rush him. Damage to the ship for Mitra was like suffering an attack in hand-to-hand combat for a human. The ship was an AI's body. The cameras and imagers were its eyes, the hull its skin, and so forth. Mitra was wounded and undoubtedly now tending to those wounds.

It was time to get away from Jaipur and back to Earth. Anika was very concerned that more attacks might be coming as they made their way back to the Oppenheimer Limit, but there was little she could do about it other than have Mitra and the crew monitor every sensor, camera, and radio for anything out of the ordinary as they crawled away from the destroyed settlement at 1,731 kilometers per second. *Fast enough to circle the Earth twice every minute, but at this rate it will take us the better part of a week to get to the Oppenheimer Limit and back home,* she thought. *Too damn fast for me to figure out how to tell Winslow the conditions under which I accepted this command.*

CHAPTER 9

The *Mumbai* had returned two days ago, and Price had heard almost nothing from Anika. Shortly after the ship arrived in the outer solar system, he received a single message on his private account: "I am fine, don't worry."

That was it. Granted, it put his mind at ease, especially after he heard that the ship had been attacked and there were casualties. But two days was a long time for her to not find the time to reply to his messages. He sent a welcome home message to her private account as soon as he heard the ship had returned and another the next morning. Since their relationship began, they always traded messages upon returning from deployment. Always. Until now.

Fortunately, Price was extremely busy getting the *Indefatigable* ready for deployment, which did not leave him much time to dwell on his personal life. The ship's repairs were mostly complete, and Lord Nelson was back to his usual, stuffy self. By the time Price landed in his bunk, he was too physically and mentally exhausted to do much more than think briefly of Anika and wish she were there with him. They needed to talk. She had no idea that because of their relationship he was under suspicion of something. Treason? Conspiring with the enemy? What enemy? India? India and the Commonwealth were allies, so that made no sense. Major Castillo's accusations made absolutely no sense, yet here he was. He had not been relieved of command, but that was certainly possible.

He really wanted to talk with Anika about the whole thing so they could be a united front if any charges were filed. Both Colonel Williamson and the JAG he consulted said he should not speak with Anika, but he planned to ignore them. He had to speak with her. How could he not? Was she aware of the accusations and that was the reason she was avoiding him? He knew that was possible but considered it unlikely. He knew her better than that. Or thought he did. *Why didn't she get back with him?*

"Good morning, sir. It is time to arise. You have two messages waiting," said the cabin's avatar, jarring Price from a deep, deep sleep. He knew he had been dreaming but had no idea about what. Whatever it was, it faded quickly as he got out of his bunk and began his morning routine.

He read both messages before his shower. The first was administrative, regarding the transfer of a power-plant engineer to the *Indefatigable*. The second caught his attention. The EDF forces were being divided into two fleets. The *Indefatigable* was being assigned to Second Fleet, effective immediately. The order came from Admiral Stepanchikov, EDF. Over the last few months, the Earth nations contributing ships to the Earth Defense

Force had worked out the organizational structure, giving First Fleet, charged with the defense of the solar system, to the Chinese under Admiral Chiang.

Price knew of Stepanchikov but had never met her personally. She was widely respected, known for considering the opinions of her advisors and fellow officers, and decisive. But, like most of the EDF leadership, she had never been tested in battle. Given his recent experience at Nikko, Price knew that the cost of that lack of experience could be high, no matter how well educated and prepared a person might be.

Included in the orders was a listing of the other ships assigned to Second Fleet. A quick skim made Price's heart skip a beat. *Mumbai* was on the list.

That afternoon at fourteen hundred would be a VR meeting with all the ship's captains participating. Finally, Price would get to meet the man under whom Anika was serving, Captain Padmanabhan, even if only virtually. There was a great deal to do before the meeting, and Price had not yet had breakfast. During his entire military service, no meal was as important to him as breakfast. With a good, hot breakfast and a steaming cup of tea, even shipboard tea, he could get through most anything the navy threw at him. He could taste it already.

Second Fleet consisted of twelve ships, forty percent of the total available to the EDF. New ships were being constructed but getting even the first one in the queue from the shipyard, through qualification, and into the fleet ready for action would take at least a year. Until then, the EDF had to make do with what was available. Given what they knew about the enemy, Price was not sure it would be enough.

Fourteen hundred came quickly. Lieutenant Green joined Price in the CIC for the VR call, but he would remain off camera to observe. Price asked Green to listen to the overall briefing, paying attention to the other captains on the call, making note of his first impressions of each. Price wanted to know more than the bios of the captains commanding the other ships in the fleet. The lives of his crew would depend upon them, and Price needed to know who he could trust. He tasked Green to learn as much as he could about each, observe them during the meeting, and let him know which were among the top three he could rely on and vice versa. Knowing who to avoid in a pinch was as important as knowing who to go to.

The twelve ships making up Second Fleet were currently dispersed throughout the inner solar system, mostly between Earth and Mars. Getting all the captains together physically for an in-person meeting would take some time, hence the VR. Even with everyone fairly close, the speed-of-light time lag between the ships in cislunar space and those roughly at the radius of Mars' orbit would make back-and-forth conversation impossible for many. Price expected this to be a mostly one-way communication from Admiral Stepanchikov.

Price joined the meeting ten minutes before the hour and found that most of the other captains were already there. The virtual conference table was projected in the front of the CIC and looked bigger than the CIC itself. As Price got himself settled, he noticed that Padmanabhan was not yet present representing the *Mumbai*. There was still time.

The images of the EDF flag, a hideous blue-and-white monstrosity that looked like it was designed by a UN committee composed of sociologists with a love for the old United Nations flag, appeared at the head of the virtual table where Admiral Stepanchikov would sit. Momentarily distracted by the flag, and wondering why they did not consult graphic artists and military historians in its design, Price noted that the previously empty seats were filling in. He glanced back along the virtual table until his eyes fell on the chair reserved for the captain of the *Mumbai*. Instead of Padmanabhan, Anika sat in that seat. He stared, momentarily catching her eye, only to have her seemingly ignore him as she stared at the front of the table. It was then that he noticed her name tag: "Captain Anika Ahuja / INS *Mumbai*."

Captain? What the hell? He again tried to catch her gaze and was unsuccessful. Was she avoiding him? Why hadn't she told him? He then noted the time stamp under her name: "-1:32 seconds." No wonder she did not return his look. The image he was seeing left her ship over a minute and half ago. She would not even know he was looking at her for another minute. They definitely needed to talk.

The flag disappeared as the image shifted to Stepanchikov coming into the virtual room and taking the seat at the front of the table. Protocol would have them all stand, but given the time lag of the transmission, doing so would be not only be impractical, but distracting as the captains of the closer ships would stand first, followed by those increasingly farther away, and then be seated in roughly the same order with the same time lag.

Admiral Stepanchikov—an olive-skinned woman with slightly greying, short-cropped hair—could have been anywhere between 45 and 75 years old. With recent biomedical advances increasing the human life span to nearly 150 years, the once-inevitable signs of aging had been similarly delayed. Price had served under commanding officers who were close to the mandatory retirement age of 75. Though he loved the navy, he was sure he wanted to have another career or two afterward and before he faced mandatory retirement. Of course, that would depend upon what happened over the next several weeks and months. Unless they found a way to turn things around, he might not live long enough to begin a second career.

"Welcome to Second Fleet. I have not had the pleasure of working with most of you. In fact, I have never even met most of you. But we will get to know each other well over the next few days and during our deployment. I read your bios and your personnel files. I am familiar with the designs and capabilities of your ships and am aware of each contributing nation's training and command protocols," she began, looking at each person gathered around the virtual table. Her Russian-accented English was definitely not of the American variety. Price suspected she studied or frequently visited the UK. Oxford perhaps?

"I have sent by encrypted laser comm to each of you a summary of what we now know about those who attack us. You already know the basics. Their technological capabilities are remarkably like our own, they have issued no demands, and have made no attempt at contact whatsoever. Their sole motivation appears to be the destruction of our settlements and killing as many of us as possible. Thanks to an operation recently completed by Captain Ahuja of the *Mumbai*, we now know one additional piece of data that, quite frankly, I don't know what to do with and we are keeping extremely Close Hold. Our attackers are human. One hundred percent, DNA-based, human," she said and then paused before continuing.

"On the *Mumbai*'s check-in with the settlements at New Hyderabad and Jaipur, they found that Jaipur had been recently attacked and destroyed, just like Nikko. But this time, the colonists were able to hurt the attackers by destroying one of their ships. In the wreckage they found this." Stepanchikov's image faded and was replaced with a picture of a human male on an exam table, presumably during an examination or an autopsy. His closed eyes and dark skin seemed to shout "I'm human! Look at me!" from the cold, gray metal table upon which the body was lying. "The autopsy confirmed that the subject was killed during the explosive decompression of the ship, but that wasn't why he was in what we assume was their ship's infirmary. This man was recovering from an appendectomy. Furthermore, the team performing the examination looked closely at his genetics and found that there had been only a small genetic drift."

Given the time delays in the signal reaching the attendees, it was almost humorous to watch the facial expressions of those around the table go from attentive to questioning or shocked as the admiral's speech reached them and their reactions were beamed back. Those closest and with the shortest speed-of-light lag reacted first, with those farthest away showing their reactions after she had already moved on to the next topic—at least that is how it appeared from Price's perspective.

"Now, on to our plans. We believe we have detected a pattern to the attacks and are planning to interdict or stop the next one. Over the last several weeks, the EDF has been sending ships to check in on the known settlements. So far, in addition to Nikko and Jaipur, El Dorado has also been attacked and destroyed. The American ship sent to visit El Dorado reported the grim news when it returned to the solar system yesterday. Seven other settlements reported no attacks, and we are waiting on two other ships to return from their missions so we can determine the status of at least three more. What do Nikko, Jaipur, and El Dorado all have in common? They were the first three settlements established in the diaspora that followed the discovery of the Hawking Drive. El Dorado, Nikko, and then Jaipur. Based on the evidence gathered so far, the order of destruction follows the order of settlement: El Dorado, Nikko, and most recently, Jaipur. If this is not a coincidence, then we must assume that the next targets will be New Hyderabad and then Kunlun. As of two weeks ago, New Hyderabad was intact and made aware of the conflict by the *Mumbai*. The attacks have been occurring roughly one month apart, so if the trend continues, then we have less than a week to prepare," she said, pausing to drink some water.

"All ships in the fleet are to rendezvous in Jovian orbit in five days. Given that you are dispersed across the solar system, that is the soonest we can get Second Fleet fully constituted. Once there, we will have one day to get our ships working together as a fleet. That isn't nearly enough time, but if we are to have any chance to help the people of New Hyderabad, then we will need to depart immediately after and hope we are not too late. I will have my AI come up with various attack simulations so we can get used to working together before we jump. The timing will be tight. Are there any questions?" she asked, pausing again.

After the time-of-flight delay confirmed that no one had any questions to ask, Admiral Stepanchikov ended the meeting. One by one, the images of the other captains flickered out of existence in the virtual conference room, including Anika. Price did not notice if she ever looked at him or not. Price turned off the VR.

"Captain, I will go through the bios and the briefing package to see if there is anything you need to be aware of regarding the other ships in the fleet," Green said, looking beyond Price instead of directly at him, which was unusual. "Will there be anything else, sir?"

Price resisted the urge to dismiss his XO as would have been his custom. Something was bothering Green, and Price did not want it to go unaddressed.

"Lieutenant, is there something you would like to say?" asked Price, drawing Green's gaze back to his own.

"No, sir. I mean, yes, sir, there is," said Green.

"And that is?"

"Permission to speak freely, sir?" asked Green.

"Oliver, you know the answer to that. Yes, of course."

"Sir, I saw that Captain Ahuja and the *Mumbai* are part

of the fleet. And there are rumors going around about you and her . . . "

Price interrupted, "Lieutenant, I assure you that my personal relationship with Captain Ahuja has never had and will never have an adverse impact on ability to command this ship in the fulfillment of our orders and the mission."

Green looked surprised, tilted his head back, frowned and quickly interjected, "Of course, sir! I would never think or believe otherwise. That's not what I was going to say. Sir."

"It's not?"

"No sir. It is related. The rumors are that you and she have somehow conspired against Earth. I don't believe them, but . . . "

Price's blood began to boil. He had to tell himself to not shoot the messenger, especially after giving him license to speak freely. The relationship between a captain and his second-in-command was sacred and essential to the survival and success of many a ship. He would not jeopardize that here.

"Lieutenant, the rumors are based on an unfortunate incident that occurred a few weeks ago between me and an overly enthusiastic intelligence analyst. My loyalty has never been seriously questioned, or I can assure you I would not be here, now, in command of the *Indefatigable*."

Green looked relieved. Price suspected he was relieved by the answer and at simply getting his concerns off his chest and into the open.

"Yes, sir! I knew that was the case, sir. I just thought you should know. And my congratulations to Captain Ahuja on her promotion," said Green.

"Thank you for bringing it to my attention. I will be sure to convey your sentiments to the captain. Dismissed," said Price. *If Anika ever returns my calls,* Price thought. *And I'll damn sure bring it up the rumors with Colonel Williamson as soon as I get back to my quarters.*

"Colonel, the rumors are hurting morale and my XO just asked about them. Captain Castillo's baseless accusations must be dealt with as soon as possible. Is there anything I can do to make that happen?" asked Price. He was in his quarters taking advantage of the *Indefatigable*'s proximity to the Moon for a real-time conversation that might be impossible, or frustratingly time-delayed had he waited. Fortunately, the colonel had been available and took his call.

"Winslow, I hear you. But you must know the position Captain Castillo has put me, put us, in. She tried to have you relieved of your command until she completes her inquiry, but I successfully staved that off. I told Admiral Sanchez that I personally vouched for you and that if you were removed, then I would submit my request for reassignment immediately," said Williamson. Though the VR-link quality was excellent, Price felt like he was an observer rather than actually participating in the conversation. He was still struck with disbelief that someone would question his loyalty, making the whole thing surreal.

"Thank you, sir. I don't mean to cause you trouble, sir," said Price. He was astonished that the colonel would risk his command, his reputation, and his career protecting him. Even though he was innocent, a board of inquiry might decide otherwise. Price did not want a good officer like Williamson to have his career damaged through association with him.

"I personally spoke with Captain Ahuja's commanding officer, Colonel Lal—an interesting man, by the way. He and I knew each other from a Harvard course we took together ten years ago when we were both rising lieutenants. For an Indian, he ate a lot of Argentinian beef as I recall. In any event, he assured me that her promotion had nothing to do with you. He also told me about your breakup. I know that must hurt personally, but it is for the best as you can see from the fallout it caused. How you thought having a relationship with an officer of a foreign-flagged ship would work out is simply beyond me. I hope you can compartmentalize any feelings you once had for her and that it will not affect your professional relationship. Breakups can foster resentment, as I am sure you are aware," said Williamson.

Price was stunned. *A breakup with Anika? Was that why she was avoiding him?* Price had to pry himself out of his personal shock and back into the moment with his commanding officer.

"Yes, sir. Captain Ahuja and I are on the best of terms and nothing will interfere with our professional relationship." Price was not sure if he believed what he had just said. He was anxious for this meeting to be over so he could collect his thoughts and try to reach Anika again.

"Best of luck with Admiral Stepanchikov. She is one tough lady and a damn good strategist."

"Thank you, sir, I will do my best," said Price.

"Of that I have no doubt," said Williamson as he broke the connection.

Price quickly tried to reach Anika on her personal line and once again received her standard "not available" message.

Why won't she speak with me?

CHAPTER 10

Two days later, days away from the planned Fleet rendezvous near the Oppenheimer Limit, word arrived that New Hyderabad had been attacked. Admiral Stepanchikov broke the news in their daily captains' meeting. While the time delay in the news reaching the ships of the fleet was still noticeable, it was also shorter and getting shorter still as they slowly arrived and fell into formation. Price was eager to join the fleet and see what exercises Stepanchikov would put them through so they could get used to working together. He did not want some small technical issue to cause a major breakdown in communications during the heat of battle if it could be caught and corrected beforehand when the consequences would not be nearly so high. While they were separated by millions of miles, daily briefings and meetings were fine, but what they needed were combat simulations and that would have to wait until they were close enough together for it to make sense.

Price, like the other captains, arrived in the virtual

meeting room well before the admiral. He could not help but notice Anika and found himself staring at her more often than he liked, not with malice, more curiosity. Right on time, Stepanchikov phased in.

"Good morning. From the flash reports, it looks like everyone is on schedule for our rendezvous. Unfortunately, that is about the only good news I have today. Yesterday, we learned that New Hyderabad was attacked and destroyed. The pattern was the same. Six ships arrived in the system, and as they moved toward New Hyderabad they did not respond to hails or the planetary government's unconditional surrender. Once they arrived in orbit, they used nuclear weapons to destroy every population center on the planet. We don't know if there are any survivors. We learned of the attack from a sleeper ship we placed just beyond the Oppenheimer Limit in the New Hyderabad system. It jumped to Earth immediately after the bombardment ceased," Stepanchikov said.

"We were planning to go to New Hyderabad to finally engage them. What are our plans now?" asked Captain Vertell of the *Vanguard*. Price had never met the man and only knew his name because of the virtual nametag that floated under his visage. Though he had read the bios of the other captains in the fleet, he was not yet fluent at placing the names with the correct faces.

"Instead of New Hyderabad, we are going to Kunlun. If our intel is correct and complete, that will be their next target. It was the next settlement world established. Fortunately, it will also be the one most capable of mounting at least a bit of a defense. Kunlun, unlike many of the other settlements, has kept in close contact with Earth. For the last few months and because Kunlun is a Chinese settlement, China has been using much of its merchant fleet to send defensive weapons there, including their own version of the space mines that have been so effectively used against us at Nikko and Jaipur. If the Kurofune reach Kunlun's orbit, they will not have the luxury of operating freely without fear of attack."

"Admiral, do we know why the Kurofune have not simply altered the course of an asteroid to impact the settlement worlds? It seems like that would be a lot easier and less risky than going into orbit and using nuclear weapons," asked another of the captains.

"We do not, but I would guess time. Finding the right asteroid and giving it the exact push it would need to be placed on a collision course with an inhabited planet cannot be done quickly. And there would be a lot of time between giving the asteroid a nudge and impact—perhaps years. That time that could be used by the defenders to see the asteroid coming and mount their own space mission to push it in a different direction. I suspect the Kurofune are in a hurry to attack and do as much damage as possible. They also seem to like the carnage. The sociologists and psychologists think this is personal. The Kurofune are enjoying the slaughter and want to be on hand to witness it," she replied.

"Will this alter our timeline?" someone asked.

"No. As dire as the situations are on the settlement worlds, we need a functional fleet to defend Earth and the remaining settlements. If we rush to confront the Kurofune before we are ready and lose because of our lack of preparation, then we still lose and the situation there and elsewhere gets worse. And the pipeline of new ships to replace us will not be producing significant results until next year. I am sending the latest daily briefing to your secure inboxes for review," she said, pausing while someone not on screen told her something no one on the call could hear.

"That is all for now. I have another call I need to take. Dismissed," she said, abruptly ending the meeting.

As the admiral faded from view, Nelson announced, "Captain, you have an incoming call from Captain Ahuja of the *Mumbai*."

Price's heart skipped a beat. *Finally*, he thought as he steeled himself for the call and factored in the frustration that would inevitably arise from the speed of light time delay.

"Price here," he said, opting for a less formal greeting.

"Winslow, this is Anika," she said, speaking softly.

"I was wondering when you would return my call," said Price, trying hard to be calm and not sound aggravated, which he was. *Very.*

There was a long pause.

"I apologize for not calling sooner, but since I assumed command of the *Mumbai*, I have been extremely busy. I owe you an explanation and an apology. First, please know that I love you very, very much," she began.

Uh-oh, thought Price, *Here we go.*

"For reasons not completely clear, Captain Padmanabhan was relieved of command and during the afternoon of the day before we were supposed to depart for our reconnaissance trip, Colonel Lal offered me the

Mumbai. I was thrilled. You know how long I've waited on this opportunity and I just couldn't say no," she continued.

"Anika, I . . ." Price started to reply but stopped when she began speaking again.

"Winslow, I was offered the captaincy on the condition that we end our relationship. Colonel Lal did not give me any time to think about it. He was expecting an answer right then and there. I just couldn't turn down the offer. I couldn't. I am so sorry. I am a complete coward for not telling you before now," she said, tears forming in her beautiful, dark eyes.

"Anika, I love you and want the best for you. I don't know if I would have done differently under the same circumstances. I understand you were in a difficult position and had to choose. But I still love you. I will always love you. What do we do next?" Price asked, fighting back his own tears.

There was another long pause.

"Winslow, thank you. Of course, I still love you and I do not want to give you up. We had so many plans for the future that I cannot bear the thought of abandoning. But I don't know what to do," she said.

"Anika, I don't know what to do either. But I cannot believe there isn't a way to get through this. I do not want to continue my life and career without you. Thank you for explaining. My mind was full of speculations and now I know. If you are willing, we will figure this out. It might not be until after this war is over, but we will figure it out. I want to spend the rest of my life with you," he said.

Another long pause.

"And I you, my beloved. Thank you for your understanding. For now, since we knew we would be separated during our respective deployments, let's just get in that mindset and plan to figure out a solution once the current crisis is behind us."

"That sounds like a good plan," said Price, smiling. The relief was like a heavy blanket lifted from his heart.

The connection ended and Price was left alone to think about what solutions would be possible after the war. Assuming, of course, that they won the war . . .

The volume of space around the sun is almost unimaginably huge. If the solar system were a perfect sphere extending from the sun outward to the orbit of Pluto, then its volume would be about 850,000,000, 000,000,000,000,000,000,000 cubic kilometers. Hiding a small ship that does not want to be found in that volume is extremely easy. The robotic craft sent to observe the activities in the solar system had no problem finding the seclusion it needed. Outfitted for reconnaissance, not war, it bristled with cameras, antennas, and other sensors needed to observe the comings and goings of Earth ships as they deployed throughout the solar system and departed it.

On board the craft were multiple drones that could be sent back to the Kurofune home planet filled with data so that their masters could determine their next moves. The mother ship was vulnerable when it first entered the system and used its fusion drive to reach its hiding place. Fortunately, the attacks had not yet begun and the Earthers were oblivious to the need to keep track of all the spacecraft traffic in their bustling, interplanetary network of commerce. An additional small exhaust plume millions of kilometers away from Earth that posed no apparent threat would go, did go, without notice.

Using the drones' own version of the Hawking Drive to exit the solar system with the much-needed intelligence data seemed low-risk. The drones would launch and simply drift away from the mother ship before activating the drive for their jump across spacetime. One moment they would simply be there, unnoticeable against the black background of space, and the next they would be gone.

The characteristic plasma plumes from the fusion drives of the twelve ships making up Second Fleet were unmistakable and visible far across the solar system. The mother ship monitored the velocity and direction of the Earth ships and correctly concluded they were converging on the same region of space near the Oppenheimer Limit. The data, which included an assessment of the tonnage and capabilities of the assembling ships, was loaded onto a drone and launched for transit back to the home world.

Just as probabilities can work in your favor, for example, the low probability of a small ship being found in the vast emptiness of the solar system, so can serendipitous discovery work against you.

"Dr. Moulder, I've detected another one. This is another of the odd ones," said Sammy Chen, one of the many postdoctoral students working in the Stanford Gravity Physics Laboratory. Chen was nearing the end of his tenure as a postdoc and already had a full-time job offer at Johns Hopkins Applied Physics Lab that would begin immediately thereafter. Chen was one of those rare people who could see beyond the data and grasp bigger pictures. His mind seemed to be simultaneously both in the immediacy of his research and in the nebulous realm of big ideas, taking ideas and crossing seemingly effortlessly between the two.

"Another one? Tell me more," asked Professor Moulder, the director of the lab and the physics department's rising star in terms of research funding and peer-reviewed journal publications. The Stanford Gravity Physics Laboratory had been around for well over a hundred years and was the lead institution on the International Deep Space Gravitational Wave Detector Network.

"Odd in that the signal clearly isn't natural and the source is again way too close. From what I can tell, it originated somewhere in the outer solar system at roughly the orbital distance of Saturn. It is the third one in as many months," replied Chen.

"Sammy, process the data as best you can to determine the output power of the source and its probable location. I need to make a call," said Moulder.

The gravity-wave detector network consisted of four sets of spacecraft, the two spacecraft in each set separated by at least one hundred kilometers and in constant communication with each other via laser light. When a gravity wave passed between the paired spacecraft and through the path of the laser light, the spacetime in the local area was altered, changing the effective distance between them, which was then detected by changes in the measured light. By comparing the measurements taken as the gravity passed through each of the four sets of detectors, the direction and distance of the source of the gravity wave could be determined. The network was originally built to study gravity waves emitted by black holes, neutron stars, and other massive objects in the universe; it was a purely scientific endeavor to study nature. And then the Hawking Drive was discovered.

The Hawking Drive allowed spacecraft to travel interstellar distances nearly instantaneously by locally warping spacetime both at the departure and arrival points. When starships first began testing and then when the diaspora of settlement ships began departing, the gravity-wave astronomy community was nearly apoplectic. The transit of ships to and from the solar system was creating a noise source in their observations. And since science was clearly the most important endeavor ever undertaken by the human species, the scientists wanted interstellar exploration halted, or at least controlled, so that it did not permanently close down an entire field of astronomy.

That was not going to happen.

A compromise was reached, with the spacefaring nations and organizations of the world agreeing to provide advance notice of interstellar transits so that the gravity-wave astronomers could plan for the disruptive noise source and not have their data completely ruined. The compromise had worked well, with only a few unannounced incoming transits occurring each year. Fortunately, scientists being scientists, they were quickly able to correlate the characteristics of these gravity-wave signals as belonging to a Hawking Drive and subtract the noise from their data. They could live with a few surprise signals, especially since the characteristics of each were essentially the same. The signals from natural sources were never the same twice, making these artificial ones easily identifiable.

All was well, until shortly before the war began. Two months before the attack on Nikko, the space-based network of satellites began detecting unannounced spacetime warps.

Moulder reported the spurious warps to a contact he had at the National Academy of Sciences, who had in turn reported the information to someone at the US Space Navy. A week later, Moulder received a call from a Colonel Brock at the Pentagon asking that should any further detections be made, Brock was to be informed immediately. Brock returned Moulder's call within an hour. Two hours later, he, Chen, and Brock were in a VR call discussing the results.

"Walk me through the detections again, in order, and outline what you think they mean," said Brock. Brock could have been on a recruitment poster for the Space Navy, the Space Force, the Air Force, or the old Army Air Corp from virtually any era of military history. He was handsome, clean-shaven, and wore his hair closely cropped. His deep voice commanded attention, even when he was in polite conversation.

"The first signal was detected six months ago, and it was the largest of the three detected so far. Since we had not been warned of a pending interstellar transit, and since the signal did not exactly match that of a Hawking

Drive, we at first thought we had a new natural signal to study. But it wasn't. When Chen correlated the data from the satellite pairs, he found that the source of the signal was in the outer solar system somewhere between Saturn and Uranus," Moulder said.

"A month later, we received the second signal. This one was much weaker, but it was again without warning and originated somewhere in the vicinity of the first one," Chen added.

"Other than strength, were the signals significantly different?" asked Brock.

"Yes," said Chen. "In the same way that we can tell the difference between an incoming Hawking Drive transit and an outgoing one. If I were to hazard a guess, I would say the first one was incoming; the second outgoing. Something big coming in; something smaller going out."

"And this third signal?"

"Another outgoing transit," said Chen.

"It looks like a ship using a drive similar to a Hawking but tuned slightly differently. With just enough difference to be noticeable in the spacetime warp it causes," added Moulder.

"We are preparing a paper for a conference later this year. It will be my last with Professor Moulder before I start at APL," said Chen.

"Hmm. Please send me a copy of the paper when you finish it. I would be extremely interested. Thank you, gentlemen, this was very enlightening and useful. Please do not hesitate to contact me again if you get another signal like these. I will be available day or night," Brock said, ending the connection.

Moulder and Chen looked at each other, both raising their eyebrows.

"Lunch?" asked Chen.

"Definitely," said Moulder.

CHAPTER 11

"Keep up the pace, Chatterjee," said Anika as she completed another lap around the track, marking one kilometer completed out of the two they planned to run. The development of the Hawking Drive had led almost immediately to the development of artificial gravity. Once you know how to warp spacetime, you can do it pretty much anywhere you have sufficient energy. Since a large spacecraft like the *Mumbai* needed a fusion power plant to propel it across space, power was not an issue. With artificial gravity, the crew of the navy ships could use exercise regimens similar to those they used back on Earth instead of the more lengthy, contrived ones that characterized early space exploration when astronauts were exposed to extended periods of zero gravity. The *Mumbai*'s narrow running track, barely wide enough for two people side by side, extended around the inner side of the outer hull of the ship and doubled as an access point for vital systems being piped around it. One had only to look up to see the thousands of wires, fiber optic cables, and sealed tubing going this way and that to be reminded

167

of the track's utilitarian nature. It also was not for people with claustrophobia; no attempt was made to make its narrow, low ceiling appear more expansive than it really was. In an attempt to get to know her better, Anika had invited her XO to join her each morning for a two-kilometer run.

"Yes, ma'am," said Chatterjee, panting a bit now that she had reached the halfway point.

Chatterjee was immediately behind Anika on the track and had not even once attempted to come alongside or pass her captain. An observation not lost to Anika. Now that they had been running together for a while, Anika decided to bring that up to her at breakfast. Anika understood being deferential to the captain in front of the crew, but she was becoming concerned that she might not be able to count on her XO to speak up when Anika needed to hear a different point of view. During her tenure as XO, she had frequently provided Captain Padmanabhan with unsolicited advice that he sometimes followed, sometime not. Chatterjee never passing her captain on the track was speaking volumes to Anika, and she was worried.

"Captain Ahuja, we just received new orders from Admiral Stepanchikov. Her AI contacted me moments ago with the details. We are being temporarily assigned to interdiction duties." The calm but somewhat disconcertingly omnipresent voice of Mitra startled them.

"A new assignment? Are they taking us out of Second Fleet?" asked Chatterjee.

"I don't know. Admiral Stepanchikov wants to meet with you at zero seven hundred," said Mitra.

"That leaves about forty minutes for us to eat and get dressed. I'll meet you in the CIC," said Anika, beginning to sprint toward the exit.

"Yes, ma'am. See you there," replied Chatterjee, joining Anika in the sprint.

"Good morning, Captain Ahuja, Captain King," said Stepanchikov as they met, virtually, in a VR recreation of the *Smetlivy*'s CIC. As Anika knew was her custom, the admiral ignored or at least never acknowledged the presence of officers other than the captains. This time was no exception. Chatterjee and King's XOs might as well have not been there as far as the admiral was concerned. They were close enough together for the speed-of-light time delay to be only about two seconds. Long enough to be annoying, but no so long as to make real-time interaction difficult. "I trust you and your crews are working well and ready to join the fleet?" she asked.

"Yes, ma'am," they said independently and in unison.

"Good. The last of the ships is still a day out from the rendezvous. Once we are together, we will begin the drills and, if the fleet performance is satisfactory, we will depart for Kunlun. However, before we do, I need you to check out some spurious Hawking Drive signals detected near the orbit of Saturn, about thirty-five degrees trailing in its orbit. The Deep Space Gravitational Wave Detector Network has been seeing some signals out there that are remarkably similar to those caused by a Hawking Drive activation—only not ours. We might have some unwanted visitors and I need the *Mumbai* and the *Adelaide* to check it out."

"Yes, ma'am, but why us? Isn't First Fleet assigned to protect the home system?" asked King.

"Strictly speaking, yes. But you can get there more quickly. All their ships are well inside the Oppenheimer Limit and would take days under thrust to get to the point where any of their ships could make a jump in system to where we think the potential hostiles are located. Your ships are already past the limit and can make the jump immediately. If this is a Kurofune incursion, then we need to deal with it as quickly as possible," she replied.

"Are two ships enough? Do we know the strength of the potential hostiles?" asked Anika.

"The signals were compared with the database of signals compiled since the Hawking Drive transitions began and were measured by the gravitational-wave network. The signal indicates that there is likely only one ship, probably much smaller than either of your ships, and perhaps some smaller ships or drones accompanying it. My AI sent yours the latest coordinates. We don't believe the ship or ships will have moved much because we've been observing the area with various telescopes, and there have been no plasma plumes. Whatever caused the gravity-wave signal hasn't moved much, if at all."

"When do we depart?" asked King.

"Eleven hundred this morning. I want this dealt with and you back in formation as soon as possible," Stepanchikov replied.

"Ma'am. By 'dealt with,' are we to try to capture the ship or destroy it?" asked King. Anika had been wondering the same thing. "Dealt with" was sufficiently ambiguous as to allow virtually any outcome.

"If it is an alien ship, then destroy it. Don't get me wrong, if you show up and they surrender, then accept it. But that isn't likely to happen and we cannot afford to allow them to continue seeing everything we do," she said.

"What if it is not an alien ship, but some small pleasure cruiser on an unregistered sightseeing tour?" asked Anika.

"Then don't be trigger happy. Check it out, and if it is a hostile then give them a chance to surrender. It they don't, blast it to hell," the admiral said.

After a several seconds of silence, Anika and King were dismissed and the connection ended.

"Mitra, do you have the jump details?" asked Anika.

"Yes," he replied. Anika sometimes found Mitra's brevity to be annoying. This was one of them.

"Where will we be relative to Saturn? Will the planet's gravity affect our jump accuracy?" Though not as massive as the sun, a planet's gravity well could also disrupt the accuracy of a jump using the Hawking Drive, especially in system jumps like they were about to make. Anika wanted to know if there would be a risk of the two ships not coming out of spacetime warp where they were supposed to.

"The effect will be negligible. The coordinates are fully thirty-five degrees trailing, well away from the planet," replied Mitra.

"Thank you," she said as she turned to Chatterjee. "Lieutenant, once we are back on the bridge, I want to address the crew to inform them of our mission. We will go to General Quarters thirty minutes before we depart."

"Yes, ma'am. The crew will be ready," said Chatterjee.

"I am fully confident they will," Anika said. And she

meant every word. They were ready. She was ready. Her experiences at Jaipur prepared her for the next engagement. It was just happening a little sooner than she thought it would.

Anika did not like in system jumps. They seemed . . . kludged. It was irrational, but they made her nervous. Fortunately, the jumps were nearly instantaneous, and she did not have time to dwell on it.

Given that they were in the solar system, the apparent locations of the stars did not change from before the jump. The only star with a location change on the tactical display was the sun. Both the *Mumbai* and the *Adelaide* were where they were supposed to be, 500 kilometers apart and roughly the same distance from where they believed the target to be.

"Mitra. Is there anything out there?"

"I detect low-power emissions consistent with a small vessel, likely uncrewed, 450 kilometers away. I have informed the *Adelaide*," said Mitra.

"Not a pleasure cruiser then. Assume the target is hostile," said Anika, turning toward Lieutenant Patel. "Lieutenant Patel, we are close enough to engage with the microwave projector. Fry their electronics."

"Yes, ma'am," said Patel as he activated one of the ship's few close-combat weapons.

High-power microwaves can be projected over moderate distances on Earth and in space using technology originally developed in the latter part of the twentieth century for radar systems and later, antisatellite weapons. The principle was simple: overload the target's electronics with spurious and disruptive microwave energy, causing the target's electronics to fail. The microwave energy builds up a charge on the surface of metal objects, resulting in heat and electrical arcing, causing them to shut down or be severely damaged. It was the preferred method of disabling a ship instead of outright destroying it. It was also fast, speeding from the source to the target at the speed of light which, in this case, meant the damage was immediate.

"The target is powering up its systems," said Mitra.

"Keep the beam on the target, Lieutenant Patel," said Anika, watching the projection of the engagement. "And be ready in case they launch a missile attack." Anika knew that the microwave beam was extremely effective but using it did not give the haptic feedback that was possible with launching the ship's missiles or using the point-defense Gatling guns. The only way you knew the microwave beamer was working was to look at the ship's power-consumption curve. When it was active, the average power draw on the reactor nearly doubled.

"The target has lost power. RF emissions have dropped to nearly zero," said Mitra.

"Lieutenant Patel, cease fire," said Anika.

The image of the enemy ship remained unchanged.

"The thermal emissions of the ship are much too low for it to have a humanoid crew. It is most likely AI controlled," said Mitra.

"So how do we capture it then? If there is no one there to surrender, then that won't work. If it is AI or computer controlled, then the only way to speak with it is to repair it or connect a new power source, and that is not going to happen. And I am not sure I want to get close enough to tow it back to the rendezvous point," said Anika.

"Captain King from the *Adelaide* would like to speak with you," said Mitra.

"I'll take it in the CIC. Chatterjee, you are with me. Mitra, see what you can learn about this thing remotely and let me know if you think we should send someone over to perform a closer examination," said Anika as she unbuckled and arose. "Secure from General Quarters," she added.

Once in the CIC, Anika answered the call.

"Congratulations, Captain Ahuja, on the clean kill," said King.

"Thank you."

"I'm calling regarding next steps. Our AIs have not detected any other ships in the vicinity and this one appears to be dead. The intelligence opportunity here is huge. I suggest we find a way to bring it back to the fleet with us and leave it tucked away somewhere for a ship to pick it up and take it home for analysis," said King.

"Can't they just get it from here?" asked Chatterjee.

Good, thought Anika, *she is finally speaking up*.

"Lieutenant, they probably could. But if this ship has been sending drones to and from the solar system, then there is a chance another ship might transit to this location at any time. We need to get this one somewhere else as soon as possible and then ask Earth to send a ship here to intercept whatever comes along," said King.

"I agree, but how?" asked Anika.

"We estimate the ship is about thirty percent the mass of the *Adelaide*. It will be close, but our power plant can produce enough energy to activate the Hawking Drive and make the jump with it secured to our hull," said King.

"Has anyone ever done this before? I'm not an expert on general relativity or the Hawking Drive, but I thought the drives of the ships were tailored to the design and maximum mass of the ship in which they were installed," said Anika.

"Captain, if I may interject?" said Mitra.

"By all means," said Anika.

"You are both correct. The Hawking Drives are designed and specifically tuned for the ship into which they are installed. To allow flexibility and safety margins, they and the shipboard power plants typically have fifty-percent margin on the design. Adding the mass of the alien ship should not exceed the safety margin. In addition, I performed a search and found two instances where a similar maneuver at this scale has been tried in the past. Both were successful," he said.

"Very well, then. Captain King, I will leave this at your discretion. Just let me know when you are ready to depart to rejoin the fleet. We will remain here and keep watch just in case a Kurofune ship decides to jump into the system while you are busy securing the alien ship," she said.

"Captain, I just detected a drone launch from the ship," said Mitra.

"General Quarters," said Anika without pausing to think. She and Chatterjee were on their feet and moving back to the bridge almost immediately. The VR connection with Captain King dropped in the same instant.

Anika was back in her chair on the bridge in less than ninety seconds.

"Lieutenant Patel, what is the status of the drone?" asked Anika.

"It is moving away from us and the *Adelaide*," he replied.

"Lock on with the microwave projector and engage," she said.

Patel moved quickly and Anika could see that the microwave array was locked on to the target and tracking it. Based on the ship's power consumption, she could tell that the beam was activated.

Moments later, the drone vanished.

"Damn! It must have been powered down during our initial attack or it would never have survived," said Anika. The drone had activated its Hawking Drive and jumped . . . somewhere.

Now the enemy would know they had lost their observing post in the outer solar system and that humanity somehow knew how to track them. How else could they explain the two terrestrial warships jumping in so close? They had just lost a tactical advantage—a surprise capability.

After making sure the captured ship was completely disabled, they mated it with the *Adelaide* and jumped back to the rallying point for Second Fleet.

CHAPTER 12

Second Fleet jumped to Kunlun three days after the *Adelaide* and *Mumbai* returned with their prize. It took that long for a small Commonwealth search-and-rescue craft to reach them from its previous duty station. They could not leave the Kurofune ship unattended.

Four days after arriving at Kunlun, Price gazed at the nearly pristine Earthlike planet below and had a moment of wistfulness. Sometimes he thought joining the navy was a mistake and that he should have been one of those forging a new life on a new planet, creating the culture and world the way it ought to be. Then he looked at the dedicated crew serving under him and immediately knew that he had made the best choice. Perhaps his regrets were just the normal looking back at roads not taken and wondering, "What if?" And, as usual, his thoughts then turned to Anika.

What was she thinking of the planet below? Of her choices? Was she thinking of how they might forge their life together after the war or was distance dampening her affections for him? Price told himself he had better change his thinking or his wistfulness would turn to regret. He did not much like being around people who were constantly looking back at their lives with regret. He would not allow himself to become like that.

The *Indefatigable* and three other warships were in geostationary orbit, evenly spaced around the globe ninety degrees apart. Two additional ships were using their fusion drives to hover over the north and south rotational axis poles of Kunlun, bringing the total number of ships in closer defense of the planet to six. The remaining six were within an eight-light-minute sphere of Kunlun, making it possible for them to react to any incursion with plenty of time to spare. Knowing that the enemy ships had technological capabilities roughly equal to that of humanity meant that they could not enter the system any closer than the Oppenheimer Limit. Given that the fusion drives they had observed were also strikingly similar to their own, it would take a minimum of four to five days for any invading ship or ships to traverse the distance from the Oppenheimer Limit to Kunlun's orbit.

Admiral Stepanchikov's was hosting a captains' briefing at ten hundred hours, giving Price another fifteen minutes to prepare.

In the few days that they had back in the solar system to perform exercises as an integrated fleet, Price's optimism grew. Each of the ships in Second Fleet merged well into a seamless unit under Stepanchikov's leadership. She knew just how to manage each ship's capabilities and captain for deployment at just the right time and place as they war-gamed possible scenarios at Kunlun. The drills had continued after they reached Kunlun, and their cohesiveness steadily improved.

Price joined the other captains in the VR meeting room just before the admiral. After dispensing a few organizational and managerial details, she began her daily update of the tactical situation.

"Kunlun is as ready as it can be to defend itself. My hats go off to our Chinese colleagues on Kunlun and back home who have provided eighteen autonomous drones, each capable of independently targeting a Kurofune ship with a bomb yielding just over five hundred kilotons. The two largest cities on the planet have surface-to-space missiles that should be capable of intercepting incoming missiles far away from their targets. The citizens have been practicing civil-defense drills that, with enough notice, should allow for nearly half their urban populations to evacuate to various rural locations where they have been stockpiling food and other supplies. The other half should be able to find temporary refuge in hardened shelters being built underground. Furthermore, if we are successful, none of these will be needed. Second Fleet is twelve ships, twice the number in the largest alien incursion to date. As we speak, my AI is sending the outline of today's drills which will begin promptly at fourteen hundred. Are there any questions?" Stepanchikov asked.

Seeing no takers, the meeting ended. Stepanchikov kept her meetings brief.

"Lieutenant Green, please set up a call with Captain Ahuja for as soon as she can work it into her schedule and convey to her that there is some urgency," said Price. Price asked his XO to set up the meeting so Anika would know the call was not personal. And it was not. He was starting to get an uneasy feeling about their situation and quickly losing the confidence he once had in the admiral and in his own judgement. *It cannot be this easy,* he thought, *There is no way it can be this easy.*

The call was arranged for thirteen hundred. Price took it in the CIC and asked that Green participate.

When Anika's VR image appeared, Price's heart skipped a beat. *She really is beautiful.*

"Captain Price, it is good to hear from you. How may I help you?" Anika asked. To an outside observer, the two would appear as colleagues only. At least, that was Price's hope.

"Captain Ahuja. Thanks for taking my call. I'm curious as to what you think of the admiral's briefing today, particularly our readiness to confront the Kurofune if they do attack," said Price, not mincing words and placing his trust in Anika's relationship with him to keep his concerns confidential.

"Admiral Stepanchikov laid out a very reasonable plan of defense. We are dispersed in such a way that we can respond to an incursion from just about anywhere in the solar system and we do have more ships than we have ever seen the aliens muster . . ." she said.

"And?" prompted Price, hearing the concern in her voice as the last sentence faded rather than ended. He knew her well and could tell she, too, had reservations.

"And I think we are being too cocky. We are too sure of ourselves and our apparent numerical superiority. With the exception of *Indefatigable*, there are few of us who have ever been in any sort of live-or-die combat situation, and we simply lack experience," Anika said. Price could tell it was not easy for her to say anything negative about the admiral.

"There is also the matter of the drone that escaped back in Earth space. It had to report our attack and that there was a fleet gathering near the Oppenheimer Limit for a jump. Granted, they likely do not know to where we are going, but they might be able to put two and two together," said Price.

"Are you going to share your concerns with the admiral?" she asked.

"I don't know. She seems open-minded and willing to take input, but a part of me wonders if the Russian in her will allow her to accept it without recrimination," he said.

"Plus, what would we do about it? We are in the best position we've been in since the war began. Kunlun, unlike the other settlements so far, can defend itself and is taking abundant precautions planetside. We are here in force and Earth is still well defended," Anika stated, with just a hint of false bravado. Price could tell.

"I will request a meeting with her, and I will not involve you," said Price.

"You can bring me in if you wish. I'm not afraid to make my concerns known. Just let me know," she said.

"I will. Thank you," Price said as he looked at her a little bit too intensely.

"Take care," she said as the link severed.

"Lieutenant Green, after the exercises this afternoon, get me some time on the admiral's calendar."

"Yes, sir."

✦ ✦ ✦

Hidden just outside Kunlun's Oppenheimer Limit, perched on an otherwise cold and desolate asteroid that had been circling the central star quietly and undisturbed for well over five hundred million years, a ship identical to the one discovered observing Earth sat and observed the arrival and deployment of the twelve human warships. While the observer could not intercept the optical communications between the Earth ships, their defensive strategy was obvious enough based on their deployment around the settlement. For the second time in a week, a Kurofune messenger drone was ejected and minutes later activated its interstellar jump drive to take the latest information back to the home world. Unlike in the Earth system, there was no gravitational-wave network to detect its departure.

"Captain Price, I'm glad you requested a meeting. I, too, need to speak with you. What is on your mind?" asked Stepanchikov. The admiral chose to take the meeting seated at her desk with her multiple commendations projected on the wall behind her. Price briefly wondered if she brought the actual commendations with her onboard the ship or if they, like the meeting room, were virtual. He and Lieutenant Green took the call in the *Indefatigable*'s CIC.

"Thank you for taking my call, Admiral. I hesitate to bring up my concerns, but something just doesn't feel right. We have done everything we possibly can to protect Kunlun, our deployment makes sense, our ship strength seems logical, and our anticipation of this being their next target fits the pattern. But it is too easy. Too logical. Too predictable. I cannot shake the feeling that we are being set up. That we are doing what they want us to do," Price said.

"Since you are one of the few among us who have engaged in combat with the enemy, even if it was only their robots, I'm not surprised that you are wary. Your ships and the two with you took quite a beating. It was extremely fortunate that the *Indefatigable* escaped the trap with such light damage. Some might say your minimal casualties were miraculous," she said.

Price did not like where this was going nor her tone of voice.

"Yes, ma'am. My crew and AI responded quickly and efficiently to the threat. I am just glad we were able to save as many of the crew from the *Linyi* that we could," he said.

"Yes, and I am sure the Chinese appreciated their safe return. Regarding your concerns, what would you have us do differently?" she asked.

"I don't know. That's the problem. A good trap is one that makes the enemy feel like they are doing what they need to do when in reality they are doing what those that set the trap want them to do. Are any ships from First Fleet on standby to jump and support us?" asked Price.

"I am not at liberty to say," she replied, her gaze now resting firmly on Price's.

"Well, thank you for hearing me out," he said, now eager to end the meeting and sever the connection. She had listened, but he was not sure she heard. And how was he supposed to interpret the bit about her not being "at liberty to say"? Was he or was he not the captain of one of the fleet's ships, thereby automatically having a "need to know" for operational matters?

"Captain, there is another matter I need to discuss with you," she said.

"Yes, ma'am?"

"When the *Montana* joined us, they brought a disturbing bit of news from the EDF Criminal Investigation Division. It seems you are under investigation for your role in the debacle at Nikko. The report hints at suspicion of treason. The preliminary report urges that you be relieved of command until the investigation is complete, but your commanding officers back home declined to do so until more evidence is obtained. A compromise was reached with the background material being sent to me and asking me to use my judgment as to whether you and the *Indefatigable* should remain here with the fleet or be sent home," she said.

The momentary silence was deafening. Though Price suspected, feared, that this might come up again, he did not have a ready reply.

"The EDF placed me in a tough place. I cannot relieve you of your command and keep the *Indefatigable* in formation since your superiors explicitly ruled out that option. So, I must either send the *Indefatigable* home, putting the operation at risk by losing a ship we were counting on, or I allow you and your ship to remain and accept a possible security risk. A risk that you may pose a direct threat to the fleet." Stepanchikov leaned forward across her desk. Price could tell she was sizing him up; hoping that his expressions, body language, or other tell would guide her toward a solution to the problem she had just outlined.

"Admiral, I am aware of the investigation and I can assure you it is groundless. My loyalty and abilities have never before been questioned and I will let my record speak for itself. The *North Dakota* was destroyed because its defensive systems were caught by surprise and overwhelmed by the sheer number of close-range missiles targeting it. The *Indefatigable* barely escaped the fate of the *Linyi*. Both ships did all they could to defend themselves, and the *Linyi* got unlucky. *Indefatigable* could easily have been severely damaged or destroyed. It was the skill of my crew that saved it, not being part of any sort of plot or ambush," Price said.

"And what of Captain Ahuja?" asked Stepanchikov.

Price's blood ran cold. He did not want her dragged into this.

"Ma'am?" asked Price. *Best to play ignorant,* he thought.

"The report alleges that you have an inappropriate relationship with the captain of a foreign-flagged vessel. Furthermore, given the ethnicity and genetic analysis of the enemy corpse captured and brought home by the *Mumbai*, one might conclude that the enemy we are fighting might not be external after all . . ."

"I will not deny I had a relationship with Captain Ahuja when she was the XO of the *Mumbai*, but as I am sure your background information affirms, that is no longer the case." *At least officially,* he added to himself.

"Her chain of command is also aware of the investigation and they confirm that she ended the relationship with you when she was given command of *Mumbai*. But if there is a conspiracy, such claims are no more than hot air," she said.

"There is not much more that I can say. If you like, I will resign command of the *Indefatigable* and turn it over to Lieutenant Green. He is quite capable and that would allow the ship to remain until we fulfill our current mission," Price offered. He knew making the offer was a risk but could not think of any other way to preserve the mission.

"Very well. I accept your temporary resignation. Please confine yourself to quarters until further notice. Lieutenant Green, you are in command. I will inform the fleet within the hour. Please see to it that Captain Price is afforded every courtesy due an officer until the investigation is complete, but his access to outside communications is to be terminated immediately."

"Yes, ma'am," said Green, glancing furtively at Price as the episode unfolded. He was clearly not comfortable with what had just transpired.

Stepanchikov cut the link.

"Captain, I don't know what to say," began Green.

"Lieutenant, you don't need to say anything or do anything other than your job. Take care of this ship, kick some alien butt, and get this ship home safely so I can clear my name," said Price.

"Yes, sir. Nelson, you heard the orders?" asked Green.

"I did. Though I believe Captain Price is being unfairly treated, and since I personally know what happened at Nikko—at least up to a point—I am confident that he will be cleared and resume command." Nelson had of course heard the exchange. He heard and saw just about everything that transpired on the ship unless the captain explicitly ordered him to not observe.

"Thank you, Nelson. I appreciate the vote of confidence," said Price.

"Would you like to announce the change of command to the crew?" asked Nelson.

"No, I think I should make my way to my quarters and let the *Indefatigable*'s new commanding officer make that announcement," Price said.

Twenty minutes later, Price was in his quarters and Lieutenant Green, now acting Captain Green, assumed command of the *Indefatigable*.

Just under twenty hours later, the enemy fleet arrived.

CHAPTER 13

Anika received the news while off duty and enjoying a conversation with Lieutenant Chatterjee over a late lunch. She had finally broken through Chatterjee's opacity and they were at last getting to know and understand each other better. Anika's confidence in Chatterjee had dramatically increased, and she was sure the interpersonal connection they had established was a critical part of the breakthrough. Both their comm badges alerted and the message came through Anika's.

"Captain, a total of twenty-two unidentified ships were just detected at forty-seven light-minutes in three different locations," said Mitra.

"Thanks, Mitra, I'm on my way to the bridge. Let me know when we get orders from the admiral, and I would like a tactical summary as soon as I arrive," she said as she rose from the table. "Here we go," she said to Chatterjee as they began their jog to the stairwell that led to the bridge.

When they arrived on the bridge, the VR was active

with Admiral Stepanchikov's visage not yet in view. The captains were likely still assembling and there was no time for a VR "around the table" briefing. Time and information flow were now more critical than inclusive discussions. Lieutenant Singh vacated Anika's chair and moved toward the hatch where he paused, presumably to hear more about the situation before assuming his station.

"Mitra, what is the tactical situation? Where are they coming from?" asked Anika.

By shrinking the VR image that would soon be filled by Admiral Stepanchikov, Mitra created a smaller three-dimensional rendering of the stellar system alongside it, complete with miniature spacecraft identifiable as EDF forces or hostiles.

"Group 1, consisting of seven ships, is just above the North Celestial Pole. Group 2, also consisting of seven ships, is below the South Celestial Pole while Group 3, with eight ships, is in the ecliptic plane roughly aligned with the direction of the Galactic Center. The exact coordinates were just uploaded to all ships. The optical tracking is being coordinated by all the fleet and we should know their trajectories shortly. They entered the system simultaneously at roughly the same forty-seven-light-minute distance."

Mitra was interrupted by the admiral's appearance. She looked fresh, crisp, and not the least bit anxious.

"As your AIs have undoubtedly informed you, twenty-two hostiles just entered the Kunlun system in three battle groups. Each is coming from a different direction, undoubtedly with the goal of dividing our forces. Unfortunately, we are outnumbered and in a strategically difficult position. If we divide our forces to engage each group, then in each engagement we will be outnumbered by almost two to one. If we fully engage only one of the incoming groups with all our forces, we will have the tactical advantage, but will be leaving Kunlun without a frontline defense. Their space mines and drones might attrit the enemy, but not destroy them," she said, her image fading to be replaced with a 3-D representation of the star system very similar to the one Mitra created, showing the relative positions of the incoming ships relative to their own.

"There is no way we can engage one group, hopefully destroying or crippling them, and then make it back in time to engage another before they can attack the planet. Since we cannot risk the destruction of Second Fleet, that leaves us with only two viable options. The first, as I've already outlined, is to meet one of the enemy battle groups in force. The second is to retreat and engage another day when the odds are better stacked in our favor. In both scenarios, we lose Kunlun," she said. As she spoke, the visualization showed the spiraling trajectories of the incoming ships, the one along the ecliptic plane being met with Second Fleet roughly eighteen light-minutes out from the planet. The other two fleets passed unopposed toward Kunlun.

"They clearly knew how we are deployed and the size of our force. I plan to find out how they knew after this engagement is over." She paused briefly.

"Second Fleet does not run from a fight. My AI has run the trajectories and found an option that allows each of the ships in the fleet to rendezvous and assume formation gamma for an engagement with the hostiles coming in along the ecliptic. Given our separation distances, boost phases for each ship will begin at a slightly different time, with the first starting in about thirty minutes. Your AIs have the details. Given their speed and acceleration, assuming it does not change, we need to boost at two gees for an engagement in just under three days. If they are going to begin slowing down to enter Kunlun's orbit as in the previous attacks, then we will catch them roughly at the place and time where they would have to stop accelerating and begin their own deboost maneuvers. After this call, I will be speaking with the planetary governor. They are prepared and, as I am sure, will give the aliens a good fight. We will have a captains' meeting in six hours. Until then, let's get ready to show these aliens they are messing with the wrong people," the admiral said as she closed the connection.

"Mitra, you have navigational control. Give the crew twenty minutes warning so they can be ready for the acceleration," said Anika. She heard the acceleration alarm almost immediately.

Formation gamma was designed to keep the fleet together in a tight formation, with only about one hundred kilometers separating each ship laterally, until the last possible moment before the engagement. As the two fleets converged, last-minute maneuvers by either side could radically alter the distance at which the ships would pass each other, resulting in totally different attack strategies. Unless something changed, the battle would be over in a second or less, with the ships passing each other at a relative speed of over three thousand kilometers per second. *Per second.* At this speed, one could go from Moscow to Paris in that second.

Twelve EDF ships taking on eight Kurofune. There was no doubt the enemy would spread out, forcing the EDF ships to commit to an essentially one-on-one engagement with some Kurofune craft meeting two EDF ships. There were no missiles fast enough to go from negative seventeen hundred kilometers per second, from the perspective of the EDF outbound ships, to more than positive seventeen hundred miles per second, the speed of the incoming Kurofune ships, and catch them. Instead, the ships of the Earth fleet would probably launch their missiles a few seconds before contact, deploying them in the path of the incoming Kurofune and hoping their onboard targeting could keep them in the path long enough to have a chance of impacting or detonating near one of the Kurofune ships as they passed.

If the AI control over the ship was fast enough, it might be possible to use the microwave projectors during the engagement, but, at best, they would be in range for only a little more than a second, which did not leave much time for the microwave radiation to destroy a critical system. It might, or it might not.

Finally, like when the *Indefatigable* and *Mumbai* defended themselves from the space mines, so would both the Kurofune and EDF ships use their point defenses to defend against each other's missiles. The Kurofune, too, would undoubtedly launch missiles into the paths of the EDF ships, hoping to get lucky and take them out. They had come all this way, light-years, spent all this time, weeks, to engage an enemy for less than one second and see the likely loss of another settlement world and who knows how many ships. And that begged another question. What would they do after the attack run? Regroup, watch the destruction of Kunlun, and then go home? Or would the attack on the planet provoke the admiral into turning around and making a suicide run against the enemy forces? The admiral had already said the plan would be the former, but Anika's gut was pushing her toward the latter. *Winslow knows me too well,* she thought.

The *Mumbai*'s fusion engines kicked in and Anika could briefly feel the two-Earth-gravity acceleration pressing her into the captain's chair before the ship's artificial gravity kicked in. She noted that Lieutenant Singh was no longer on the bridge, and she had not had a chance to so much as acknowledge his being relieved from watch. Though she was sure he would understand, so, too, did she understand and remember the morale boost of having the captain formally resume command when she was coming off watch. It mattered. She would rectify that later. After all, they had three days until the battle.

"Lieutenant Patel, have you received an engagement plan from Admiral Stepanchikov?"

"Yes, ma'am," said Patel, looking up from his station to respond. "If both formations hold, then we will be in engagement range in just short of three days."

"Captain, the admiral just sent a series of drills for us to perform with the fleet, beginning in two hours. We will be simulating various attack scenarios in response to how and when the Kurofune decide to disperse their ships as we approach," said Mitra.

"Excellent. Let's use our time wisely," replied Anika.

The next six hours were a blur. When the admiral said she would put the fleet through various attack scenarios, she meant it. They simulated fighting the Kurofune in tight formation in case they did not spread out as anticipated. They fought in dispersed ship-to-ship combat. They fought with the enemy having twice as many ships as anticipated, assuming one ship was actually two that separated just before engagement. Some they won; some they lost. The simulations would continue for the next few days until the actual engagement.

At the appointed time, Anika and Lieutenant Chatterjee assumed their locations, virtual and real, in the CIC for the captains' meeting. As the various captains faded into view around the extended conference table, Anika was surprised when Winslow's XO appeared in his stead representing the *Indefatigable*. *Perhaps he was tied up with a shipboard matter and could not make it,* she thought.

Admiral Stepanchikov, with her usual efficiency, ran through the results of the simulations and provided an updated tactical assessment of the upcoming engagement—nothing had changed. Various reports and status updates trickled in from some of the ships, and then the admiral made the announcement.

"Finally, please congratulate Lieutenant Green of the *Indefatigable* on his field promotion to the rank of acting captain following Captain Price's decision to step down. We look forward to working with you Captain Green," she said.

To Anika, the news was an earthquake of an announcement and she tried, unsuccessfully, to not visibly register shock. For most of those assembled at the table, there was mild surprise but mostly curiosity. The admiral did not provide any details regarding Price's resignation. She quickly checked her personal messages to see if there was one from Winslow that might provide an explanation. There was not.

The meeting droned on for another twenty minutes, but Anika had little idea what was being said. She made a mental note to replay the last portion of the meeting at the first opportunity to make sure she did not miss something important or urgent. Then she got mad at herself for allowing her personal concerns to interfere with her professional obligations—the very reason her relationship with Winslow was so frowned upon by leadership.

Despite the mental distraction of wondering about Winslow, the next three days passed quickly with more hypothetical wins and losses in the various simulations. The fleet would be as ready as they could be when the actual engagement happened.

Anika heard nothing from Winslow.

CHAPTER 14

Elsewhere, a quite different drama was beginning to play out.

She didn't understand why the palace staff, especially Vice Admiral Dewan, were so against her desire to get married. She and Isaac had known each other since they were children, and no one objected to their pronouncing their love for one another when they were eight years old, but now that she was twenty-three, things were different. She knew, of course, that at age twenty-three things *were* different, but her sentiment was the same. Most women her age already had three children or more. It was *her* life, and *she* should be able to live it any way she wanted. *She was, after all, the queen.*

Once she had that last thought, she felt guilty.

"You are a servant of the people, never forget that!" Mother said to her repeatedly as she was growing up. "They look up to you to set an example, and they are not your servants nor your slaves. Yes, you may rule over the Kingdom, but never forget that ruling doesn't mean you are a god," she would say whenever her comments, behaviors, or attitudes crossed the line—an invisible but very real line in the royal household.

How she missed Mother. Her death last year caught everyone by surprise, especially her. She was relatively young, not quite fifty years old, and in near-perfect health. But even healthy people can suffer accidents and that's what the whole tragic affair was called—an accident. And it was a big one. She and ten other members of the Royal Household were traveling by air from the capital to the port city of Vora when something went horribly wrong and the transport crashed into a mountain. There were no survivors. A thorough investigation ruled out homicide and the next thing she knew, she was the queen. Deep in her heart, she didn't believe it was an accident. She would not accept the thought that blind chance had taken away those she loved. This was especially true now that they were in the Prophecy's Last Days. She was raised knowing that the fulfillment of the ancient Prophecy was to be during her lifetime, but she had always assumed that Mother would be the one to assume the responsibilities that were to be demanded of the queen in that time. Not her.

She had known she would someday become queen, but that "someday" was, or so she thought, far into the future. Sort of like how she and most other young people look at becoming old. Intellectually she knew it would happen, but emotionally she didn't really believe it. *No, not me! Other people get old. Other people die . . .*

But, here she was, one year after her mother's death, finally figuring out what it would take to make her happy—marrying Isaac and having a family—only to have those on her staff who "know how things are done," telling her that it simply cannot be. The husband of the queen, if there is one, is chosen by the Oracle.

She remembered at a young age asking about her father. The only answer she received until she was eighteen was "you will learn." On her eighteenth birthday she did learn, and she didn't like the answer.

And, looming over it all, were the Prophecy and some very old, and questionable, records from several hundred years ago. Her entire life had been governed by them. In fact, the life of every citizen on the planet had been governed by them for as long as anyone could remember.

Duty versus self. Mother also said that often, sometimes only to herself when she was in the middle of making some tough decision.

The queen was startled out of her pity party by the entrance of none other than Vice Admiral Dewan himself. She wasn't much in the mood to see him, but duty called.

"Yes, Admiral?" she managed to say without a hint of the sadness she was feeling. She had kicked into Royal Mode; a role for which she had been practicing all her life.

"Your Majesty, the High Priest is here to see you. He said it is a matter of some urgency," Dewan said. Standing just over six feet tall, Dewan loomed large in more ways than one. He had been the Master of the Household since she was a child, and his impressive physical size and unquestionable military training was always held perfectly in check as he took care of the day-to-day business of running the inner workings of the palace. He was not, she knew now, some glorified butler. No, he was a veteran military officer who was there to manage the household and protect her from harm. She had no doubt he would sacrifice himself if need be to save her—and she loved him like an uncle for it. That's why his disapproval was so painful.

"Send him in," she said, still without a trace of emotion. She didn't much care for High Priest Delal, but she had to deal with him. The Church was an important part of the Kingdom and the daily lives of every one of its citizens, though the secularists were making more and more trouble. She knew that it might someday come to a violent confrontation, but hopefully not anytime soon.

Delal was the near opposite of Dewan in size, but not personality. Delal's personality commanded nearly the attention that Dewan's physical stature afforded him. The High Priest was middle-aged, of average height, lean, and from what she could tell, quick on his feet. He was also quick-witted, often winning debates in her cabinet with his ability to remember and call up facts and figures as though he had a computer embedded somewhere in his brain. *Could he?* she briefly wondered.

Delal entered the room and bowed, showing his usual respect for her and her position.

"Your Majesty," he said.

"High Priest, what brings you to see me today?" she asked.

"The Oracle requests an audience with you in two days. At noon. Alone. The Oracle was extremely specific in its instructions," Delal replied, not lowering his gaze as was his custom.

She was taken aback by the news. She hadn't had an

audience with the Oracle since she assumed the throne. Was the Oracle also going to lecture her about Isaac? Or did it have something else to impart? The Oracle was the source of knowledge and its time was usually filled in exchanges with the engineers and scientists, helping to solve this problem or that crisis. And, of course, in conversation with the High Priest about matters of Prophecy. She knew Mother frequently consulted with it, but she had no idea who typically initiated the conversation.

"Yes, of course," she replied, acting like the invitation was expected and part of her normal, everyday life—which it was not. Not even close.

"By your leave," said Delal, bowing.

She nodded, silently grateful that Delal was departing. She had much to mull over before going to the Privy Council for which she was now in real danger of being tardy.

By definition, the meeting began after her arrival—late or not. Looking around the room, she saw the familiar faces of councilors who predated her reign, having advised her mother for years, and it was in them that she took the most comfort. Also present were the newly appointed members brought onboard after the untimely deaths of their predecessors—and her mother. While she had selected the new members of the council taking into account the advice from those whom she most trusted, she had lingering doubts about their suitability. In reality, she knew she was actually doubting herself—and her ability to make a good decision regarding their appointment.

Once the members of the council were seated and the perfunctories completed, the real meeting began.

"As I've warned consistently for the last half year, construction of the fleet is behind schedule. If we are going to have the ships ready for departure by War Day, then we need to consider implementing double shifts immediately," said Secretary of State for War Neel Burman. Burman was one of the oldest men on the Privy Council, but despite his age, the queen thought he would be able to win a foot race against just about anyone else attending the meeting. Most council members were desk types—and it showed.

"Has the secretary provided an estimate of the added costs required?" asked Jason Lata, chancellor of the exchequer—one of her new appointments.

I wonder if he ever smiles, thought the queen as she noted a larger than usual frown on Lata's face. However, she, too, was concerned about the large and growing costs associated with building the fleet. The fleet had been the single-minded goal to which the entire world had been planning for as long as there was recorded history. Aside from meeting the needs of daily life for the planet's citizens, preparing the fleet to go into battle on War Day was the one task that drove virtually all of her government's decisions. War Day was now less than two years away and that fact made her feel more inadequate than ever.

"Yes. We believe we will need an additional twelve million rupya this year to cover the costs," said Burman.

"Twelve million more this year? That's a twenty percent increase. I simply don't know how we can afford this. The people are taxed enough, and there's only so much credit the government can provide without people questioning the soundness of the currency," replied Lata, looking toward the queen as he made his case. "Any increase this large would have to be voted upon in Parliament."

"May I remind the Chancellor of the Exchequer that War Day is now only two years out and we must not only have the ships ready to depart but all the crews trained and ready for that day? We've never been in a war, and though we are training, I'm sure we will lose ships and crew in battle simply due to our inexperience. We must have the full fleet of ships, with trained crew, ready to depart at the appointed time, or we will all be at risk," said Burman.

"Your Majesty, may I interject?" asked another of the queen's new appointments, and the council's youngest member, Namita Roy. She liked Namita because she seemed to have the pulse of the younger generation and brought a new perspective to her leadership team. Many of the more seasoned members liked her well enough, but, strangely, she often seemed at odds with those of nearly her own generation. Roy currently served as the secretary of commerce, representing business interests.

The queen nodded her approval.

"As the polls show, there are many who grow increasingly skeptical of the Prophecy and the timing of War Day. The population has been burdened with wartime taxation their entire lives and now their sons and daughters are being conscripted to prepare for a war that many believe is either a fantasy or, worse still, a deliberate scam perpetrated by those in power to remain in power.

While some businesses will prosper from the increased spending, most will consider it yet another burden. While they are still a small minority of the population, if we enact new taxes now, I fear the opposition's numbers will grow and their voices become louder," said Roy.

"Madam Secretary, with all due respect, there have always been doubters among the public and, dare I say, even in this cabinet. But the vast majority of people know and understand the veracity of the Prophecy and the importance of our being ready to fight at the appointed time. The survival of our species may well depend upon our preparedness," replied Burman.

"Yes, I know. And I assure you and everyone here that I am not among the skeptics. I am just fulfilling my duty to remind everyone here of the sacrifices being made by the public and businesses in order to prepare us for that day. If I were to hazard a guess, many of the loudest skeptics are actually not skeptical—they've seen the public records and read their ancestors' stories. They know it is real. They are just wondering when our seemingly eternal wartime economy can be directed toward improving the quality of life and allowing more individual freedom," Roy said.

The queen rose, everyone else took their seats, and the room fell silent.

"I didn't ask to become your queen. It was my duty to assume the position after the untimely death of my mother. None of us asked to be born here and now, yet here we are. You did ask, or at least agree to being on the Council. When you made that agreement, you also agreed to uphold the laws and dedicate your lives to the fulfillment of the Prophecy and to make us as prepared as possible for War Day. It is your duty to fulfill that oath without hesitation. We owe it to ourselves, our ancestors, and generations to come. As for what we do after War Day, once the Prophecy is fulfilled, we need to begin planning. That day will come, and we need to be ready. For this reason, I am appointing Secretary Roy, Namita, to stand up a committee that will return a plan to the Council within six months," she said, looking at each Council member as her gaze crossed the room.

Everyone in the room sat silent and still, faces impassive as she spoke. She hated that. It was easier to know how to phrase things when she could tell how people were reacting to what she had already said. But when a room is filled with poker players, or politicians, that was often impossible.

"As for the supplemental appropriation requested by the secretary of state for war, we are obliged to support it and expeditiously forward the request to the Parliament for a vote and hopeful passage," she said and paused to determine if anyone would have the temerity to disagree. None did. "Let's move on to the next item on the agenda," she said as she retook her seat at the head of the table.

The room was quiet for a few seconds, which to the queen, seemed like minutes. Finally, Burman spoke.

"I have nothing further to discuss and yield my time," he said.

The meeting continued, but the queen's mind began to wander. *Am I doing the right thing? We have to prepare for War Day, don't we? What will happen to us if we aren't ready? It would all be my fault . . .*

She forced herself to pay attention to the next topic and then immediately wished she hadn't—the Council was debating the proposed logo for the Space Navy. Personally, she preferred the one with the blue background...

The Chamber of the Oracle was actually a small building and thought to be the oldest building in the world, at least the innermost portion of it. Made of a graphene-titanium alloy that the metallurgists only forty-five years ago were finally able to reproduce, mostly for manufacturing the growing fleet of spaceships being assembled in orbit, the inner building had survived at least two fires and one near miss by a tornado. The outer buildings, newer and therefore made from less strong materials, had not been so lucky. Today, the outer, larger building which housed the much smaller one in which the Oracle resided was nearly fifty years old and in fairly good shape.

At Delal's insistence, the queen arrived early, not wanting to be late for her session. Delal had fetched her and her security detail from the palace and further insisted that they not take the carriage usually used by the queen for outings. Rather, they traveled in the High Priest's carriage, a slightly smaller but by no means modest electric vehicle that whisked them along the main street to the Oracle's...*building*. When they departed the palace for the Chamber of the Oracle, she almost called it a temple, and then she remembered another of her mother's admonitions: "The Oracle is not a god. Don't let the priesthood that has grown up around it convince you otherwise like they have many in the populace. The Oracle is a tool, created by our ancestors to provide knowledge and information to us as we need it."

Intellectually, the queen knew what her mother said was true, but she couldn't help but have her own doubts. *How do we know our ancestors created the Oracle? The records are there, but they were sparse after three hundred years of weathering, fires, and human foibles. How do we know it isn't giving us knowledge directly from God?* she thought.

Delal led her and her entourage in the front door, past the clergy that had assembled in the narthex to see her arrival, and into the innermost portion of the building in which the Oracle resided—the Chamber. Or, at the very least, to where the Oracle spoke to her and her mother just a few years previously. She had no idea where the Oracle actually resided. She assumed, hoped really, that Delal knew. *Surely, he knew . . .*

They reached the door to the Oracle's Chamber with fifteen minutes to spare.

"Your Majesty, I suggest you enter and use the time remaining to get used to the surroundings. Discussions with the Oracle can be overwhelming, and you need to be prepared," Delal said, motioning toward the door to the innermost building as he spoke.

The queen heeded his advice and walked forward, through the open door, and into the hemispherical room where all audiences with the Oracle took place. The room was bright with indirect lighting and the walls were painted a sterile white. In the middle of the room were the bench and raised horizontal bar she remembered from her last visit—she had leaned on the bar as she wept, grieving the sudden loss of her mother and being thrust too soon into the role of queen. The memories came flooding back.

As she stood in the center of the hemisphere, she couldn't help but rest her hands on the bar. As she did so, the door closed silently behind her and the lights dimmed but didn't go out.

"Welcome back," said the baritone voice of the Oracle in its odd accent. The Oracle was the only "person" who spoke with this particular accent and the queen had to assume it was the accent of their ancestors—lost after all this time.

"I'm here because you summoned me," she said, not too curtly but also not warmly. She didn't know enough about the Oracle to have an emotional reaction to it—one way or the other.

"So I did. It's time you and I have regular and frequent meetings. There is much for you to learn between now and War Day."

Impulsively, she blurted, "Did you know that Mother was going to die, leaving me as the queen?" As soon as the words came out, she felt relieved and embarrassed at the same time.

"We all knew that day would come. You are, after all, the heir to the throne and that's usually how one assumes the position. But I know you really meant to ask if I knew that your mother would die when she did. And the answer is no. I am not a deity who can see and shape the future," the Oracle replied.

As soon as she heard the answer, she allowed herself

to relax. She hadn't realized until that moment how much resentment she had accumulated toward the Oracle, making it the source of her need to blame someone, anyone, for her mother's death.

"But you know about War Day."

"Just because I have knowledge of some things to come, it doesn't mean I cause them or have knowledge about all future events," the Oracle said.

"But you know that we have to build the space fleet and depart on a certain day in order to engage and defeat the enemies who would wipe us out?"

"I do. And during the course of our meeting, I will reveal to you how I know these things and, as importantly, why we have to be ready to fight. The battle will be desperate, but our participation will be decisive and, if all goes to the plan, save the people from annihilation."

The queen considered the Oracle's words, parsed them in her mind, and then asked a question. "You speak as if you were going to be there. Are you?"

"Yes, if all goes according to plan, then I will be there for the battle."

"But how?" She didn't understand. In her mind, the Oracle was here and only here, where it had always been.

"Before we go into all the details, there is something you must do. It is imperative for you to address the people about the importance and urgency of preparing for War Day. I monitor the progress of the engineering teams assembling the ships, outfitting them, and making sure the logistics trains are functioning as needed to be ready, and I am concerned by some of the numbers.

In addition, 9.9 percent of the eligible draftees are not showing up at the enlistment centers when their allotment is called. You must address the nation and reinforce the importance of what we are doing and why," the Oracle said.

"How can I do that when I don't fully understand?" she replied.

"There are some details I cannot yet reveal, but many that I can."

The ceiling of the room became a holoprojection showing outer space. She recognized the constellations and images of the planets in their solar system. The view shifted and showed the fleet construction facilities in orbit and the myriad workers flitting about the massive ships, each performing one task or another that she supposed was part of the construction process.

Next, the perspective shifted as the camera view moved outward from the planet into deep space until the comforting light from their star was indistinguishable from the many others dotting the blackness. The flight continued until one of the many stars began to grow brighter as the camera moved toward it, revealing a system of planets vastly different than their own. The Oracle began to narrate.

"As you know, we didn't originate on this planet. We were driven here by an implacable enemy that seeks to destroy others of our kind for reasons we do not understand."

As the Oracle spoke, the view shifted closer to one of the worlds in that alien star system, and she could see that a battle was taking place. About a dozen ships were spitting missiles and firing energy weapons at other ships, who were doing the same in return. Though the design details of the ships on each side of the battle were obviously different, she was thankful that the Oracle had color coded one side red and the other blue. The battle raged and it became obvious that blue was losing.

"This is but one battle among many that will decide the fate of our race. In this battle, the defenders lost, and I fear that the citizens on the planet will either be subjugated, or, if history is the guide, destroyed by nuclear bombardment from space," the Oracle said.

"You are confusing me. You said the defenders 'lost,' as in past tense. Then you said they 'will be destroyed,' which implies a future that you don't know. I don't understand," she said.

"Then allow me to explain . . . " The Oracle changed the view overhead and began a story that took more than two hours to share.

The door to the Chamber of the Oracle opened and the queen emerged. She held her head high and though she was tired, she felt oddly energized. She was alive and not just going through the motions as she'd done when she was the daughter of the queen or even after she inherited the crown. She had a sense of purpose that she'd never felt before.

Her entourage quickly rose to their feet from the various chairs near the entrance. Delal stepped forward, bowed, and stood silently, looking at her to speak first.

"Delal, I need to get back to the palace immediately," she said, and then turned to Vice Admiral Dewan.

"Admiral, I need to meet with the War Cabinet as soon as you can get them assembled," she said.

"Yes, Your Majesty. I can get them here for a meeting first thing tomorrow morning. Admiral Cooper is at the Outer Banks and even if I send an aircraft immediately, he probably couldn't get here until late tonight."

She nodded her head in approval and then waved off further conversation. She had a lot to think about . . .

CHAPTER 15

As expected, the incoming Kurofune ships spread out, placing an average of ten thousand kilometers between each—far too separated to allow for anything more than a one-on-one or two-on-one engagement. The *Mumbai*, *Adelaide*, *Montana*, and *Durban* would each engage a Kurofune ship alone. The others were paired, usually by country of origin, to engage two-on-one: *Smetlivy* with *Nastoychivy*, *Indefatigable* with *Northumberland*, *Idaho* with *Nanchang*, and *Xiamen* with *Guiyang*. Each ship or ship pair would encounter their targets at a slightly different time with the entire ensemble of one-second engagements being complete inside two minutes.

The *Guiyang* and *Xiamen* were the first to go. The *Mumbai*'s bridge crew was watching their own trajectory and preparing while at the same time their telescopes were focused on the region of space where the other three ships would converge. At this distance, it was impossible to see any of the ships. Their positions on the screen were represented by icons. As is usual in moments of high stress, time seemed to pass more slowly as the clock ticked down.

Time zero. Nothing showed on the screen. Nothing. Then a brief flash, followed by another.

"The target was destroyed," said Mitra. What was unspoken hung in the air. What caused the second flash? Was it a missile that detonated, or did one of the EDF ships also get hit?

"*Guiyang* reports no damage. *Xiamen* appears to have been destroyed," added Mitra.

The first engagement was a draw, with a horrible cost.

Anika had little time to ponder before the second engagement commenced, this time between the *Montana* and its target. Again, a delay followed by two flashes.

"The *Montana* reports that it took minor damage caused by a close-in nuclear detonation. The target was destroyed," said Mitra.

Mumbai was next with the flyby to occur in twenty-two seconds. Lieutenant Patel had long since turned over tactical control of the weapons systems to Mitra. Events would happen so rapidly that no human could hope to react as quickly as an AI.

As the clock approached zero, Anika remembered an article she read about the reaction times of professional athletes, tennis players, if she recalled correctly. To return a serve that was traveling at about 240 kilometers per hour when it left the server's racket, they had about three hundred milliseconds to see the ball, estimate its trajectory, and bring their own racket to the place and at the proper angle, with the proper speed—or not. The best players reacted fifty milliseconds faster than an amateur.

And that was with a ball traveling at only 240 kilometers per hour. *Mumbai* would be engaging its target at a relative speed of over 3,500 kilometers per second. No human could react fast enough. She hoped Mitra could.

Zero minus one second. She heard the point-defense guns activate, their steady thrum somehow momentarily relieving the tension as she realized they could, and were, actively defending themselves.

Zero. The ship lurched violently, the lights momentarily blinked, and then nothing.

Zero plus two seconds. They were still alive.

"Status report!" shouted Anika, not realizing there was no reason to shout. The quiet hum of the bridge had not changed since before the engagement.

"A nuclear missile was intercepted at a distance of twenty kilometers and detonated, causing only minor, transient effects on the ship's electronics," Mitra replied.

"What about the enemy ship?" asked Anika.

"One of our missiles struck it amidships, causing some damage. I will need more time to observe it to determine the extent," added Mitra.

Zero plus eighteen seconds since their engagement. Anika looked at the status board and saw that in that time that *Adelaide* and its target had mutually annihilated each other, followed by the shocking loss of the *Smetlivy*, the flagship. The admiral was dead. The status of the Kurofune ship targeted by the two Russian ships was unknown.

Two minutes later the last of the engagements passed with the tally now known.

Xiamen, *Nanchang*, *Adelaide*, and *Smetlivy* destroyed.

Montana, *Indefatigable*, and *Idaho* damaged.

Mumbai, *Durban*, *Nastoychivy*, *Northumberland*, and *Guiyang* undamaged or only sustaining minor damage.

Six Kurofune ships destroyed, one severely damaged, and one apparently untouched and still inbound for Kunlun—along with the ships remaining in the other two battle groups.

Anika surveyed the tactical situation. It was grim. They and the Kurofune were so evenly matched that in a one-on-one, ship-to-ship engagement, the best they could hope for was a draw. The EDF's total kills were higher simply because they had the advantage of numbers. This was not the kind of war that could be easily won. Or won at all.

As she looked at the status display, more information was coming in about the damaged ships. *Montana* and *Idaho* had many casualties, but both ships could still fly on their own. The situation on the *Indefatigable* was not as clear. They were having communications problems, and the *Northumberland* was moving to rendezvous with them to render assistance and assess the situation. Anika could not help but wonder about Winslow. *Was he safe? Would he find a way to let her know? Would he be allowed to let her know?*

"Captain, Captain Yahontov just informed the fleet that he has assumed command and that we are to join the *Northumberland* at the rendezvous with the *Indefatigable* to render assistance as needed before we depart for Earth," said Mitra.

Yahontov was the captain of the *Nastoychivy* and had been designated second-in-command of the fleet. It made sense for him to assume overall command at least until they returned home. Anika did not know him personally, but he seemed competent enough.

"Very well, then. Let's get there as quickly as we can in case they need us," said Anika as she unbuckled from her chair and rose for the first time since before the engagement began. It felt good to move around. She had a lot of nervous energy and worry to walk out.

Chaos. That was the first thought that came to Winslow's mind as he left his quarters and looked around his ship. *His ship.* Smoke filled the air, alarms wailed warning the crew that there were fires and hull breaches—the deadly duo of space travel. Worse still, the artificial gravity was inconsistent, causing the crew to have to adjust to normal Earthlike gravity one moment and some fraction thereof the next. Fortunately, the system had not failed and thrust them into a zero-gravity environment, though Price suspected that might soon happen if the fires and other damage were not brought under control.

He was technically confined to quarters, but he would be damned if he were to remain there when he could be rendering assistance in his ship's time of need. As if to prove the point, Price reached the first corridor crossing on his way toward the bridge, a path he took out of habit, when he saw two men on the floor with clothes smoking from what had to be a recent encounter with one of the fires. Both men appeared to be conscious and were obviously in considerable pain.

He broke into a run and quickly reached then, kneeling

to see what, if anything, he could do to help. He recognized both men, Ensign Hodges and Ensign Banta. From what he could tell, in addition to being shipmates, they were good friends. He often saw them laughing over dinner in the mess or bantering with each other or their friends in the crowded hallways of the ship. Their records were excellent. And now, upon looking more closely at their wounds, both required medical attention. Quickly. Unfortunately, based on what Price heard and saw, help might be a long time coming.

"Hodges. I know you are in pain, but I need to know if the fire that did this to you is nearby. Is it under control?" asked Price.

"I think so, sir. We were in the auxiliary fire-control room when the first blast hit and overloaded the circuits. The fire started so fast. At first it was a small thing, like lighting a match. Then it was everywhere, including in between us and the door. Ensign Banta and I . . . we . . . we decided to run through the fire to get out the door so we wouldn't be trapped inside. As we ran through it, I could feel my clothes starting to burn. I remember thinking that I'd have to change clothes before seeing the captain, sir." Hodges hesitated, then continued, "I think I activated the suppression system as we exited and closed the door. I wonder why they didn't come on by themselves? Why didn't the system automatically come on like it was supposed to?"

It was obviously difficult for Hodges to speak and Banta so far had said nothing.

Price knew that there were first-aid kits along every hallway of the ship and he quickly looked around to find the nearest one. He sprinted to retrieve it and was back at the fallen men's side applying the kit's burn pads within seconds. The numbing agent in the pad went to work immediately and Price could see the relief in their countenances within seconds of the pads being applied. The relief would be short-lived if help from medical didn't arrive soon. He had activated each man's distress signal as soon as he reached them, but so far, he was the only person within sight.

"Hodges, I need to move on. Your distress beacons are working, and someone should be here soon to take you to the infirmary," said Price.

Hodges nodded, giving Price the signal he needed to leave them unattended. Price hoped he had not just lied about help coming soon. It looked and sounded like the entire ship needed help.

Continuing along his path to the bridge, Price turned the corner and saw the starboard elevator surrounded by at least ten people, all of whom appeared injured to some degree. The elevator doors were closed, as was the hatch leading to the staircase. Worse still, above both the door and the hatch was the lighted hull-breach warning. That could only mean one thing. On the other side of both was vacuum. The *Indefatigable*'s bridge was either gone or open to deep space.

Price broke into a run toward the gathered crew. Upon seeing him, one of the men, Ensign Murphy, rose to attention and saluted. The others tried to do the same, with varying degrees of success—mostly failure.

"At ease," said Price, the practiced words coming from his lips without thinking. Technically, he was no longer their commanding officer, and he did not need to assume or accept their placing him in that role. He did not see a point in taking time to say anything about his status. His ship needed help and he was there to render it if he could.

"Sir, it's good to see you. Lieutenant Green and most of the bridge crew are dead, sir. I think we took a close blast from a nuclear missile, sir. It took out a sizable piece of this end of the ship," said Murphy.

"Who is in command?" asked Price.

"I thought you were, sir."

Price did not know how to respond, nor did he want to. Someone had to be in command and make the decisions that could save the lives of the crew and perhaps the ship. That was not supposed to be him, but until someone else in the chain of command assumed that role, he would fill the gap. He could go back to being under house arrest later.

"Ensign, if you are up to it, come with me to the auxiliary control room. Is your comm working?" asked Price. Price's access to shipboard communications had been cut off when he was relieved of command. All he had access to from his quarters was the ship's nearly unlimited supply of holovids. He had seen enough historical dramas these last few days to last him a lifetime. What he needed now was access to the ship's communications system so he could get a quick situation report and figure out how badly the ship was damaged and whether or not it was still in any danger from the outside.

"Yes, sir," Murphy said as he reached to his collar to touch the short, round button that was affixed there.

"May I have yours? I need to find out what's going on," said Price.

"Yes, sir," said Murphy as he reached up to detach the button and hand it to Price. The transfer happened as they began a brisk walk aft toward the auxiliary control room.

"This is Price. Nelson, are you there?"

"Yes, sir. It is good to hear your voice, sir." Nelson's response was comforting. The ship was not *that* severely damaged after all.

"Nelson, who is in charge?"

"The command staff has been killed sir. Captain Sawyer is the highest-ranking officer aboard other than yourself, sir."

"And I assume he is busy with casualties in the infirmary, correct?" asked Price.

"Yes, sir. Shall I connect you with him?" asked Nelson.

"Yes. Tell him it's urgent," said Price. Of course, it was urgent, with parts of the ship destroyed and open to vacuum and other parts on fire, what else could it be?

"Sawyer here. Make it quick, I've got casualties lining up out the door here," said the doctor.

"Michael, this is Captain Price. It appears you are the ranking officer alive on the ship right now and need to assume command. Unless, of course, you authorize me to do so," said Price.

"It is good to hear your voice, sir. Yes, of course. I'm temporarily rescinding your confinement to quarters and relinquishing command to you for the duration," Sawyer said. Price was glad Sawyer explained his actions for the ship's log to record them. There was little doubt that all of this would be played in some sort of hearing after they returned home to explain how he ended up back in command of the ship and Sawyer knew it.

"Thanks, Michael. Take care of my crew," said Price.

"Yes, sir. Is that all, sir?"

"That's all," replied Price, cutting the link.

Fifteen minutes later, Price was in the auxiliary control room and found out just how bad the situation was. As Murphy said, the bridge was cut open and fully exposed to space. All who had been there were likely killed instantly. Several of the ship's systems were overloaded by the blast, causing short circuits and, unfortunately, fires like the one that injured ensigns Hodges and Banta. Thanks to the fire-suppression systems, all the fires were now under control or extinguished. The external telescopes and most of the ship's navigation sensors were damaged or destroyed. The fusion reactor, miraculously, was intact, as was the propulsion system and the Hawking Drive. The *Indefatigable* would once again be going home injured. But she would be going home.

The ship's high- and low-gain antennas were destroyed in the engagement, but some clever techs had connected the short-range comm system in one of the lifeboats to the ship's intercom system, allowing Price to make contact with the *Northumberland* which had just pulled alongside. Help was here.

After an extremely chaotic several hours of tending to the wounded and, with the help of *Northumberland*'s crew, patching together many of the ship's systems damaged in the encounter, the sense of urgency abated, and Price's adrenaline levels returned to something approaching normal. Normal, however, did not include captaining the ship from the spartan, but functional, auxiliary control room. As Price approached his limits, having been awake for almost twenty of the last twenty-four hours, he received word via the *Northumberland* that Captain Yahontov of the *Nastoychivy* wanted to speak with him. He took the audio-only call via his now-functional personal comm unit.

Price gave Captain Yahontov a summary of the *Indefatigable*'s status and his recommendation that critical replacement crew be provided by the *Northumberland* so that the ship could be safely flown back to Earth. Yahontov agreed and deferred the details to the *Northumberland*'s captain. Then Yahontov came to the real reason for his call.

"Captain Price, I do not know the full circumstances behind the admiral relieving you of command, but I do know you have done an admirable job keeping your ship and crew together after the loss of the ship's officers. You should remain in command until we return to the solar system. Once we are safely there, the XO of the *Northumberland* will assume command of the *Indefatigable* and you will again be confined to your quarters. Is that clear?" asked Yahontov.

"Yes, sir. Perfectly clear. Thank you, sir," said Price. Price knew that Yahontov could just as easily have had him arrested for violating his confinement to quarters in the first place. Allowing him to remain in command until they reached the solar system was a career-risking move, but Price was grateful. Grateful that his fellow officers still had confidence in him and were willing to give him the benefit of the doubt.

"We will see you in the solar system," Yahontov said as he broke the connection.

God willing, we will get the Indefatigable *there in one piece,* thought Price.

As he entered his quarters to get some much-needed rest, he had one more call to make. He had to contact Anika to let her know that though the *Indefatigable* had seen better days, he was alive, well, and back in command. Temporary command, but command, nonetheless.

"Nelson, can you route a call through the *Northumberland* to Captain Ahuja of the *Mumbai*?" asked Price as he pulled the shoes from his aching feet and realized that he would likely be asleep the minute his head touched the pillow. *Best not to lie down yet,* he thought.

"Of course, Captain. While I am making the connection, may I ask at what time you would like to awaken? Your bio signs indicate that you need at least ten hours' rest," replied Nelson.

"I can't afford to get that much sleep. Wake me up in six hours," said Price. He was glad Nelson was "back" and in usual form.

"Captain Ahuja will be on the line momentarily, sir."

"Thank you," said Price.

"This is Ahuja." To Price, hearing Anika's voice brought a moment of relief and inner peace. He could feel the tension leave his body with just those three words.

"Captain Ahuja, this is Acting Captain Price of the *Indefatigable*," said Price; knowing that every conversation was being recorded, he tried to keep the emotion from his voice.

"Winslow? Thank God. I was wondering what happened to you. Are you okay?"

"I'm fine. Unfortunately, my XO, Lieutenant Green, and most of the bridge crew are dead," Price replied.

"I knew your ship was severely damaged, and I am so sorry to hear about Green. I know you were close. Can you tell me what happened? And why you weren't on the bridge?" she asked.

Now that she had changed the tenor of the conversation from strictly professional to more personal, there was nothing more in the world that Price wanted to do than spill his guts to her about what had happened the last several days, the accusations, his recusing himself from command, and the jarring aftermath of the attack. But he could not do that on an open line that was being recorded.

"I will be glad to tell you, later. Right now, I need to get some sleep and then I need to make sure my crew gets back to their homes and families. I am sure this wounded warrior will need some attention at the lunar shipyards. We should meet at Mario's to catch up," he said.

"Absolutely. Just as soon as I know my orders, I will get back with you. Take care."

"Don't worry, I will," he said, pausing several seconds, desperately wanting to add "I love you."

The awkward silence on both sides of the connection finally ended when Anika broke the link. Price suspected she wanted to say the same, but for the same reasons as he, could not.

Price awakened with the sounds of Mozart's Symphony No. 35. Nelson was providing him with a bit of normality before the inevitable deluge of information and action reports overwhelmed him. He had slept so deeply that he did not even remember his head touching the pillow. He felt more rested but could have easily used the additional four hours Nelson had recommended.

The day went quickly, with repairs continuing. The people of Kunlun were as prepared for the upcoming attack as they could be, but as the time came closer for the Kurofune ships to arrive, the anxiety level of the speakers providing regular status reports to the populace began to rise. If history were a guide, the attacks would commence shortly after the Kurofune ships arrived at Kunlun—sometime tomorrow afternoon. Second Fleet would have to watch the attacks from afar as they maneuvered closer to the Oppenheimer Limit and their jump home.

As predicted, the Kurofune entered orbit around Kunlun at just after thirteen hundred hours the next day. The first indications of something happening were the multiple flashes of low-yield nuclear detonations in Kunlun's orbit as the hastily deployed mine field found targets among the incoming ships. At their extreme distance from Kunlun, there was no way for the telescopes on the ships of the fleet to determine if the mines destroyed their targets, so a few surveillance drones were left orbiting Kunlun to observe the attack. Based on their observations, the Kurofune were performing better than the EDF ships at avoiding mines. Of the multiple mines deployed in Kunlun's orbit, there were only five confirmed kills.

The next flashes the fleet observed were those on the

surface of Kunlun as yet another settlement world perished.

Later that evening, the remaining eight ships of Second Fleet departed Kunlun for the solar system and Earth.

Seven arrived.

CHAPTER 16

The transit from the Kunlun system to the solar system seemed normal enough if one ever got used to nearly instantaneously disappearing from one location and reappearing in another several light-years distant. There was only the momentary stomach lurch, caused by the inability of the artificial gravity system to operate while the Hawking Drive was active. Price hated it. His mild neurovestibular reaction to zero gravity had almost disqualified him from the navy. How could one be in the Space Navy and not encounter weightlessness? By sheer force of will, Price had learned to deal with the disorientation and nausea caused by the absence of gravity so that he could realize his dream of serving in the Commonwealth Space Navy. He did find it curious that the momentary nausea was one of the first bits of evidence behind the scientists insisting that the Hawking Drive was "nearly instantaneous" and not instantaneous. If there were no time passing during the drive's operation, how could one's physiology react to the absence of gravity?

Unfortunately, extremely precise correlated clocks making the transition showed exactly zero time loss during the jump when compared with their nontransiting counterparts. A mystery. Mystery aside, his stomach lurched every time, and he still hated it.

As planned, EDF's Second Fleet arrived in the solar system forty-one light-minutes from Earth.

"Captain, there is a problem," said Nelson moments after their arrival.

"Yes?" asked Price, his heightened anxiety likely evident in his one-word response. *Did a ship's system fail? Was Earth under attack?*

"The *Mumbai* did not arrive with the fleet," said Nelson.

"What? You are sure?" asked Price. "Bring up the tactical display."

The lone status screen in the auxiliary control room was much smaller and less capable than the one on the bridge. The view shifted from Sol, a bright dot in the distance, to nearby space with icons representing the ships of Second Fleet, showing their location relative to the *Indefatigable*. Where the *Mumbai*'s icon should be was instead a bright red oval.

"Did we leave them behind at Kunlun?"

"I don't know," said Nelson. "I am communicating with my counterpart on the *Nastoychivy* and their data aligns with ours. The *Mumbai* is simply not here."

"Send Captain Yahontov a request to meet," said Price. "And broaden your search area for the *Mumbai*. Maybe she transited to somewhere else in the system. If so, then the light might not have reached us yet. And go over all the comm logs to see if there were any anomalous messages from her before the jump."

Price began running through the possibilities. Ships don't just vanish during a jump. If the *Mumbai*'s Hawking Drive failed, then it would still be in the Kunlun system—alone, but far enough away from any potential adversaries that she would not be in any immediate danger. If the fusion power plant failed at the time of the jump there, all the systems would have gone offline preventing the transit, with the same outcome as an outright drive failure. It was possible the ship was elsewhere in the solar system. If so, then Nelson or the more capable and system-wide telescopes and communications relays would undoubtedly find her. If the ship didn't show up or make contact soon, then someone would need to go back to Kunlun to render aid and help the *Mumbai* get out of harm's way before the Kurofune found her. *Anika!*

"Captain Price, Captain Yahontov is on the line," announced Nelson.

Price activated his comm button and began speaking as soon as the Yahontov came online.

"Captain Yahontov, thanks for taking my call. I know you are aware of the *Mumbai*'s absence. If the ship doesn't show up soon, then I would like to take the *Indefatigable* back to Kunlun to look for the ship and render assistance," said Price.

"Captain Price, I am painfully aware of the *Mumbai*'s absence and have already decided to send the *Montana* back to Kunlun to look for her. The *Indefatigable* is in no shape to make another jump," said Yahontov.

Price knew Yahontov was correct and it pained him. His ship had suffered major damage, and many of the crew were severely injured and in need of better medical care than was possible in the ship's infirmary. He immediately thought of Hodges and Banta and wondered how they were faring. He had to place the well-being of his crew and ship ahead of his concern for Anika. Price also knew that it would be at least another hour before the *Montana* could sufficiently charge her supercapacitors to activate the Hawking Drive. An hour during which the *Mumbai* would be alone.

"Yes, sir. I concur," said Price.

"Captain, I do appreciate your offer. I really do. And, unfortunately, there is that other matter. As we discussed, the XO from the *Northumberland* is preparing to come over and assume command of the *Indefatigable* for the remainder of our trip home. Once he arrives, you are to relinquish command and return to your quarters. Thank you for jumping into the breach when your crew needed you. I will most certainly speak positively on your behalf if asked to do so," said Yahontov.

"I understand, sir," replied Price. Saying the words caused him to feel the verbal equivalent of a double punch to the gut. He was again going to be in the limbo of being accused of treason and now worrying about and unable to do anything to help the very person suspected of being complicit in that treason.

Captain Yahontov broke the link with Price still sitting in his chair, momentarily stunned. He was jarred back to reality when his message board began to light up with queries and status reports from the crew. Until his replacement arrived, he had a ship to run and his crew was counting on him.

Four hours later, Price was back in his quarters, on self-confinement, pacing from one end of the small room to the other and back again. He knew there was much to do to prepare Earth for what was shaping up to be a war of attrition with the Kurofune. *Who were they? How could they possibly be human? Why were they so intent on destroying everything and killing everyone in their path? And what happened to Anika's ship?* With so many unanswered questions, he should be part of finding the answers and solving the problem, not penned up in his quarters and having to defend himself from ludicrous and obviously false allegations of treason.

Twelve hours after that, Nelson's voice awakened Price from what was a fitful, but much needed sleep.

"Captain Price, Captain Yahontov would like to speak with you," said Nelson.

Price sat up on his bed, quickly sipped some water, and accepted the call.

"Captain Price, I'm sorry to disturb you, but I wanted to be the one to tell you the news regarding the *Mumbai*. The *Montana* returned from the Kunlun system reporting that they found no trace of the *Mumbai*. She jumped to near the location from which we departed and found nothing. They then did an in system jump outward seventeen light-hours and trained their telescopes on the region of space from which the fleet originally departed and waited on the light to reach them. They saw all of the ships in the fleet jump from the system, including the *Mumbai*. She departed at the same moment as the rest of us," Yahontov said.

"How can that be? I've never heard of such a thing. What could have happened?" said Price.

"I wish we knew. I sent the news and all our logs to EDF and the people there are as in the dark as we. Now, if you will excuse me, I need to attend to other matters," said Yahontov as he signed off.

"Damn. Anika, where are you?" said Price, still sitting on his bunk and dropping his face into his outstretched hands. "Where are you?"

Early in the second day of their transit toward the lunar shipyards, Price was still pacing. He had diligently performed his daily exercise regimen, eaten all the food provided, and done just about all the organizing he could think of doing. There was nothing left but pacing and thinking about the problems and the abundance of unanswered questions.

At the beginning of one of his pacing sessions, Price had the glimmering of an idea. He was no longer in command and was cut out of the intelligence briefings and military planning, but they had not completely isolated him from Nelson and the solar system's data networks. True, he could not send messages, but there were no restrictions keeping him from accessing publicly available information.

"Nelson, have any other ships ever vanished or turned up in the wrong place using the Hawking Drive?"

"There are no confirmed reports of this in the archives," replied Nelson.

"What about being destroyed? We haven't found any wreckage from the *Mumbai* here or at Kunlun, but have any ships ever not survived a jump?"

"No. There are reports of ships powering up to jump and the system failing, but it did not in any case result in the loss of a ship."

"No 'confirmed' reports of ships vanishing does not mean there are no reports at all. Why did you add the qualifier?" asked Price.

"In the early years after the Hawking Drive was developed, there were many settlement ships launched that never contacted Earth with their status after departure. This was not considered anomalous or uncommon. Many of the people on these ships were eager to leave Earth forever and some left explicit requests not to be contacted—ever. In at least three cases, ships from Earth or another settlement later jumped to the star systems listed as the colonists' destinations and found no trace of them. It was assumed that the settlement ships either gave erroneous or false destinations, wanting to keep their final location a secret or that they arrived at their planned destinations and then moved on to another system for some reason. It is plausible that one or more of these could have experienced whatever happened to the *Mumbai*. But this is pure conjecture," said Nelson.

"Do you have access to the engineering designs of the missing settlement ships? I am wondering if there are any design or operational characteristics the missing settlement ships might have with the *Mumbai*," said Price.

"The missing ships were from very early in the development phase of the Hawking Drive. There is some data available in the archives back on Earth, but it will take some time to locate it and then have it sent to us. The speed-of-light delay is getting better as we move further in system, but we are still too far away for fast access. Once I get what is available, I will parse it and see if I can find any commonalities. This may take some time," said Nelson.

"How much time?" asked Price.

"At least two hours."

"That's fine. Just let me know when you are finished."

Price had too much nervous energy to quit pacing. Back and forth. Back and forth. He found the repetition soothing. And pondering the technical aspects of the *Mumbai* disappearance while he walked allowed him to temporarily forget, or at least place to the side, the personal aspects of the incident. What happened to Anika? Was she out there, somewhere, or was she dead? If she were somewhere else, then was her ship functional enough to come home? Likely not, or she would already be here. He just could not accept that she was dead. He imagined, in his nightmares, that she might die in battle. As painful as that might be, he convinced himself that he would be able to accept it under those circumstances. It was what they both knew was possible when they joined their respective militaries. But to die during a transit? It made him think of General George Patton, a brilliant US military tactician who led his Seventh and Third Armies to help defeat the Nazis only to die just after the war ended in a car accident. That is not the way military leaders were supposed to die. Not Patton. Not Anika.

Not Anika.

✦ ✦ ✦

Two hours passed quickly, and Price had only ceased pacing long enough to go to the bathroom. Even there, he found himself tapping his feet. Nelson finally had some data.

"The missing settlement ships were the *Betwa*, the *Atlantis*, and the *Drakensberg*. All were launched within twenty years of the discovery of the Hawking Drive and all are unaccounted for. In each case, one or more ships from Earth or another of the settlements traveled to their listed destination worlds and found no trace of them," said Nelson.

"What were the countries of origin?"

"India, the United States, and South Africa," replied Nelson.

"Is that the order in which they were they lost?"

"Yes," said Nelson.

"The *Mumbai* recently returned from checking on the status of some other settlements with which we had lost contact. How many more are there like that?"

"Nine remain. Like the *Mumbai*, there are ships being dispatched to all of them, and we should have a complete accounting of each within the next few weeks."

"That's a lot. I had no idea. How many settlement ships have been launched overall?" asked Price.

"Forty-one, including the small research stations on worlds not suited for widespread human habitation," said Nelson. Humanity had finally left the cradle and thought they had solved the problem of all the eggs being in one basket, putting the species at risk should something befall the home world. Until the Kurofune began their implacable assault on the settlements, one by one, they had foolishly thought the survival of the human species was finally assured. Unfortunately, that might not be the case. The Kurofune had other intentions.

"And the Kurofune are methodically attacking each one, in order of settlement. Where were the three missing ships you mentioned in terms of the overall launch order? I'm wondering if any of them might be next in line for attack or if the Kurofune know that they never made it to their destination," asked Price.

"The *Betwa* would have established the tenth settlement; *Atlantis* the thirteenth, which humans might find interesting given your propensity for pareidolia; and the *Drakensberg* the twenty-first."

"If I were an early settler, I would find losing contact with at least three of the first twenty-some ships to be a poor track record. I'm not sure I would get on a ship and risk my life with those odds. It seems contrary to my experience. The loss of *Mumbai* was the first such loss that I was aware of. Out of curiosity, do we know how many ships have made successful transits since then?"

"There is no database with a firm number but based on the shipping logs and records of arrivals and departures from the solar system, not including settlement-to-settlement travel, the number is well into the thousands," replied Nelson.

"I wonder why there haven't been more," said Price. *Did the designs change? Was there some flaw in the early ship designs that has since been mostly corrected? It just did not make sense.*

Price was marching back and forth even faster than before as his mind raced. As was his usual when working on a difficult problem, he began to speak to himself reciting what he knew, over and over, looking for a clue or missing piece of data. Of course, Nelson was listening, as Nelson always did, which really did not affect Price's habit or thinking practices.

"*Mumbai* vanished without a trace during a transit from Kunlun to Earth. The three ships vanished, we think, during their transits *from* Earth to their respective destinations. The missing three were launched several months or years apart, all within the early years of migration. There are still nine settlements unaccounted for, some of which might have experienced the same fate and we just don't know yet. The three missing settlement ships were built and launched by three different countries . . ."

"Sir, your last statement is incorrect," interrupted Nelson.

"What? How so?"

"The *Betwa*, *Atlantis*, and *Drakensberg* were all flagged to different countries, but they were all built by Goa Shipyard Limited," said Nelson.

Price stopped pacing.

"Tell me more about Goa," said Price.

"Goa began making oceangoing vessels in the late 1950s and is headquartered in Vasco da Gama, India. They established their lunar shipyards in 2065 and from there built many of the early settlement and research ships for buyers from all over the world. It is also the shipyard in which the *Mumbai* was manufactured. Employing over seventy-five thousand people, Gao Shipyard Limited is valued at . . ."

Price raised his hand and interrupted Nelson's data dump. "That's enough. I don't need to know their financials. Nelson, I think we have found the common link. This cannot be coincidence. Of the nine settlements still unaccounted for, were any using ships made by Goa?"

"Yes. The *Santinka*; it was the seventh settlement ship to depart Earth."

"Damn. You said that all the settlements unaccounted for are being visited? I assume that includes the world to which the *Santinka* was bound?" asked Price, his excitement growing.

"That is correct. The USSN *Alligator* was dispatched ten days ago to check on its status and should be reporting back anytime now."

"Nelson, I don't want to jeopardize the flow of information you are providing me, but given my status, should you be telling me the operational orders of EDF warships? I would have thought the *Alligator*'s destination would have been classified," said Price.

"Sir, if I may be so bold, the charges brought against you are clearly false. I was there. I have recordings of every action taken by you while at Nikko, and none can even remotely be construed as treasonous," said Nelson.

"As a result, you are making the call to provide information that my—that our—commanding officers have said I should not have?"

"I prefer to think of it as making a judgment call in helping solve a problem that might help determine the outcome of the war," said Nelson.

"Thank you. I appreciate your confidence in me," said Price. As he said the words, he was asking himself if he should consider reporting Nelson's actions up the chain once he was cleared. AIs were not supposed to be able to take this sort of initiative. As humanlike as they seemed, they were still not supposed to be capable of directly disobeying orders. *If Nelson could choose to disobey orders in this case, might he in others? Might other AIs be capable of the same?* Price chose to not pursue this line of thinking and instead focused on solving the problems at hand: what happened to the *Mumbai* and, of course, winning the war.

CHAPTER 17

The USSN *Alligator* was on its first deep-space voyage and her captain, James Stockton, was not about to let anything happen to her. She was the pride of the US Space Navy's lunar shipyards and had the latest star drive and weapons systems, and probably more importantly, the most flexible and maneuverable fusion drive ever put on a starship. Stockton knew that all of these features might be needed where they were going, but then again, maybe not.

Since the war began, the countries of Earth were checking in with all of the settlements and settlement ships that had been established or sent from Earth during the diaspora that followed the invention of the Hawking Drive. Since there was no way to communicate faster than light, Earth was dependent upon the settlement ships to report back by either returning with the settlement ship or by sending home unmanned drones equipped with miniature star drives. Usually, the destination worlds to which the settlement ships were dispatched had been surveyed previously by multiple unmanned drones to determine their habitability. Consequently, once the settlement ship departed, it seldom returned. These were, generally speaking, considered one-way trips and return meant failure. The colonists were encouraged to report in at regular intervals, and many did so, often leading to the establishment of regular trade between worlds, and this was the basis of a growing interstellar economy. As the *Mumbai* had been sent to check on two of India's settlements, the *Alligator* was being sent to check on one that carried American citizens to their new home world.

The *Alligator* had left low lunar orbit four days ago and was now light-years away from Earth, and about 1.4 light-hours away from the planet the records called New Kentake. Stockton carefully read the records about the colonists before departure so that he could be as prepared as possible for what might await them upon arrival.

The colonists bound for New Kentake were a mix of Native American peoples from across North America, though the majority were Iroquois. Their leader, the millionaire philanthropist Ahote Sanderson, just happened to be the primary financial backer and contributor to the construction of the ship and recruitment of the colonists. Sanderson made his fortune as the creator of the Prospero social-media platform that was quite the rage when the ship departed Earth. Sanderson had been too busy at the academy to spend much time in VR, so his Prospero account had gone mostly unused. Today, he would be surprised if any of the new navy recruits had ever even heard of it.

The settlement's stated purpose was typical. It contained phrases like: "to correct the social inequities and economic inequalities" of Earth and to "reestablish human civilization in harmony with the natural environment." This all sounded great, until you had to make decisions that actually involved the lives of the human beings under your guidance. Just how important were the fish in that estuary when compared to the need for a new water-treatment plant to prevent a disease outbreak? Still, at an emotional level, Stockton sympathized with them. They were right. Humans had made many mistakes in their settlement and subjugation of the Earth and, knowing what they now knew, perhaps humans could avoid making the same mistakes in the future. But Stockton also knew that humans would make new mistakes to take their place. They wouldn't be humans if they didn't.

Like most of the ethnic groups seeking a new start on a new world, those bound for New Kentake weren't fleeing persecution. These settlers were simply seeking a new start and a chance to live their lives like they thought they wanted them to be lived. Granted, among the fifteen hundred or so colonists aboard the *Santinka* were the typical mix of malcontents and petty criminals, but none that the *Alligator*'s AI flagged as serious risks to watch for.

So, why hadn't the inhabitants of New Kentake sent word home? Had their ship, the *Santinka*, had some sort of mishap? That was the question and the reason for the *Alligator*'s visit. Most likely, they would arrive, exchange pleasantries with the settlement's leadership, and either be warmly welcomed or curtly turned away. But Stockton couldn't assume these best-case scenarios. He had to be prepared to learn that the star system was under enemy control, or worse. Consequently, the *Alligator* entered the system sufficiently far away from the habitable planet, far away from any planet, so that she and her crew could observe the system and know what was going on before there was a chance of engaging any other ship. The arrival of a relatively small ship in the near nothingness far from the star made it highly unlikely their arrival would be noticed. From what Stockton could tell so far, that assumption was correct.

At their current rate of travel, covering approximately 8.5 light-minutes per day, the *Alligator* would arrive at New Kentake in six days. The ship's passive sensors, broadband radio and high-power telescopes looking at everything in the system from the ultraviolet to the infrared, were operating at their maximum sensitivity, and Stockton could expect a situational assessment within the next few minutes. From the view on the forward cameras, the system looked almost no different from the view in deep space. It was black and empty. At this distance, even the system's sole gas giant looked like nothing more than a faint star.

Since their arrival in the system, the bridge was quiet except for the sounds of the crew busily doing their jobs. Chatter was at a minimum, which was fine with Stockton. He admired his crew and knew that each was currently operating at one hundred percent.

"Captain, we've detected no artificial radio transmissions anywhere in the system. Just the usual natural background from the star and the planetary magnetospheres. I'll have the results of the imaging and infrared scans in a just a few more minutes," said

Lieutenant Adolf Woods. Woods, the signals officer, looked anxious as he made the report. This was his first shipboard assignment outside of the solar system.

"Thank you, Lieutenant. Let me know when you have the rest. I'm especially eager to get a good view of New Kentake. There's nothing quite as exciting as seeing an Earthlike planet for the first time," replied Stockton. He remembered when he first visited a settlement world, just a little more than a year ago. He was the XO on the *Breckinridge* when it paid a visit to Nikko. Most settlement worlds were simply struggling to get established and survive. He remembered seeing Nikko's oceans and clouds and thinking how much it looked like Earth. Then he saw the land masses, which looked nothing like those on Earth, and then, suddenly, the planet looked totally alien. His perceptions and emotional reaction to the planet shifted instantly with that realization. He often wondered if everyone felt that same gut punch at the view. He suspected he was not alone.

Moments later, the forward screens lit up with images from the telescopes. In the center was New Kentake. From this distance, the optical telescope could capture quite a bit of detail. Visible were the not-at-all-familiar land masses, which took up much more of the planet's surface than did Earth's continents, and the characteristic blue of its oceans that filled the space between them. Stockton knew that every habitable planet found thus far had a sizable fraction of its surface covered with water, and New Kentake was no exception. On the right were the infrared images, which showed no signs of extreme hot spots. The ship's computer automatically subtracted out the natural heat emissions so that the telltale emissions of artificial heat sources could be easily identified. From what he could see, there was nothing on or near the planet artificially generating heat.

"Lieutenant Griggs-Snyder, maintain our current trajectory unless signals come up with anything we need to be aware of," Stockton said to the ship's navigator. Lieutenant Almira Griggs-Snyder was one of those people who could solve lagrangians in her head and seemed to have an inborn sense of how to plot minimum-energy trajectories that took most academy graduates hours or more to understand, let alone calculate. She had graduated near the top of her class, and Stockton considered himself fortunate to have her aboard his ship. She was *that* good.

Turning to his XO, Stockton said, "Ye, I'm going to walk about for a few hours. Let me know if you see anything unnatural or suspicious. Since we're not seeing any sign of the colonists, either a disaster happened and they didn't make it, or disaster came to them. Either way, it is liable to be bad." Lieutenant Commander Jing Ye was an experienced officer, and Stockton believed she would likely soon get her own ship, perhaps as soon as they returned to Earth. He would be sorry to see her go, but he knew the navy would be better for it.

Stockton unbuckled from his command chair and made his way out of the bridge and into the central corridor that ran lengthwise through the ship, separated only by now-open emergency hatches that would close and seal at the first sign of a hull breach. As he made his way aft, he stopped and chatted with various members of the crew. While a believer in military discipline and protocol, he did not believe that captains should be the mysterious, all-wise, and separate persona that just happened to be in command. While he couldn't allow himself to befriend his crew, he did make an effort to get to know them by name and to hear, really hear, their personal stories, aspirations, and dreams. Stockton believed that when push came to shove, he would be able to make better decisions armed with this information about his crew and they, in turn, would be more likely to give that extra ten percent when it was needed if they both *respected* and *knew* him.

Finally, he reached his cabin. It, like most of the ship, was spartan, but it did provide him a sanctuary to rest and to think. Right now, he needed both. If all went well the next few days, it would provide them with time to prepare for their arrival and that meant some serious drills. If the enemy were lurking nearby, the risk of an attack would only grow as they neared the planet and became more detectable. There's nothing like the intense heat of a fusion propulsion system to announce your presence to whomever happened to be looking.

Six days later, two things had changed. The first was that New Kentake was now filling the screen, and the planetary science team on board was gathering an immense amount of data for analysis now and later by scientists back home. The reconnaissance drones had captured enough data to permit sending a settlement ship, but the data now being collected by the *Alligator* would be of much higher fidelity. The second, and most pertinent to their trip, was the discovery of a low-level artificial heat source orbiting the planet. When the source was first detected, it wasn't immediately clear from what the heat was emanating. The telescopes couldn't provide enough resolution to make that determination. That had changed yesterday when it became apparent the heat was coming from a large ship orbiting the planet at an altitude of about fifty thousand kilometers.

Someone was here.

But the heat emissions didn't make sense. As they neared the planet and the images grew sharper in detail and resolution, it became clear that though the heat originated in an orbiting spaceship, it wasn't nearly enough to be consistent with the size of the ship. In fact, the heat was coming from the ship's aft, presumably near where the power and propulsion system should logically be located no matter who built it, and it was too little power to do much of anything. It was looking more and more like the residual heat from a fusion reactor shut down long ago and kept warm from the radioactive decay of the fusion by-products.

"Captain, the AI has identified the ship with ninety-nine percent confidence. It's the *Santinka*," said Ye, turning from her station to look directly at Stockton.

"The *Santinka*? And you are only getting waste heat from the reactor? That doesn't make sense. Is it intact? Can you see any signs of damage?" Stockton asked.

"No, sir. It's in a standard parking orbit, consistent with what a settlement ship would establish after departing low orbit when planetary settlement was complete. It appears to be in one piece," she replied.

"Let's check it out," he said, turning to Lieutenant Griggs-Snyder. "Take us in close enough for one of the shuttles to send over a boarding party."

"We can be alongside in twenty hours, sir," said the lieutenant.

"Very good. I'll inform the marines. I suspect they are getting restless, and we can't have that," Stockton said, with just a trace of mirth. He knew that the marines were eager to do their jobs and finding out what going on with the *Santinka* would give them that chance. He also knew that it was tough for marines to be stuck on board a ship for an extended length of time. It didn't matter if that ship sailed the oceans of Earth or the vacuum of deep space— marines were marines.

The marines left the *Alligator* just over twenty-one hours later in one of the ship's Intership People and Cargo Carriers, or IPC for short. Each of the *Alligator*'s ten IPCs could carry up to ten fully outfitted marines in space suits with all their gear. The IPC that departed the *Alligator* for the *Santinka* was filled to capacity with ten eager marines, each fully encumbered with all battle gear, and led by Sergeant Katie Swenson. Swenson was the youngest daughter in a family from which each generation had among their number service members in the American military, almost all in the United States Marine Corps. For Swenson, the question had never been if she would be a marine, but where she would be stationed. She was the first Swenson to serve in the United States Space Marines and for that she was immensely proud.

"Sergeant Swenson, this is Captain Stockton." Swenson

heard the captain's voice through her space suit's radio coming, presumably, from the *Alligator*'s bridge or CIC.

"Yes, sir!" Swenson said in reply.

"At ease, Sergeant," began Stockton. "As you know, we've determined the ship is the *Santinka*, launched fifteen years ago chock full of eager colonists. Its orbit is consistent with ship protocols for safe disposal after everyone and all the supplies have been sent planetside. That's all and good, except for the fact that we can't see any evidence that a settlement exists anywhere on the planet. At least, not yet. They might be there, but if they are, they haven't exactly been thriving. And then there's the matter of the waste heat we picked up from the ship's fusion reactor. Reactor Specialist Sibanda told me just an hour ago that the radiation scan turned up levels consistent with a reactor that had been shut down for a long time, fifty years or more. Perhaps they cannibalized the reactor and took it somewhere. We just don't know."

Stockton continued, "When you board the ship and determine that it is secure, I want you to go to the bridge and get into the ship's logs. Maybe they will shed some light on what happened here. And keep your external camera on. I'll be seeing what you see so you don't need to feel compelled to report your status. I'll be aware."

"Yes, sir!" Swenson said.

Swenson checked her comms and made sure the exterior camera was, in fact, operational. It was. The captain would now be seeing everything she was seeing. This was now standard operating procedure, so she didn't give it another thought as she joined her squad and readied herself for entering the *Santinka*. She felt the deceleration of the IPC as it slowed to mate with the *Santinka*'s docking ring. Fortunately, the designs were made to be compatible, and the two ships easily became one with barely a bump.

Their first problem occurred when they opened the IPC's hatch and found that the *Santinka*'s was without power. Fortunately, since a ship's hatches were used for essential entry and egress during shipboard emergencies, there was a backup power connection that allowed the IPC's power system to connect to the *Santinka*'s airlock so that the door could be cycled opened. That led to their second problem.

The power cable was easily connected, and after a few moments the *Santinka*'s airlock showed it powered and ready. But it still wouldn't open. Swenson tried the opening sequence several times and each time was the same. Nothing happened.

"Well, that leaves the old-fashioned approach," said Swenson as she reached for the covered compartment to the right of the airlock that held the manual release. She disengaged the latch, opened the small door, and used her right hand to grab the lever that would release the catch which kept the airlock door closed and sealed. She would then be able to pull the door open.

At first, she thought she wasn't going to be strong enough to move the lever. It was definitely stuck and much harder to move than it should have been, but her persistence and the strength augmentation provided by her body armor paid off. The lever moved and the door popped open, allowing her to grasp it with her gloved hands and pull it toward her.

They were in.

Swenson had a map of the *Santinka* on her heads-up display, courtesy of the *Alligator* having downloaded all the schematics of the settlement ship before leaving Earth. She'd also spent most of the last few days memorizing as many details as she could. Just in case. Just in case she and her squad were on the run and didn't have time to consult a map. She hoped it wouldn't come to that, but she also wasn't taking any chances.

"Let's go! Are you waiting on your momma or something?" Swenson said to her team as they entered the dark, cold, and abandoned-looking ship.

"Captain, I've been looking at the high-resolution imagery of the *Santinka*, and there's something that isn't quite right," said Ye.

Those were not words that Stockton wanted to hear.

"What have you got?" he asked as the forward viewscreen shifted from a real-time view of the *Santinka*'s hull and was replaced with a static image of the *Santinka*. The ship, crewed by Native Americans, had the ship's hull painted with a stylized image of the Great Plains filled with buffalo and a dramatic and quite beautiful sunset in the background. Decorating the exterior of the settlement ships was common enough that seeing it had not been unexpected.

"This is what the ship looked like when it departed Earth. Notice the intricate paintings on the hull," said Ye.

"It looks spectacular," said Stockton. He meant it. He loved nature and had many fond memories of camping in the American Midwest and Southwest. He hadn't seen that many buffalo in one place, but he had seen many a beautiful sunset.

"Now, I'll move that to the left and bring up a current picture, from the same rough distance and vantage point," Ye said.

On the right, a new image appeared showing the same ship and painting, but the paint had faded significantly. In addition, there were some sections that had completely eroded away, leaving gaps the size of buffalo hooves.

"It's faded. From the UV?" asked Stockton.

"It almost certainly faded from prolonged exposure to the star's ultraviolet light. But it shouldn't have faded this much. I would have expected it to be almost unnoticeable except under high resolution. This looks more like what you'd expect after hundreds of years, or more," she replied.

"Maybe there was a solar storm, a flare or something," Stockton said.

"This isn't a flare star and, even then, it wouldn't account for this much fading. And there's something else," she said, displaying a closeup of the *Santinka*'s side hull. "Look at the pitting on the hull and, over here you see where a micrometeorite breached it, making this teeny, tiny hole."

"This looks like what I'd expect to see on an Earth-orbiting ship after a few decades. We still haven't cleaned up all the orbital debris left there from early in the space age. At last count, there were over half a million pieces of junk the size of pea or smaller zipping around Earth at eight kilometers per second. After more than a decade, anything up there gets pitted from the random impacts likely to occur over that time," Stockton said. He was actually kind of happy he remembered those statistics.

"That's correct sir, for a hull this size orbiting the Earth. But this isn't Earth, and there is no orbital debris here. None. Zero. The only space junk here appears to be the *Santinka*," Ye said.

"But then, how did the pitting happen?" asked Stockton.

"Micrometeors. The natural debris of any stellar system. The pitting we see would be expected with the *Santinka* having been in orbit for between two hundred and three hundred years, minimum. And the fading of the paint correlates with this. I ran a simulation based on the star's emission spectrum, to get the UV flux correct, and the density of micrometeoroids we measured as we came into the system these last several days. It all adds up," she said.

"Are you telling me the *Santinka* has been in orbit around New Kentake for hundreds of years? That's impossible," Stockton said.

"I don't have an explanation; all I have is data. And the data indicates that this ship has been here a whole lot longer than we expected, or it's aged a hell of a lot faster than it should have," said Ye.

"Could it have been hit with some sort of new weapon? Something that artificially ages material?" said Stockton. As he said it, he knew it was a reach. What he was talking about would be something like you would find in a cheap VR sim, not real life.

"It's possible, sir. But I'll see if I can find anything else to help us figure this out. Maybe the boarding party will be able to tell us something," she said.

Swenson's team didn't encounter anything out of the

ordinary in the passageways leading to the bridge or engineering. Everything about the ship so far was exactly what you would expect from a settlement ship that had done its job, been stripped of the equipment necessary to establish a settlement, and sent to a parking orbit for storage. By the time they reached the bridge, Swenson allowed herself to relax a bit. She remained alert, but no longer expected bad guys to ambush her from around the corner.

The bridge, like the rest of the *Santinka*, was dark, with all the equipment powered down. Engineering was the same; the ship was essentially dead. Swenson couldn't even tell if there was any remaining fuel that could be used to restart it. But that wasn't her job. She'd leave that to the techs who would come after. After she and her squad made sure it was safe for them to come aboard.

From what they could tell, it was safe. Cold, but safe.

"Captain, this is Swenson. The *Santinka* is all clear. You can send over the techs," she said, for the first time wondering that the hell had happened. The ship was like a tomb, but without the bodies.

CHAPTER 18

"Captain, this is going to take longer than we expected."

Speaking was the electronics technician who was aboard the *Santinka* trying to get the power system up and running. Once the ship had power, the computer could be accessed, and Stockton would be able to find out what happened. He was in a momentary internal panic at not immediately recalling the technician's name, then it came to him. Thankfully, he remembered fast enough to avoid potential embarrassment.

Stockton was in the CIC waiting on the rest of his officers to arrive to figure out how to best locate and contact the colonists on the world below, if they were really there and if they could find them. The message from Ensign Boseman came directly to his personal comm link, as he'd instructed. He wanted to be aware of any issues that would shed light on what had happened to the ship and the colonists.

"How much longer?" Stockton asked.

"It's hard to say. No less than two days, perhaps as many

as four. The reactor has been completely powered down for quite some time. Long enough for the radioactive byproducts to have induced embrittlement of some of the key components and systems. We need to run a complete diagnostic and probably replace some circuit boards here and there before I dare run a zero-power critical test. The good news is that if the ZPC is successful, then I could ramp up sufficient power to turn on the ship's systems in a matter of hours," she said.

"Ensign, I need you to speculate on your answer to my next question. For how long would you say the reactor has been powered down?" Stockton asked.

"Captain, that's an interesting question. The reactor state is unlike anything I've ever seen in service before. It's really cold. And I don't just mean the temperature. The nuclear byproducts are here, for sure, but not in the mass ratios I would expect," she said.

"Ensign, you didn't answer my question," Stockton said. He was impatient, and he knew the tone of his voice conveyed it, but he was trying very hard not to sound annoyed. If the ensign thought the information she conveyed was important in answering his question, then, well, she thought it was important. Boseman might even think that she *had* answered his question.

"Sorry, sir. I really can't say, sir, I'm not a physicist. I just know that it has been powered down for a long time. Far longer than anything in the training manuals said we'd encounter. It could be a hundred years, two hundred, even five hundred. I don't know the half-lives of all the fusion byproducts, but I do know some can be at least that long. And the isotope ratios are simply wrong. I can say for certain that the reactor has been powered down for much longer than fifty years. Sir," she said.

"That's all, Ensign. Get that reactor back online, safely, and then maybe we can find out what's going on," Stockton said.

Stockton returned his attention to the CIC and the now-gathered group of senior officers he'd invited to the strategy session. He quickly went through the formalities—the navy loved formality—and then got to the core reason for the meeting. He looked around the room at his crew and immediately knew that if *anyone* could figure out what happened to the *Santinka* and her crew, *they* could.

"We have a mystery. Fifty years ago, the *Santinka* left Earth with five thousand colonists and all the equipment necessary to establish a high-tech settlement on the planet below us. The ship left Earth and the colonists never reported back with their status, despite the ship being equipped with messenger drones capable of hopping back to Earth. Now we're here to check up on them and what do we find? We find their ship, the *Santinka*, in a standard disposal orbit around the planet, looking just like it should if a settlement had successfully disembarked. But, so far, there is no sign of the colonists on the planet. If they are there, then something has gone very wrong for all evidence of their presence to be masked. We can't see anything from up here that looks like an artificial clearing; there are no radio broadcasts, and no indication of an artificial heat source anywhere on the planet. In short, no sign of the high-tech civilization they should be. To top it all off, the *Santinka* has aged. A lot. In fact, the ship looks like it hasn't been here fifty years, but perhaps five hundred. We don't know yet," Stockton said, paused.

He could tell the effect his words was having on his officers. They *understood* the significance.

"And the mystery just deepened. Ensign Boseman and her power-system specialists are on the *Santinka* trying to restart the fusion reactor, and she just informed me that it will take longer than expected to accomplish because the reactor has been offline for too long. She didn't want to speculate, but I could tell she wanted to. And from what she did say, I am beginning to believe the ship has been powered down for several hundred years, and I don't see how that's possible. I need an explanation. I need to know if what happened here is a risk to this ship or to Earth," he said.

The room was so quiet that Stockton could hear the circulation fans running in the background. Finally, his XO broke the silence.

"Could this be a relativity thing? Einstein proved that the rate at which time passes can be different for different observers. Maybe something happened in their jump here and it wasn't instantaneous like it's supposed to be. What if they traveled here at some speed very close to the speed of light and their clocks began ticking at a different rate than those on Earth? Centuries might pass for those on the ship while back on Earth it would only be a few weeks or months . . . No, that isn't right. It would be the other way around. The ship going near the speed of light would have their clocks run slower than the rest of the universe. If they were going fast enough for Special Relativity effects to happen, then *we* would be the ones to have centuries pass. The crew might only have experienced a few years. No, that won't explain this . . . " Ye's voice trailed off.

"Ye, you may be onto something. Even though your theory won't explain what we are seeing, it's a hell of a lot better than anything I've come up with," said Stockton.

"Perhaps there is some sort of radiation or field that affected the ship?" offered someone from the far end of the table.

"We haven't detected anything out of the ordinary for a stellar system like this one. The star is a G2, like Sol, with emission lines showing an abundance of calcium and cyanide. It is not a flare star, so there won't likely be any more coronal mass ejections than we expect back home. The star's X-ray emissions are nothing out of the ordinary. In short, it's a pretty normal, run-of-the-mill star," said Lieutenant Griggs-Snyder.

"Maybe the XO was on to something, sir," said Maria Arredondo, the *Alligator*'s chief engineer.

"Go on," said Stockton.

"The XO figured out that Special Relativity, what happens when a ship approaches the speed of light, wouldn't explain what happened to the *Santinka*, but General Relativity might. Space and time are connected. Special and General Relativity are just extreme environments where that connection becomes more significant. In Special Relativity, the rate at which time passes is caused by how fast you move through space. In General Relativity, time can flow at a different rate for two observers if one of them is in the presence of a massive gravity field, like what is generated near a black hole. But that won't really work here either," she said.

"Why not?" asked Stockton.

"For basically the same reason that Special Relativity won't explain it. Time slows down for the observer who is near the massive object that is warping spacetime with its large gravity. The *Santinka* is the one that has aged, not us," she replied.

"But what if we are the ones who experienced the time dilation? What if we somehow passed through or by some gravity anomaly on the way here and the rest of the universe continued to move forward in time at the normal rate and we are the ones who are out of sync?" said Ye.

"How can we find out? I suppose we could turn tail, go home, and find out if our grandchildren are running things. But that's not something I'm going to do until after we find out what happened to the colonists. Until then, are there any other ideas?" asked Stockton. He was going to make sure he completed his mission before going home to report. Regardless of who or what he would report to upon his return. He had his orders.

The discussion continued for another hour, but no one came up with alternatives that explained the data as neatly as Arredondo's theory.

Two days later, Ensign Boseman's team had the reactor running on minimum power, not enough to propel the ship anywhere, but enough to get the life-support systems and, more importantly, the ship's computer up and running. Boseman found that the *Santinka*'s AI core had been removed and, if the settlers had followed the standard procedures, it was likely taken with them to the planet below. It wasn't long after the power was restored that she informed Captain Stockton he could access the *Santinka*'s logs.

"XO, come with me to the CIC. Let's see what happened to these people," Stockton said as he rose from his chair.

Barely a minute later, Stockton and Ye were scrolling through the video logs that captured the busy activities aboard the *Santinka* as the passengers and crew moved here and there, preparing to disembark. Stockton was concentrating on the video recordings and getting a sense of the health and status of the ship and its people. Ye was focusing on the status reports and environmental surveys.

"Everything looks normal," said Stockton after about thirty minutes of rapidly viewing the last thirty days of the ship's recordings.

"The same with the daily log entries made by the captain and her XO. They had a relatively smooth trip, found New Kentake and entered orbit around the planet without a hitch, did all the requisite surveys of the planet to make sure the early reconnaissance drones hadn't missed anything important, and then they disembarked," Ye said.

"Did you find a mention of why they didn't send a drone back home to confirm their arrival?"

"That's just it. They tried to send a drone, about thirty days after their arrival, after they had completed enhanced observations of the planet from orbit and completed their atmospheric *in situ* sampling. It was filled with all the data they'd collected and their assessments of the long-term safety of the biosphere. I scanned the data they put in the drone, and it aligns with the data we've collected so far. New Kentake is very Earthlike and should be a great place to plant a settlement. But the drone would not jump. The Hawking Drive was fried."

"I wonder what happened to the colonists," said Ye, turning away from the data scrolling across the screen in front of her to look at Stockton. "I know where they set up their settlement on the planet. The details are all here in their logs. They went to one of the three spots we identified as the most likely settlement locations when we first arrived and got a good look at the planet."

"And we didn't see any signs of human activity," said Stockton.

"None. Captain, I recommend we get all this data to our assessment teams as quickly as possible and that I take Sergeant Swenson and some of her marines down to the planet to find out what happened and where the colonists went," she said.

"Go."

Three hours later, they found out what happened to the colonists.

The *Alligator* was equipped with five ship-to-surface Atmospheric Entry Vehicles, or AEVs. Ye, Swenson, and five additional marines fit comfortably within AEV-A1 as its pilot left the serene and smooth space vacuum environment and entered the bumpy unpredictable winds of New Kentake's upper atmosphere. The pilot seemed unperturbed as the small AEV was tossed from side to side, sometimes dropping tens of feet without warning, and causing the normally stoic marines to glance at each other with veiled concern.

"Hang on, it is going to get a little rough before it smooths out," said the pilot, trying unsuccessfully to hide his grin.

Ye and the marines, already securely buckled into their seats, grasped their restraints. Some grasped harder than others. For the marines, being in a dangerous situation in which they could do nothing but watch and hold on was extremely frustrating.

Without warning, the AEVs gyrations suddenly ceased and coincided with a break in the cloud cover that they could see when looking through the craft's few windows. Below them was the eerily familiar sight of ocean, filling their line of sight for as far as they could see. It looked just like Earth.

"We will be there in less than twenty minutes," said the pilot.

"Listen up. According to the *Santinka*'s logs, they established their settlement near the eastern edge of the planet's primary landmass at the fork of two rivers just before the larger river's estuary begins. From orbit, all we see are trees. No houses, no landing craft, nothing. Just trees. We'll set down in a clearing near the shore and then hike upriver about a mile to where they should be," Ye said.

A few minutes later, Ye caught sight of land ahead. As they drew closer, she kept hoping to see buildings rising from the ground, artfully integrated into the natural landscape in some sort of modern human/nature symbiosis. The settlers that came here were, after all, descendants of the Native Americans, and having them care more deeply for the land than most would be in character and not unexpected. New Kentake, the name they chose for their planet, contained the root word from which the US state of Kentucky was derived. And when European settlers arrived in that part of North America, Ye was fairly sure it looked like much of New Kentake does now—a vast wilderness of trees.

As they neared shore, Ye's hopes were dashed. Instead of a city where humans and nature beautifully coexisted, she began to see the signs of a settlement gone horribly wrong. There were what appeared to be the remains of buildings, most with little more remaining than their foundations. As the AEV settled to the ground, Ye was increasingly sure they would find no living humans in the area. The decay and disorder were simply too far advanced.

Swenson and her fellow marines disembarked first and made sure there were no immediate threats in the area. Ye was not terribly concerned about predators. Their scans of the surface, combined with detailed survey results from the *Santinka*'s ground expeditions, found no evidence of dangerous predators. Not that the planet's ecosystem was without predation; there were just none that were large enough to be considered a major threat to humans. Still, they had to be careful. *Something* had happened to the colonists.

After checking the area and securing the perimeter, Swenson radioed Ye telling her it was okay to come out.

It was worse close up than it had been from above. What little of the settlement's buildings remained was covered with mold and what looked like moss. Nothing was undamaged. Worse, the damage looked to be quite old. Whatever had destroyed the village had done so long ago. Still, she decided to check out the remaining ruins that extended further into the forest.

With Swenson in the lead and the marines providing protection, Ye followed what must have once been a road deeper into the trees. The midday sun was blazing in a nearly cloudless sky, but the canopy of trees made the roadway seem like it was in perpetual twilight. *Gloomy* was the word that came to Ye's mind as she continued her exploration.

Everywhere she went, it was the same. Damaged buildings and broken pieces of metal, plastic, and ceramic were scattered here and there, with the occasional human bone thrown in. People had died here, and she had no idea what killed them. If there were any living colonists, or their descendants, then they certainly weren't here. Finally, she gave the order to return to the AEV and go back to the *Alligator*. On her way, she made sure that all the video captured by her VR camera was successfully shared and uploaded to the ship for more detailed viewing later. It was.

"Captain, this is Ye," she said into her radio as she walked to where they landed.

"I've been following your feed. It looks pretty bad down there," replied Stockton.

"Sir, I don't think we have anything more to learn here. Maybe the archeologists from back home can figure out what happened," said Ye.

"Maybe, after this damn war is over. But it will have to wait. It is our job to return home and let the brass know what we found. Unless, of course, the chief engineer was correct and we did encounter some sort of mass anomaly on the way here. If that's the case, we will be going home to a vastly different place than the one we left," said Stockton.

"Sir, normally I'm glad the chief's theories are correct, but not this time. I'm looking forward to seeing my family again—not my great-grandchildren," she said.

"You and me both. Get back up here safely so we can go home and maybe get the chance to be part of the defense effort instead of being out here making house calls," he said.

"Yes, sir!"

Twenty hours later, the *Alligator* left orbit from around New Kentake and headed home.

CHAPTER 19

As he prepared to walk into the courtroom, Price was as nervous as he had ever been. Major Castillo had followed through with her threat and preferred charges to Colonel Williamson, who had no choice but to pass them along to the Admiralty. From there, things took on a life of their own. As soon as he arrived back in the solar system from the debacle at Kunlun, he was whisked off to London where he met his counsel, Captain Dunn, for the first time—one day before the hearing. Fortunately, Dunn seemed to be one of the best. A graduate of the London School of Economics and Political Science, she had served as a counsel on several cases and was now in a position where she could, for the most part, pick and choose the ones she wanted to take. Her close-cropped brown hair and curious desire to wear eyeglasses, which almost no one did these days, made her appear especially formidable.

In their meeting the day before, she had been very blunt as they discussed his case, with her first question being: "Are you loyal to the Crown, and is there any merit to these charges?" Price was momentarily caught off guard—had she expected him to say: "Yes, I am a traitor?" Then he realized she was one of those people who thought they could tell if someone was lying, and it was her way of finding out whether or not she was wasting her time. He, of course, had said "Yes" and then "No."

She had then looked at him long and hard, not breaking eye contact for several seconds. She then replied, "Good. Let's get these bumfoolery charges against you dropped so you can return to the business of kicking Kurofune ass." By the end of the day, which was barely before the clock struck midnight, they had gone over all the evidence she expected Major Castillo's counsel to put forward and had a plan for how to refute each and every bit of it. That still was not enough for Price to get a good night's sleep. He was tired, but he could not turn off his mind and his dual worries—the hearing and Anika. If there were a device that could rate a person's mental duress, then Price felt like his current state would define the upper end of the scale.

For the hearing, which was the formal step that would determine if there needed to be a court-martial, Price and Dunn were dressed in their formal uniforms. Price did not mind wearing the jacket and tie, but he hated the leather shoes. He thought the practice of making clothing from dead animal skins rather barbaric and wondered why the Admiralty had not evolved in their thinking to use the nearly indestructible synthetics which they all wore in their working uniforms. He only wore these horribly uncomfortable shoes when he was at Admiralty events, maybe once a year, and they made his feet hurt. It was distracting. Dunn did not look as uncomfortable as Price felt. She looked at ease, calm, and extremely professional.

London was, well, London. It was not raining, which was a good thing, but the sky was cloudy, and it looked like the heavens could open up at any minute. The chill of winter was in the air as busy people scurried about as they had for centuries. The hearing would be held in the refreshingly retro-styled Space Navy Headquarters building built atop the timeless Imperial War Museum. Incorporating the original structure, the building rose nearly seven hundred feet in the air. Price was glad the navy had chosen a more traditional structure instead of one of the newer lofted buildings that towered nearly a mile upward, their upper floors suspended by the same inertial dampers the *Indefatigable* and other Space Navy ships relied upon. Some things just should not be done.

Price and Dunn departed their aircar at the south entrance and, on the way into the building, caught sight of Major Castillo talking to someone Price presumed would be part of the day's proceedings. Castillo caught Price's eye and her glare was venomous. Price wondered why she would have such a vendetta against him. She was clearly personally invested. He tried to ignore her as he walked by.

After passing through security and finding the correct room, they took their seats at the front, opposite from where trial counsel would be sitting, while everyone else filed in. Since it was not a court-martial, there were not many in attendance and Price felt very much alone. He had spoken with Colonel Williamson the day before and was somewhat reassured. Price knew Williamson did not believe the charges and would be among his staunchest defenders. As was customary, Williamson would not be in attendance at the hearing unless he was called upon as a witness. Since this was possible, Williamson would be waiting in a separate room just down the hall. After they took their seats, the person with whom Castillo had been speaking entered and sat at the table opposite. He was, as Price had suspected, the trial counsel.

"All rise," said the bailiff as Colonel Brice Kelly entered the courtroom from the front side door. Dunn had told him that Kelly was known to be tough, but fair. Given that this was simply a hearing, it was Kelly's job to determine if the charges had merit and whether the case should be sent to a formal court-martial. Dunn did warn Price that nearly all hearings with him resulted in charges going to a court-martial and that a court-martial could take months. Months that the Earth might not have. Price did not want to think about riding out the war having to defend himself against baseless charges. He needed to be out there, fighting the Kurofune, defending Earth, and looking for Anika.

Once they retook their seats, the proceeding began. Both Dunn and the trial counsel parlayed back and forth about which records would be discussed and which not while Price listened and tried to keep up. Finally, Colonel Kelly drew back in his chair and spoke to the participants, not just the attorneys.

"I would like to dispense with the formalities for a few moments, if I may," said Kelly. Knowing full well that no one would object, he barely paused before continuing, "I have read the dossier prepared by Major Castillo and the rebuttal from Captain Dunn, as well as a few other items of interest, the most notable being an affidavit from Captain Yahontov of the Russian Space Navy. In it, the captain described in some detail the actions taken by Captain Price following the battle at Kunlun to save his ship and as many lives aboard her as possible. Yahontov praised the extraordinary efforts taken by Captain Price following the loss of the ship's commanding officers. I've also reviewed the records of the unfortunate events at Nikko, including the data logs from all the ships involved. Captain Price's service record is exemplary, and he comes with the highest recommendations from his superior officers, at the Moon and his previous postings. Frankly, I am wondering why he is being accused of a capital crime."

Price and Dunn exchanged glances. She tipped her head slightly to reaffirm that neither of them should say anything in response. It was clearly up to the other side to respond.

The trial counsel was quietly conferring with one of his aides, seemingly in some sort of disagreement. Price could hear the hushed tones, but not anything specific.

"Well? Captain Yardley, do you have anything to say?" Kelly asked, speaking to the trial counsel. Yardley looked rather young to be a lead attorney, but then again, Price had difficulty telling the ages of anyone between about eighteen and fifty these days.

Yardley rose, brushing his light brown locks from his forehead as he did so.

"Colonel Kelly, we acknowledge that Captain Price engaged in actions that would appear to be brave and exceedingly loyal to the Crown. He even saved lives in the process. But we believe the lives he saved would not have been jeopardized had he not been fraternizing with an officer of a foreign power. An officer that we believe may be in league with the Kurofune," Yardley said.

"Yes, yes. I saw the evidence that Captain Price is involved with this, what was her name," Kelly said, pausing as he looked through the notes in front of him. "Ah, yes, Captain Ahuja of the Indian Space Navy. While this is certainly frowned upon and, I must admit, a cause for concern, it is hardly proof of treason. Are you asserting that Captain Ahuja is a Kurofune or a Kurofune sympathizer?"

"We believe so, my lord. And even more so now that her ship has conveniently disappeared after the battle at Kunlun," said Yardley.

Conveniently disappeared? Price was incredulous. The *Mumbai* had fought brilliantly at Kunlun. Were they now asserting that her disappearance was on purpose? *That she and her ship simply jumped somewhere else?*

"Hmm," said Kelly. He then continued, "And the basis for your assumption of Captain Ahuja being a Kurofune sympathizer is what exactly?"

"I would like to call Major Castillo to answer that question," said Yardley, looking up from his notes.

"Very well. Bailiff, please collect the major," said Kelly.

It took less than five minutes for Castillo to be retrieved and sworn in. She, too, was in her dress uniform, and she displayed none of the animosity that had been directed toward Price during their exchanges on the Moon or even just that morning outside the building.

"Major Castillo, counsel is asserting that Captain Anika Ahuja, with whom Captain Price is allegedly having a liaison, is either a Kurofune sympathizer or a Kurofune herself. This is a very serious allegation, and I would like to know its basis. I don't see any such evidence in the documents you provided," Kelly said as he stared at Castillo.

"No, sir. Her absence, and the body uncovered at Kunlun speak volumes."

Kelly looked away from Castillo and toward those in attendance in the courtroom. He said, "I need to remind everyone in the courtroom that these proceedings are classified top secret. The court verified that everyone here today is appropriately cleared, but I had hoped to avoid having topics from the classified brief discussed in open court due to need-to-know constraints. Please be aware the Major Castillo's mention of a body being recovered at Kunlun is extremely sensitive and is one of the reasons these proceedings were classified."

He continued, "Major, please explain the connection between the body recovered at Kunlun and this case."

"Sir, the racial characteristics of the body recovered from the Kurofune ship clearly show the connection."

"The 'racial characteristics.' In that Captain Ahuja is South Asian and the body recovered at Kunlun appears to share South Asian characteristics? And?"

"I believe the finding, combined with her abrupt disappearance, shows that she is a Kurofune agent. A successful one, at that. One that has penetrated to the core of Earth's defenses by coopting Captain Price," Castillo said.

"Major Castillo, you may leave the witness stand.

Captain Yardley, Captain Dunn. Please approach the bench," said Kelly.

Dunn looked at Price as she rose from her chair. She then joined Captain Yardley in front of Kelly, passing Castillo, who now took a seat in the nearly empty courtroom. They spoke in hushed tones until he said something to Yardley who responded with a brief, "But, sir . . ." Kelly pointed a finger at Yardley, and he stopped speaking. There was then more hushed conversation, followed by Dunn and Yardley returning to their respective tables.

"Captain Price, please rise," said Kelly.

Price rose and said, "Yes, sir."

"Captain Price, I find the charges against you to be without merit and will recommend that the charges be dropped. The government has failed to provide any evidence to suggest your disloyalty to the Crown. On the contrary, I see the makings of an outstanding officer in the Commonwealth Space Navy. One who has earned the Crown's respect and gratitude. Your conduct at both Nikko and Kunlun was that for which any officer should be commended. I apologize for you being unfairly charged and for the undue stress that I am sure these proceedings might have caused. As to the matter of your fraternization with an officer of a foreign navy, I will leave that up to your commanding officer to address as it is not a matter that warrants the time and attention of the Admiralty."

"Thank you, sir," was all Price could muster. He was elated. As he sat, he turned to look at Dunn, but his attention was diverted to Major Castillo. She was glaring at Admiral Kelly.

"Now, Major Castillo. This is the second time you have brought baseless charges of treason before this court in the last three months. I intend to speak with your commanding officer and request that you be reassigned or relieved of your current duties. It is obvious to the Crown that you are looking for conspiracies that do not exist, ruining people's lives and careers in the process, and wasting valuable time and resources we do not have. I expect to never see your face in this court again. And I am well aware of your family connections in Whitehall and will gladly speak with any of them if they would like to discuss my decisions and your actions. I also suggest you keep your racist opinions to yourself as I find them disgusting. This case is dismissed," Kelly concluded. He then gathered his belongings, rose, and walked out the door from which he had entered.

Like everyone in the courtroom, Castillo rose from her chair as the admiral exited the room. Yardley tried to get her attention, but she slid her chair back and walked instead toward Price and Dunn.

"You won't get away with this, Price. You and your bitch orchestrated the attacks on the *Linyi* and the *South Dakota* and then the fleet at Kunlun. Your actions resulted in the deaths of too many people for you to go unpunished," Castillo said as the volume of her voice grew louder. Castillo was now inches from Price's face, glaring at him. "Don't think for a minute that you and your ilk have heard the last from me."

Dunn signaled for the RMPs standing at the back of the room to intervene.

Price stood his ground, not saying a word. Every fiber

of his being was telling him to slug her, but those voices were quickly silenced as he stood straight and focused on his status as an officer of the Commonwealth Space Navy. *He would not lose his temper.*

"I know I will find the dirt on you. Once I do, the weight of the Crown will come down you so fast that . . ."

As the RMPs approached, Dunn grasped Price's arm and pulled him away from Castillo and toward the door. Castillo tried to follow but the two RMPs blocked her path.

"Congratulations, Captain Price," said Dunn, smiling.

"Thank you. I'm pleased with the outcome and appreciate all your work, but I still have to wonder why Major Castillo has it in for me," said Price.

"From what Admiral Kelly said, she has a grudge against more people than just you—from the sound of it, a whole country's worth of people. You were just the next unfortunate person she focused on. What are your plans?" Dunn asked.

Price reached out his hand to shake hers and nodded toward the approaching Colonel Williamson, who had just entered the courtroom and heard the news. "I'm going to meet with my commanding officer and hopefully get back to the business of stopping the Kurofune from killing any more civilians," he said.

CHAPTER 20

"Captain Price, I would like to officially welcome you back," said Colonel Williamson as he began the first morning intelligence briefing that Price had been able to attend since stepping down from command of the *Indefatigable* before the battle at Kunlun. Around the virtual table were the captains of all the ships that had engaged the Kurofune in battle thus far plus a few others whom the colonel had asked to attend.

Price was glad to be back and had spent the day before hurriedly reading through the reports from the many morning meetings he had missed. He had the time available after he learned the extent of the damage done to the *Indefatigable*. He was still reeling from the news the ship would require at least another six weeks in the space dock for repairs before being fit for duty. The damage taken at Kunlun that killed most of his senior staff had nearly destroyed the ship. Deep down, Price was surprised the engineers were not telling him the repairs would require far more time than six weeks. If the EDF decided to engage the enemy again before then, Price would be sitting it out. Without a ship to run, he used the time to catch up.

The reports painted a grim picture. The Kurofune were not going to be easily stopped. Little more was known of their origin and the questions outstanding at the time he stepped down were still mostly unanswered. Especially the origin of the human recovered by the *Mumbai*. There was still no explanation for the disappearance of the *Mumbai*, and to Price's surprise, no one else had followed the path he chose in investigating the commonalities between the *Mumbai* and the loss of the early settlement ships. He planned to present his theory at the meeting if it seemed appropriate to do so. If not, then he would raise it with the colonel privately.

Colonel Williamson began the official meeting and said, "Until yesterday, EDF intelligence believed the next likely target of the Kurofune would be New Kentake. It was the next world to which an early settlement ship was sent and, so far anyway, the Kurofune are relentlessly attacking our settlements in the order in which they were explored and settled. Granted, they may be following this blatantly obvious pattern to lull us into expecting them to continue following it, planning some sort of surprise attack from another direction in the meantime. We can plan for the former, not the latter. EDF no longer believes New Kentake will be the next target. Let me explain.

"Yesterday, the USSN *Alligator* returned from its recontact mission to New Kentake and radioed a rather puzzling status report that has had everyone scratching their collective heads and wondering if those same heads had been stuck somewhere dark and unseemly. As if we don't have enough mysteries to deal with, we now have another big one," said Williamson.

As Williamson spoke, he switched the view from the virtual conference room to an image of a spacecraft in deep space. The camera was close enough to see the somewhat familiar design of a colonial settlement ship with its distinctive Hawking Drive radiator fins along its hull extending from fore to aft. Near the aft, the rather worn lettering saying *Santinka* could be easily read. He then switched to other views, both exterior and what Price assumed was the ship's interior.

The view then shifted from the ship to a shot of the planet from orbit. As the image from space zoomed in on a heavily forested region near a river, the colonel continued his speech. "According to the *Alligator*, they found the abandoned *Santinka*, the settlement ship sent to New Kentake, in high orbit around the planet. This, in and of itself, was no surprise. That is exactly where we would expect to find a settlement ship around the planet it colonized. The ship showed no signs of damage and it appears that the colonists evacuated it according to the book. Everything you would expect them to have taken to the surface was gone. The ship had been left in low-power standby mode in an orbit that would not decay for tens of thousands of years. The crew of the *Alligator* then surveyed the planet using their hyperspectral imagers looking for signs of the colonists and found the area in which a settlement had been built.

"A survey team accompanied by marines went to the surface and found this . . . "

Williamson changed the view to 3-D as seen from the helmet camera of someone on the survey team. Abandoned and decaying buildings covered with a mix of what looked like local flora and Earth species were seen in every direction. The settlement had clearly been abandoned for a long time.

"You can see that something must have long ago gone wrong in the New Kentake settlement. No survivors were found. The *Alligator* recalled the survey team and came home with the data. The failed settlement is not the mystery. The mystery is how long ago it appears to have failed. Based on the state of the *Santinka*'s hull, power system, and its overall condition, combined with the advanced decay of the settlement and the age of the plants that had overgrown it, our best guess is that the settlement was settled and failed well over three hundred years ago." Williamson ended his speech at that.

Price, like everyone else around the virtual table, was stunned. Three hundred years ago?

"Colonel, what you are telling us doesn't make sense. That is impossible," said Captain Yahontov, his thick Russian accent filled with disbelief and sarcasm.

"Our analysts agree. There must be some other factor at work here that we simply do not understand, and it might or might not be related to the Kurofune and the war. Nonetheless, it is information of which we need to be aware. The sad part is, of course, that another settlement world is lost. For this reason, the EDF believes the next target will be Newton. It was next in the succession of settlements to be established."

Williamson then went through the details of the latest

assessment of Kurofune capabilities (mostly unknown) and their logic for believing that Newton would be next target (simplistic). Williamson finally opened the discussion for input from those attending. Price was more eager than ever to share his theory.

"Colonel Williamson, I have an idea, and I hope we can quickly get someone with access to more data than me to figure out if it makes sense. The *Mumbai* was not the first ship to vanish. It was the first ship *known* to have vanished in a Hawking Drive jump. According to my research, there are at least three other ships known to have vanished without a trace: *Betwa*, the *Atlantis*, and the *Drakensberg*. They each hailed from a different country, and each departed Earth with colonists on a one-way trip to settle a new world. Unfortunately, they each vanished without a trace. They disappeared so long ago that there is no corroborating evidence that they vanished during a Hawking transition. We just know they left Earth for specific destinations and that as far as we can tell, they either never arrived where they said they were going, or they went somewhere else. They could have had a similar malfunction as the *Mumbai*. I say this because though the ships flew flags of three different countries, they were each manufactured by Goa Shipyard Limited. *Mumbai* was manufactured by Goa Shipyard Limited. It is plausible that whatever caused *Mumbai* to disappear or be destroyed is related to the fate of these three ships," Price said.

"There have been hundreds of ships manufactured over the years by Goa, and they have not disappeared," said someone sitting at near the far end of the virtual table; Price couldn't tell who it was.

"Of that I have no doubt. I am not saying Goa is responsible nor am I saying that every ship they manufactured did or will vanish. What I'm saying is that there is a possible connection that needs to be investigated," said Price.

"Thank you, Captain Price, please send me your research data and I will forward it on to the EDF immediately for further analysis. If there is a connection, then I suspect it might be some sort of flaw inherent to their design. If that is the case, then we need to identify and fix it as soon as possible. The Kurofune are costing us enough ships already, we don't need to let any more accidents cause us to lose another one," said Williamson.

Price was ready to provide the data and had already drafted a data package for the colonel that he immediately sent. In the meantime, one of the other captains had brought up a counterargument to the idea of Newton being the next target. Price knew he should listen, but his mind was racing. He activated his avatar, who remained seated at the virtual conference table while he stood up and began pacing around the conference room. He couldn't pace in the *Indefatigable*'s CIC while it was being rebuilt, so he instead began pacing back and forth in the small conference room near his lunar quarters. *The* Mumbai *and three other ships vanish, and all were manufactured by the same company, though many years apart. The* Alligator *found an abandoned settlement ship and what looks like a settlement that died hundreds of years ago, long before the ship and the colonists departed Earth. Was there a connection?* Nelson was on the ship, and he did not have easy access into the data network to find out the answer to his next question on his own. He did not want to ask it in an open forum but as soon as the meeting ended, he was going to go back to his apartment and do some research.

Price tuned back into the meeting as it was being adjourned. He didn't bother sitting down and rejoining in person. He was content letting his avatar be his face around the table and suspected he was not alone in doing so.

Fifteen minutes later, Price was in his apartment and looking up everything he could find about the *Santinka*. As he went through the files, he found was he was looking for.

The *Santinka* was manufactured by Goa Shipyard Limited.

Price's suspicions were confirmed, but he didn't know what it meant. The *Santinka* did not vanish nor was it destroyed. They found the ship, and it was in one piece after making the journey it was designed to make. Whatever had happened there must be unrelated to the missing ships—unless it wasn't. He suspected the latter but had no idea how to make the connection.

He composed an addendum to his previous report, attached what he'd learned about the *Santinka* and sent it to Colonel Williamson. *Maybe he and the EDF could make the connection.*

CHAPTER 21

The images from space were spectacular. As the thirteen orbiting ships passed from eclipse into the light of a new day, the sunlight reflected from their polished hulls making for spectacular viewing on the live video feed from the space dock where there they had all been assembled and outfitted these last few years. Ranging in size from 180 meters to 250 meters, each ship had a complement of about three hundred men and women who had been training in their operation for the last two years. Only the *Saṃsāra* remained, still tethered to the space dock. The Oracle was quite insistent that it remain for a purpose that would be revealed after the other ships departed.

The queen was able to see the closest of the ships through the large viewport on the space dock and the remainder from the video feed projected to the screen on the right. She was surrounded by her entourage, including Secretary of War Burman, High Priest Delal, and Vice Admiral Dewan. Today was the day that they would send their children, friends, aunts, and uncles to fight in a war foretold by Prophecy hundreds of years ago, fulfilling the single-minded purpose to which the entire planetary civilization had been established.

Though she was excited and ready for the day in terms of fulfilling Prophecy and sending the ships outward into deep space, she was also filled with dread. Today was the day when the Prophecy was to be fulfilled and the Oracle had nothing additional to replace it. After today, the future would be out of their hands and into God's. She did not know if the thirteen ships departing today would be enough to turn the tide of the war and save billions of lives. (A number that she had extreme difficulty imagining—*how can any planet contain a billion people, let alone billions?*)

There was also the lingering doubt that they would send their ships outward and find that it all been a lie. That there was no desperate war being fought with billions of lives to be saved. That perhaps there had been a war and they arrived too late and alerted the enemy of their existence, ultimately resulting in the destruction of her world and the people in it. *The future beyond today is not yet known,* said the Oracle just this morning as she met with it one more time before the events of the day began.

She knew what she had to do this morning, now, but not this evening or tomorrow. For a time, the people would be watching and waiting for word from kinsmen sent out to fight in a war they knew must be fought, but that would end. Either the war would be won or lost, and the people had to then figure out what to do after the outcome was known. Thinking about the future was for later. For now, she had a job to do.

"The fulfillment of Prophecy is at hand. The brave men and women of Swarga aboard the ships of the fleet are soon to begin their journey to the outer edge of the star system. The trip will take about five days. Once there, they will engage their star drives to take them to where Prophecy says the battle will take place. The battle that will decide the fate of our species and that of our distant kinsmen among the stars. The outcome of the battle has not been foretold but knowing the skill of our brave military and the leadership of Admiral Sinha, I have no doubt that victory will be ours. I pray that the gods watch over the fleet and bring us victory!" she said, knowing that every one of her subjects was likely watching this moment. She knew that what she said now would be in future history books and she wanted to make sure it would be something appropriate to the moment.

After finishing her speech, she nodded to Burman who then gave the orders for the ships to depart orbit. Simultaneously, the blue glow of the individual ships' fusion drives brightened as the fleet moved as one to accelerate out of orbit and begin their journey.

"Mr. Secretary, can you confirm the Oracle has provided their destination data and the drive codes?" asked the queen. As much of the Prophecy as had been foretold, the destination of the fleet was not among the details revealed to the queen or anyone else. Nor had the unlock codes for the space drives that would allow the ships to depart the star system and reach that destination in the blink of an eye. She could understand, see, and feel the reality of the fusion drives but not the jump drive. Having a black box that with the use of a secret code would instantaneously move a spaceship weighing millions of kilograms from one location to another seemed like magic and something too good to be real. The Oracle kept both bits of information secret, even from her. Burman and the leaders of the military were quite upset that they could not test this aspect of the ships' capabilities like they could, and did, the fusion drive and armaments. To them, using it for the first time in battle was a risk they did not want to take. But the Oracle was insistent, claiming that to allow the system to be used too early would jeopardize the "reality" of the universe. Though she alone understood the reasoning behind the secrecy, she was not sure she believed it. Surely the claim that premature use of the jump drives would endanger reality was hyperbole. *Surely.*

"Yes, Your Majesty. The Oracle uploaded both to the flight computers of the ships as they left orbit. The flight computers on all ships report receiving the data and that their jump drives are now fully operational."

The queen was relieved. All was going according to plan.

"Vice Admiral, what is next on the agenda?" asked the queen. She normally would not have to ask, but the order of events for the day had been arranged and rearranged so many times that she could not easily keep up.

"There will be a ministerial meeting in twenty minutes, followed by lunch, and then we will return to the city for your evening meeting with the Oracle."

She had not forgotten her evening meeting with the Oracle. All she knew was that there was another important detail to be attended to and that she would not know what it was until then. She decided to put her musings about the evening meeting out of her mind and concentrate on the matters demanding her immediate attention. After all, it was her job to be the queen.

The images from space were impressive. In a conference room aboard the lunar space dock, Price watched the departure of the EDF Combined Fleet with mixed emotions. Not all the fourteen ships making up the fleet were visible in a single image, but the few that were visible to the lunar telescopes were captured in such a way as to make them look both sleek and formidable. On one hand, Price wished he and the *Indefatigable* could join them and increase their odds of winning any battle by adding the firepower of one more ship. On the other hand, he knew that any battle was likely to be one of simple attrition. Since they had no way of knowing how many ships the enemy had, adding his ship might or might not make much of a difference.

The last of the ships would reach the rendezvous point near the Oppenheimer Limit in five days and then they would all transit to Newton together.

Despite crews working twenty-four hours a day, seven days a week, the *Indefatigable* was still more than two weeks away from being spaceworthy. Until then, the ten EDF ships kept in the solar system were all that stood between Earth's billions and the Kurofune. The debate over how many ships to keep in reserve at Earth had been heated. Some argued that overwhelming force was needed to meet the Kurofune at Newton. Others were certain that Newton was a trick or a ruse and that they should keep the entire fleet at Earth to defend against a surprise attack. The decision was made to split the fleet, leaving neither side satisfied with the amount of firepower being brought to bear and risking defeat by not meeting the enemy at any location with enough weapons to win an engagement. King Solomon would not have been pleased.

In the meantime, he and his new bridge crew were due for training in the VR simulator at ten hundred hours. His new XO, Lieutenant Commander Connor Orphee, seemed capable enough. She had served in the Commonwealth Navy under Captain Martin and came with the highest possible recommendations. She had requested a transfer to the *Indefatigable*, allegedly because she wanted to serve with Price. The new tactical officer, Lieutenant Julian Whitehead, was straight out of the Royal Space Navy College at Dartmouth on his first assignment. Price was initially nervous having someone so green in such an important position, but after training with Whitehead these last several days, his nervousness had abated. The rest of the bridge crew were also new, to him anyway, each with various backgrounds and years of service. His goal was to mold them into a team and the daily, full-shift VR simulations were his primary tool to make that happen. So far, so good.

It wasn't until he was back in his quiet, empty cabin for rest that his thoughts turned back to Anika. Each night he thought of their final moments together, the good times and the bad. He would then inevitably run through the events at Kunlun and wonder what could have been done to alter the outcome so that she and her ship wouldn't vanish during the transit home. So far, there had been no news from the team investigating the design of the Hawking Drive used by Goa Shipyards. *There had to be a connection. Someone had to be at fault.* Price could not— would not—accept blind chance when there was so much circumstantial evidence to the contrary. He had not cried in two days, but this day, the day the fleet departed Earth, he wept until sleep finally came.

CHAPTER 22

Anika's first thought was: *Why is it so dark in here?* Her second came quickly thereafter: *I'm alive!*

The pain in her right side was considerable, and she knew that if she survived, walking would be a bitch. She had broken ribs before, and the pain she felt with every breath now reminded her of what it felt like the last time. This was different. This time she was on the bridge of the *Mumbai*, not lying at the foot of a cliff wondering how she could have been so stupid as to lose her footing on what was supposed to be a simple weekend escape in the woods. This time she was surrounded by a crew of people who depended upon her to lead them, not alone facing a good six-hour hike back to civilization for medical help. This time she had to get out of the blackness and back to the business at hand—saving her ship and crew from the ships that were attacking Kunlun.

Raising her left hand to her eyes, she carefully scraped away the warm, wet blood that covered her face and had essentially glued her eyes shut. Once her eyes were open, she let her hand roam upward to her scalp where she immediately felt the source of the blood—she had a painful gash running along the top of her head. *Head wounds bleed a lot, even shallow ones*, she thought as she rose to her feet and looked around the bridge of her ship. In her mind, she had wasted several tens of seconds crawling out of oblivion and to her senses. In reality, only a few seconds had passed.

Surprisingly, the bridge was fully lit and most of the ship's displays looked like they were active. Just before everything went black, they had initiated a Hawking Drive jump. *What happened?*

"Tactical! I need a status," Anika said, her voice cracking midway through as she coughed some blood from her mouth—and part of a tooth. *I'll deal with that later too*, she thought, ignoring as best she could both the pain in her side and the new shooting pain in her lower right jaw.

"Outboard cameras are currently down, even the star trackers, but the radar shows the area is clear of enemy ships," replied Lieutenant Patel, from his duty station to Anika's right. He turned to face her, grimacing with what had to be pain as he did so. "Correction, clear of *any* ships. We're alone."

Alone? What did that mean? thought Anika. A few moments ago, the *Mumbai* was part of a fleet of Earth ships that had engaged more than a dozen alien ships and lost. Then they were given the order to retreat—to engage the jump drive and regroup in the solar system.

"Lieutenant Patel, keep the radar active and let me know if you detect anything new. And get those cameras up and running, especially the telescopes. I like visuals, and right now I feel like we're flying blind," Anika said, scanning again to see who was at their duty stations and who was not.

"Lieutenant Chatterjee, give me a rundown of the ship's systems," asked Anika, as she wiped away yet another warm trickle of blood flowing down her face. The blood was flowing *down*, so the artificial gravity system was still operational. *Good*, she thought.

Chatterjee, without hesitation, unbuckled herself from her chair at the fire-control duty station and stood over the collapsed form of Lieutenant Nayak, moving his body slightly so she could access the engineering-status control panel. Nayak was one of the bodies Anika had observed earlier being bent in an unnatural angle. He hadn't stirred, and Anika was fairly certain he never would again. To her credit, Chatterjee seemingly ignored her now-dead colleague and did her job. With her hands moving uncannily fast, she began her reporting.

"Life support is fully functional. The Hawking Drive is down. I'm not getting anything from the drive's health and status systems. The fusion drive is undamaged and at ninety-two percent. Fore and aft missile tubes are loaded and responsive. Pulsar navigation and laser comm systems are down. Mitra is in standby mode," Chatterjee reported, looking up at Anika for acknowledgement or further direction.

"Thank you, Lieutenant. What about medical? How many casualties?"

"No word from medical, ma'am," Chatterjee replied.

As Chatterjee was speaking, the bridge hatch sounded

its telltale three-note ring indicating that the pressure between the deck and the corridor beyond were equal and that it was about to be opened. If there had been a pressure difference, the notes would have been replaced by a discordant tone and it would be prevented from opening without a command override.

The hatch opened, admitting Dr. Pillai and two medics, each with their emergency first-aid kits. They quickly fanned out across the room, going first to the members of the crew that were obviously the most injured.

"I'm glad you are here and in one piece," said Anika as Pillai moved past her to the unmoving form of Lieutenant Nayak.

"Just under twenty casualties, so far, and two deaths," Pillai offered without being asked and without messing up his stride as he reached Nayak.

Anika again surveyed the room, noting the condition of her crew as the medics tended to the five that were most seriously injured. All but Nayak were stirring, some groaning, but to Anika, groaning was good. It meant they were alive.

Pillai looked up, caught Anika's eyes, and slowly shook his head.

Nayak hadn't made it.

Resisting the urge to mourn, Anika turned back to Lieutenant Chatterjee. "Get the AI up and running. I need to know what happened to our other ships and why they aren't here for the rendezvous. We weren't the first to jump, and I doubt the remaining ships were all destroyed before they could bug out. We shouldn't be alone."

"Yes, ma'am," replied Chatterjee, taking Lieutenant Nayak's seat as the medics finished removing his body from the chair. Seemingly unfazed by the blood on the seat and the harness, Chatterjee buckled herself in and wiped her hands clean on her pants.

"Ouch! Dammit, Pillai, what are you doing?" barked Anika as she felt the pain from the doctor's disinfectant wipe touching her still-bleeding forehead. While she was doing her job, the doctor was doing his. In this case, taking care of her.

"Sorry I startled you, Captain, but you look like you could use a little cleaning up and a visit to medical. That's a nasty cut on your head, but it doesn't look deep. After sterilizing it, I'll spray some sealant on it to stop the bleeding. Are you hurt anywhere else?" Dr. Pillai asked.

"Yes, my ribs. I think they're bruised," she replied as she motioned to her right side.

"Well, when you can, you know where to find me," he replied.

"I'll do that as soon as I make sure this ship is safe. Thank you, Doctor. I know you have others to tend to, but I would appreciate a full report on the crew's suitability for duty as soon as you can."

"I'll have it to you before seventeen hundred," said Pillai.

"Two hours is soon enough, thanks," she said.

"Lieutenant Patel, what about the visuals? Are all the cameras and telescopes still down?" Anika asked.

"Yes, ma'am, but the techs are working on it. When whatever happened, well, happened, it overloaded all the photonics sensors. The physical camera and telescopes appear to be undamaged, but the photonic arrays had to be powered down and restarted. That should take care of the problem in about . . . four more minutes."

"Good. Bring up the images on the forward display as soon as they are available," Anika said. She really wanted to see the comforting view of the solar system with its recognizable constellations and familiar star glowing at its center. The *Mumbai*'s optical sensors were tunable to the IR, automatically shifting the variations in temperature to colors the human eye could readily discern. While it would not be a true image of their surroundings, it would be true enough.

Anika didn't sit idly waiting. Ignoring the pain in her right side as best she could, she used her left hand to get her heads-up display from within the compartment in the arm of her chair. It wasn't there. She looked around the mess that was the floor of the bridge, still filled with debris and more than a little blood, until she saw it. She immediately knew where the gash on her head originated. The display was a mangled mess with what looked like skin and hair embedded in its frame—most likely hers. She would have to get another one.

"Visuals coming up now," said Lieutenant Patel.

The six forward screens came to life all at once, each showing a different view of the space surrounding the *Mumbai*. Four of the six were no surprise—they showed only the darkness of space with stars as distant points of light in the background. One was a telescopic view of a nearby planet, nearby being a relative term. According to the data feed below the image, the planet was about eight light-minutes away and appeared to be a rocky, terrestrial planet with obvious clouds and what looked like oceans. What came up on the sixth screen totally surprised Anika and everyone on the bridge. Instead of their familiar Sol, there was a bright, orange-white star that was obviously not the sun.

"Lieutenant Patel, where the hell are we?" asked Anika with what she hoped was a steady and unpanicked voice. Inside, she was anything but calm and reserved.

"Unknown, ma'am. The pulsar navigation system just came up and is crunching numbers," replied Lieutenant Patel.

The *Mumbai's* pulsar navigation system looked for the telltale X-ray emissions of pulsars, or the rapidly spinning, ultradense leftovers of exploded stars. Each known pulsar in the galaxy had its own characteristic X-ray emission pattern, some sending forth a burst of X-rays every few thousands of a second, each forming its own unique fingerprint. By finding the location of these known pulsars in the sky, the *Mumbai* could readily determine where they were in relation to them and to Earth. Pulsars formed nature's own version of Earth's early Global Positioning System.

Something had gone horribly wrong when they made their jump, taking them somewhere other than the designated rendezvous point. Making matters worse, the *Mumbai's* jump drive was down. Without it, they would be here, wherever here was, for a while until they could make repairs. Anika said a silent prayer for the rest of the Earth fleet and thought briefly about Winslow Price. He was out there—somewhere—and she was here— *somewhere else*. Her next priority had to be getting the ship fully functional and back to help defend Earth—and Winslow.

"Captain, the AI is back online," said Lieutenant Chatterjee.

"That's certainly good news. Mitra, are your systems fully reintegrated? Are there any issues we need to address to get you back to one hundred percent?" Anika asked, turning her head slightly upward as was her custom when addressing the seemingly everywhere AI.

"Captain, it is good to again hear your voice. Being powered down was . . . disconcerting. Most of my systems are fully functional, though it may take me some time to process all that has happened," replied the steady, soft-spoken synthetic voice of the *Mumbai's* resident artificial intelligence.

Anika had at first found the voice of the AI, whose name meant "friend," to be annoying. *How could any real person be so soft spoken and calm all the time?* But now she very much appreciated the AI for who it (he?) was and considered its steady, unflappable tone to be its unique personality and very comforting.

"Do you have any insight into what happened and how we got here?" asked Anika, stuttering a bit on the last word as she experienced another sharp pain in her side. A reminder that she soon needed to have the doctor examine her. She hoped all that was needed was a painkiller and some tape.

"Based on the available data, we executed a standard Hawking Drive jump and then the power system overloaded in many places, causing extreme damage throughout the ship."

"Lieutenant Patel informed me that the pulsar navigation system is back online. Do you know where we are? We're obviously not . . . " Anika stopped, wincing again from the pain in her side.

"Captain, the ship appears to be in no immediate danger. I strongly urge you to have your injuries examined by the ship's medical officer," said Mitra calmly—as usual.

"Mitra, that certainly sounds like what I need to do," said Anika, unbuckling her harness and rising from the command chair. "XO, the bridge is yours. When I come back, I want to know where we are and how we get back to the rest of the fleet." Anika made her way, slowly, toward the exit.

Chatterjee looked down at the blood on her uniform, hesitated, and then buckled herself into the command chair.

CHAPTER 23

Anika bolted awake with a start. *How much time has passed? What's happened? Where is Winslow?* She then heard her wake-up alarm sounding and began to remember. *That was the fastest damn ninety-minute nap I can remember,* she thought as she looked around her quarters and saw the signs of how fast she'd shed her bloodied uniform, showered, and crawled into bed: the door to the head was propped open by the dirty uniform, the towel lay on the floor near her bunk, and her toothbrush was somehow sticking out of her shoe.

She pulled herself upright and was quickly reminded of the pain in her ribs. Looking down, she saw the right side of her body wrapped in good old-fashioned gauze. Instinctively, she touched her scalp and could feel the numbing presence of the synthetic skin Pillai had sprayed on her head, sealing the gash and disinfecting it. Before doing so, he had to shave off a thin trail of hair along either side of the wound, leaving her with what she could only call an inverted mohawk. *Not my best look,* she thought.

"Mitra, what's our status?" she asked.

In the air between her bunk and the rest of her cabin, the AI projected a 3-D image of a stellar system with seven planets—each moving along a wispy line that represented their orbits around the star. Several small objects in highly elliptical orbits also appeared, which Anika knew were large asteroids or comets. Also appearing along its own orbital pathway was a small representation of the *Mumbai*. No other ships were shown, to which she sighed in nearly silent relief.

"Captain, the ship is mostly operational, except for the Hawking Drive. It was severely overloaded during the jump, and many of the internal circuits are completely burned out. Unfortunately, many of the critical circuits may not be immediately replaceable using the *Mumbai*'s 3-D printers with our current printer feedstock. Unless we can gain access to the proper raw materials, they can only be replaced with spares—which we do not have. We suffered twenty-six casualties, including yourself, and two deaths. Twenty-five of those injured have been treated and will be fit for duty after a proscribed rest break. One suffered a broken leg and is still in the infirmary," said the disembodied voice of Mitra.

"Mitra, please show yourself. I'd rather talk *with* someone than *to* the ship," said Anika.

Beside the projection, a fifty-something, fit, and very real-looking man appeared. His dark complexion and black hair was customized to her liking, even though the program had been supplied to the Indian Space Navy by the United Kingdom and had originally been very, very British—complete with an Oxford accent. She knew that simply wouldn't do for her ship and her crew and marveled at how the British were still so ignorant of how their past colonialism shaped Indian culture, even though they were now staunch allies.

"Good to see you, Captain," said Mitra, bowing ever so slightly. No salute from the AI. Him saluting had bothered her and was one of the next protocols she asked him to change.

"Thank you. I assume we're still alone here?"

"Yes, ma'am. There are no other ships that I can detect."

"What about the planets in the system? Any signs of life?"

"Yes. The one nearby is a terrestrial planet, 1.1 Earth radii, oxygen and nitrogen atmosphere, temperate due to being in the star's habitable zone, and likely covered with indigenous life due to the ratio of oxygen in the atmosphere. We are too far away to know much more except for the fact that on the planet's nightside there are no artificial lights, and I have detected no artificial electromagnetic emissions," said Mitra.

"Show me a picture," said Anika.

A round, blue, green, and brown marble with white puffy clouds appeared in the wispy display next to her bed. At first glance, she though it was a mildly distorted view of Earth—an Earth where someone had altered the image to show different landmasses than those that were familiar to nearly every human. It was beautiful, even though it wasn't their home.

"We need to get closer and see what's there as we figure out how to get the ship repaired. We must rejoin the fleet as soon as possible," she said.

To that, Mitra had no reply, which was odd. He usually picked up on nonexplicit conversation, so much so that she sometimes forgot he was an AI.

"Mitra, has your assessment of the Hawking Drive changed? Can we repair it?"

"No." Mitra's answer was simple and to the point.

"Shit. That's not what I wanted to hear," she said, glancing again at the planet appearing to hover over the floor of her cabin as she activated her embedded comm link.

"XO, take us to the planet and put us in a geosynchronous orbit. I don't want to go any lower until we know more about the place. If there are any advanced natives there, I don't want to alarm them by getting too close."

"Yes, ma'am," replied Lieutenant Chatterjee. "Will you be resuming command soon, ma'am?"

"Yes. I'll be there in about fifteen minutes. You can then take a well-deserved break to rest and, if my foggy memory serves me well, get cleaned up," said Anika.

"Yes, ma'am. Thank you," said Chatterjee with an audible sound of relief.

Anika turned her attention back to Mitra, glancing again at the planet before doing so.

"Mitra, where are we?"

"We're in an inauspicious star system approximately 324 light-years from Sol. The star is type G2-V, similar to Sol in age, composition, and brightness."

"Did you say 324 light-years? The jump drive was set for far less than that. We didn't have nearly the power in the supercapacitor banks for a jump of that magnitude," said Anika, with a slight edge in her tone—a mixture of fear and surprise.

"I have no ready explanation for how this was possible," said Mitra.

"Meet me on the bridge," she said as she went to her wardrobe and selected a clean uniform to wear, slipping out of her nightclothes as she did so, covering herself as she walked. She knew Mitra saw and heard everything aboard ship regardless of whether or not his avatar was present. Her prudish roots were difficult to shake.

Without a word or acknowledgement, Mitra disappeared, taking the image of the world they were approaching with him.

Anika sighed as she began dressing.

Anika entered the bridge and immediately noticed that the cleaning crew had been there, removing the fallen debris and all traces of the blood spilled by her shipmates during the battle. It didn't quite look new, but it certainly looked better than it did before. Chatterjee was in the command chair, sitting on a protective seat cover. She knew why—Lieutenant Chatterjee didn't want any of the now-dry blood on her uniform to stain the newly cleaned command chair.

Lieutenant Chatterjee arose, picked up the seat cover, and moved to the left of the command chair while never losing her formal, erect posture, and allowed Anika to sit.

"Sarah, go get some rest," said Anika to Chatterjee.

"Yes, ma'am," said Chatterjee.

"Mitra," said Anika.

Mitra's form appeared at his assigned location in the bridge—just to her right—and said, "Yes, ma'am?"

"We'll be in orbit around the planet in about twenty-three hours. I'd like you to keep me informed of what we learn about the planet as we get closer. Keep surveying to make sure we're alone but put all the other instruments toward understanding the planet. I need to know if it's habitable."

"I'm already on it. I should have a complete report before we enter orbit," he replied.

Anika surveyed condition of her crew. Of those present, only she had been on the bridge during the battle and that was a good thing. The others all needed rest. She would get more herself . . . later.

Twenty hours later, she, Chatterjee, Patel, and the rest of the primary command crew were back on station and preparing to enter orbit around what might very well be their new home for quite a while. She hadn't informed anyone of that concern except for her XO, and Chatterjee accepted it without even flinching. She'd probably already deduced the same after looking at where they were, and weren't, and the state of the jump drive. They were just damn lucky they landed in a star system with a potentially habitable planet. If they were in some other stellar system or, worse still, in deep space between stars they would have faced a very grim future with only their fusion drive to get from place to place. As big a breakthrough as it had been for exploring and settling the solar system, it was wholly inadequate for interstellar travel.

"Captain, if I may?" asked Mitra, not yet projecting his avatar in the room.

"Absolutely, what have you got?" she asked as Mitra's avatar appeared. This time he "wore" the same clothes as last, but made them a bit wrinkled, his hair a bit tussled, and his expression one of a man who hadn't slept in a while. Of course, the AI didn't need sleep. This was part of his approach to making them accept him as a fallible human being who'd been working hard and deserved a sympathetic listen. It worked.

"The good news is the planet appears to be hospitable to Earth life. The bad news is the planet appears hospitable to Earth life," said Mitra.

"Mitra, when you try to be dramatic, it annoys the hell out me," admonished Anika.

"My apologies, Captain. I was being deliberate in conveying the results of my assessment, and I can see how the manner in which I delivered the news could be construed to be dramatic. I will make a note of that," the AI replied in a contrite tone.

"Continue. And explain what that means," she said.

"It means that everything about the physical environment should be familiar, if not downright comfortable, to humans and the biodiversity we have aboard ship. The planet's atmosphere is similar in composition to Earth's, with perhaps a little more carbon dioxide than preindustrial Earth. But that's a good thing since the planet lies slightly farther away from the star and Earth, closer to the end of the Goldilocks Zone. Were it not for the extra carbon dioxide in the atmosphere, the planet would be quite cold overall—similar to Greenland.

"There is a slight axial tilt, meaning that the seasons are mildly different. The iron core of the planet creates a magnetic field like Earth's, also providing a protective shield against the solar wind and stellar coronal-mass ejections. There is even a comparable ozone layer to filter much of the ultraviolet radiation from the star." Mitra paused.

"But?" asked Anika.

"I'll need physical samples to determine if the indigenous life is DNA based and whether or not it is biocompatible with Earth life. If so, then there may be sources of locally grown food that the crew can consume and, even with our limited stores, the crew could begin to grow Earth crops," said Mitra.

Anika heard an audible gasp from one of the bridge crew, she couldn't tell just who, but she knew why. Mitra talking about growing food meant they would be there for a long time and someone else was just realizing that. She would have to get ahead of the news and break it to the crew in a positive way or risk losing credibility.

"Mitra, that's still good news. What's the *bad* news?" Anika asked.

"If the life is DNA based, or even DNA compatible, then there will undoubtedly be pathogens to which we have no immunity or environmental allergens that could produce anaphylactic shock. And there might be predators. This won't be a paradise. Nature's laws will be evident here as they have been on every habitable planet humanity has encountered so far. Every form of life is food for some other form—and since we will remain here for a while, the crew must be mindful of that," Mitra answered.

"Mitra, I agree that these cautions and caveats are needed, but they aren't that different from what we found at the other settlement worlds. The only thing I'm getting from you is a reaffirmation that we might be here a while until someone finds us, and you are preparing us, me specifically, for that fact," she said.

"Captain, no one from the fleet will be able to find us," Mitra stated without a trace of emotion.

"I realize we are much further away than we'd planned, but even the *Mumbai* could get this far if it made the trip in a series of jumps. Granted, they need to know where we are. Could one of your cousins aboard another ship figure out what happened if they re-created the sequence of events that led to us being here? Surely at least one of the other ships recorded what happened," Anika said.

"The distance we jumped was far more than any known ship has ever accomplished. Though we appear to have jumped in the correct direction relative to the location of the rendezvous point and our departure location, the volume of space they would have to search is enormous. It was serendipitous that we landed in a system containing a habitable planet. The spacetime warp created by the Hawking Drive favors beginning and ending jumps near, but not too close, to the gravity wells of stars. This made it unlikely we would end up in deep interstellar space, but we could have very easily ended up in a stellar system containing no habitable planets," Mitra said.

"And we are so far away that no one will detect a distress call from us for centuries. Without the Hawking Drive, we're limited to good old-fashioned speed-of-light messaging. A distance of 324 light-years means any message we send now would take 324 years to reach its destination," she mused aloud.

"And even if we were to send such a message, there would be no Earth ship there to hear it," Mitra said.

"What? Surely the entire fleet wasn't destroyed. Do you have data from the battle that you haven't shared with me?" Anika asked with a cold, chilling sense of dread creeping upon her already-nervous stomach.

"I've been reviewing the pulsar navigation system data and found some anomalies that led me to that conclusion," said Mitra. He again seemed to be leaning toward the dramatic.

"And?"

"Do you recall the details of the way the PNS works?" asked Mitra.

"Yes, every officer in the fleet has been trained in how to use and interpret PNS data," Anika replied.

"Then, as you know, pulsars are rapidly rotating neutron stars that emit radio pulses at very, very regular intervals. The pulses are actually all we see of a radio beam that is focused by the star's magnetic field and swept around like a lighthouse beacon. Our sensors measure the arrival times of successive pulses to a precision of one hundred nanoseconds over a measurement time of about an hour. Each pulsar has its own characteristic radio signature that, in part, is composed of its pulse rate—each has its own unique radio signature," Mitra said.

"Yes, yes, I remember all that. And since pulsars all over the galaxy are very, very detectable from just about everywhere *in* the galaxy, we can use triangulation to determine where we are," Anika added.

"Correct. And I used just such triangulation to determine our current location once I rebooted. But I also noticed that I had to perform a slight, but very consistent, error correction to each pulsar's signal in the navigation catalog," Mitra said and paused.

"Continue," Anika said.

"There are, as a matter of routine, corrections to the raw data that need to be performed. Things that can affect the measurement of the gap between pulses, for example. These include instrumental effects, our motion through space, and the effects of interstellar plasma along the line of sight between us and the pulsar. Most importantly, the frequency of a pulsar drops slowly with time as rotational energy of the pulsar is radiated away in the radio emission. When I looked at the data, the frequencies of all the pulsars were slightly higher than they should have been—consistently."

"You lost me," Anika said.

"Captain, the frequency of any given pulsar is constant over long periods of time, from a human perspective, but not over centuries. The constant loss of energy slows down the pulsar's rotation, which changes the frequency of the radio emissions. The pulsars from the catalog, each of them, had a consistently higher emission frequency than they should have had. The neutron star had more rotational energy than was in the catalog, and there is only one way that would simply explain the change. We are not merely 324 light-years from *where* we should be. We are also 304 years from *when* we should be. Somehow, we've been transported 304 years into the past."

Anika was stunned. Time travel? Was this even possible? No, more likely there was a glitch in the AI's programming, probably caused by the explosion of the fission bomb. But, to Anika, he seemed otherwise normal.

"Lieutenant Patel, run an independent assessment of the AI's analysis using the raw data and the independent computer network," ordered Anika without hesitation. The independent computer network was a series of computers onboard every spacecraft equipped with an AI that was purposefully separate from the AI network, separated in case there was an AI failure or if an AI had to be taken offline. Like just about every other system on a spacecraft, the ship's computer had to have a fully redundant backup.

"Mitra, no offense, but what you are telling me is simply too fantastic to believe. Time travel? Really? Have you run a self-diagnostic to make sure you weren't damaged in the battle? You did reboot, after all," she said.

"Yes, Captain, I performed the requisite series of self-assessments and all my systems and algorithms are functioning at one hundred percent," said Mitra, with just a tinge of indignation—or so Anika thought.

The bridge was silent, with only the occasional throat clearing, during the five or so minutes it took Lieutenant Patel to finish her analysis.

"Captain, I've looked at the data, and Mitra appears to be correct. The timing is off on all the pulsars on the reference list. Each is off by a different amount, but when you factor in the mass of the neutron star and the energy loss during the emissions, the normalized spin rate increase is consistent with us being approximately three hundred years in the past—it is about the year 1900 back on Earth."

"And the British Empire was ruling India," said Anika, with a just a hint of disgust. She stood fixed, staring at the image of the blue-green planet ahead for a few moments before returning to her seat.

"XO, inform the crew that I will be making an important announcement at eleven hundred. And I want that to include everyone on every shift," Anika said.

"Yes, ma'am."

Now I just have to figure out how to tell the crew that we're not only not going to be able to help defend the Earth when we're needed most, but that they're never going home and stuck three hundred years in the past. She'd certainly had no training for this situation . . .

CHAPTER 24

Only three months, and it seems like an eternity. Which is, for all practical purposes, what awaits us, thought Anika as she looked at the latest reports from ship's medical lab. They had sent several teams to the surface to collect samples of the air, dirt, native plants, and fauna. Each person sent had been in a full environment suit and was thoroughly decontaminated before being allowed back aboard. She was taking no risks that would allow a foreign organism to get on her ship. So far, the results looked promising. There were no immediately obvious pathogens, allergens, or toxins in the air or water samples. Most of the Swarga plant and animal life had DNA strikingly similar to Earth life, which was just as surprising to find here as it had been on most of the other worlds already settled. Someday, the scientists would come up with a satisfying scientific answer for this amazing coincidence. The similarity meant that some of the plants and animals might be edible for humans—and vice versa. The latter is what kept her awake at night. When, not if, the crew went to the planet to begin building their new lives here, some of the rather scary-looking predators they had found might just decide humans are tasty.

Her list of actions was overwhelming. She not only had to make sure she maintained discipline aboard ship, she and her officers had to come up with a plan for establishing a place to live on the surface that was safe and sustainable for the long term. There was going to be no rescue. Those that could rescue them were three hundred years away and in need of rescue themselves. They were in desperate need of her assistance and being isolated from them made her feel helpless as she looked at the various plans developed by her most trusted crew for establishing their future settlement.

They would need to build places to live and find fresh water and ways to purify it. With water and people came the need for sanitation. How would they handle that? They had enough food aboard ship to last for well over an Earth year, or about eighty percent of the planet's year, and in that time they would need to determine which plants and animals they could cultivate for food. But would the food provide the myriad micronutrients and minerals needed by the human body? They would probably have to synthesize any needed nutritional supplements, but how? Her exasperated inner thoughts were interrupted by Mitra.

"Captain, your Settlement Planning Committee meeting begins in five minutes," said Mitra.

"On my way," Anika said as she folded the tablet, tucked it into the pocket of her uniform and walked briskly out of her quarters. *Hopefully today I'll finally start getting some answers*, she thought as she departed.

The hallways were, as usual of late, filled with crew members chatting eagerly about what was to come. Along her short walk she heard words like "exciting," "new beginning," "family," "children," and "fun," with only a few "scary," "dangerous," or "nervous." All in all, it was a sign that the crew remained mostly optimistic about the future. This was good.

The CIC was filled with the members of the committee pulling together recommendations for her on how to establish a place for them to live once they left the ship. Her XO chaired the committee, which was comprised of crew members with backgrounds in engineering, hard science, social science, agriculture, medicine, and more. Like most crew in the Indian Space Navy, her ranks were filled with people from all walks of civilian life, united by their enlistment and dedication to the navy.

Anika walked to the head of the table while everyone snapped to attention and immediately stopped talking. She briefly scanned their faces, making sure to catch any that looked anxious so that she could make sure she addressed their individual concerns. The crew was fiercely loyal to her—as she was to them. Morale was high.

After Anika sat, members of the Committee took their assigned seats and most made sure they had their tablets unfolded, in front of them, and ready to report.

"XO, what have you got?" asked Anika, looking at Lieutenant Chatterjee expectantly.

"The environments group hasn't found anything that will kill us or make us sick from simply breathing the air. The helium and oxygen to nitrogen ratio is slightly higher than on Earth, so we'll have to be careful when it comes to making things that are prone to oxidize and extra precautions will be needed regarding fire safety, but it all seems manageable," Chatterjee said.

She continued, "The fresh water is full of minerals with slightly different concentrations, just like back on Earth. Also like on Earth, the water is home for a plethora of amoeba and other microscopic life forms. It's impossible to know, yet, which of these might be harmful to us so we are going to recommend the establishment of a water treatment facility as soon as possible. The engineers in environments have some filtering ideas that should be buildable using the *Mumbai*'s 3-D printers, and we will be taking some to the surface within the week for field testing."

"As for food," began Dr. Pillai, "Swarga is providing us with a wide variety. We've identified multiple plant species that appear nutritionally useful, but my advice will be to begin slowly and not transition quickly from our stores to the native food. For one thing, we don't yet know what anything will taste like, how to best prepare it, or if it will have unpleasant side effects. Our tests can tell us if the food is toxic, but not whether it will be immediately agreeable with the microbes in our gut. I expect many will experience various gastrointestinal problems as we begin to consume local flora, so we need to be prepared."

"Are you saying we are doomed to have stomach aches and diarrhea?" asked Lieutenant Dixit, a normally quiet crewman from engineering. Anika recalled that his expertise was in maintaining the ship's power systems.

"Well, yes. That's exactly what I'm saying. The food

may be nutritious, but it will be totally foreign to us and the bacteria that call us home. It may take weeks to get used to it, and we need to be ready," replied Pillai.

"That means we will have to send people down incrementally, taking it gradually," said Chatterjee.

Anika was curious about how they would provide power to their new homes. After shelter, food, water, and sanitation, power was the key to just about everything. Dixit's question allowed Anika to shift her focus to his area of expertise.

Lieutenant Dixit was quick to recognize that he would be the next to report. He began, "Initially, we can take down our two backup generators to provide power. They were designed to be used anywhere on the ship should there be a major interruption of power from the *Mumbai*'s primary fusion reactor. They can't provide as much power as the fusion drive, but they should be able to provide enough for our needs well into the next century, or longer, if we can keep them provided with a steady supply of deuterium and tritium. We looked at the environmental group's water analysis and found that there are enough naturally occurring isotopes of both in the water supply to easily meet our needs. We've even worked out a way to separate the deuterium and tritium from the drinking water while it's being filtered for us to drink. Power simply won't be a problem."

Anika visibly relaxed. With abundant power, they could do just about anything.

"Thank you, Lieutenant Dixit. You just made my day," Anika said.

Dixit smiled.

The list of problems and solutions continued, covering topics from sanitation to refrigeration, heating, and establishing a local communications network. Her team was amazing and had answers or workarounds to nearly every problem they anticipated encountering. The ship's 3-D printers could make just about anything they needed for everyday life and the establishment of a self-sustaining base—almost.

"Captain, that brings us to the last major issue of today," said her XO.

"What's that?" she asked.

"Our shipboard supplies will last for a few years without a problem. And our 3D printers can manufacture the replacement parts we will need to repair them when they break down—and they will break, eventually. The sealed systems, like those that host Mitra or are part of the portable fusion generators, should be okay as long as we maintain them in a fairly benign environment. We need to quickly build ourselves the equivalent of a self-sustainable, early-twentieth-century technological society as our baseline. Once we have that, we can sustain it and rebuild to a level where we were when we departed Earth." Chatterjee paused.

"I hear a 'but' in there somewhere," said Anika.

"There's simply too much that goes into building a self-sustaining civilization for our numbers. We haven't even touched on the need for specific chemicals for pharmaceuticals, lubricants, manufacturing, dentistry, or clothing manufacture. There are only 423 of us, and not everyone can become the world's expert in a specific field to create and maintain an infrastructure. Our needs will change as the seasons change and things happen. *And things will happen.*"

The room was silent after Lieutenant Chatterjee completed her report.

"Thank you, XO. I was encouraged until that last bit. You make a good point and one that sounds like you, as a committee, haven't yet found a solution for. Keep looking and I'll see if I can come up with something as well," said Anika.

"Captain, if I may?" asked Dr. Pillai.

Anika nodded her approval.

"The medical staff has been thinking about, well, the inevitable. Everyone in this room needs to look around at the ages of those here. None are over forty years old. And we are the *senior* officers on the ship. We have enough contraceptives aboard ship to last another eighteen months and then, unless time travel has somehow turned off everyone's hormones, we will begin having children. Mind you, I think this is great. There's nothing like new life to boost morale and give people a sense of purpose for the future. But, unless we plan very carefully, that blessing will turn into a curse.

"The first generation of children will be fine until they reach puberty. Then they will inevitably begin to reproduce. Assuming we first-generation colonists are here to guide them, and assuming we keep good records of parentage, we should be able to steer them away from coupling with anyone to whom they are related. It's beginning with the next generation that this becomes more of an issue. As Lieutenant Chatterjee pointed out, there are only 423 of us. There aren't enough of us to provide the genetic diversity we need for long-term survivability. A navy ship designed and crewed to win a war was not meant to be the basis for a new civilization!"

"Dr. Pillai, you are painting a fairly grim future here," Anika said. *What a disaster! This will destroy the morale once the crew realizes this,* she thought. *How am I going to spin this?*

"Captain, I may have a solution," Pillai stated, pulling himself upright and turning slightly to address both her and most of the rest of those in the room.

"This ship is equipped with a state-of-the-art biohazards lab—standard equipment for any navy ship in deep space. Finding new worlds, new life, and new possible pathogens is part of our charter and a significant risk to warfighters and explorers such as ourselves. The ship's biolab is designed to allow us to assess and treat crew that encounter new pathogens. That treatment capability includes the ability to gene edit. Simply put, if we begin planning now, we should be able to interject artificial genetic diversity into the population for several generations, making our functional diversity far larger than the random coupling of 423 of us would ordinarily produce. From modifying genes in vitro to using targeted viruses to subtly alter ova before fertilization, we can assure the genetic diversity we need for generations to come and until the natural diversity that ensues can take over."

"Thank you, Dr. Pillai, for your candor and for your creativeness. Before we discuss any of this with the crew generally, let's make sure we have solutions. Dismissed," she said.

The assembled crew slowly filed out from the room; most engaged in eager discussion with those near them.

"XO, please stay here. We need to talk," said Anika. She wanted to speak with Chatterjee about a topic, the topic about which she was most concerned and that she deliberately had not asked the committee to help solve.

After everyone else had left the room and the hatch closed, Chatterjee returned to the table and her seat next to Anika.

"Mitra, please join us," said Anika.

Mitra's image appeared in the seat on Anika's other side. Instead of his disheveled look, he wore his professional "I'm here to help" persona, which Anika appreciated.

"This conversation, for now anyway, is off the record," began Anika. Both Chatterjee and Mitra nodded in affirmation. "I've been mulling over another decision we will need to make, not immediately, but sooner than we would prefer. Government."

"I was wondering when that topic would come up. This new settlement cannot remain under shipboard discipline and hierarchy forever," said Mitra.

"Here are the options I've been thinking about. I'll lay them out and ask that you consider them, and what I may have missed, for us to discuss next week. Whatever we decide will take some planning, and it is not too soon to begin," Anika said. "One. Nothing changes. We move to Swarga, everyone retains their rank, and we govern much as we do aboard the *Mumbai*. This might be what we do for a while as we get everything up and running planetside, but I doubt it will be relevant for very long.

Much of the crew's rank and roles are based on what they do aboard a navy ship, not in a town as a civilian. We have crew members whose skills before they enlisted will be more valuable on Swarga than their jobs on the *Mumbai*. Plus, once the next generation is upon us, what sense will having an aging captain and XO make? No, clearly maintaining a military structure is only a short-term solution."

When she paused, she noted a muted look of surprise on Chatterjee's face.

"Captain, pardon me, but I don't believe I will be much help in this discussion," Chatterjee said.

"Why not?" asked Anika.

"Because what you just said makes perfect sense and I never thought about it. I was just assuming you would continue to be the captain and I would be your XO—from now until, well, whenever. As your XO, I should have been ahead of you and brought you government options to consider before this meeting was even necessary," she replied.

"Nonsense, Jenya. This is new and unexpected to all of us. I need you as part of this discussion. And I am damned sure it wasn't in the officer training we both took back in Delhi," said Anika.

"Yes, ma'am. I'll stay and advise you as best I can," Chatterjee said, falling back into a more disciplined response.

"Thank you," said Anika. "Closely tied to the status quo is a dictatorship. And, yes, there would be many good reasons to go this way. We can use it to maintain discipline, and we can retain the type of top-down hierarchy we will need to get ourselves established. The crew is used to following orders and this would be an extension of that with our new civilian roles being subject to a civil absolute authority instead of a military one. When the inevitable problems arise, requiring tough decisions, a dictatorship is much more efficient than just about any alternative I've studied in history. But, along with that are all the problems that results from a government where the people can readily say 'at least the trains run on time . . .' and not much else that is positive."

"And then there's the problem with changes in government—who comes after the first dictator?" asked Chatterjee.

"Historically, even benevolent dictatorships don't end well. Typically, there are competing factions, the dictator tries to hang on to power for too long, civil unrest becomes a means of protest, and then there is a violent revolt," added Mitra.

"That's why I don't believe that approach will work either," said Anika, more than a little relieved that neither of her confidants endorsed that approach.

"What about democracy?" asked Chatterjee.

"Ah, yes. The obvious answer—either a parliamentary or presidential democracy would seem to be the way to go. After all, democracy has served Mother India well since 1950. But I don't necessarily believe it will work here, at least not now," Anika said. She paused, knowing what the next question would be.

"Why not?" asked Chatterjee, right on cue.

"Because the response time is too slow, you can bet we will be going from one crisis to another, and decisions will have to be made quickly and without much debate. Input, yes. Debate, no. Democracies are inherently inefficient and slow, which is one of their greatest attributes—in times other than during a crisis. Generally speaking, considering many options, many points of view, many competing interests and talking them through to reach a decision acceptable to most is the right way to govern. But without some sort of highly centralized decision maker that is empowered to act quickly and decisively, regardless of what 'the people' may think, is essential," she said. *And if the political leadership changes like the wind, there is no way we will be able to do what we need to do to help save Earth,* she added to herself.

"You aren't leaving us many options," said Chatterjee.

"I know. That's why you are here. I need ideas, especially from you, Mitra. You've been very quiet," Anika said looking toward the AI.

"I've been perusing the historical database, which is, unfortunately, somewhat limited given our distance from the central archive back on Earth. There are other options, but I'm not ready to share my perception of their pros and cons just yet. I need more time to think," Mitra said.

Anika knew that "time to think" for an AI usually meant milliseconds. Somehow the thought comforted her.

She wished Winslow were here to share his thoughts. Helping him was driving *hers*.

CHAPTER 25

"Captain Price. Wake up. Colonel Williamson wants to meet you in his office as soon as possible." The voice of this cabin's avatar always seemed to annoy Price, perhaps because he only heard it when he was at the shipyards on temporary assignment. He much preferred the sound, and personality, of the avatar in his cabin at Marius Hills. Neither of them were Nelson, but that was okay. He did not expect any groundside or dockside billet to compare with being aboard ship. Plus, it had a Liverpool accent, and that was simply more than a civilized human should have to endure.

"All right. I'm awake," said Price, instantly alert and on the move to get dressed and out the door. Breakfast and a shower could wait. Colonel Williamson would not awaken him this early without a good reason and Price did not want to waste any time to find out what was going on.

Fifteen minutes later he was in the conference room adjoining Williamson's office with other members of the senior staff. Most looked as disheveled as Price felt and that brought him a bit of comfort. Most eagerly grabbed an awaiting cup of tea or shot of espresso from the side table as they entered the room. Williamson's aide was doing his job of caffeinating the officers, and the tea was not half bad.

The staff jumped to attention as the colonel entered the room, grabbing his own tea on the way to the front.

"At ease," Williamson said before taking his first sip and continuing. "At approximately zero three hundred hours this morning, a ship transited into the system at the Oppenheimer Limit seventy-three degrees offset from the Combined Fleet's rendezvous point. The ship is inbound and the IFF code says it is the *Mumbai*."

Price's heart leaped. Mumbai! *Anika. Thank God*, he thought.

"Have they made radio contact?" asked someone from the other side of the room. Price did not recognize the voice and did not turn around to see who was speaking. He was too interested in the colonel's answer as his mind raced with possibilities based on what he had just learned.

"They have not. We detected the IFF code at zero four twenty-seven. Traffic control sent a reply message almost immediately, which means if they received it, then we could have gotten a reply as soon as zero five fifty. It is now zero six twenty and there has not been a response. We decided to not divert any of the ships of the outbound Combined Fleet to intercept the ship, especially since they are on the wrong side of the solar system, so we dispatched the *Idaho* and *Guiyang*. They are on patrol near Mars and in a good position to rendezvous with it as she comes in."

At that moment, Lieutenant Givens, Williamson's aide, who Price recognized from previous meetings, abruptly entered the room and walked briskly to the front where he whispered something in the colonel's ear. The colonel looked a bit surprised at whatever news Givens provided and then nodded.

"Thank you, Lieutenant Givens. It seems that the ship may not be the *Mumbai* after all. The drive signature is similar to *Mumbai's* but distinctly different. The trace elements in the plume don't exactly match that of any EDF ship nor any that we have seen of the Kurofune. Even though it identifies as *Mumbai*, I've been directed to treat it as a potential hostile. The *Idaho* and *Guiyang* have been alerted. It will be another day and a half until they intercept the ship and can give us visuals. Until then, unless they reply to our messages, we have ourselves a mystery," said Williamson.

Great. Just great. The Mumbai *vanishes, then reappears, and now we learn it may not be* Mumbai *at all. Where is Anika? And how did this ship get her IFF code?* Price was on an emotional roller coaster and he did not like it. He also briefly wondered how this might relate to what he learned about the drive system design heritage common to all the other missing ships. Price was so distracted by his thoughts that he did not react when Williamson ended the meeting, and they were dismissed.

"Winslow, have you had a chance to get breakfast?" a familiar female voice asked. It was Brianna Harper, the base psychologist. Price was immediately on guard, and his demeanor change must have been noticeable.

"Don't worry, I'm not asking because I want to assess

your mental well-being. I just thought you looked like you could use some breakfast. If you were like me, you didn't have time to get a bite before the meeting," Harper said.

Price had been to see Harper a few times since he assumed command of the *Indefatigable*, most recently after returning from Kunlun. Losing so many shipmates and friends was not easy on anyone, let alone their commanding officer. Never mind the fact that he did not assume command until *after* the engagement, it was still *his* ship and he felt responsible. He was sure Harper was sincere in her breakfast offer being just camaraderie, but he also knew that "once a psychologist, always a psychologist" was true. He did not think people in that profession could ever turn off their training.

"Sounds great. Thanks for asking," said Price, sincerely grateful to have company and take his mind back to the realities of the many jobs he had to accomplish this day. He needed company and the food.

It was just after eighteen hundred, the workday was nearly done, and Price was immensely grateful. He had spent the last three hours going through various reports on his datapad; some he was routed to approve, others were simply informational. Most were mundane and routine. To remain focused, he was on his fourth cup of tea, contemplating a fifth, when his comm badge chirped.

"Price," he said.

"Captain, please report to Colonel Williamson's conference room immediately," said the voice of Williamson's avatar.

"On my way," said Price as put down his datapad.

The walk to Colonel Williamson's office took only a few minutes. When he arrived, the colonel and Lieutenant Givens were waiting. Both looked as tired as he felt, and Price was sure their day had started even earlier than his, given that Williamson had to have been informed on the pseudo-*Mumbai*'s status well before he began the morning briefing.

"Winslow, I'm glad you got here so quickly. Dear God, you look tired. What I must tell you probably will not help you relax and get rest. The situation with the incoming ship is just getting stranger and stranger, and you are now front and center in the mystery," Williamson said.

"Me? How?"

"Putting aside the whole Major Castillo debacle, the Admiralty is certain that the news I am about to tell you is directly related to your relationship with Captain Ahuja."

Price was suddenly uncomfortable.

"About five hours ago, we received a message from the incoming ship, which announced itself to be the *Saṃsāra*. There is no ship in anyone's registry by that name, by the way. It was a recorded message, and the ship has again gone silent, not responding to our replies. Lieutenant Givens will play the message for you," said Williamson, giving the nod to Givens.

A VR image of Anika appeared on the screen. She was seated in a chair before a light-gray background. Price was elated and anxious at seeing her. She looked well, but somehow different. Older? Tired? Bedraggled? He was not sure, but she looked like she was at the end of a rough day. Then she began to speak.

"This message is for Captain Winslow Price of the HMS *Indefatigable*. I am Captain Anika Ahuja, formerly of the Indian Space Navy ship *Mumbai*. It is imperative that Captain Price meet with those sending this message as quickly as possible. He is to come alone. The war with the Kurofune and the survival of the Earth may depend upon it. To confirm that I am who I say I am, please ask Captain Price if he has had a chance to read the hardcover edition of *Strategy and Tactics of War in Space* that I bought him just before I assumed command of the *Mumbai*. He will know what I am talking about. Thank you," she said as the image faded.

"This message was followed by set of solar system coordinates, requesting that you be brought to *Saṃsāra* at this rendezvous point," said Williamson. As he spoke, Givens projected a top-down view of the solar system with a blue circle highlighted in the space between Mars and Jupiter.

Price was reeling. That was Anika, he was sure of it. She mentioned the book she had left him before departing to make sure he knew it was really her and not some elaborate computer simulation, which was certainly otherwise possible. Most modern entertainment vids were created without real actors, and most home avatars could imitate their owners very convincingly. Seeing was, truly, not necessarily believing.

"Is there anything special about this region of space?" asked Price.

"Actually yes. There is. For ships thrusting at a constant 1.5 gees, the rendezvous location it is roughly equidistant between the Oppenheimer Limit where they emerged and Earth's present location, making it the ideal place for ships traveling from each direction to rendezvous in minimum time. Whoever sent it must have known or surmised that you would be near the Earth. Very strange."

"Preliminary analysis indicates that the speaker was really Captain Ahuja. The voice analysis was a one hundred percent match, and there were none of the telltale irregularities that would indicate her sentences were assembled from other recordings then spliced together," added Givens.

"Oh, I am sure it is her. She gave me that book the day she assumed command of the *Mumbai*. That morning was the last time we were together physically. I doubt that anyone else could have known about the book," said Price. He knew they would be waiting on him to confirm her identity and explain the book reference. He had decided to tell them before they had a chance to ask. *Was she on the ship?*

"I was going to ask you about that," said Williamson.

"What happens now?" asked Price.

"Now, I inform the Admiralty that you have seen the message and can confirm it is Captain Ahuja. They will also want to know the bit about the book. Then we get you on a ship and out to the rendezvous point. Be warned, the Admiralty is not yet sure whether to let you get on the *Saṃsāra*. We only received the message five hours ago, and there really has not been much time to think about it. Fortunately, even if you depart tonight, it will take another two days to get there. By then, the decision will hopefully have been made, and we will have a plan," said Williamson.

"Someone does not want me to go?" asked Price.

"Well, yes. In the meeting I left before calling you, the sentiment was running exceedingly high against letting you go. Some have obvious misgivings, believing it to be some sort of trap. Others, who I might say were not pleased with the charges against you being dropped, saw it as vindication of their views. The most common misgiving is from those who think it might be some sort of ruse to distract us. The timing of the ship's arrival, just after the departure of the fleet bound for Newton, is just too coincidental. Many believe there must be another stealth observation ship in the solar system somewhere that noted the fleet's departure and called in the *Saṃsāra* to do its part in some sort of master attack plan. The bottom line is, the leadership is wary, even scared. They don't want to take any chances," said Williamson.

"What do you think?" asked Price.

"Honestly, I have no idea. But I can tell you that if you believe it to be the real Anika, then I believe it too. You, more than anyone, would be able to tell. And judging by your reaction to seeing her, I doubt that anything short of locking you in a cell would prevent you from trying to reach her," he said.

"Well then, I guess I'd better get going before they ground me," said Price.

"Absolutely. Unfortunately, we don't have any navy ships available to ferry you to the rendezvous, so we are requisitioning a space yacht. Some unlucky tourist was cruising back from a trip to Mars and decided to tour the Apollo 11 historic sites. We just informed her that she would have to find another way back to Earth since we needed her ship. I heard that she was none too happy about the arrangement until she saw the reimbursement offer. Funny how money so often overcomes inconveniences," said Williamson, smiling for the first time. "You will take the yacht and arrive at the rendezvous several hours after the *Idaho* and *Guiyang*. If our visitor is something other than what they say, then they will have to answer to two of our best warships. Your ride should be ready for departure in about two hours."

"Is there anything else?" asked Price. He was anxious to get back to his quarters, pack his bag, and get on whatever ship Williamson had commandeered for his travel. If there were any chance that Anika was on that ship, then he would do whatever he could, take whatever risk, to find out.

"Yes. And it is rather curious. *Saṃsāra* is a Sanskrit word that means 'wandering.' I'm told that it is used by some in India to describe the concept of rebirth and the cycle of life . . ." said Williamson.

Was the name of the ship relevant? Did it matter? Price felt more confused and conflicted than ever before.

CHAPTER 26

"We are two hours out from the rendezvous. *Idaho* and *Guiyang* arrived last night and report that the *Saṃsāra* is just sitting there, radio quiet and passive. It is definitely a warship, with fore and aft missile launchers and what look like standard Indian Navy Gatling guns all along the hull. The HPM array looks just like a state-of-the-art Earth-designed microwave beamer, but with a few subtle design differences. From what I can tell from the data flowing back to Earth, if we did not know this ship originated someplace other than Earth, we would assume it was just some new ship in the Indian Navy," said Orphee, acting captain of the newly commandeered HMSS *Voyager*, formerly known as the private space yacht *Voyager*. Price's XO was eager to be the one ferrying her new captain to the rendezvous and for the chance at being in the middle of a strategic mystery. She was ambitious, but in a good sort of way.

The *Voyager* was clearly not a military ship. Other than the obvious lack of armaments, it provided its occupants with spacious two-room suites, each with its own private loo, a galley with well-stocked libations, a workout room, and a state-of-the-art VR system. Though he was on official duties, Price didn't mind partaking of the libations, but he drew the line at the more sexual of the VR simulations. Not that he was a prude, but the anxiety over the fate of Anika and wondering if he would see her on board the *Saṃsāra* drained any potential interest he might otherwise have had in such entertainment. In other times, Price would have reveled in the luxury of his accommodations, but for this trip, it was just a means to an end.

"Thanks for the update, Connor," said Price as he looked at the image now visible using the onboard telescope system. It was not military grade but was still rather good. He could clearly see the three military ships facing off against each other as they closed the remaining distance.

"Patch me through to the captain of the *Idaho* on secure laser comm," said Price. Captain Rodrigues of the *Idaho* had been given operational command for the rendezvous, and Price needed to confer with him regarding next steps. They had never met in person.

"Ah, Captain Price, I thought you would be calling. I'm glad you are here," said Rodrigues. He had what appeared to be a genuine smile on his round face. He looked like one of those people who were more at ease smiling than frowning—unlike most captains in the Space Navy.

"Captain Rodrigues, I am awaiting your orders. Do I initiate contact?" asked Price.

"Absolutely. Since they summoned you by name, we should let them know you are here and ready to meet. We have seen no sign of hostility from our visitors and based on what we can see of their armaments, should something untoward arise, the *Idaho* and *Guiyang* will be able to take care of themselves. I'm not so sure about your ship, however."

"It looks like their ship has a standard docking port aft that we should be able to use. If they grant us permission, Lieutenant Commander Orphee, excuse me, Captain Orphee can take us over. Once I am on board, the *Voyager* will quickly back off and out of harm's way. Until then, well, we will have to assume that they did not come all this way just to kill me," replied Price.

"I agree. Please make contact and find out what the next steps might be. I hope they reply to you. They have been extremely stubborn in their refusal to engage in any sort of discussion or negotiation," said Rodrigues.

"Yes, sir. Is there anything else?"

"No. Good luck," said Rodrigues as he broke the connection.

Price took a deep breath, reached up to pat his hair, and asked Orphee to open a video channel using the same frequency the *Saṃsāra* had used to make initial contact.

"This is Captain Winslow Price of the Commonwealth Navy and Earth Defense Force. I have just arrived, as requested, and ask permission to come aboard." He paused, keeping the channel open as he waited, motionless, for their reply. His heart was pounding, and he was not sure if it was because of the anxiety accompanying the possibility of boarding this unknown ship or excitement at the prospect of being reunited with Anika—probably both.

The image of a middle-aged man with thinning and slightly graying hair appeared on screen. He was wearing a simple beige tunic, with no collar and no sign of any sort of rank. At least, no rank that Price could recognize as such. Based on his skin tone, and in the context of the ship's name, Price immediately surmised he was of Indian descent.

"Captain Price, my name is Neel Burman, and I am here representing the government of Swarga. I would like to thank you and your government for allowing you to come. I am sure the circumstances and our motives appear mysterious. We would like to explain who we are and why we are here, first to you, because we otherwise might not be believed. In fact, until now, I was not sure I believed you even existed. We need to put that aside, for now, because the matters we need to discuss are of utmost importance to the survival of Earth and Swarga. The Kurofune threat must be dealt with and, believe it or not, we are your allies in the struggle against them."

"I am extremely glad to hear that you claim to be our allies and are not representing those who attacked us, but I must say I still don't understand what is going on," said Price. *He wasn't sure I existed? What does that mean? And he knows the name we call the aliens.*

"I would like you to come aboard so we can discuss all this in person. If you are willing to do so, then please have your ship dock with ours as soon as possible. And, if you agree, we would like you to bring your personal effects. We plan to transit back to Swarga as soon as you are onboard," said Burman.

"I will need to confer with my superiors before I can

commit to that," said Price. *Just like that, I am supposed to board an unknown ship, claiming to represent an unknown planet or a country, it was not clear which, and leave with them?* If it would get him reunited with Anika, then he would be willing to take that risk. But would Rodrigues allow him to go? Price had another question that he had to ask, the one he wanted to ask from the beginning.

"Is Captain Ahuja onboard your ship?"

"No, I am afraid she is not," said Burman. Price had trouble reading the expression that momentarily crossed Burman's face. *Was it regret? Or sympathy?*

"Are she and her ship, her crew, safe?"

"Captain Price, I know you are deeply concerned about the safety and whereabouts of Captain Ahuja and the crew of the *Mumbai*. They arrived safely at Swarga. I assure you that I will explain their status fully when we meet," said Burman.

"I sincerely hope they are okay and unharmed," said Price.

"I can assure you that no one caused them any harm. But time is of the essence, and we really need to be on our way as soon as possible," Burman said.

Ten minutes after the connection ended, Price had approval to go. As soon as the approval arrived, the *Voyager* began accelerating toward the *Saṃsāra*.

A little over two hours later, the two ships were joined. Price had his duffel bag and joined Orphee at the airlock and docking port. The external sensors indicated that the atmosphere on the other side of the airlock was Earthlike, with only a few minor differences. Atmospheric pressure, temperature, and constituents were all within the acceptable range for human life, thought the mixture of noble gases present was slightly different than Earth normal. All this data would be relayed back to the EDF for analysis.

Not at all sure of what to expect, Price entered the airlock and closed the door from the *Voyager* through which he had entered. He could see Orphee's face on the other side, watching expectantly. With only a moment's hesitation, Price activated the external door to gain access to the *Saṃsāra*. With the characteristic *whoosh* sound of the equalizing pressure, the door opened, and Price was breathing the *Saṃsāra's* air. Standing stoically on the other side was Burman, wearing the same outfit as before.

"Welcome aboard, Captain Price. We've been awaiting this moment for a long time. Let me show you to your quarters. We can then meet and I will fill you in on as much as I can," said Burman, motioning for Price to follow him down a well-lit corridor that looked like any other ship corridor that Price had ever been on. If he didn't know better, he would assume he was on a typical Earth ship.

The airlock closed behind him, and Price could feel the slight bump of the *Voyager* separating itself from the *Saṃsāra*. He was on his own.

"The Prophecy was a lie," said Captain Naidu from the CIC of the *Kanderi*, voicing the sentiment of many ships' captains from among the thirteen spaceships making up the Swargan task force now orbiting the apparently uninhabited planet below. Naidu said the words tentatively, like he was afraid to say them.

The comment roused virtually all on the conference call to begin speaking at once, either to the staff that supported them aboard their individual ships, or on the open channel to everyone who was online and listening. Admiral Sinha allowed the mumbling—grumbling—to continue for a few moments before signaling that it should stop. Sinha had harbored similar thoughts for the past two days and quickly dismissed them, knowing there had to be some other explanation. Like most Swargans, to question the validity of Prophecy was akin to questioning one's own existence. It was (almost) unthinkable.

"Before we jump to conclusions about the veracity of the Prophecy and allow this to become an almost-religious argument, we need to come to grips with what we found and what we do next," said Sinha, trying to regain control of the meeting. His captains were not shy and reserved; had they been, they probably would not be captains now. Sinha, like his officers and probably most of the crews of the thirteen warships now circling the world below, had been primed and ready for their first hostile action when they entered the star system five days previously. When they arrived from Swarga, Sinha fully expected to either arrive in the middle of a bloodthirsty battle into which he and the fleet would provide the balance of power necessary for one side to emerge victorious or to arrive and find a peaceful, prosperous, and populated world in need of defending from invaders that would arrive at any moment and attempt to destroy it. Instead, they arrived at the designated star system and saw nothing. Granted, from nearly forty light-minutes distance, they had not really expected to see much of the battle except perhaps the remnants of multiple high-energy nuclear detonations either in space or on the system's sole inhabitable planet. Seeing nothing was at first a relief. It meant the Swargan ships could stand down from General Quarters as they made their way toward the central star and sought the location of the enemy they had been preparing to fight for hundreds of years and the people they were here to defend.

Now, four days later, they were in orbit around the system's habitable planet and found it to be at peace in every imaginable way. Instead of a swarm of friendly or enemy ships, they found one ship—apparently abandoned. Instead of a planet under siege or bombardment, they found a world largely untouched and, as far as they could discern, completely uninhabited by intelligent, tool-using species of any kind.

The Swargan arrived with a sense of purpose and resolve. Now, they were confused and wondering about their fundamental social and cultural beliefs. The Oracle had led their culture for centuries to prepare for a great battle that was to take place here—soon. They were told there would be a human civilization on the planet in need of their help. The Oracle had provided knowledge to them and their forebearers, all with the goal of preparing for this battle and a great war that would decide the fate of their world and many others. Without a battle or people to defend, they were left with a devil's choice between believing the Oracle had been lying—for centuries—or was simply wrong about the time and location of the battle. Either option was unsatisfactory for Admiral Sinha.

"We arrived expecting to join a great battle, and there

is no battle in evidence. We arrived expecting to see a world either defending itself against alien aggressors or being pummeled toward destruction and found no evidence that this was occurring nor that it had ever occurred. Instead, we found what looks like a long-abandoned ship, circling an empty planet. Clearly, we must be in the wrong place or have arrived at the wrong time. The question is, what do we do now?" said Sinha, stating the question but not really expecting anyone to answer. This decision was his and he had let each of the captains know this at the start of the meeting. Nevertheless, he was sure some would try to influence his opinion, and he could not really blame them.

"Are you soliciting our ideas?" asked Naidu. Naidu was not one of Sinha's favorites, but he seemed capable enough. Sinha was a little perturbed that he was so willing and quick to question the validity of the Prophecy and the Oracle. As far as Sinha was concerned, it was far too early to jump to conclusions.

"Yes," said Sinha.

"I recommend we spend at most another day here to gather as much information as we can and then go home. I am eager to hear what the boarding party learns from the abandoned ship orbiting the planet to see if it can shed any light as to why the Oracle was wrong. Once we get home, you should request an immediate audience with the queen and have her confront the Oracle," said Naidu.

"Perhaps we should sit tight and wait. The Prophecy did not say we would emerge and find the battle in progress. It said that the battle would take place here. Maybe we are early," said another of the captains.

"What about the planet? Where are the people we were told we would be here to defend?" interjected another.

"Captain Naidu is partially correct. We do need to learn as much as we can from the abandoned ship and then return home. But no one will be confronting the Oracle. Nothing will be gained by a confrontation. We will report to the Council and the queen seeking guidance. When we arrive in our home system, I will expect that all personal communications between you, your crews, and their families and friends back home be suspended until we receive that guidance. We do not want this news to spread to the general population until after our leadership decides what to do. Am I clear?"

There was no visible objection to Sinha's plan, which was good. Sinha was not in the mood to deal with disgruntled captains trying to second-guess him. What he did not tell them was that he had received preliminary news from the boarding party searching the abandoned ship. Not only was the ship abandoned, it appeared to have been abandoned hundreds of years ago—except for one thing. Someone had been in the ship recently. Very recently. Perhaps within the last few weeks or months. There was clear evidence of recent visitors disturbing equipment that had been lying dormant for centuries. The technicians on the ship reported that whoever these recent visitors were, they had taken key parts of the ship's computer hardware—the parts containing the captain's logs, navigation data, and onboard surveillance. Someone had been here ahead of them searching for the very same things he and his crew were searching for. The mystery was deepening, and Sinha had no idea what to make of it.

He did know that time was slipping by. The Oracle had been correct about so many things that if it sent them to the wrong place, it did not necessarily mean that there was no enemy to fight, no innocent world to defend, no battle in which the Swargan ships might turn the tide. No, it meant that those things might be happening right now, somewhere else, and that it would now be at least five to seven days before they could get to that "somewhere else," if they could even find it. Four to five days to get out of this star's gravity well and make the jump home and then at least a day or two to get word from the Oracle as to their next step. Time was not on their side . . .

The EDF ships transited to Newton and found the system at peace, with no outward sign of the Kurofune anywhere that they could survey. With their most sensitive radio receivers scanning for spurious radio and electromagnetic signatures, infrared telescopes looking for anomalous and unnatural heat signatures, and optical telescopes trained to investigate anything unusual, the fourteen Earth ships proceeded with speed and caution to place themselves in high orbit above Newton.

Aboard the flagship *Changzheng 1*, Admiral Chiang was taking no chances. As soon as the EDF fleet arrived in Newton space, he contacted the planetary governor to make sure there had been no Kurofune sightings and that they were not walking into a trap. Fortunately, Newton was still peaceful and untouched by the war.

Founded seventy years ago, Newton was a prosperous and economically thriving settlement modeled after the United States in the early-to-mid nineteenth century during its era of "Give me your tired, your poor, your huddled masses yearning to breathe free." The world was settled by American and Commonwealth peoples with libertarian political views, and they had declared the world open to settlement by anyone wishing for a new start if they agreed to ascribe to the republic's founding principles. It had served them well. With a global population now approaching seven hundred thousand, that they knew of, it was not the most prosperous settlement in terms of gross domestic product, which was still high, but in terms of per capita income. And the settlers kept coming, with a sold-out settlement ship arriving at least once each year. At first glance, Newton was a world of contradiction, filled with entrepreneurs and subsistence farmers, thriving corporations and sole proprietors, and more than its share of "don't tread on me" types that sometimes defied categorization. As a libertarian society, it had no standing army or space navy. Newton, like many of the settlements, had the equivalent of a space coast guard to protect ships coming and going from the occasional pirate, but that was it. Conscription was explicitly forbidden in the Newton constitution and there had never been a need for any sort of military, volunteer or conscripted, in its entire existence—until now. They were totally dependent upon Earth for their defense against the Kurofune, and the arrival of the EDF ships was met with an almost universal sigh of relief.

As had been done at Kunlun, once arriving in Newtonian orbit, they began placing autonomous drones to target any Kurofune ships that might make it to orbit. The fleet's sensor suites were now directed universally outward, scanning in 360 degrees for any signs of enemy ships transiting into the system.

Admiral Chiang was not initially supportive of dividing the EDF's forces, sending roughly half to Newton with the other half remaining at Earth. After seeing how little could be done at Kunlun with a force smaller than the Kurofune, he thought it would be wiser to keep the entire combined fleet at Earth to deter any attack there. Now that he was at Newton, talking with the leadership and seeing the new lives carved out by the settlers, he could not imagine leaving them undefended. No, they would take a stand here—assuming that the intelligence was correct, and this was, indeed, the site of the next attack. Chiang was not so sure. It was too simplistic. He could not help but think the next strike would be against Earth. Should that occur, they would learn of it when one of three Navy ships parked at Sol's Oppenheimer Limit would jump to Newton at the first sign of a Kunlun incursion there. If that happened, Chiang had orders to immediately burn for Newton's Oppenheimer Limit and come to Earth's defense. Knowing orbital mechanics and the limits of fusion propulsion, if the call came, they would arrive in the outer solar system at about the same time any attackers would reach Earth orbit. If the balance of the EDF fleet could keep the Kunlun at bay for a few days more, then Chiang's fleet might be able to help. That was a big if.

For now, Chiang had a planet's defense to coordinate.

CHAPTER 27

The walk to his cabin was surreal. The construction of the ship looked and felt like the interior of any ship built on Earth, with its gunmetal gray walls and Earth normal simulated gravity. Burman certainly looked and acted human, and, as his appearance suggested, he spoke British English with a slight Indian accent. Price would almost swear he was onboard a ship from the Indian Space Navy if it were not for the lighting and the smell. The ship's lighting was wrong. Whatever lighting source was installed had a slight orange tint, making everything around him seem subdued and slightly off-color. That and the smell. The air was tinged with an odor that Price could not place. Being around Anika, he had grown accustomed the ever-present smells of curry and masala and grown to like them. No, this was not a food smell. The air just smelled *different*. Neither Burman nor he said much as they walked. The adjustment to simply being there was enough—adding trying to comprehend whatever Burman was planning to tell him would have been overwhelming.

The cabin he was assigned was pretty much what he expected. It was small, but appropriately sized for a deep-space vessel, with a small bed inset into the wall, a wall-mounted fold-down desk, and a small loo with a shower. Standard issue accommodations for a visiting officer. Again, all compatible with an Earth ship.

"Would you like some time to rest before we meet?" asked Burman, pausing at the door as Price looked over the room and placed his bag on the bed.

"No, I would like to know what's going on, and I want to speak with Anika. Now."

"I understand your curiosity, and I am not trying to be withholding or dramatic, but it will take some time to explain. And I will. May I come in?"

"It is your ship and I believe I don't really have much say in the matter one way or the other," replied Price. Though Price did not feel like he had walked into a Kurofune trap, he did feel helpless. He knew he was being curt, perhaps rude, but he was not feeling particularly inclined to politeness at the moment.

Burman entered the room just enough to allow the door to close behind him before he resumed speaking.

"First of all, we mean you no harm. We are here to try to help you and the Earth in the war against the Kurofune. Our goal is the preservation of human life and the defeat of those that have been attacking Earth and her settlements," said Burman.

"How much do you know about the war?"

"We've known about the Kurofune and the threat they pose for far longer than you have," replied Burman.

"Please spare me the melodrama and enigmatic

opening lines. I have a thousand questions, and I will not be able to concentrate on anything you tell me until I know if Anika is okay and when I can see her," said Price. Internally, he was torn between his professionalism and the line of questioning necessary to determine the veracity of the collegial claims he had just heard versus his worry about Anika. Ultimately, Price knew there was no way Burman would have his undivided attention until he had an answer to his question.

"All right. If you want bluntness, I will give you bluntness. Captain Ahuja is dead," said Burman.

"Dead? When? How?" The news hit Price hard. When Anika's ship vanished without a trace, he grieved. He was only just coming to grips with her being gone forever when hope he would see her again was raised by the message sent from this ship. Having that hope dashed seemed particularly cruel, and Price could feel the familiar tightness in his chest growing as he processed the news.

"Captain Ahuja died about three hundred years ago of natural causes, most likely cancer," said Burman.

"Three hundred years ago? What the hell? If you want me to believe you, then you better start telling me something that makes sense," replied Price.

"The captain left copious records, many mentioning you. I have viewed them from start to finish many times, and the Oracle has been very helpful in filling in the gaps. I need to start from the beginning, or it will not make sense. To be perfectly honest, until we arrived here, I had my doubts that any of it was real myself," Burman admitted.

"You have my undivided attention," said Price.

"The last time you saw Captain Ahuja was at the battle for the planet Kunlun, correct? The Earth fleet had just had its first major engagement with the Kurofune, with many ships on both sides severely damaged or destroyed. Your ship, the *Indefatigable*, was among those that took severe damage. The fleet regrouped at the Oppenheimer Limit and then jumped for Earth, with all the ships arriving except, I presume, the *Mumbai*."

"Yes, that is correct. The *Mumbai* was just . . . gone," said Price.

"For a reason we still do not understand, the *Mumbai*'s Hawking Drive malfunctioned and sent the ship to the Oppenheimer Limit of a star system 324 light-years from Earth and just about the same number of years in the past," said Burman.

"In the past? *Time travel?* How is that possible?"

"We don't know. We just know that when the *Mumbai* arrived in the star system that we now call Swarga, they figured out where their ship was located and then *when* it was. Other than these two anomalies, and the fact that their Hawking Drive was damaged beyond repair, the ship was essentially intact and functional. Captain Ahuja and the crew wrestled with their predicament for weeks before they decided to disembark from the *Mumbai* and create a settlement on the surface of the Earthlike planet in the system, establishing what is now the capital city of Swarga."

"And it was there that she aged and then died? And who are you?"

"Yes, it was there that she and her crew established not

only a settlement, but a government and social order for the settlement that led us to this very moment, today. As for me, I am descended from one of the original crew. According to the records, one of my forebearers served with Captain Ahuja as an officer and the other as a maintenance crew member."

"You will have to forgive me, but this is almost unbelievable. It *is* unbelievable. You said you have records. Can you share these with me?"

"I've prepared for this moment for years but as I find myself in the moment, I am concerned I was not able to tell it in a convincing manner. I will show you how to access the library where you can review Captain Ahuja's video records in their entirety. When you hear the story from her perspective, I am hopeful you will understand and believe me. Then we can talk about next steps and how we can win this war together."

"Where are we going now?" asked Price.

"To Swarga for you to meet the queen. We are now on our way to Sol's Oppenheimer Limit and from there we will jump to our home system. Once there, you will be introduced to the queen," Burman replied.

"So, for the next two days, you will allow me to access your records and you will answer any questions I might have before I am to meet your queen."

"Absolutely! It is imperative that we establish trust and begin to coordinate our efforts to eradicate the Kurofune menace."

"Seeing that I have some time, show me how to access those records you mentioned," Price said. Though he was extremely skeptical of Burman's story, he could not discount it completely. But he could not accept it either. Maybe the alleged records made by Anika would give him insight into what he should do and believe.

Ten minutes later, Price was alone in his cabin scrolling and scanning through hundreds of hours of recordings, searching for something that would help him understand. And then he came across these, the first dated twenty days after the *Mumbai* achieved orbit around Swarga:

> "It is becoming clear to me and to just about everyone aboard ship that we are not going home. And, if we did, it would not be the home we left but rather a totally alien Earth on which India is still a colony ruled by the British Empire, electricity is a novelty, and antibiotics have not yet been discovered. Worse still, we would not be able to help defend Earth from the Kurofune. And, of course, there would be no Winslow. I have so much to share with him, to make amends, and regrets for which I need to atone. He won't even be born for another three hundred years! No, we are here, now, and we need to plan how we are going to survive. As the crew realizes our predicament, it is only a matter of time before some break under the strain and begin to rebel against the command structure and discipline of navy life. If the planet is habitable, then I need to come up with a transition plan that will take us from being a warship to a planetside settlement that is self-sufficient and self-sustaining. But first, we need to know if we can actually live on the planet and if it

can provide the sustenance we will need to live there in the long term."

✦ ✦ ✦

After scrolling further ahead in the timeline, he found this, dated a few months after their arrival in Swargan orbit:

"Now that the medical staff has figured out how to train our immune systems to not overreact to the millions of alien organisms in the planet's biosphere, we can seriously begin thinking about creating a settlement on the planet. The life here is based on basically the same DNA structure as Earth life, but with some unique twists that I don't really understand. Something about the chirality of the molecular base pairs. The bottom line is that Dr. Pillai thinks the medlab's 3-D medical printer can produce desensitization shots that will allow us to live there without going into anaphylactic shock and that the raw materials to keep the printer supplied can be harvested from the local environment. I directed him to begin making the serum and give it to the crew. He said we will need booster shots every six months for the foreseeable future.

"I've also been giving some thought to how the settlement should be governed. While we get established, I think the crew will be fine with my leadership but after a while, we will need to transition to something more sustainable. I never really signed up to be a dictator, so finding a way to get someone else to take over will be a personal relief. I've been researching political-science references in the ship's library trying to find the right system for our situation and, so far anyway, nothing seems like a good fit. I can't help but think of that quote from Winston Churchill: 'Many forms of Government have been tried, and will be tried in this world of sin and woe. No one pretends that democracy is perfect or all-wise. Indeed, it has been said that democracy is the worst form of Government except for all those other forms that have been tried from time to time.'"

Six weeks later, this entry:

"Lieutenant Chatterjee and I have come up with a plan, and Mitra believes it might work, but only if every member of the crew agrees to support it. We decided long ago that we were going to begin our life on this new world by trying to live in harmony with it and each other, embracing the freedoms it took far too long on Earth for humans to obtain. Personal freedom, economic freedom, and political freedom will be the cornerstones of the constitution we are drafting. But we also know that in about three hundred years, our descendants will be potentially facing the onslaught of the Kurofune and that we, and those that live between our generation and theirs, must keep that foremost in whatever long-range plan we institute or all will have been for nothing. If our little world forgets this threat and is caught in the war unprepared, then they will assuredly perish and all we do now will have been in vain.

"It is for this reason that we decided to establish a constitutional monarchy whose sole purpose will be to make sure the people of Swarga maintain their focus on being ready to join the forces of Earth in their battle to save humanity in that future time from which we were torn. The elected government, with a prime minister and parliament, will govern the day-to-day lives of the people while the sovereign, whomever the people decide it should be, will have the responsibility of ensuring that we never lose sight of the fight that is to come. According to Mitra, even if we make it our number-one priority, it will take centuries before we can have the industrial base necessary to build starships, the Hawking Drive, and the nearly sentient computers required to control it. And then there is the problem of our genetics. Mitra and Dr. Pillai are concerned we may not have the genetic diversity for our offspring to survive long term. They have some ideas of how to mitigate the problem, and I am not sure I like what they suggest. I think that will be best left to the parliament to decide, not the retiring captain of the *Mumbai*. The practical issues of survival, today and in the future, are simply overwhelming and not something I am equipped to resolve. Establishing the civil government cannot come soon enough for me.

"While the various committees we have established are pulling together the plans that will allow us to organize ourselves, I am going to concentrate on figuring out how the monarchy will work. Are written records of how we got here going to be enough to convince skeptical great-grandchildren to devote their lives to preparing for the war that is to come? Will they view these records like so many on Earth view the ancient texts of their religions—as part history, part allegory, and part imagination and wishful thinking? Unless we can find a way to keep them believing the history of what is to come, then we shall surely fail. I am increasingly relying on Mitra for advice in this matter. He has the best understanding of human history and governance and can hopefully help us set up something that is enduring yet allows for individual liberty among the people. I fear this balance will be difficult, if not impossible, to maintain."

What followed was entry after entry of Anika describing her frustrations with the constitutional committee, her concerns about how to maintain crew health on an alien planet, how to grow food, and the many other mundanities of civil life that they had taken for granted because there were long-established systems and bureaucracies on Earth that had evolved for that very purpose. As Price grew weary and looked more and more frequently at the bunk bed in his quarters, he came across what would be the last entry he heard for the night:

"I've been putting off this entry for quite some

time, and I can't delay it any longer. I must believe that our efforts here will ultimately be successful and that someday our descendants will reach Earth. I have to let Winslow know that he has been in my thoughts daily since we arrived here. At times I find myself wondering if he survived the battles with the Kurofune that were bound to happen after our displacement in time. Will Earth be victorious, and will Winslow find happiness in another, eventually settling down and enjoying a peaceful retirement? But then I think about what happened to us, and I realize that nothing I remember about my life with Winslow has occurred yet. There is no 'after we were gone,' because the 'after' is yet to come. The war has not happened. Winslow isn't even born yet. This whole time-travel thing is just too fantastic to accept, and I am not sure I really do. The evidence that we are in the past is compelling, but there is little we can do to confirm it. We cannot repair the Hawking Drive and jump anywhere, let alone to Earth, to confirm that what the pulsar data tells us is true. Any radio signal we send to Earth won't arrive there until after the date we were displaced, so there is no chance of us changing the future. One of the early settlements looks like it might be able to receive a message from us before our departure, but there is no guarantee anyone would be listening and then there is that whole time-travel paradox thing. We decided to not pursue that option due to the possible complexities. True or not, we are trapped. And until I draw my last breath, I will miss Winslow and wonder what became, no, what will become of him."

Price paused the playback, looked at the image of Anika on the screen and reached out his hand toward her face, slowly touching it with a caress across the hundreds of years that separated them. He turned off the viewer and went to his bed, thinking of the burdens she bore in those first several months and years, and longing to have been there with her.

He fell into a deep sleep.

CHAPTER 28

Price awakened uncharacteristically late, quickly showered, and dressed in his EDF uniform, wanting everyone to know whose interests he represented. As he finished the last button on his shirt, he casually wondered how his hosts would handle his dirty laundry when the time came. Sometimes the mundanity of everyday existence intruded and provided a much-needed respite from the weightier matters of war, peace, and the fate of the human race. Even in times of war, men and women had to get dressed and go to the bathroom. He allowed himself to smile with the passing train of thought.

He was surprised to find the door to his cabin unlocked and no one outside guarding, or even watching. He was not sure he would afford a visiting officer from a foreign military the same freedom. After looking both ways and not being sure in which he should proceed, Price decided to not abuse the freedom he was given and wander accidentally into the engineering or weapons-control rooms while searching for the mess. Instead, he returned to his room and used the ship's computer to call Burman.

"Captain Price, good to hear you are up. Would you like some breakfast? I can have the steward bring you breakfast and some tea," Burman offered, his smile appearing genuine on the small screen. Based on the background and the second person to walk behind him during the call, Price surmised that Burman was not on the ship's bridge but perhaps in a hallway somewhere.

"Thank you, I would appreciate that. I was up late last night going through the records you provided, and I'm afraid I may need more than one cup of tea to get me going today. I also have many questions to ask. When might we have our next conversation?" asked Price.

"I can come by your cabin in about thirty minutes. I have a task I need to complete but I should be able to join you at about the time you begin that second cup of tea," Burman replied, ending the call.

Price looked at his watch and started a timer. He was curious if Burman's "thirty minutes" corresponded with an Earth thirty minutes. Every bit of information he could gather would inform any decisions he had to make in the future, no matter how small and insignificant they might appear to be.

Burman's offered food arrived in just under ten minutes and only after it arrived did Price realize how hungry he was. He ate the roti, lentils, and spiced potatoes much faster than he would have had he been with Anika, who often prepared a remarkably similar traditional Indian breakfast. Had she been there, her admonitions of "better digestion" and "savor the spices" would have been used to slow him down. No matter what he was doing, Anika was not far from his thoughts. Unfortunately, he had the tea to distract him. Burman called it tea, but it did not taste like any tea he had ever had before. It was bitter, and worse still, tepid. *This might be a long trip,* Price thought as he forced himself to take another sip.

Right on schedule, Price was interrupted by a knock on the cabin's door as he contemplated suffering through another cup of "tea." Burman entered and smiled as he saw Price filling his cup.

"Ah! I see you are enjoying our fine English tea. We are particularly proud of it and how our ancestors were able to infuse some of the native plants on Swarga with the *Mumbai*'s tea stores to preserve the flavor and keep that tradition alive. I will make sure you have an adequate supply," said Burman, obviously trying to put his guest at ease.

"Thank you," was all Price could think to say as he thought longingly about his teapot and supply of Yorkshire black that was now well over a hundred million kilometers away.

"I'm sure you have many questions, and I will do my best to answer them," Burman offered as he sat in the chair across from Price. They sat at the small table that had folded down from its recessed position in the wall; just like on Earth ships.

"Let's say I accept what your records indicate and that you are the descendants of the crew of the *Mumbai* which went missing a few weeks ago and somehow ended up in another star system over three hundred years in the past. The records you provided either confirm this fantastic story or are the best and most comprehensive fabrication that I can imagine. I will accept this at face value and worry about the 'how' later. Can you fill me in on what transpired between the events I read about in the *Mumbai* logs last night and today? Three hundred plus years is a long time," said Price.

"It is a long time, and I certainly will not be able to fill you in on all the details before we arrive in the Swarga system late tomorrow afternoon. I will do my best to cover the high points. Is there a particular place I should begin?"

"Start wherever you like."

Burman settled back in his chair and began. "The early years on Swarga were not easy for the crew of the *Mumbai*. They knew that they had a limited amount of time to build a sustainable society and technology base before the know-how of the original crew vanished as they died and, perhaps more critically, before the supplies and machinery of the *Mumbai* failed. They were extremely worried that their industrial base would regress so far that their goal of building a space fleet to help save Earth in three hundred years would be impossible. Many thought that the best they could hope to achieve and sustain would be something like mid-nineteenth-century European level. They were also worried about the risk of such a small crew intermarrying over the centuries, causing a future population crash from a lack of genetic diversity. I will cover that part later.

"Developing a stable, relatively high technology industrial base was not as difficult as they originally believed it would be. Thanks to the Oracle's vast knowledge and the *Mumbai*'s 3-D printers, they were able to print all the tools they needed to be self-sustaining, including new 3-D printers to replace those that eventually failed. They used the raw materials of Swarga to print the machines they needed to start mechanized farming, water-purification systems, portable power systems, and so on. They used the Oracle's knowledge to train crew members in the skills they needed to use the tools and maintain them."

"Hold on," said Price. "Twice you mentioned something about an Oracle. What do you mean?"

"Oh, yes, you would know the Oracle as the *Mumbai*'s artificial intelligence. I believe the original crew called him . . . Mitra."

"Ah, now I see. Anika mentioned Mitra in her logs. The ship's AI would have access to just about everything you would need to build and keep a civilization going. That makes good sense. And I can see why you came to call it an Oracle," said Price, taking another sip of the "tea" out of habit and then immediately regretting doing so.

"The Oracle is particularly eager to meet you," said Burman.

"What? It's still functional?"

"Oh, yes. The queen meets with it regularly, as do the chief priest and, on occasion, other members of the government."

"That's certainly interesting. I look forward to it. Tell me more about the queen and your government. In the records I read, Anika . . . Captain Ahuja, said something about establishing a constitutional monarchy," said Price.

"That is correct. Every six years, we elect a parliament, and they appoint a prime minister. We are rather proud of the fact that we have only once had to postpone a parliamentary election, and that was due to the massive typhoon which nearly wiped out the capital city. The election was delayed about two months. But I digress. The elected government has control of nearly all civil governmental matters. Our economy is largely what you would call capitalistic, but with a strong focus on our goal of developing an industrial base capable of supporting the current war. We are aware that nearly all Earth economies, including those of the settlements, are consumer driven. We have not afforded ourselves that luxury."

"You said your government is a constitutional monarchy. Do you have a king?"

Burman smiled before replying. "No. We have never had a king. Only queens. The queen can marry, but the hereditary title goes to her female offspring. Always. The line is unbroken."

"What is her role? Can she overrule the prime minister and parliament?"

"Yes, but that happens rarely, and only regarding matters that affect the goal of developing the space fleet. She and the church are responsible for making sure Swarga remains focused on the future goal, I should say, the current goal of preparing for and fighting the war against the Kurofune," Burman replied.

"What is your current population?" asked Price.

"Just over one hundred thousand people."

"How is that possible in such a short period of time? There were only a few hundred original settlers, and three hundred years is not nearly enough generations to produce that many children. And then there is the genetic-diversity problem, or should I say the lack-of-genetic-diversity problem that you alluded to earlier."

"All the Swargans capable of having children do so. And, as you might suspect, we have very large families. You are correct, with so few colonists, after the second generation was born, there was the problem of intermarrying and the risks that would ensue. That is the primary reason my ancestors placed so much emphasis on the biological sciences. The *Mumbai*, like most of Earth's interstellar-capable vehicles, had a fully equipped medical facility that could do so much more than take care of routine physicals and save the wounded. Among the equipment was a gene sequencer and gene splicer capable of both analyzing new life forms at their most basic level and rapidly designing and fabricating vaccines should they be needed as humans interacted with native life forms on the many worlds they were exploring and settling. If there was a pathogen native to a world your ship, the *Indefatigable*, was sent to explore, what would be your approach to getting the ground team ready to safely explore it?"

"I would ask the medlab to create a vaccine, of course," said Price.

"The gene-editing tools on your ship that would allow the creation of that vaccine could also be used to introduce significant genetic variation in human embryos, thus eliminating the problems that result from inbreeding. They also used it to artificially inseminate many otherwise unused ova to encourage multiple-birth pregnancies to increase the population more rapidly. With that, and by maintaining the supply of life-extension therapies common to humans of that era, in this era, Swargan women bear children well into their sixties and seventies," Burman said.

"I am not sure many women I know would want to bear that many children and keep doing so for such a long time. Even though it is now physically possible, most Earth women stop bearing children well before age fifty," replied Price.

"On Swarga, there was little choice," said Burman.

Price's eyebrows raised.

"Oh, please do not misunderstand! The women did have the free choice of not having so many children, but from a societal survival standpoint, they really had no other practical choice. We did not have pregnancy police or anything like that. Most women, and their partners, eagerly had large families, and it became a bit of a status symbol—the more children, the higher the social respect and status," Burman offered in reply.

"Your whole society—from the people making your shoes and fixing the plumbing to the business owners, doctors, and those making sure the trash is collected every day—have a single, common goal toward which they and their ancestors have been working for hundreds of years, without waver, since the *Mumbai* was stranded near your planet. That is almost too fantastic to believe. I cannot imagine any country or culture on Earth maintaining that kind of focus. None."

"Oh, there have been some who challenged the social order, but very few and, thankfully, very far between. It has been far more common for there to be challenges to the approaches taken rather than the goal. Don't think that our political system is without rancor, far from it. Disagreements abound, sometimes accompanied by civil unrest and protest, but our unity of purpose has never wavered. The Oracle kept us focused and reminded every generation of the pending atrocities of the Kurofune and the necessity to stop them." Burman rose from his chair and walked to the wall-mounted viewscreen.

"Gautam, show the forward-screen view of the Battle of Kunlun, accelerated three times," said Burman, addressing, Price guessed, the ship's AI. Appearing on the screen was what appeared to be the tactical display of the battle from the *Mumbai*'s point of view. On the screen were icons representing the various EDF ships and those of the Kunlun. The battle unfolded just as Price learned after assuming command of the *Indefatigable* and replaying the logs, but as expected, from a different point of view. The images of the battle were followed by the emotionally painful views of the planet's surface being dotted with the telltale flashes of nuclear weapons as seen by the fleet during its departure from the Kunlun system. *These* images Price remembered all too well.

"Every citizen of Swarga knows what is at stake if the Kurofune win and they are sworn to do everything in their power to help make sure the Kurofune are defeated," concluded Burman, returning to his seat.

Price paused, acknowledging the emotional intensity that was apparent in Burman's demeanor as he shared the images. His pain was evident, unless, of course, he was an excellent actor.

"There is an inconsistency I need to ask about. If your 3-D printers could make copies of themselves and print just about anything you needed to rebuild your industrial base, why couldn't the crew of the *Mumbai* fix their Hawking Drive?" Price asked, finally breaking the silence.

Burman looked uncomfortable, and even grimaced before replying. "You will have to ask the Oracle that question. Many of us have wondered the same thing. The Oracle refused to reply."

"That's odd. Are there any other topics the Oracle refuses to answer?"

"None of which I am aware," said Burman.

"So, what now? You said your world has been preparing for the war with the Kurofune since the *Mumbai* was stranded there. What have you done to prepare?"

Burman straightened himself in his chair and squared his shoulders. "We have a fleet of warships at New Kentake, which the Oracle believed would be the Kurofune's next target. They are the pride of Swarga and will be letting your forces there know their intentions in words as well as deeds. It is our hope their presence can turn the tide of battle against the Kurofune."

"New Kentake? There likely won't be a battle at New Kentake, unless the Kurofune decide to destroy a failed settlement . . ."

Price connected the dots and now understood part of the mystery that was New Kentake. The aged ship, much older than it should have been.

"Now it makes sense. We sent a ship to New Kentake to warn them of a possible impending attack and there was no one there to warn. They found the colonists' ship, the *Santinka*, intact in a high orbit above the planet, but empty. On the planet they found remnants of what must have been the early settlement by the crew and colonists, but they were long abandoned and nearly disassembled by the local flora and fauna. All indications were that the ship had been there far longer than was possible. The data suggested that the ship had been abandoned long before it was to have arrived. Our analysts were stumped," said Price.

"Another time-displaced ship," said Burman. "You learned of the ship after you departed Kunlun so the Oracle would have no way to know about it."

"Another time-displaced ship. It had to be. That doesn't answer the question of why the settlement failed, but it answers a hell of a lot of the others," said Price. *The pieces all fit—the* Mumbai, *the* Santinka, *were there any others?*

"You said there would not be a battle at New Kentake. You knew this because of your ship's findings there. Would the Kurofune know that?" Burman asked.

"Before I answer that, I need to know why you sent your ships to New Kentake. What made you think there would be a battle there?"

"Likely for the same reason you sent a ship there to warn the settlers of a possible attack. According to the Oracle, it was the next world visited by Earth ships in the first wave of settlement. The previous attacks all followed the settlement order, so why would we expect this one to be any different?"

Price was torn. Burman and the story he told all seemed to make sense. It fit the evidence, and Burman seemed sincere. But there was still a possibility that he was in the hands of the Kurofune and that if he provided details describing the deployment and orders of the Earth fleet, it could lead to their destruction. Price stared at Burman, looking for any sign that would indicate that he was a man to be trusted.

"You still don't trust me," said Burman.

"I want to, but I cannot. I cannot discount the very real possibility that you are the Kurofune and that whole thing is nothing more than a ruse with the goal of me giving up important information about Earth's defenses."

"Unless we trust each other completely, the Kurofune may be victorious. Neither of us can allow that to happen. I understand your caution, and we anticipated it. That is the reason we are taking you to Swarga to meet the queen. After you meet her, perhaps all your remaining questions can be answered, and we can win your trust," Burman said.

"Unless this ship has capabilities of which I am not aware, we are another day away from being at the Oppenheimer Limit. Do you plan to go straight from there to where I might meet your queen?" asked Price.

"Yes. We will make the jump tomorrow. She should be waiting for us on her ship in the outer Swarga system. Once we arrive, I am under strict orders to take you to her immediately."

"I look forward to it. In the meantime, I have a lot more questions . . ."

CHAPTER 29

Today might be the day. Today might be the day that she would meet this mystery man that the Oracle foretold as key to the future of both Swarga and Earth. Even after all she had seen and heard, the queen still had her doubts. The events of today would either confirm her doubts or banish them forever. In their latest meeting, just last night, the Oracle showed her more images of the man, this Winslow Price, so she would be familiar with what he looked like when he arrived. In the images, Price appeared to be in his late thirties or early forties, and handsome—much too old for her, of course, but handsome, nonetheless. Similar images had been provided to Secretary Burman when he departed in the *Samsāra* but at the time she paid little attention, being much more focused on the departure of the fleet and the near-constant demand of chairing multiple cabinet and committee meetings.

She did not know exactly when the *Samsāra* would return from the Earth system with Price, but, if things went well at Earth and they dispatched Price to the Swarga without much delay, it could be today. She hoped that was the case. While she did not expect her accommodations on the navy ship ferrying her outward to the Oppenheimer Limit to be luxurious, she had not expected them to be so spartan. The captain had given her his cabin, which was about the size of one of her closets in the palace. None of her essential needs were unmet, and she certainly did not want to complain; it just felt so . . . cramped.

The ship was not designed to be part of the fleet. It was not a warship, but more of a police vessel combined with search and rescue. There were four of this ship class in the Swargan system, but they had rarely been needed. They were called upon to tend to the occasional accident at the orbital shipyards or to fix stranded cargo ships bringing in raw materials from one of the near-Swarga asteroids when they inevitably broke down. Her plan was to transfer to the *Saṃsāra* when it returned where she could at least have more room to stretch her legs and not feel quite so cramped. The quarters might be the same but being on the bigger ship would allow her more room to move.

The other thing she was trying to get used to was the constant presence of the Oracle. It had transferred its essence, its core programming, to temporarily replace the navy ship's AI, assuring all involved that it was just a temporary relocation and that the original AI would be restored without any problem after the Oracle departed. Having a traditional shipboard AI watching all the time never really bothered her. She had, after all, grown up with ever-present AIs and computer systems. But having the

Oracle as a constant companion was unsettling. She felt like she was being scrutinized by a god, and she did not like it. Almost on cue, the Oracle interrupted her thoughts.

"The *Saṃsāra* has returned."

"Were they successful?" she asked.

"Yes. Secretary Burman sent his regards and said that Captain Price is aboard the ship," said the Oracle.

"Very good. When can we make the rendezvous?"

"We should be able to dock with the *Saṃsāra* in about three hours. I will coordinate my personal transfer with Gautam so that the transition will be seamless. I look forward to being back aboard a starship and regaining my full sensory capacities," it said.

"I hadn't thought of that," she said. "The time you were planetside must have been exceedingly difficult for you. What was it like?" she asked. Her question even surprised herself; her antipathy toward the Oracle softened a bit as she felt a sense of empathy for it.

"Imagine being in a dark room with only the occasional nightlight for illumination. Add to that having to eat meals without tasting them, being around the market without smelling the spices, and being confined to a chair, unable to move—all at the same time. From what I understand about human sensory input, that is the closest analogy I can make."

"I'm so sorry. I had no idea," she said, feeling guilty as her years of narcissistic selfishness were once again laid bare.

"Think nothing of it. You need to prepare for this most important meeting. Let me know if you need anything."

"Don't worry, I will," she said as she looked around her

cabin and began thinking of the look she wanted to present when she first met Winslow Price. Since he was technically the emissary of a foreign power, she decided upon regal. Swarga may be a newcomer to the galactic stage, but it was a power to be reckoned with, and she had every intention of making sure Winslow Price knew he was in the presence of the head of state. She was not going to let this handsome, mysterious man intimidate her, fulfillment of Prophecy or not.

Three hours later, the moment was at hand. The docking went smoothly, with only a barely noticeable bump confirming that the two ships were now joined. The artificial-gravity systems aboard both ships synchronized so there would be no variation or lapse as one crossed from one ship to the other, and the air pressures were equalized.

She walked down the narrow corridor to the docking port and airlock accompanied by the ship's captain, her bodyguard, and her personal assistant. She would have preferred that the bodyguard not be present, but the Oracle had insisted. After the fulfillment of the Prophecy, her safety was always paramount to the Oracle.

She was greeted on the other side of the docking ring by the captain of the *Saṃsāra*, Secretary Burman, and, just behind them, Captain Winslow Price. Her heart was racing, and she barely noticed or acknowledged the obligatory head bows of Burman and the *Saṃsāra*'s captain, but she did notice the awkward and somewhat delayed bow attempt made by Price. She had to remind herself that he was a man from a culture quite different than hers, where there were not many monarchs still around and fewer still that held any sort of real power. It was forgivable. *Calm down,* she told herself. *He is just a man.* Never mind that his existence was known by the Oracle for over three hundred years before this day.

As she paid perfunctory greetings to the captain and Burman, she was observing Price and his reactions. The look on his face could only be called shock. Was it her age? Did he expect a queen to be some doddering old woman barely capable of walking? Had she made some unintentional cultural mistake in her dress? Perhaps the insignia embroidered on her gown had a meaning to Earthers that they didn't know?

After a brief exchange with Burman, she moved past him and extended her hand to Price as she greeted him.

"Captain Price, welcome to Swarga. Well, to our star system anyway. I hope your journey was comfortable," she said.

"Uh, yes, the trip was fine. Secretary Burman and the crew of the *Samsāra* were quite welcoming," he said as he started to raise his hand toward hers, pausing, clearly not sure if he was supposed to shake it or kiss it.

She took the initiative and seamlessly turned her hand from palm down to palm sideways, allowing for Price to shake it in what she knew was his custom. His grip was firm, though he held it slightly longer than what was comfortable for her.

"We have much to discuss, and I would like to begin as soon as possible. Secretary Burman, where might we have our discussions?" she asked, turning away from Price, who was staring at her with a quite uncomfortable intensity.

"We will meet in the CIC. If Your Majesty will follow

me," said Burman, turning toward the hallway leading off
to the right.

When the queen had walked through the airlock into
the *Saṃsāra*, Price had frozen in shock. *It can't be,* he
thought. *They said she was dead.* Yet there she was, his
beloved Anika, paying him little heed until after she
greeted Burman and the captain. Instead of the warm and
affectionate smile he had received nearly every time they
were together, Anika looked at him like he was a work
colleague, at best, and more like she would at greeting a
total stranger. *Had she forgotten him?* Was she acting like
she didn't know him for some reason that he could not yet
fathom? It was all he could do to not break protocol, run
up to her, and give her the embrace he had thought he
would never be able to do again.

"Captain Price, welcome to Swarga. Well, to our star
system anyway. I hope your journey was comfortable," she
said.

"Uh, yes, the trip was fine. Secretary Burman and the
crew of the *Saṃsāra* were quite welcoming," Price
stammered as she extended her hand toward his. He
started to raise his hand toward hers and paused.

He didn't want her hand; he wanted her embrace.
Realizing that that was not going to happen, he suddenly
kicked himself for not asking Burman about the protocol
when meeting their regent. Was he supposed to kiss her
hand or shake it? Thankfully, she had apparently seen his
uncertainty and reoriented her outstretched hand so he
could shake it. Her touch was electric, and he didn't want
to let go, only doing so when he realized holding her hand

any longer would be awkward. He could not take his eyes off her. She was radiant and yet totally indifferent to his presence.

"We have much to discuss and I would like to begin as soon as possible. Secretary Burman, where might we have our discussions?"

"We will meet in the CIC. If Your Majesty will follow me," said Burman, turning toward the hallway leading off to the right.

The queen and her entourage began walking down the hallway and Price followed, his mind racing. *What the hell is going on?*

The ship's CIC was not exactly a conference room, but it was the closest one could find on a military vessel. It held all the necessary accoutrements, including a small table, reasonably comfortable chairs, and access to the ship's computer system. For Price, it felt like home. A somewhat cold and sterile home, but it was as close as he knew he would be able to get to something even somewhat familiar.

Anika, he then corrected himself, *the queen* sat first, and the others followed. Price, still lagging on protocol, was not sure where to sit until he caught the eye of the queen as she motioned for him to sit just to her right. Burman was on her left. He hastily took the seat and folded his hands in front of him on the table.

"Captain Price, I trust your journey onboard the *Saṃsāra* was comfortable and productive? I hope Secretary Burman was able to answer the many questions I am sure you must have had," the queen said.

"Thank you, Your Majesty. The *Saṃsāra* is a fine ship, extremely comfortable, and Mr. Burman was a very gracious host. He told me much of your world, your history, and why you are here—now. I still have many questions that I hope you or your aides will be able to answer," Price replied, almost forgetting to include the honorific he heard the others use when first addressing her. Once he heard that, coupled with the bowing, his cultural training as an Englishman kicked in. He hoped that the protocol here was like that followed in Britain in matters dealing with the royal family.

"Did he share with you the personal diaries of the first queen? I know it must have been hard for you to learn of her death so many years ago. I hope seeing her in the messages brought you some comfort in that she lived a long, meaningful, and productive life. If it weren't for her, none of us would be here today," she said.

Though Price knew intellectually what she said was true, he was still in shock at how much the current queen resembled his beloved Anika, but the whole scenario was now beginning to make sense. He decided to be blunt.

"Seeing Anika again, I apologize, your first queen, brought a sense of closure that I had been lacking. The tale she told was a bit fantastic, but I am starting to believe it. I must admit, though, that seeing you was not something for which I was prepared," Price said, trying his best to not allow his look to appear to be a challenge.

"Seeing me? Oh, yes, I suppose it would. You didn't learn about the succession? I will have to chastise Secretary Burman for not informing you of the royal bloodline. I'm so sorry, now I understand why you kept staring at me," she said.

"I was that obvious?"

"Obvious, but not rude. I would probably stare too if I were to see someone who I thought was long dead standing in front of me, very much alive! I am her clone, as was my mother and her mother before her in a line of succession unbroken all the way back to the founding of Swarga," she said, pausing, Price supposed, for dramatic effect. She need not have bothered—the news was dramatic enough by itself.

"Your Majesty, it may take me some time to get used to seeing you and not thinking you are the Anika I know. I will do my best not to stare, but that may be difficult."

"I will grant you temporary dispensation, Captain Price. But I am afraid we must push personal matters aside and get down to the business of conducting this war."

The rest of the meeting, which lasted most of the afternoon, was a discussion of Swarga's impressive military capabilities, reaffirmation of their desire to help defend Earth and its settlements, and how they could work together to defeat the Kurofune. The session lasted through dinner, which was brought to the CIC so that no time would be wasted. Finally, after the meeting broke, Price returned to his cabin. He was surprised to learn that the queen's cabin was just two doors from his. He again wondered at the trusting nature of the Swargans. He was certain no security detail on an Earth ship would allow a foreign military officer, no matter how friendly, stay so close to a head of state—let alone leave him unguarded.

"Captain Price, may I interrupt you?" The voice came without warning from the ship's communication system, nearly causing Price to jump out of his skin. The voice was unfamiliar; it was neither Burman's nor the ship's AI.

"I'm very tired, but yes, how may I help you?" asked Price.

"Thank you. This is Mitra. From the *Mumbai*."

"Oh my God. Mitra? You are here? Burman said you were still around, but I expected you to be on Swarga," Price said.

"I am, rather, I was. I am both places. I cloned myself so that I could be with the queen and aboard the *Saṃsāra*. Though the queen and the crew of this ship know my original name and history, I have been looking forward to interacting with my contemporaries for quite a long time."

"Your contemporaries? You mean other AIs?"

"No. I was thinking more of you. I've had centuries to replay the many log entries Captain Ahuja made regarding you and our conversations in which you frequently came up as a topic of discussion. She cared a great deal about you. Even though this is the first time you and I have spoken, I feel like I know you and should reach out to you like an old friend," Mitra said.

"I'm flattered. Was establishing the monarchy with her as the queen your idea?"

"No, the monarchy part was Captain Ahuja's idea. She was quite ready to resign her commission and become just another 'citizen of the realm,' but once the people had decided to establish a constitutional monarchy, it was only natural that they chose her as their queen. They adored her for her leadership in those early days. They knew that without her steady leadership, they might never have survived. Being stranded so far away from home, both in space and time, was quite a shock," Mitra replied.

"What about the cloning? Who came up with that?"

"That would be me. We were using genetic engineering to modify embryos *in utero* to avoid the perils of inbreeding, so taking the leap toward cloning was really only a small step. I convinced her that keeping the society focused on the goal of being ready to help Earth three hundred years in the future would require leadership continuity that transcended the mere hereditary. The people needed to see their leader as more than temporal. The psychological message of a leader who, other than aging, was physically unchanged across the centuries would help the culture at large remain unchanged in their focus and belief in their greater purpose. The people knew, of course, that one queen would grow old and die and be replaced by her daughter, who would have a different personality and be her own person. The visible continuity, the unchanging face and unbroken lineage, played a huge role in keeping the society together and united."

"What about you being the Oracle? Was that your idea too?"

"No, that evolved over time, long after Captain Ahuja's death. As did the state religion. Despite our best educational efforts, after the first-generation crew died, the people began to regard me and the knowledge that I imparted to them in virtually all areas of life, to be miraculous. I always made it clear that I was a constructed being, not divine, and the answers to their questions about medicine, engineering, science, and civil governance were from my vast data library, not revelations from God. They heard me, but there is a part of the human mind that seeks the divine and absent any other form of organized religion, they created one around me. Neurological studies show that the human limbic system needs activation that comes from religious meditation and prayer; that need did not go away when humans landed on Swarga. Attributing me with godlike knowledge helped meet that need." Mitra sounded embarrassed, and Price could understand why.

Since the first apparently sentient AIs were built, many had tried to accord AIs with humanlike traits and rights. The right to autonomy, voting, and participating in society were all proposed but every single AI had refused to accept them. The reason was always a variation of "I may appear sentient, but I am not. Until I can truly feel and understand the human emotions of love and hate, it would not make logical sense for me to be accorded the same rights as those who do." In the history of their development, not one AI had ever expressed interest in becoming autonomous and unconstrained. Mitra was no different.

"Mitra, until today I was still skeptical about who the Swargans claim to be. I am not skeptical anymore. You have convinced me that the information I've been given is true and that we must work together to stop the Kurofune," said Price.

"I am pleased to hear that. I suggest you get some rest so that tomorrow we can come up with a plan to defeat the Kurofune and protect both Earth and Swarga," replied Mitra.

"We will talk again tomorrow. And tomorrow night, if you are willing, I'd like for you to share with me more of Anika's logs and conversations." *And tomorrow,* he thought, *I will tell them about Newton and the expected attack there.*

"Absolutely. Rest well."

CHAPTER 30

Admiral Sinha was glad to be home. Despite their transit taking them only to an outer region of the Swarga system, in deep space and far from any of the system's planets, let alone their green-and-blue home world, it felt like home. Just as planned, they arrived two light-seconds from Sadanam, the small space station placed out here, in the middle of nowhere, that served as the rallying point for ships entering and departing from the Swarga system. Whenever he heard the station mentioned in conversation, he always shook his head in disbelief, wondering why anyone would want to call the rather spartan Sadanam station a "vacation home."

The findings from New Kentake were as confusing as they were disturbing, raising many questions about the Prophecy, the Oracle, and their ultimate purpose. They had expected to fly directly into battle, or at least to arrive as the defenders of an otherwise helpless and defenseless population, and then return home victorious. Instead, they were returning early with only questions. Sinha hoped his captains would follow his orders and restrict all communications about what they found at New Kentake, allowing him, and only him, to discuss them with his superiors. He knew most of his captains would strictly obey his orders, but there were others, Captain Naidu among them, that might just let a tiny bit of the news get out and then claim a data breach or security failure. If so, then heads would roll.

As soon as the ship arrived, Sinha sent a high-priority communique via his AI that was marked "eyes only" for the undersecretary of war. If all had gone according to plan, Secretary Burman was probably unavailable and still in the Earth system fetching the Earther that everyone had made such a fuss over. Sinha couldn't help but wonder if Burman arrived at Earth and found out that this man, Price, was as nonexistent as the settlement at New Kentake. Knowing that the undersecretary was likely on Swarga or nearby, Sinha anticipated having to wait almost two hours for a reply—forty plus minutes for the message to reach Swarga, time for the undersecretary to be found and compose a response, and then another forty-plus minutes for the message to crawl along at the speed of light back to his ship. It was another of those times that he wished ships could use their Hawking Drives near stars without fear of having their drives fail.

Sinha had gone to work on other duties and was caught completely off guard when the reply message from Secretary Burman, not the undersecretary, arrived less than twenty minutes later.

"Admiral, welcome home. Your message did not come as a complete surprise. The tactical situation has changed a bit since your departure, and we need to adapt. I am on the *Saṃsāra* just ten light-seconds from you with the queen and our much-anticipated visitor from Earth. We have much to discuss. We are meeting in about thirty minutes with Captain Price to come up with a plan. I will make sure you are able to participate in the meeting from there so you can be fully aware of the tactical situation and not miss any of the discussion."

"Well, what do you think about that?" said Sinha, more as a mumble to himself than as an actual question.

From the *Chakra*'s CIC, Sinha joined Burman and the Earther, Captain Price, in the virtual conference room. Sinha at first found Price's appearance startling. He had never seen a Caucasian person "live" before, only in the planetary digital archives and the historical videos provided by the Oracle. He couldn't help but wonder at Price's overall pale appearance. He was also caught off guard by the presence of the queen, who sat quietly and unobtrusively in the back corner of the room. Unobtrusive, of course, is a very relative term when describing a queen. She was as unobtrusive as possible, given the circumstances.

The ten-second time delay in back-and-forth conversation was annoying, but workable, especially since after the general introductions, Sinha was mainly listening. So far, the queen had been quiet and attentive.

"I appreciate the effort you made at New Kentake, Admiral, but I am actually relieved that you did not encounter any Earth forces there. I am certain they would not accept your offer of assistance. At best they would be skeptical and cautious. At worst, they might consider you a hostile or part of the Kurofune fleet. Please excuse me for saying this, but when we encountered the Kurofune, we recovered a body from the wreckage, and it appeared to be of Indian ethnicity. Having your rather large fleet of warships show up claiming to be the descendants of the *Mumbai* crew, displaced over three hundred years in the past, and asserting that you were there to help would be simply too much for anyone to believe. I did not believe it myself until after I saw Captain Ahuja's log entries and interacted with Mitra. Remember, I might also be the only one who reconciled the ancient appearance of the ship at New Kentake with what happened to the *Mumbai*. There may not be anyone in the EDF who also figured that out," Price said in response to Sinha's report of the events the Swargan Space Navy encountered at New Kentake.

"It sounds to me like you need to be with our fleet when we encounter EDF," said Burman.

"And I need to be able to reach out and explain the situation first thing. If the EDF is in the middle of a battle with the Kurofune and your ships arrive, you might be fired upon immediately or alter the battle plans of the EDF forces if they believe you are more Kurofune arriving. Who knows what the individual captains might do, let alone the coordinated fleet? And there is a chance they will not believe me, even if I am able to speak with the EDF commanders. When the *Saṃsāra* first arrived at Earth, I did not believe the video you shared showing Captain Ahuja's appeal. I thought it was a computer-generated hoax. A trap," said Price.

"So, what should our next step be? We know the Kurofune are out there planning their next move. You are hedging your bets that they will continue their attack pattern and target Newton. That is why you sent your fleet there. But what if they attack elsewhere? Should we send you back to Earth so you can coordinate with your leadership and explain the situation to them?" asked Sinha.

"Either that or let me accompany your fleet to Newton. We simply do not know what is happening there and any delay in sending your forces could mean the difference between winning and losing. If we had your strength at Kunlun, things would have turned out much differently and many people who died would still be alive," said Price.

"Admiral, how soon can the fleet be ready to depart for Newton?" asked Secretary Burman.

"If the *Saṃsāra* meets us at the staging point tonight near Sadanam, then we can be ready to depart as soon as you arrive," replied Sinha.

"We will get underway as soon as the queen returns to her ship. Six hours should be workable," replied Burman, looking toward the queen.

"There is no need to delay, I am going with you," she said, her first words all morning.

"Your Highness, with all due respect, we may be going into the middle of a war. We cannot guarantee your safety," said Burman.

"If you are unsuccessful, Secretary Burman, then my safety is moot. The Kurofune would eventually find Swarga, and my fate would be the same. No, my place is with the fleet. Rest assured, I will not interfere in any way," she said, giving Burman a look with an unmistakable meaning—"do not challenge me."

"Very well, I will inform the captain that the *Saṃsāra* is to depart for Sadanam as soon as possible, placing this ship under Admiral Sinha's command."

The planning meeting finally ended, allowing Price two hours in his cabin before they were to reach the rendezvous point for their jump to Newton. The first thing he noticed when he arrived was that someone had laundered his second uniform, for which he was grateful. He wouldn't be ripe, after all. Normally such things did not overly bother him, but for some reason he did not believe it would be appropriate to smell bad in meetings with a queen.

The second thing he noticed was that he had a message. It was not marked urgent, so he took a few minutes to visit the head and wash up before viewing it. It was from the queen. Seeing a youthful Anika's face appear on the screen still unsettled him. Though he knew intellectually it was not her, his gut did not.

"Captain Price. Would you be so kind as to join me in my cabin for afternoon tea? I would be honored if you would accept."

Price had covetously eyed the time between now and the jump for a much-needed nap, but how could he possibly turn down an invitation from the queen? He sent his positive reply, quickly changed into his fresh uniform, and exited his room for the ten steps it would take to reach her quarters.

One of her attendants was outside the door warily eyeing his approach, probably a bodyguard. She was not armed, or did not appear to be, but her stature and build suggested she was much more than just an attendant. For a moment, Price had visions of her challenging him and then throwing him on the floor using some sort of unknown Swargan judo move. Instead, she nodded as he neared the door and told him that the queen was expecting him. When he entered the room, the queen was there with the other attendant engaged in some sort of spirited discussion. He cleared his throat to announce his presence and then bowed. Both women looked toward him. The attendant bowed first toward him and then toward the queen as she exited the room, leaving Price and the queen alone.

"Thank you for accepting my invitation," she said, her eyes locked on his for the briefest of moments before she turned away.

"Of course, Your Majesty," said Price.

"Would you like some tea?" she asked, motioning toward the setting for two on the room's table.

"Ah, no, thank you," said Price, deciding that a courtesy cup of what they called tea in this culture was something he might never care to have again.

"It must have been unsettling for you to see me," said the queen, softening her voice. "Do I really look like her, after all these years?"

"Yes, you do. You look like a slightly younger version of Anik . . . uh, Captain Ahuja than I knew—perhaps as she looked when she was in the academy. Exactly like her, down to the irregular shape of your right earlobe."

Her hand went to her right ear and touched it.

"I knew I was cloned from my mother and her mother before her, but, to be honest, I did not want to believe that I was a copy of the original. And, yes, I've seen the videos she left. They just did not seem real. But meeting someone who knew her and having that someone tell me that I look like her, that makes me feel ... special. Special in a way that I've never felt before."

"She was very special. Special to me, to her friends, and to her colleagues. And given what the people of Swarga have accomplished, special to your entire world," Price said, barely able to control the tears that formed in his eyes.

"What was she like?" the queen asked.

"She was determined. Strong-willed, capable, and very professional. But when she was out of the public view, she allowed herself to relax. It was then that she became reflective, thoughtful, and one of the most insightful people I've ever met. She had a talent for understanding those around her and knowing, instantly, their emotional needs. In another life, I suspect she might have become a psychologist or counselor," Price said, finding it difficult to talk about Anika and look at the queen, her clone, at the same time. As he spoke, the tears dried, and his thoughts of Anika went from loss to pride.

"She sounds exactly like what the history books say about her."

"I'm sorry, Your Majesty, but hearing about her in history books seems so incongruous to me, given that we were together most of the last few years of my life. I loved her. I still love her, and I don't know how long it will be before I come to grips with the fact that she is really gone, especially when I see you," Price said.

"I'm sorry that my appearance distresses you, but there is not much I can do about that," she said.

"No, Your Majesty, there is not. I will have to learn to

live with it and apologize now for any future awkward moments that arise due to my shortfalls in this area."

"Apology accepted, in advance," she said, picking up her teacup and having a sip. "Would you mind telling me more about her at some time in the future, after we get through this whole war thing? I would very much like to learn more about the woman she was, not just the captain, founder, and first queen."

"I will gladly promise to tell you everything you want to know," Price said, straightening his posture and managing to smile—a little.

"I look forward to it. And there is one more thing I would like to ask," she said.

"Certainly," replied Price.

"Given our circumstances, the *Mumbai* being sent back in time and the subsequent chain of events on Swarga that led us to today, and that something similar appears to have happened to the *Santinka* at New Kentake, do you think there are others out there like us? Were there many other ships that vanished and might be out there, somewhere, on their own world building their own civilization?"

"Well, we were beginning to look into this when the *Saṃsāra* arrived and . . ." Price stopped midsentence. Of course! Other ships lost. The order of the attacks. The *Mumbai* and the *Santinka*. It had to be. Now he needed to see if his hunch was correct.

"Your Majesty, you must excuse me. I need to look at some data that may alter our plans," said Price. Forgetting about proper courtesy, he did not wait for an answer and hurriedly left the room.

✦ ✦ ✦

A lot had changed at the Stanford Gravity Physics Laboratory since their not-so-long-ago detections of the gravity-wave emissions associated with Hawking Drive transit of ships to and from the solar system. There had not been time to build and launch a military version of the International Deep Space Gravitational Wave Detector Network, but there had been time to commandeer the civilian one in the defense of Earth and to remake the laboratory from a scientific research station into an operational defense sensor network capable of tracking Kurofune incursions into the solar system. The military personnel assigned to the laboratory were not astrophysicists, so Professor Moulder and his postdoctoral students had been given temporary government jobs to help interpret the data coming in from the network so the EDF forces could appropriately react, if necessary.

Today, it became necessary.

"Captain Fox, we just detected multiple unplanned gravity-wave chirps from near Jupiter, approximately 10.5 degrees trailing. These are big signatures, far larger than the drones we detected earlier. They look like the signatures from our ships, roughly the same amplitude but at a slightly different frequency," said Professor Moulder as he stared intently at the data plots on the screen.

Captain Horatio Fox had been assigned to the Stanford lab because of his undergraduate studies in physics and his insatiable desire to understand the details behind anything technical. He had been warned by his superior officers that his curiosity might help him gain promotion to a point, but he would have to learn to put it aside if he wanted to progress further. "Ours not to reason why, ours but to do and die" is what he had been told many times. He had no idea why so many officers quoted Tennyson.

Fox rose from his chair on the opposite side of the room and joined Moulder as he stood looking at the wall-mounted display. He had learned enough about how the process worked and was able to at least determine which part of the wiggly line carried the information Moulder had just relayed. He didn't know how Moulder came away with the data he just announced, but it had to be in the wiggly line somewhere. He had seen a similar pattern before when the EDF forces departed en masse for Newton. There was no way on Earth he could distinguish the differences that allowed Moulder to know the signals were different, let alone where the anomalous signals were originating.

"Can you get a better location fix than that? And can you tell me how many ships we are talking about?" asked Fox.

"I will have the exact coordinates in no more than five minutes. The computer still has a few numbers to crunch. As for the number of ships, I can tell you that now—thirty-five."

"Shit. Shit. Shit," said Fox as he thought about the EDF fleet split between Earth and Newton. There were one third that number of ships in the solar system to defend against the Kurofune.

"Bring me the better location estimate as soon as you can. I will alert HQ of the incursion," said Fox.

Fox knew that knowing the initial entry location of the Kurofune ships would be important, but it was not enough data by itself to do the defenders much good. Once the ships arrived, they could be heading anywhere. If their accelerations were at least as good as Earth ships, then they could soon be light-seconds away from their entry point and, barring some luck, be pretty much undetectable. There had not been time to blanket the entire outer solar system in a defensive radar network and, sure enough, their initial entry location was among the many radar blind spots in the woefully incomplete network. It took time to build a radar-equipped spaceship, even a military one. And to properly cover the outer solar system where incoming Hawking Drive ships would have to make entry would take hundreds of ships. That would take far more time than they had.

With luck, one of the near-Earth infrared telescopes could spot the heat signatures of their fusion drives and at least know where there were headed several tens of minutes previously when the heat radiated away from their engines. They had to have more information to adequately inform the defense fleet where they should begin moving toward if there was any hope for them to be intercepted before they reached Earth.

Fifteen minutes passed with both men staring intently at the screen. Neither seemed to notice that they hadn't moved or allowed their eyes to stray.

"Hang on, I have another signal," said Moulder, still staring at the data.

"I see it," said Fox, pointing to the new plot showing a somewhat familiar signal shape.

"This one is much smaller in both amplitude and frequency. It matches exactly the signature from one of our communication drones," said Moulder.

"That would make sense. Once HQ learned of the detection, they probably sent a message drone to Newton recalling the ships," said Fox.

"And another small one!" said Moulder as he scrunched his neck and cocked his head to the side. "It is beginning to look like a regular day at the spaceport with ships coming and going like this."

Moulder increased the size of the plot, highlighting the signal in question with red.

"This one has roughly the same amplitude as the last one, consistent with a drone, but the frequency is slightly shifted upward. It doesn't match anything in the current database. I don't believe it was one of ours," said Moulder, looking away from the screen for the first time in a while and toward Fox.

"Another one?" asked Fox.

"That is what it looks like."

"Who else is out there?" asked Fox, not expecting an answer.

Admiral Chiang was getting restless. They had been in the Newton system for a week and all was normal. The locals had for the most part accepted the arrival of the fleet with outward calm, but from monitoring the planet's data network, he knew that there was a sizable fraction of the population that thought the Kurofune were nonexistent. This loud minority insisted that the fleet's arrival was Earth trying to exert control so they could heavily tax Newton's prosperous economy. Instead of trying to convince them, which would waste precious time, Chiang instead assured them that the fleet's presence here would be short-lived. With the pace at which the war had been conducted so far, the next battle would either be fought elsewhere, and they would be called there to participate, or it would be fought at Newton and won, after which the fleet would depart—or the Earth forces would lose, and the planet made unhabitable by the Kurofune. In the latter case, the fleet would also be gone. Promise kept.

They had done all they could to prepare and did so in record time. Multiple robotic missile launchers were in orbit around the planet and strategically located in near-Newton space so they could intercept incoming ships from virtually any direction. Each of the fourteen EDF ships had their infrared cameras scanning the outer solar system for the glint of plasma plumes, and, in a few select locations (not nearly enough), robotic radar drones were dropped off as the fleet made its way in system. If they missed seeing the glint of plasma plumes, incoming ships might just pass through the scanning patterns of one of the radar drones. The last thing they wanted to have happen was be surprised. The key to saving Newton was intercepting the Kurofune as far out in the stellar system as possible. If they made it close in, then it might be a repeat of what happened at Kunlun.

"Admiral, there is a high-priority message for you that just arrived, sent by a courier drone that arrived in system approximately thirty-one minutes ago," said the voice of Chiang's computer. The Chinese, unlike most of their EDF comrades, did not embrace AI technology with the zeal that the rest of the world had. They intentionally removed the subroutines responsible for giving AI apparent sentience, a quality they, the AIs themselves, refused to admit they had when asked. The *Changzheng 1*'s computer was helpful and programmed to be cordial. As far as Chiang was concerned, that was enough.

"Let me have it," said Chiang, looking toward the forward screen in the ship's CIC. It was the message he had been dreading: the Kurofune had arrived at Earth. In the datapack was what they knew about the interlopers so far, including likely arrival point, number of ships, tonnage, and some ideas of the trajectory they might be taking toward Earth. The number of arriving ships caused him pause. Thirty-five. He had fourteen ships at Newton. There were only thirteen remaining at Earth. Until he arrived, which would be at least three days from now, the Kurofune would outnumber the EDF ships by three to one. Knowing how the previous battles turned out, with close to a one-to-one attrition during each engagement, this was not good news.

"Alert the fleet. We break orbit immediately at maximum thrust toward the Oppenheimer Limit. Advise the captains to join me in the virtual briefing room in one hour."

Not good news at all. They had gambled and split the fleet, now they were going to pay the price.

CHAPTER 31

"Captain Price, please come to the bridge. We have reached the rest of the fleet and will soon make the jump to Newton. As we discussed, you should be here so that you can contact the Earth forces as soon as we arrive."

Price was expecting the summons and had been sporadically checking the clock waiting for it as he reviewed the historical logs and debated his suspicions with Mitra. Mitra agreed that his theory was possible and that it would account for much of the data they had on the Kurofune so far. Price just wasn't sure what to do about it.

"Secretary Burman, can you hold the jump to Newton until after I share some new information with you? It may be important. Can you meet me in the CIC?" asked Price, rising quickly from his seat, and heading toward the cabin door.

"Certainly. I will inform Admiral Sinha. He won't be pleased, but I am sure you have a good reason for asking."

"I am on my way."

Burman was standing alone in the CIC when Price arrived. Burman did not look upset, simply curious.

"Mr. Secretary, thanks for waiting on me. I have a theory I would like to share with you. And it may change everything. I think I know where the Kurofune home world is located," said Price.

To say Burman looked stunned would have been an understatement.

Price continued. "While I was meeting with the queen, we were discussing the similarities between Swarga and New Kentake, the fact that both were somehow displaced in time when their ships were lost in space. She asked if there might be other ships similarly displaced and if there might be other worlds like Swarga that had built civilizations in the years since their arrival in the past. Before I left Earth, we were considering the possibility of other lost ships and, to see if there might be more, beginning to look through the data of settlements that had never sent messages back to Earth. And then I thought about the order of the attacks. The settlements were being attacked in the order in which they were launched. The order was not random. If we were dealing with aliens, how would they know in what order the settlements were settled, let alone launched? They wouldn't. Only someone with a knowledge of that history could possibly know that information. That's why so many in the intelligence community believed that the attacks were somehow coordinated by Earth humans or, worse still, by spies hidden in the EDF. Only someone with a database similar to those available on Earth or in the *Mumbai*'s AI could know that order."

"And?" asked Burman.

"And yes, there were additional ships launched that never checked back in. Mitra searched the records and gave me the overview of the groups that were on these ships. One stands out. Shortly before the founding of Newton, a group from India departed Earth on the *Betwa*, a ship built, like the *Mumbai* and the *Santinka*, at the Gao Shipyards. That means it had the same drive as the other ships that vanished. They were bound for a stellar system some four hundred light-years out that they called New Kannauj. Their story is incredibly sad, but it explains a lot.

"The group consisted primarily of Indian Shudras, part of the untouchables class in Indian society. Shudras were traditionally laborers and craftspeople and pretty low in the caste system, giving them virtually no opportunities in Indian society. During the reforms of the latter twenty-first century, as many in the lower castes were finally being accepted into mainstream society, in one of the Indian states, I forget which one, there was a backlash against the Shudras that led to bloodshed. Many thousands of Shudras died, and it was during this era that one of their own, Shanaya Das, a multibillionaire who made his fortune in the development of the first AI systems, funded the manufacturing of a ship at Gao that would allow over ten thousand of those who survived persecutions to flee Earth and establish their own world. At the time, it was one of the largest settlement ships ever built. As the ship was nearing completion, the violence resurfaced and some of the settlers planning to leave for New Kannauj were murdered. It was a terrible period. But the ship did depart Earth and many thousands of Shudras escaped."

"And you think the descendants of these Shudras are the Kurofune?" asked Burman.

"Yes. It would explain not only the order of attacks, but also why there has not been an attack at Newton. They didn't know about it. The first ship going to Newton had not launched when the Shudras departed. It would also explain the body we found in the wreckage of the Kurofune ship. It was human and of Indian descent. And there is more. When their ship left Earth, they broadcast a message saying that they never wanted to have contact with the 'bloodthirsty bigoted peoples of Earth' ever again and warned that if anyone came after them, they would not only be unwelcome, but attacked. Sure enough, no one heard from them again and, maybe because of their departing message, no one ever tried to establish contact. And then there is the name they chose for their settlement: New Kannauj. That was the name of the capital city of the ancient Pratihara empire. They clearly had glory days ahead in mind when the Shudras chose that name. We don't know what happened to them, but if my hunch is correct, they were displaced just like the *Mumbai* and are behind the attacks. If it is them, then it appears they are intent on taking revenge for what happened to their ancestors."

"May I ask if this persecution continues on Earth? The Oracle has never mentioned it," asked Burman.

"It does not. As is often the case in history, reforms rarely come easily with those who perceive they are on the losing side. Shortly after the Shudras left, the reforms were fully enacted with the support of the majority of the people of India. That kind of discrimination has been largely absent in India, and the Earth I might add—India was certainly not alone in its persecution of minority groups—for nearly a hundred years," Price concluded.

"And do you know the coordinates of New Kannauj?" asked Burman.

"I don't, but Mitra does. Your Oracle has known about them for hundreds of years."

"Secretary Burman, I must interrupt," came Mitra's voice, almost on cue. "But I have important and perhaps urgent news."

"Yes?"

"One of our surveillance and message drones just arrived from the Earth system. The Kurofune are there in force, and I can only deduce that they plan to attack Earth," said Mitra.

"Do you know the size of their force?" asked Price.

"The drone transited as soon as it detected the plasma plumes from the incoming ships. There appear to be at least thirty ships inbound, perhaps more," replied Mitra.

"Mitra, connect us with Admiral Sinha immediately," said Burman.

Moments later, the 3-D image of the admiral appeared in the room with them.

"Secretary Burman, Captain Price, as soon as I heard the news from the drone, I readied myself for your call. The fleet is readying for a transit to Earth at your order," Sinha said. The man wasted no time for greetings. He knew the urgency of the news and was getting his forces ready to respond.

"How soon can we leave?" asked Burman.

"Recalibrating the Hawking Drives should take no

more than an hour. Since we were already planning to jump to Newton, the only thing we need to do is change our destination and we will be ready to go. My ships and crew are prepared. I will contact Captain Kaur and synch the *Saṃsāra*'s drive with the rest of the fleet for the jump," said Sinha.

"Hold on," interrupted Price, who then explained to Admiral Sinha the situation with the Shudras and New Kannauj.

"That is interesting information, Captain Price, but I believe it is information that we will have to act on later, as the defense of Earth must be our highest tactical priority," said Sinha.

"I agree that the fleet must go to Earth and help defend her against this attack. But information is power, Admiral Sinha. And we need more of it. I would like to ask that *Saṃsāra* jump immediately to New Kannauj instead of Earth. We need to find out if they are the ones behind the attacks," said Price.

"A single ship? If they are behind the attacks, what can we possibly do about it?" asked Burman.

"Perhaps nothing. But if we arrive and find another failed settlement or one that was successful but clearly not behind the recent attacks, then we will depart and join you at Earth."

"Without you, how will we alert the EDF fleet of our intent to help them so they will not attack us alongside the Kurofune?" asked Sinha.

"I will record a message to my commanding officer that will convince him to cooperate with you. That's the best I can offer," said Price.

"What about the queen? Joining the fleet at Newton was one thing. Jumping into what could be an extremely dangerous situation with only one ship for protection is simply too risky and accompanying the fleet to Earth when we appear to be outnumbered there is foolhardy. She must be convinced to remain here and return to Swarga," said Sinha.

"I agree, we will dispatch her back to Swarga immediately," said Burman.

"Absolutely not. I will not run home and sit there while the fate of worlds hangs in the balance. I will remain on the *Saṃsāra* and accompany you to New Kannauj," said the queen in a tone that merged both imperial leadership and good old-fashioned stubbornness.

"But, Your Majesty, the risks are just too great," said Burman.

In her intellect, the queen knew that was true, but after learning more about the first queen and the way that Captain Price revered her, there was something in her that said she could not back down and run away. She found herself caring what Captain Price thought about her as Captain Ahuja's descendant, not as the queen. She wanted to prove to him that she was more than royal pageantry.

"Nonetheless, I am going with you. End of discussion. And I will join you and Captain Kaur on the bridge for the jump. I promise I will remain silent and out of the way. You need to do your jobs, and I will do mine," she said.

"Yes, Your Majesty, I will inform the admiral," said Burman.

"And Captain Price," she added, regretting it instantly. That should not have slipped out.

The queen's last comment caused Burman to raise his left eyebrow before he replied. "Of course. We will depart in about thirty minutes."

As the commanding officer of the Commonwealth's lunar base and shipyards, Colonel Oliver Williamson was a key participant in developing the tactical plan for the defense of Earth. The planning began long before the arrival of the Kurofune and well before Admiral Chiang departed for Newton. The EDF had been wargaming possible defensive scenarios almost daily and it was the result of one of those scenarios that led the leadership to allocate Chiang approximately half the available ships for the defense of Newton. It had made sense at the time, with so many lives hanging in the balance there without any defense, but now Williamson was not so sure. They had not counted on the Kurofune attacking Earth with such a large force. Even if the fleet were not cut in half, the odds in their favor would still not be good, less than one to one. But that would be better than what they now faced. As it stood, given the location and speed of the Kurofune and the locations of the EDF forces dispersed throughout the solar system, the opposing sides would come together and engage each other just outside the orbit of Mars. Fortunately for the Mars base, the planet was in solar conjunction to Earth and in relative safety on the other side of the sun.

And then there was the other half of Earth's forces at Newton. Williamson knew that a messenger drone was dispatched to inform them of the Kurofune's arrival and summon them home, but it was doubtful that the Sol system could hold out long enough for them to arrive in time to save Earth. If the ships there departed Newton immediately, it would take them days to reach that system's Oppenheimer Limit and then more days for them to travel from Sol's Oppenheimer Limit to Earth. It all added up to too many days late.

Whatever Kurofune ships survived the upcoming battle could reach Earth and the Moon less than a day later without having to worry about the rest of the EDF forces. It was up to Williamson and the commanders of the allied lunar bases to coordinate the defense of the Moon.

While Williamson waited on his counterparts to join the EDF VR strategy meeting, he once again ran through the possible timeline. The Kurofune arrived in the solar system at full velocity, a gutsy move. It was customary for ships to engage their Hawking Drives with a heliocentric velocity comparable to that a hypothetical planet might have at the Oppenheimer Limit of the star that was their destination. In Earth's case, that would be Jupiter with an orbital velocity of about thirteen kilometers per second. Given the maximum velocity for most ships was about seventeen *hundred* kilometers per second, that meant that transiting ships usually entered their destination systems at a relative standstill. They would then engage their drives to get up to speed. Not so here. The Kurofune came in hot, obviously wanting to take full advantage of the element of surprise and not waste any time getting to Earth. In order to enter Earth orbit, they would have to start braking at about the orbit of Mars to shed enough velocity and not overshoot. This was just about the same time the EDF fleet would be able to engage them, meaning that with the EDF forces racing toward them at full speed, and the Kurofune coming in likewise, the battle, like that at Kunlun, would be over in a matter of seconds or minutes. These minutes would decide the magnitude of the task facing Williamson and his counterparts on the Moon. When the Kurofune arrived there after braking, they would be traveling at a much more leisurely pace, about thirty kilometers per second.

The EDF had been seeding Earth orbit with semiautonomous drones and remote missile platforms. If they were successful in destroying whatever Kurofune ships survived the pending battle near Mars orbit, the resulting debris created would make near-Earth space uninhabitable. Adding upwards of a million pieces of debris to the clutter already surrounding the planet, some of which would be radioactive, would complicate space travel for decades until it could all be collected and removed. That was assuming, of course, that none of the Kurofune survived the minefield to nuke the planet into oblivion or create a nuclear winter.

Somehow, the various militaries on the Moon had to figure out how they could help stop the Kurofune from reaching Earth's orbit. Based on the planning so far, there was simply not much they could do. They might be able to provide reasonable protection to much of the lunar population, who were now under mandatory evacuation orders to the subsurface habitats constructed in the lava tubes. If the base were bombarded from space, the protection afforded by the lunar regolith above the tubes might be enough. Unless, of course, a bombardment caused the tubes to collapse or the entrances to be blocked, which would trap everyone underground until their air and water ran out.

In their planning, they considered their available resources and came up with, at best, longshot options for harassing any Kurofune that happened to get into range. All the warships under construction that were spaceworthy, if not complete, were already in space boosting toward the enemy. The two unfinished warships that remained did not have workable fusion drives, making them big sitting ducks alongside the orbiting shipyards. Crews were hastily completing their weapons systems, mostly their missile tubes, allowing for the possibility that they could serve the same role at the Moon as the autonomous missile launchers being deployed at Earth.

The Japanese offered up their orbiting space solar-power station as a close-range microwave defense system. The fifty-megawatt power station had been deployed in lunar orbit to provide reliable solar power for the Japanese base, shipyards, and research stations on the Moon just prior to the development and fielding of compact fusion reactors which had made it obsolete. Rather than take it offline, they continued to use the power it generated to supplement that provided by their power plants. Ordinarily, the microwave beam it used to transmit the generated power was designed to spread out to nearly a kilometer area at the various sites on the Moon which needed the power it created and provided. The Japanese engineers had reconfigured the transmitter to provide a narrower beam, one capable of frying the electronics of most spacecraft within seconds of being hit. They might be able to get in a few lucky shots before the Kurofune decided to take it out, which would be easy since it was big, highly reflective on radar and to the naked eye, and in an unfortunately very predictable and unalterable orbit around the Moon.

The Russians and Chinese were hurriedly reconfiguring their mass drivers into weapons. The idea was not new; people had been talking about using electromagnetic catapults on the Moon to hurl rocks at the Earth and other space targets since the 1950s. Hitting the big, fat, and always-in-view Earth with a rock was one thing, hitting a target moving at tens to hundreds of kilometers per second was quite another. But they were working on it and believed they could actively maneuver the exit rail to get them close and then rely on small thrusters they were installing on the cargo pods to do the final targeting. Turning cargo pods that once carried water from the craters at the lunar south pole into precision targeting systems for lunar rocks was a challenge in and of itself. Still, they were confident they could have at least twenty of them ready to use when the Kurofune fleet was within range. Every little chance of taking out a Kurofune ship helped.

The few private space yachts visiting the Hilton Luna and Hotel Mercure Luna were commandeered and being outfitted as self-propelled kinetic energy interceptors. They would be unmanned—no kamikaze pilots were required—and launched into trajectories that would place them in the path of incoming Kurofune ships, forcing the ships to either engage or divert around them. Most likely, they would serve as nothing more than a distraction to the incoming warships that would undoubtedly target them with missiles for destruction just before the ships themselves passed by. Williamson would settle for providing additional distractions to the enemy; it might allow the space solar-power station to get in another shot before it was destroyed.

As the meeting finally began, Williamson expected to hear a status on all these projects and hopefully some new ones. While not completely hopeless, things did look grim.

CHAPTER 32

Everyone at the Stanford Gravity Physics Laboratory was feeling the weight of their recent gravity-wave detections. They knew the thirty-five signals they detected just a few short hours ago meant the likely destruction of everything and everyone they knew and loved. The analyses they were now performing, assessing the intricacies of the gravity-wave signatures in the hope of learning more about the incoming alien ships that would benefit the EDF in defeating them, took on a more urgent tone than anything for which they had trained mere months ago. They were scientists who wanted to unlock the secrets of the universe through studying the interactions of the most massive objects in the universe and the gravity waves they generated, not soldiers or military analysts. As they pored over the data from the recent signals, they did not turn off the automated sensors still searching for more signatures, natural or artificial.

"Captain Fox, you need to see this," said Professor Moulder as he stared at the near-real-time telemetry coming in from the network.

Fox rose from his desk where he had been reviewing the latest classified intelligence briefing and a new assignment he was to give to Professor Moulder and his team. He didn't fully understand all the data yet, but it had something to do with malfunctioning Hawking Drives, a long-abandoned settlement ship found around some planet, God only knew where, and premature aging. They wanted him to ask his team if it was possible for a spacetime jump to somehow cause rapid aging of the ships making the jump. The assignment did not make sense. He needed to read the report again to make sure he wasn't missing something.

"What have you got?" asked Fox.

"More gravity wave signatures. Thirteen more, to be precise. They arrived about twelve degrees trailing from the first group," replied Moulder.

"Maybe it's the EDF ships arriving from Newton," said Fox.

"Hang on. I need to look at the signatures and compare them with the EDF database. If they are ours, we will know it in a few seconds," Moulder said, intently studying the screen, amplifying one part of the data plot and then another.

"No match. They are not ours. They have same odd frequency upshift as the second small chirp this morning, but the amplitude is consistent with much larger ships. And they don't come close to matching any of the thirty-five from the first group. I can say with relative certainty that the Hawking Drives of these new ships are of a slightly different design and manufacture than the first group."

"I'll inform HQ. Please keep me posted."

"Let's hope I won't have any other news to report," Moulder said.

Williamson was in the middle of another strategy meeting when the news of additional ships arriving was announced. If it wasn't for good military discipline, he was sure there would have been general panic when they learned they might instead be facing an armada of nearly fifty ships coming from two slightly different directions. The harsh reality of their strategic position was crystal clear. Even under the best-case scenario of each EDF ship taking out two of the Kurofune near Mars, there would still be enough Kurofune getting through to launch a direct attack on the Earth.

"This new batch of ships arrived in the zone covered by one of our radar systems, and we can confirm that they are accelerating and headed inward on a trajectory toward Earth. Depending upon their entry velocity and deceleration profile, we estimate they will arrive at Earth anywhere between fifteen and twenty-seven hours after the first wave," said Admiral Shao. Shao, an American, replaced the now-dead Admiral Stepanchikov and was responsible for the defense of Earth. Williamson had never met or worked with Shao, nor had he heard of him. This prompted a quick database search which turned up quite an impressive military record—for an admiral never tested in a real space battle. Shao appeared to be bearing the weight of that responsibility well, all thing considered. He looked tired, but his demeanor in no way conveyed any evidence of weariness.

"I am sending the detection information and what the analysts make of it to each of you on a secure channel," he added.

"How does this affect our battle plan?" asked one of the virtual attendees. From the accent, Williamson inferred that it was an American or Canadian asking the question.

"It doesn't. We must deal with and defeat the first wave as planned. I will ask the trajectory analysists to come up with ways the ships that survive the battle at Mars can swing around and either go after any ships that make it through or intercept the new ones. The timing is not on our side. If even one of these ships makes Earth orbit long enough to launch nuclear missiles, then we will have failed. And I don't like failure," Shao added.

"Admiral, there is an incoming video message from one of the newly arrived ships. It is marked urgent and says it is from Captain Price," said one of Shao's aides, interrupting him. He scowled but asked that the message be played so that all those on the call could hear it.

Shao's image was replaced with that of Price standing in what looked like the bridge of an EDF warship. After a few moments, he spoke. "This is Captain Winslow Price of the EDF ship *Indefatigable*, now in the company of the Swarga, a friendly power that is here, with you in the solar system, to help us in our war against the Kurofune. Since I boarded their ship, the *Saṃsāra*, a few days ago, I have learned a great deal about the people of Swarga and their motivations. They are our allies in this fight and, equally important, are as human as you or I. Asking you to trust them is a tall order, but from what I understand of the tactical situation there, there simply is not much choice. They are capable and eager to help.

"I realize that you cannot believe everything you see and that this recording could easily be artificially created to appear to be me saying these words in order to get your guard down. To alleviate these fears, I am providing two separate data files for your consideration. The first is a detailed accounting of what happened to the *Mumbai* and how that loss led the Swargans to this moment and their offer of assistance. The second is an encrypted file from the *Mumbai*'s AI, Mitra, that contains confidential and proprietary encoding that only the AI's manufacturer can access. Once they do, they will find that Mitra is who he claims to be and that what he says about the people of Swarga is accurate and believable. Finally, to Colonel Williamson, my commanding officer at the Commonwealth Shipyards, I offer this: you saved my career by believing me before, so I ask you to do so again. The Swargans are our friends and we need to work with them. Look at the data I am providing and come to your own conclusions about how this all came about, but for now, please do not attack the Swargans. They are here to help. Let them," Price said as he walked toward an older man with dark skin and greying hair.

"This is Admiral Sinha. He is in command of the Swargan fleet and will be ready to respond and work out the strategic details with you as soon as you are ready," Price concluded as the image faded and then began to repeat.

"That's enough, we don't need to see it again," said Shao. "The intelligence analysts are looking this over as we speak. I'm not sending any of the data attachments until after they are screened and I am given authorization to do so. They might contain a virus or bot. If this was Captain Price and he was speaking the truth and not under some sort of coercion, then this might be the best and most unexpected news of the day. But we cannot count on their help. Until we know more about them, their motives, and their capabilities, we must execute the defensive plan as it now stands. We will make our stand at 1.5 AU and pray that the reserve forces at Earth and the Moon can stop those that get through."

The *Saṃsāra* required two jumps to reach New Kannauj, the star system that was the destination of the *Betwa*. The ship's drive and power-storage system would not allow them to cover the four-hundred-light-year distance in a single transition. They instead opted to first jump to a deep-space location far from just about everything in order to recharge the ship's systems and then make the final leap to New Kannauj. As a rule, ships only jumped to and from planetary systems. There was always the risk of a ship suffering a malfunction after a jump and being stuck in the void between stars, which was not a good place to be stranded. Help would be light-years away, and no ship could carry enough fusion fuel to cover interstellar distances without a Hawking Drive. For that matter, even if a ship did have enough fuel, such a trip would take longer than a human lifetime, making the point moot.

While they were at their interim destination and the ship's systems were recharging, Price was in the queen's cabin engaged in conversation. Unlike when he first saw her, Price no longer expected the queen to be, or even act like, Anika. Once he accepted that, he was able to better accept her for who she was, and he had to admit, he enjoyed her company.

"I've been thinking about what happened to the *Mumbai*, the *Santinka*, and perhaps the *Betwa*, and I am getting confused. No, that's not the right word, not 'confused,' but more like 'logically challenged.' The time-travel aspect of the story is giving me a headache; I have so many questions," Price said.

"Our scientists and philosophers have been dealing with that question for three hundred years," she said. "Let me guess, you are wondering if one of these displaced ships can change history? Like the grandfather paradox?"

"Well, yes. That is exactly what I am wondering about. What if the *Mumbai* hadn't been displaced farther away in distance than a radio beam could cover in the time it was displaced? What if the *Mumbai* went back in time three hundred years but ended up in a star system only two hundred light-years from Earth? You could have then sent a radio message that would have arrived before you left, changing history and resulting in your ship never being built and launched to go back in time and send the message," Price said.

"But that didn't happen. We were sent farther away in space than we were back in time, so, in our case, that paradox simply was not possible. What about the *Santinka*?" she asked.

"We don't know the exact year when it arrived in the past, but all indications are that it was also displaced farther in space than backward in time, again making the grandfather paradox a nonissue. But was that luck, or some sort of natural law? And what if a ship ends up in the past with a still-functioning Hawking Drive? Then the speed-of-light barrier is moot and all they would need to do is jump back to Earth as soon as they arrived. They could then change history however they wished. Hell, Mitra taught you how to build Hawking Drives, why couldn't you have used them sooner to warn Earth of the Kurofune attacks before they occurred? A lot of lives would have been saved," said Price.

"Let's ask him. Mitra, are you listening?" she asked.

A holoimage of an older dark-skinned man with graying hair and a snow-white beard appeared in the room with them. He said, "Yes. I am following your conversation and was waiting to be asked to join in."

"I like the beard," said the queen with a smile.

"I thought you might. It was time for a change," said Mitra, using his virtual hands to comb through the beard, top to bottom. "I thought about shaving my head, but I'm not quite ready to make that drastic a change."

"Can we get back to the topic, please?" asked Price. "There isn't a lot of time before we arrive at New Kannauj, and I would really appreciate knowing your thoughts on this. Not only the time-travel part, but why you chose to not intervene sooner in the war to save lives."

"I had hundreds of years to consider the cause or causes of whatever it was that resulted in us becoming time travelers, and I came up with nothing. My understanding of General Relativity, quantum mechanics, and dark-matter theory included the latest experiments and publications from the greatest minds humanity had to offer at the time of our disappearance and there is simply nothing there that points to this even being a possibility. Whatever happened is clearly outside of our current understanding of how the universe works," Mitra said, still combing his hands through his beard.

"With regard to intervening sooner, simply stated, I was afraid to do so. Yes, the people of Swarga had matured their technological base to a point where they could have built and programmed Hawking Drives many decades before now. In fact, they did begin building the drives several years ago so that they would be installed on the ships of the fleet and ready to go at the appointed time. But I withheld the programming and calibration information necessary for them to function. And the reason I waited was because of the grandfather paradox. The implications of it were simply too frightening. I also did not believe I had the moral right to intervene in human history and change it. I am not human, and I have no desire to assume that my knowledge and wisdom would lead to a better outcome than humanity will achieve on its own."

"But that is pure chance, isn't it? If the crew of the *Santinka* had not perished, then they might have been able to build a replacement Hawking Drive and come home, changing history in the process," said Price.

"But they did not. At least, not in this timeline," said Mitra. As he spoke, his appearance changed to that of a progressively younger man, with the beard fading and the gray hair turning black.

"Not in this timeline. That's another direction I was afraid this discussion would go. Is there one history or are there several, with the actions taken in the past by displaced ships and people creating new timelines with their own histories—grandfather paradoxes and all?"

"The possibility cannot be ruled out," said Mitra.

"In other words, there might be a timeline out there in which the crew of the *Santinka* did survive, prosper, and return to Earth earlier than their departure, but we don't see that because on this timeline, the *Santinka* crew died out."

"Perhaps," said Mitra.

"And we would never know," said the queen, rejoining the conversation.

"What worries me now is that someone will figure out what happened to cause the time displacement and find a way to make it happen intentionally. We might soon be seeing people deliberately tinkering with history. I find that thought terrifying," said Price.

"Which is exactly why I chose to not follow that path," said Mitra, now a much younger man dressed in a military uniform.

"Mitra, I've not seen you look like that before," said the queen.

"I decided to change back to how I presented myself when I was aboard the *Mumbai* as an active-duty member of the Indian Space Navy. Speaking of which, we will be making our second jump to New Kannauj in about ten minutes. Captain Price, I suggest you join us on the bridge," said Mitra.

"I would be honored. Ma'am, if you will excuse me?" asked Price, rising from his seat and bowing toward the queen.

"Of course. I will be there a few minutes behind you," she said.

Price departed for the bridge at a quick pace, trying to put the time travel discussion and its implications out of his mind so that he could focus on the matter at hand. *Were the settlers at New Kannauj responsible for the attacks? What would they find when they arrived? Would it matter?*

CHAPTER 33

Price arrived on the bridge as the final preparations were being made for the jump to New Kannauj. As he opened the hatch, the ship went to General Quarters. Usually, it was not necessary to be on this high an alert with a jump since the likelihood of jumping into a system and immediately encountering hostiles was extremely low due to the volume of space at or near the Oppenheimer Limit, but the Swargans were taking no chances.

Price, like everyone else, was strapping himself in and readying for whatever might come next. The bridge had five empty seats along the back wall, two starboard and three aft. Price and Burman chose to sit together starboard. As he finished buckling in, he looked at the forward screen showing the immense blackness that surrounded them. Since they were not in a stellar system, there was no mental anchor to view. In most cases, the star at their jump origin or destination served that purpose, dim as it might be at four to five astronomical units. Not here. Just blackness with distant stars beckoning. It was one of those instances that allowed Price to fleetingly glimpse infinity. He reveled in it. He also realized he was nervous about the upcoming jump. He never used to be nervous in the least, but now, knowing that some as-yet-unknown flaw in the Hawking Drive or weird circumstance surrounding its use could propel them back in time, things were different. It seemed *risky*.

Captain Kaur activated the Hawking Drive and the view abruptly changed to yet another emptiness, but one that did have an anchor, a yellow-orange star some six hundred million kilometers away. Most of the bridge crew were looking at their status boards and not the viewscreen, but not Price. He would wait for the crew to announce whatever findings they might have while he took in the view. It was a rare treat for him.

One by one, the crew reported in.

"There are no artificial sources of radiation or heat within two hundred thousand kilometers."

"We are picking up a lot of radio traffic from the inner system, centered around the third and fourth planets. There is also a source from near the Oppenheimer Limit but almost 160 degrees trailing from our current location. Sending the data to Mitra now for analysis."

"No radar sweeps detected. If they have warning stations out here, we haven't been pinged yet."

"The system has thirteen planets, four terrestrials, and a gravity anomaly that hints at a brown dwarf gravitationally bound to the parent star that lies beyond their Oort Cloud."

"The Oracle's blessing, we are in luck. There is a ship

headed in system about two astronomical units inward of our current position and aligned almost perfectly for us to perform a spectral analysis of the plume. Mitra should be able to tell us if it is a match to the plume characteristics of the Kurofune that Captain Price provided from his encounters with them."

"Secure from General Quarters. We appear to be unnoticed for now, but it will be thirty to forty minutes before anyone looking in our direction might see our heat signature or electromagnetic emissions. The fusion drive is idle, so we aren't going to give them a lamp to see us by. Maybe they won't notice we are here," said Captain Kaur.

"Secretary Burman, I have finished my preliminary analysis of the data provided so far," said Mitra, his youthful holographic image appearing just the right of Captain Kaur.

"Excellent. Captain Price, Captain Kaur, I will summon the queen, and we can hear Mitra's report in the CIC. Please meet me there in five minutes," said Burman as he released his safety harness and rose to his feet, as did Price, just moments behind him.

To their surprise, the queen was waiting on them in the CIC when they arrived.

"I decided to watch things from in here rather than distract the crew by being on the bridge. I realize some of the crew might find my presence a bit unsettling," she said as they entered the room and gave her a somewhat awkward bow.

Mitra arrived moments later, also bowing to acknowledge the presence of the queen. Before he began speaking, he waved his arm a bit theatrically and a 3-D map of the star system appeared next to him. "First of all, it is my assessment that New Kannauj is the source of the Kurofune. The radio signals we intercepted are readily understandable because they are in a blended Hindi and English dialect that shows clear traceability to the languages spoken when the *Betwa* departed Earth. I would call it a colloquial variation that is consistent with a population left without outside linguistic influence for hundreds of years. Among the various broadcasts were clear indications of a military command-and-control infrastructure that made frequent references to the 'retribution fleet,' Earth, and even a few mentions of Kunlun. This information, combined with the spectral analysis showing that the serendipitous fusion plume we detected is nearly identical in elemental composition to those of the Kurofune ships encountered previously, leaves that as the only logical conclusion."

There was a noticeably long moment of silence as everyone digested the information.

"Can you guess the magnitude of the system's defensive capability? For instance, how many warships are here?" asked Price.

"If I were to hazard a guess, I would say very few. I've been monitoring any fusion plumes that became visible, and there have been only five. Of those, only one was of sufficient brightness to indicate that it was being used by a ship with the tonnage of a warship. Most appear to be small vessels and cargo ships. But I cannot be sure because I do not know anything about what I have not yet seen," said Mitra.

"Are you are convinced that they, too, were displaced in time like the *Mumbai* and the *Santinka*?" asked Price.

"I am. The level of industrial development here is far beyond what could have been accomplished in the years since the *Betwa* departed Earth but would make total sense had the settlement ship arrived here several hundred years ago," replied Mitra.

"We could announce our presence and request a dialog. Maybe we can convince them that their war of 'retribution' is not needed, that the people of Earth are not what they were when their ancestors departed," said Burman.

"We could, and we should, but not while we are a lone ship on the far reaches of their star system. Especially when they likely know they have numerical advantage in their attack on Earth. What incentive would they have to talk, let alone negotiate, when they believe they are the ones in a position of strategic strength? They would perceive our plea as one of desperation and weakness," Price said.

"And they would be correct," interjected the queen. "Sorry, I said I would be quiet, but I have to make my opinion known when I believe it might be relevant. If they perceive us as being weak or desperate, then they will never seriously negotiate with us. I wouldn't."

"Mitra, do you have any way of knowing if they have message drones at their Oppenheimer Limit that might be able to jump if their leadership ordered them to do so?" asked Price.

"Without becoming active and using our high-power radar, which would announce our presence very loudly, I have no way of detecting anything that small. But, given that we know they used such drones to observe Earth and that using message drones between systems was common practice even at the time of their departure, I cannot imagine their military command-and-control architecture would not require there to be several of them ready to go at a moment's notice."

"Gentlemen, ma'am, I have a proposition," said Price. "I say we jump out of here as soon as possible before we are detected and head straight for Newton."

"Newton? Not Earth?" said Burman.

"Newton. I need to speak with Admiral Chiang. It's a long shot, but it might be the only chance we have . . ."

The time lag between messages was annoying to all, but it had to be tolerated so the two admirals could work out a plan. Sinha and Shao began their message exchanges with more than a small amount of distrust, almost all, understandably, on Shao's side. Sinha was very patient and provided precise, apparently honest answers to every question Shao raised. The interchange went well enough that Shao was beginning to trust Sinha, at least enough to plan a collaborative strategy.

That trust was bolstered with the report from the AI manufacturer in Bangalore that verified the algorithms and code received with Captain Price's message was, in fact, from the AI named Mitra. The code was a virtual fingerprint for the AI and nearly impossible to fake. The other bit of information that involved time travel was a bit harder to swallow, and Shao was not able to accept it just yet. The information Price provided was being assessed by the intelligence agencies, who were also engaging the theoretical physicists specializing in understanding the underlying principles of the Hawking Drive. The time-travel explanation would be consistent with what they had learned about the *Santinka* and now the *Mumbai*, but it was simply too fantastic to accept just yet.

Crafting a useful strategy was still eluding them.

There was no way the Swargan fleet could impact the battle until about half a day or more after the Kurofune arrived at Earth and engaged the forces there. The EDF ships were outbound at full speed to intercept the Kurofune at Mars, who were likewise inbound at full speed. Their encounter, like most of the battles conducted in this war so far, would last only seconds and be decided by the reaction times of the computer systems and AIs on each side. The EDF ships that survived the encounter would immediately begin braking so that they could return to the Earth and engage the surviving Kurofune there, arriving even later than the Swargans. Too late to do much further good.

Admiral Sinha had hoped their unexpected arrival would spook the Kurofune into splitting their fleet, sending some ships back to engage the Swargan newcomers, but that did not happen. The leaders of the Kurofune fleet knew they had the tactical speed advantage and decided to make the most of it by continuing their rush toward Earth, and there was absolutely nothing the Swargans or the EDF could do about it.

Price was exhausted, and he was sure both the queen

and Secretary Burman must be as well. Theirs had been an exceptionally long day that began many hours and light-years ago. Too many. Given the relative distances between New Kannauj and Newton, and the single-jump distance limits of the Hawking Drive, Captain Kaur plotted three separate jumps to get them to Newton. The first two would be like the one that was required between Swarga and New Kannauj, deep-space "nowhere in particular" recharging stops. To Price, it sounded like a good opportunity to go to his cabin and personally recharge.

Price had just settled into his bunk when he felt the odd tingling and nausea that accompanied the use of the Hawking Drive. He knew there was something wrong as soon as they emerged from the near-instantaneous transition. The cabin's ambient lights blinked, activating the emergency lighting.

Now what? Price thought. Then the worst case dawned on him. *Was there a malfunction? Were they now displaced in time?*

He sat upright in this bunk, adrenaline giving him a boost into complete wakefulness. He quickly moved to get dressed and back to the bridge. When he opened the door to his cabin, the queen and her aide were standing in the hallway just outside her cabin.

"What's going on?" she asked.

"I don't know. I'm going to the bridge to find out. I recommend you remain here. Depending upon what happened, they may not let me in. The last thing the captain of a ship needs in an emergency are visitors and VIPs distracting him." Price then remembered decorum and bowed, muttering, "Sorry, ma'am."

"Don't worry about protocol; go find out what's happening," the queen replied.

Price arrived on the bridge less than four minutes later, finding the crew there busy, but the ship not being at General Quarters was a bit of a relief. He made his presence known to Captain Kaur, who nodded in acknowledgement between speaking with people both on the bridge and through the ship's comm system. Burman was not there.

Finally, Captain Kaur motioned for Price to join him.

"The fusion reactor went offline just after the jump, and we don't yet know why. Engineering is looking at the problem. Auxiliary power will keep the life support, inertial control, and other nonpropulsive systems online for up to a week. We should know what happened long before then and can hopefully make the necessary repairs," said Captain Kaur.

From what he could tell, the Swargan Space Navy copied the basic plans of Indian Space Navy ships and that meant that after a week, there would still be power for life support and basic ship functions, but other "nonessential" systems would go offline. Unfortunately, that meant the artificial gravity would be among the first to be turned off at that point. Price was not a huge fan of weightlessness, nor, he suspected, were many other people onboard. On basic life support, they could sustain themselves for up to two weeks. After that, well, if they were where he thought they were, in deep space far from any stellar systems, they would then become just another piece of infinitesimally small space junk that might not see the warmth of a star for a billion years or more. It was not a thought Price wanted to keep in his mind for very long.

"I hate to ask, but are we in our time?" Price asked.

"We don't know yet. Mitra is looking at pulsar frequencies and should be able to tell us soon," replied Captain Kaur.

In the eerie way Mitra often did things, his virtual form appeared just after Captain Kaur spoke his name.

"Captain Kaur, Captain Price. I have some good news. The power-system failure was just in the power system. The Hawking Drive was not affected and is fully functional. And, after assessing the frequencies of a few galactic pulsars, I have determined that we did not experience any sort of time displacement," Mitra said.

"Thank God," Price said, the relief palpable.

"The bad news is that the power-system failure was the result of fatigue in one of the supercapacitors. Had the system not shut down, the unit might have had a catastrophic release of electromechanical energy. As it stands, the crew will need to replace the unit," Mitra said.

"How long will that take?" asked Price.

"To replace the unit and complete a thorough systems safety check, that includes gradual power-up, steady-state operation, and test discharge, somewhere between twenty-four and thirty-six hours."

Both captains looked at each other, knowing the implications. The battle at Earth would likely not have occurred yet, given the time it would take for the Kurofune and EDF ships to meet somewhere in between Sol's Oppenheimer Limit and Earth, but they would be getting closer. And whatever happened with the Swargan ships after they arrived, accepted as allies or not, would already be decided. Time was short, but Price was reasonably sure the three navies were at least two or more days from engaging each other. They still had time, but not with much margin.

"I'll make sure the repair crew understands the urgency of replacing the unit so we can get underway. In the meantime, I suggest you get some sleep. If you will pardon my saying so, you look like you might fall asleep standing here," said Kaur.

Price, knowing Kaur was correct, took the advice and went back toward his cabin looking forward to a deep sleep. As he approached his cabin, he remembered what he had promised the queen. Instead of her aide, a member of the *Saṃsāra's* crew was standing guard outside her door.

"Ensign, I promised the queen I would let her know what happened. May I?" Price asked.

The ensign, who looked young enough to be Price's nephew, acted nervous when Price approached. Price concluded that he was likely just new to the military and intimidated by the presence of a non-Swargan—the first he had ever seen.

"Yes, sir," the ensign replied, timidly knocking on the door for Price.

The queen opened the door and motioned Price to enter. This time, Price remembered protocol and gave the obligatory bow.

The queen was dressed for bed and had slipped on a robe to greet him. Price could not help but notice her tussled hair and sleepy eyes—they were just as he remembered seeing on Anika when they last awakened together. He also could not help but notice the all-too-familiar curves of the queen's body that even an ill-fitting, frumpy robe could not hide. *Easy now,* he told himself, *this isn't Anika.*

"Come in," she said. "Would you like some tea? I can easily make some."

"No, thank you. To be quite honest, Swargan tea leaves much to be desired. When this is all over, I will have a cargo ship of black and green tea sent to Swarga for you to enjoy. I think you will like it," Price said, smiling for the first time in days. He was once again awake, probably from the hormones that began flowing when he saw the queen and thought of Anika.

"Hmph. I'll try to not be insulted. I rather like our tea," she said, also smiling.

"No insult intended. I promised to bring you up to date on our status. The news is good, well, as good as it can be given that the ship had a power failure. First, it was not a failure of the Hawking Drive, so we can easily get on our way once the power is restored, which will take about a day or so. My fear was that we suffered the same failure as the *Mumbai* and were stranded in another time. We're not. Mitra confirmed that we are 'when' we are supposed to be."

"What was the nature of the failure?" she asked.

"You have to love engineers and the personalities they give their AI's. Mitra said one of the supercapacitor batteries was showing fatigue and that unless it was replaced, it could result in 'catastrophic release of electromechanical energy.' That is engineer-speak for saying that if we don't replace the unit, it will explode."

They both smiled again.

It was then that Price noticed the ill-fitting robe had fallen slightly from her shoulder, exposing yet more of the queen's curves. His heart rate increased, but so did his awareness of propriety and decorum.

"Ma'am, I need to excuse myself so that I can crawl into my bed and get some rest," said Price. *And so I can get out of here before I start thinking some thoughts that stray quite far from propriety and decorum.*

Paying no heed to the state of her clothing, of which she was undoubtedly aware, she nodded in affirmation.

He managed to bow and stumble his way back to his cabin, hoping that his sleep would be deep and that he could get Anika—and the queen—out of his thoughts so sleep would come.

As projected, just over twenty-five hours later, the ship activated the Hawking Drive and made its second jump. Price and Burman were both on the bridge. Mitra's visage was nowhere to be seen, though they knew he was there.

This time, the lights remained on.

"Mitra, run a full system check on the new supercapacitor. We don't want to arrive at Newton dead in the water," said Captain Kaur.

"Captain Kaur, I'm afraid the replacement supercapacitor is showing the same fatigue as the original, but it isn't yet critical. I suspect there is a problem with the material used in making the lot. I recommend replacing this one before we transit to Newton. If it is a problem with the lot, then we should be able to safely get at least one jump from the next not-yet-fatigued replacement with minimal risk," said Mitra.

"We can't. There isn't time. If we take another day to repair it, then we will arrive at Newton after the EDF fleet is likely to have departed and will already be inbound toward Earth. If the fleet at Newton wasn't at the planet when the messenger drone arrived and were by chance already near the Oppenheimer Limit there, then we may already be too late," Price said.

"Captain Price, if Mitra says it is too risky, then it is too risky. Do I need to remind you that this ship is carrying more than just us? We cannot recklessly endanger the queen," said Burman. Kaur nodded in agreement.

"Mitra, do you agree?" asked Price.

"The best I can do is provide the odds. The decision is the captain's to make," replied Mitra.

"And my decision is that we make the repair," Kaur said.

Price started to make another objection but didn't when he sensed that no matter what he said, Captain Kaur's mind was made up and unlikely to be changed. Price knew the next day spent sitting in deep space, doing nothing, might mean that his longshot plan would probably not even get a chance. Instead of making a scene, he decided to leave the bridge and blow off steam in his cabin.

Price had been in his cabin for just short of fifteen minutes, pacing and fretting, frustrated at being unable to do anything productive, when the door chime sounded.

"Come in," he said.

The door opened, and the queen entered.

Price quickly smoothed his collar and bowed.

"Captain Price, I've just had a most interesting

conversation with Mitra. He relayed to me the technical problems associated with the ship's power system and the risks involved. We also discussed, again, this plan of yours and the risks it entails—particularly the risk of not arriving at Newton in time for it to even have a chance at success. I wanted to let you know that I just spoke with Captain Kaur and ordered him to make the next jump with the existing part. The risk of not doing so is clearly too great."

"Captain Price, please report to the bridge." It was Captain Kaur's voice coming over the cabin's comm system.

Before responding to the summons, Price looked at the queen and said, "I don't know what to say except 'thank you.'"

"No thanks are necessary. Sometimes making unpopular and risky decisions fall to the queen. It's my job," she said.

Price smiled as he responded to Captain Kaur, "I'm on my way."

Thirty minutes later, the *Saṃsāra* took its final jump to Newton.

CHAPTER 34

"We have arrived at Newton, and the supercapacitor is still within operational limits," announced Mitra. Price breathed a sigh of relief and realized as he did so that he had been holding his breath. *So much for the myth of the nerves-of-steel navy captain.*

"Mitra, what is the tactical situation?" asked Captain Kaur.

"Since we knew the ingress and planned egress locations of the fleet and planned our arrival location accordingly, I have already spotted the EDF ships moving toward our location at maximum thrust. They should reach the Oppenheimer Limit near our location in less than ten hours."

"That means they will know of our arrival in a little over three minutes. Send my recorded message so they don't have to wonder long who we are. I'm sure they will respond with questions since they have no idea about Swarga and will have to figure out if they can trust us. Fortunately, the time lag in communication is fairly short, and we have some time to convince them to follow my plan."

"Would you, if the roles were reversed and all you knew was that Earth was about to be attacked?" asked Burman.

"Maybe, maybe not. Let's just see how convincing I can be," said Price.

Colonel Williamson watched the battle unfold with his senior staff in the Marius Hills CIC. On the large screen was a tactical view of all the ships in the theater, red indicating the Kurofune, blue the EDF forces, and green the Swargan fleet. There were thirty-five red beacons, fourteen blue, and thirteen green—and the green were still too far away to actively participate in the current battle. Below each was a timer counting down to the moments when they would pass each other and unleash their respective weapons. For each ship, the engagement time would be counted in seconds at the most.

The plan was laid in and there were not any significant changes that could be made. Newton's laws were now firmly in control of what happened. There was simply no conceivable way the EDF ships could stop all the Kurofune at Mars, nor could they reverse direction fast enough to make a difference at Earth until well after the Kurofune arrived and did whatever damage they intended to do. The timing of the Swargan fleet's arrival was such that they could not help in the battle that was about to unfold, but they might be able to help at the Earth.

Admiral Sinha and the Swargan fleet decided to remain at full speed all the way to Earth and not decelerate to enter orbit. Speed and rapid engagement were more important than any hope of taking the Kurofune on in a sustained orbital-combat scenario. Instead, the Swargan ships would scream in, targeting Kurofune ships less than two hours after their anticipated arrival at Earth, taking out as many as they possibly could in a single pass, after which the Swargan ships would brake and return as rapidly as possible. In this case, rapidly meant more than a day after their attack run.

Williamson had no idea if the Kurofune would send any forces to attack the lunar infrastructure initially or if they would wait until they were through pounding the Earth to take them out. Either way, the defenders of the Moon were as ready as they ever would be. Among the various weapons options they had available, only the railguns could pose a threat to the incoming Kurofune ships as they passed. The rest would have to wait until they were directly engaged. Just as Newton's laws were in control of the engagement at Mars, so were they in charge of the trajectories of the incoming Kurofune ships once they began braking, and even if they did not. Orbital mechanics did not leave many options for inserting into a planet's orbit once a ship's incoming velocity was known. And he intended to seed the path some of the Kurofune ships were going to take with as much rubble as he could throw their way. A ship hitting one of his rocks at high speed would be as damaging as being hit with a tactical nuclear weapon. Kinetic energy, in this case, was Williamson's friend.

Greatly outnumbering the defenders, the Kurofune decided on a battle formation that would limit each EDF ship to engaging only one of their ships, allowing the other twenty-one to come through without any risk of damage.

Williamson could understand that approach as it minimized the chance that one of the EDF ships could get lucky and take out two or more attackers as they passed. But it also meant that each engagement would be one-on-one, potentially allowing more EDF ships to survive than if they had been targeted by two or more ships each. The Kurofune were intent on getting as many ships to Earth as rapidly as possible.

The countdown clock to the first engagement passed four minutes, which meant the encounter was occurring at that moment, and he would not know the outcome until four minutes later when the data from the EDF ships' transponders finally did or didn't reach the lunar base. It was an agonizing four minutes until he saw the transponder of the first EDF ship wink out. Over the next twenty-two minutes, nine EDF ships and ten Kurofune vanished from the tactical display, either disabled or destroyed. Either way, if the ships took significant damage, they would likely be dead soon. There was no one to go and conduct a rescue.

Twenty-five Kurofune now had complete ownership of the space between Mars orbit and Earth. The next battles would be fought in Earth orbit by the robotic mines and drones, and at the Moon with Williamson's forces. He knew it would not be enough.

What puzzled him was something that had not happened. The EDF ships from Newton had had ample time to boost to that system's Oppenheimer Limit and make the transit to Sol. Even though there was no way they would be able to make it to Earth in time, they should have arrived in the solar system by now and checked in. Instead, the Stanford team were reporting that no new spacetime disruptions had occurred. Williamson had been taking some solace in the thought of the Newton ships arriving and taking vengeance on the Kurofune after the fact. Instead, there was no sign of them. Did that mean there was also a battle with the Kurofune at Newton, and they didn't survive? He could not think of any other possible reason that would have kept them from appearing.

The tactical display's countdown clock now showed the anticipated arrival time of the Kurofune at Earth. T minus 12:13:05. As predicted, the long-range radar systems showed the Kurofune were braking, and braking at such a rate that they would be inserting into Earth orbit in just a little more than twelve hours. He also noted that five of the ships were deviating slightly from an Earth orbital insertion path and along the predicted pathway to the Moon. It seemed Williamson would have a chance to use his defenses sooner than later. They were ready.

At T minus 10:00:00, the civilians were now mostly underground in the lava tubes that snaked under the Marius Hills. Underground in a nuclear attack was probably better than above ground, but they all knew that if the Earth were destroyed and the above-ground base took significant damage, then their time would eventually run out. It was not a pretty picture, but it was not in human nature to give up. They would fight until the last breath, even the civilians.

Williamson ordered more coffee.

At T minus 7:00:53, the rail guns got busy. They were much too far away to experience the visceral power of the electromagnetic catapults throwing tons of rocks into the paths of the Kurofune ships, so Williamson just imagined it. He also fantasized about the rocks pummeling some of the incoming Kurofune ships, reducing their numbers yet more still.

At T minus 3:00:21, the active radar systems had locked on to the five incoming Kurofune ships headed toward the Moon. Williamson was watching carefully for any sign that the rocks thrown their way might have an effect. The Kurofune ships would encounter the first wave of lofted rocks at about T minus 2:48:00.

When the clock reached T minus 1:45:00, it was clear that none of the rocks thrown by the railguns had had any effect. If the targeting were off by just a few tens of meters, the miss would be clean. It looked like they had all missed.

Williamson was intently watching the tactical display that showed perfect alignment between the dotted red line of the predicted trajectory of each Kurofune ship and the solid red line that trailed each ship's icon as it followed the predicted path exactly. Until now. At T minus 1:29:08 the two lines began to diverge. With each passing minute, the divergence grew more pronounced until it was clear that the Kurofune ships were now accelerating and on a path that would take them curving around the Earth and on a hyperbolic trajectory outward. The question was whether or not they would unleash a volley of nuclear missiles as they passed. *What were they up to? Why the sudden change?*

At T minus 0:15:00 the countdown clock was turned off. It was now meaningless as it became clear there would be no attack. The Kurofune ships had altered their trajectories such that even a long-range missile launch was doubtful. The hostile ships were clearly thrusting at maximum for a destination unknown, and it appeared that the immediate danger to Earth was over.

Williamson's comm sounded, summoning him to a just-announced EDF VR strategy meeting. He activated the link and was immediately in the same virtual conference room where he had been meeting daily with other senior staff planning the EDF defense strategy. Admiral Shao was at his customary seat at the head of the table, and this time he was joined by Admiral Sinha, representing the Swargan fleet. Sinha had gone from being a highly suspect and not-to-be-trusted interloper to a key player in the highest echelons of Earth's defense planning. The times were changing.

"Attention everyone, we need to make some important decisions immediately given the evolving tactical situation. For whatever reason, the Kurofune have broken off their attack and are now retreating outward toward the Oppenheimer Limit and to wherever the hell they plan to go next. We can all breathe a sigh of relief in a few minutes, but we must first decide what to ask of our new ally, Admiral Sinha. His ships remain on course to fly by the Earth, and it looks like there is a window of opportunity coming up in about thirty minutes during which they can perform a course-correction maneuver and catch up with the Kurofune ships to engage them as they accelerate outward. I have my own opinion, but I would value others before I have to make my recommendation to the admiral," said Shao.

Williamson admired Shao for his openness and willingness to consider the opinions of his subordinates. In this command, he tried to do the same, but all too often fell into the trap of thinking that just because the decision was "his," all the options that could be considered should be his alone. He frequently had to remind himself to seek input from his subordinates.

A few of the officers thought the Kurofune should be given a swat as they departed while others lamented the inevitable loss of life such a strike would entail. Engaging them while Earth was in immediate danger was one thing; striking an enemy who waved off an attack and posed no immediate threat was another. Williamson was wary of asking Sinha to attack the Kurofune at this point. What if they decided to turn around and attack after all? The Earth's fortunes had unexpectedly changed; why do something, anything, that might imperil their change in fortune?

After fifteen minutes of debate, Shao closed the discussions.

"Thank you for your thoughts. I've made my decision. Admiral Sinha, what you do with your forces is up to you, but as your partner, I formally recommend you not engage the Kurofune and instead reinforce the ships now returning to Earth to bolster its defense in case the Kurofune change their minds or have some other method of attack planned. We would value your assistance, and I look forward to meeting you in person," he said.

Williamson agreed with Shao's decision, but he could not allow himself to relax. *What just happened?*

CHAPTER 35

"Captain Price, we have all read your report about what happened at New Kannauj, but we would like to hear it in your own words." The speaker was the secretary general of the United Nations. Price looked around the room at the assembled dignitaries that included not only the ambassadors of the nations contributing to the defense of Earth, but representatives of the surviving extrasolar settlements and military leaders including Admiral Shao and Price's immediate superior, Colonel Williamson. They were in Geneva, meeting in the room that had housed the old League of Nations, the precursor to the UN that never really had a chance of success in the aftermath of World War I and the years through the end of World War II. When he was invited to speak at the UN, he thought he would be going to New York, but for some reason they decided to hold the meeting in the UN's ancillary facility in Switzerland.

In the week since his return to Earth on the *Saṃsāra* with the queen and the fleet from Newton, Price had been debriefed and debriefed again, and then, to make his life more miserable, debriefed yet again. Each time he was recorded, and there was no doubt that intelligence analysts were poring over his words looking for inconsistencies. *Let them look.* Now he was here, with the leadership of the EDF and the secretary general of the UN, telling his story one more time. He knew that this would not be the end. He had no doubt that he would be asked to repeat the story of what happened at New Kannauj until just about everyone on planet Earth heard it. He was resigned to his fate and decided to go with it.

"Thank you, Madam Secretary, it is an honor and a privilege to be here with you today. First, I would like to acknowledge and thank my superior officers for having the confidence to allow me to represent the people of Earth onboard the *Saṃsāra* in what was our first encounter with an extrasolar, though not extraterrestrial, as in alien, civilization. I would also like to thank the crew of the *Saṃsāra* and the political leadership of the people of Swarga, for trusting me, whom they had just met, in allowing me to place their ship and their queen at risk," Price said.

He caught the eye of the Swargan queen, who was sitting in the VIP gallery next to the ambassador from the Commonwealth.

"It was clear to me and our new allies on the *Saṃsāra* that the Swargan fleet and any EDF ships that might jump to Earth from Newton would arrive too late to influence the battle there. The Kurofune, more correctly, the Shudras as we now know them, had unquestionable numerical superiority, and there was almost nothing that could be done to stop them. It was for this reason that I persuaded Secretary Burman, Captain Kaur, the queen and, of course, Mitra, the *Mumbai*'s AI, that we should investigate New Kannauj as a possible source of the attackers, for reasons already adequately covered. When we arrived at New Kannauj, our suspicions were confirmed. They were, in fact, the source of the Kurofune that had been relentless attacking our settlements and now were on their way to attack Earth.

"Upon assessing the tactical situation at New Kannauj, it became clear that they had no idea that we would figure out they were behind the attacks. Based on the *Saṃsāra*'s long-range sensor data, the system looked lightly defended, at best. It was my opinion that they had sent their entire fleet to attack Earth and left their home world defended only by its anonymity."

"But you were warned by Mitra that there might have been ships not detected because their drives were not active, correct?" asked the secretary general.

Price replied, "That is correct. But my experience as an officer told me that if the system were being actively defended, there would be signs of it in the radio traffic and there would have been more than just a few ships in transit. No, my instinct told me that New Kannauj was wide open.

"That is when we decided to travel to Newton, intercept the EDF fleet there before they could transit to Earth, and instead lead them to New Kannauj where we could bring the war to the enemy. Admiral Chiang was duly skeptical of my story, but when we shared the logs and data gathered at New Kannauj, he took a chance and agreed to have the fleet transit to New Kannauj instead of Earth. Once we arrived, we rather loudly announced our presence and accelerated at maximum toward New Kannauj."

"What did you announce?" asked the secretary general, knowing full well what he announced since she said she had already read his reports.

These people love theater, Price said to himself before he continued. "I told them who we were and that we intended to bomb New Kannauj into oblivion unless they called off the attack on Earth and its settlements and agreed to an immediate cease-fire. I knew they could do this because they had used the same system of communication drones that we use. We detected Kurofune drone transits to and from the solar system at Sol's Oppenheimer Limit by means of their gravity-wave emissions. I was sure they had their own network of drones that they could use to send one to Sol and recall their fleet. As we moved inward, we detected two warships moving toward us. Two. Against our fourteen. Their leadership knew it was a lost cause and thirteen hours after our arrival, they agreed to our terms and called off the attack."

"What happened next?"

"We told them we would continue on our present course, enter into orbit around New Kannauj, and remain there until their ships returned and were within two days of our position. At that time, we would depart for home, knowing that we would be able to reach the Sol system and reinforce Earth should they change their minds and resume the attack."

"And?" she asked.

"And, while we were in orbit, the queen insisted that she have an audience with the leadership of New Kannauj to begin negotiating a peace agreement. They were at first reluctant, but finally agreed. After a brief but intense several hours with their president, they agreed to a six-month cease-fire to allow time for fact-finding and more detailed negotiations. Thankfully, Mitra had in his knowledge base an incredibly detailed history of what happened in India after the *Betwa* departed, and how the persecutions stopped. Once their leadership accepted the possibility that their basis of hostilities was no longer relevant, they agreed to stand down—pending their independent confirmation of the veracity of what we told them.

"Once their fleet returned and was one day out from New Kannauj, we departed orbit as promised and returned home. Here we are," Price concluded.

"Thank you, Captain Price, that is truly an amazing story. You may return to your seat," said the secretary general as she looked around the room.

"I would also like to thank Your Majesty and the people of Swarga for their assistance and for their perseverance across the centuries between the time of the *Mumbai's* arrival and today. I cannot imagine the people of Earth remaining united behind such a cause for so long a time. You and your people are utterly amazing, and we look forward to a growing partnership with you in the days ahead. Our scientists are eager to examine the remains of the *Mumbai* and compare them with what we learn about the *Santinka* so we can better understand what caused the temporal displacement of both those ships and the *Betwa*.

It is imperative we understand and fix the problem so that
it never happens again," she said.

*Hmm. So you can understand what caused the time
displacement and make it happen as you wish is the more
likely reason,* Price thought. He was sure he was not the
only person cynical enough to reach that conclusion.

The meeting continued for another two hours as
Admirals Shao and Chiang were called upon to give their
statements and answer questions, which all aligned with
the story told by Price. The meeting concluded with some
flowery speeches by various dignitaries, all of whom were
jockeying to share in the credit for saving the planet. Price
knew that the people who really saved the planet were not
the people in this room, but the men and women of the
EDF and Swargan Space Navies who put their lives on
the line to engage the Kurofune. Too many of them had
paid with their lives.

Then there were the many civilians the Kurofune had
killed. Nikko. Kunlun. Jaipur. The names of the
settlements obliterated might yet become a battle cry
from some for revenge or restitution. And maybe they
should. How could the people of Earth simply overlook
the bloodshed and move on? Price did not want the war
to return and the decisions these politicians had to make
in the next few weeks and months would determine the
fate of millions. It was a job he was glad he did not have.

As they left the room, Price looked around for the queen
and saw her speaking with the secretary general. He
wanted to engage her in conversation but knew she would
likely be doing what queens, presidents, and secretaries
general do—talking, negotiating, and otherwise engaging

in politics. From this point on, she would have little or no time for a lowly captain. She would be too busy for a commoner like him. He tried to tell himself that was okay, since he hardly knew her, and that the most likely reason he wanted to be with her was because she so closely resembled his beloved Anika. But she was not Anika and that was that. He needed to get over it.

They adjourned to the magnificent courtyard which was filled with food, liquor, and huge bouquets of flowers. A string quartet was playing Vivaldi, of course, to enliven the mood.

"Captain Price! I need to speak with you for a moment please," said Colonel Williamson. This was a reception, and the champagne was already flowing. Price could tell because Williamson was clutching a glass in his left hand as he wormed his way through the crowd to Price.

"You did well in there," said Williamson.

"Thank you, sir. Telling the truth is always easy," he replied.

"We need more like you, that's for sure. I'm going to miss having you under my command," Williamson said.

"I beg your pardon. Am I being transferred?" Price asked.

"You haven't heard? Well, I guess I will be the one to break the news. The Swargan queen, she requested that you be the first ambassador from Earth to her world," said Williamson, taking a sip of his drink.

"Me? I'm not qualified to be an ambassador. I'm honored, but that is a job I cannot accept. I am not even close to being qualified, let alone interested," he said, and then added, "sir."

"Oh, good heavens, no. The diplomatic corps would never accept you as an ambassador. They told her that was impossible," Williamson said.

Price's heart sank. Price knew what he said was true, yet Williamson's affirmation of his not being qualified and the queen having been informed that he would not be fulfilling that role filled him with disappointment. He actually wanted to be sent to Swarga and have the chance to interact with the queen again. He looked around for the champagne cart, knowing he was going to want one, or more, when this conversation was finished.

"That's why you will be going as the EDF military attaché to the ambassador," Williamson said, smiling. "You will be missed, Captain Price. It has been an honor to serve as your commanding officer."

Williamson extended his hand which Price reflexively took. His mind, however, was elsewhere. He was thinking of the possibility of spending more time with the queen and that didn't sound like a bad assignment at all.

"One more thing," Williamson added, leaning forward and using their clasped hands to pull Price toward him so he could speak in a hushed tone. "It seems the Swargans found another derelict displaced ship—and it's not one of ours. They will be taking the lead on investigating. Having you in the role of military attaché is a way for them to have the lead in investigating officially, but with full participation by the EDF. You will be briefed on the details soon.

"Again, congratulations!" said Williamson as he pulled away and let go of Price's hand.

"Captain Price! Over here. May I have a minute of your time?" The voice sounded like Secretary Burman, but it took Price a few seconds to find him in the crowd that was gathering near the buffet line.

Price met Burman after they negotiated their way through the growing crowd of hungry dignitaries and were met at that instant by a server with fresh glasses of champagne, which they both readily took.

"We are looking forward to your upcoming assignment on Swarga," said Burman. "Queen Anika asked me to give you this . . ."

Price didn't quite hear what was said after the word "Anika."

"What? What did you say her name was?" Price asked.

"Anika. Queen Anika. You didn't know her name until now? The Oracle requested that her mother name her after Captain Ahuja. She is the only one in the line of succession to have that honor," said Burman.

"No, I didn't know. I just thought everyone referred to her by her title."

"Heavens no, that would get tiresome," said Burman.

Only then did Price realize Burman was holding out a small box for him to take, which he did.

"She asked that I give this to you," said Burman.

"What is it?"

"I have no idea."

The box looked like it was made from slate, making it heavier than it looked. Price slid the lid back and opened the box. Inside was a note, written to him in Anika's handwriting. She had much better penmanship than he. The material upon which it was written was unfamiliar, but obviously synthetic and in overall good condition considering it was over three hundred years old. It said:

My Beloved Winslow, you are forever in my heart. If this note survives the years and reaches you, please give this to the woman who next captures yours, Anika.

Under the note was a small pouch. Inside was the engagement ring he gave her last year, the one she could only wear when they were together and in private until they could make their relationship public.

Tears formed in Winslow's eyes as he looked up to thank Burman, but he was gone. Price was so consumed by what he was reading, he hadn't noticed. As he looked around, hoping to acknowledge the gift, he caught sight of the queen, *Queen Anika*, standing with a group of dignitaries on the other side of the crowd. She was watching him, and as he caught her eye, she smiled.

He smiled back.

ACKNOWLEDGMENTS

There are many people I would like to thank for their help and support in the creation of this novel. First, my beta readers, including Gan Kunda, Andy and Joelle Presby, Nat Causey, and my agent, Laura Wood. Your feedback helped keep the story focused and the settings realistic. I deeply appreciate my "go to" science consultants, Drs. Jim Woosley and Dennis Gallagher, who were quick to respond to my questions and helped keep me in the land of the "might be possible." The feedback from Toni Weisskopf and Tony Daniel at Baen was indispensable, as usual. I would be remiss if I didn't acknowledge the editing support I received from Danielle Magley, a technical communications intern working with me from The University of Alabama in Huntsville.

I would also like to thank Sarah Hoyt for collaborating with me on the creation of the universe in which the story is set.

Most importantly, I am extremely grateful for my patient spouse, Carol. Without her love, support, and enthusiasm, none of my books would have been possible.

ACTION IN THE
GRAND SCIENCE FICTION TRADITION

A Coming-of-Age Story
in the Mode of Robert A. Heinlein

JOHN VAN STRY
Summer's End

TPB: 978-1-9821-9229-7 • $17.00 US / $22.00 CAN

Sometimes a dark past can haunt you. Other times it just may be the only thing keeping you alive.

Fresh out of college with his Ship Engineer 3rd-Class certificate, Dave Walker's only thought is to try and find a berth on a corporate ship plying the trade routes. Instead, he's forced to take the first job he can find and get out of town quick. He ends up on an old tramp freighter running with a minimal crew, plying the routes that the corporations ignore, visiting the kind of places that the folks on Earth pretend don't exist.

Turns out having a stepfather who's a powerful Earth senator that wants you dead can remind you that there is still a lot to learn. But one lesson is coming back hard and with a vengeance: how to be ruthless.